To:
My guy Bruno
control-alt-dele

T. D. B[signature]

SAPIEN

THE DAWN OF OBVILION
T. O. BURNETT

Copyright 2018 by T. O. Burnett

All rights reserved. No part of this book may be reproduced or transmitted in any form or by any means, electronic or mechanical, including photocopying, recording, or by any information storage and retrieval system, without permission in writing from the copyright owner.

This is a work of fiction. Names, characters, places, and incidents either are the product of the author's imagination or are used fictiously. Any resemblance to actual persons, living or dead, events, or locales is entirely coincidental.

ISBN: 978-1986038300

Cover Design by Mark Bailey, Yellow Dogg Designs

www.Sapien.World

Thanks:

First and foremost, I want to thank LaKesha Womack. Your work on this project allowed me to focus on the creative aspect alone. I needed that focus and you allowed me to operate with an unbridled mind. You're the best! Thanks.

To Anthony Smith, thank you for challenging me every step of the way. You didn't let me off the hook. We debated, we argued, and sometimes, we agreed. You pushed me, brother. I needed that.

To Adrian Curtis, your ear was an invaluable asset. I knew I had to keep this story exciting for you. You were with me every step of this journey. You rock, bro!

To Wendell C. Brantley, your friendship and wisdom kept the fire burning. I could not have had a better sounding board. You knew exactly what to say and when to say it. For that, I am grateful.

I owe a special debt of gratitude to Priscilla Magnusen. You're the definition of a true friend. Your belief in me is more valuable than you could ever imagine. I'm glad you're in my life. I could never repay in one thousand lifetimes the cost of the impact you've had on my life. Thank you!

Dedication:

I dedicate this book to two very special people. First and foremost is Mrs. Rose Ellis, my twelfth grade English teacher. You saw something in me that no other teacher before ever recognized. You were the first to let me know that what I was putting on paper wasn't normal. I had no clue, I thought everyone could write. I wish you were here to read this.

Last, but not least, I want to recognize the most impressive man I've ever known, Jeddo D. Bell. Dad, I love and miss you. Everything I am is because of you. You will forever be at the forefront of everything I do from this day forward. I won't let you down.

SAPIEN: DAWN OF OBLIVION

CHAPTER 1: WELCOME TO HADES! ---- 7

CHAPTER 2: THE ONISHI EMPIRE ---- 25

CHAPTER 3: POLITICS AS USUAL ---- 36

CHAPTER 4: JUST IN TIME ---- 55

CHAPTER 5: WHAT'S OUT THERE? ---- 76

CHAPTER 6: MYSTERY LADY ---- 86

CHAPTER 7: GOODBYE, EVROPA; HELLO, NASTY ---- 107

CHAPTER 8: IT'S ALL CLEAR NOW ---- 121

CHAPTER 9: EYE FOR AN EYE ---- 130

CHAPTER 10: THE CALM BEFORE THE STORM ---- 141

CHAPTER 11: DECEPTION ALL AROUND ---- 151

CHAPTER 12: THE FRANCOIS FAUX PAS ---- 161

CHAPTER 13: BJORN TO BE MAD ---- 178

CHAPTER 14: BIRD OF PREY ---- 193

CHAPTER 15: THE EVE OF ETERNITY ---- 204

CHAPTER 16: THE DANGEROUS DUO ---- 222

CHAPTER 17: UNCONVENTIONAL ---- 241

CHAPTER 18: THE RECKONING ---- 260

CHAPTER 19: BLOOD IN THE BASTILLE ---- 283

CHAPTER 20: THE END? ---- 305

ABOUT THE AUTHOR ---- 321

Chapter 1: Welcome to Hades!

Location: The city of Iniquity, Elba County, Zasnezene Province, planet Hades
1500 hours

Three crew members of the Starship Whisper sat in a dimly lit corner of the parlous Sumner Tavern. The seedy watering hole was moderately sized but filled to capacity. It was a popular place for mercenaries and smugglers, such as the crew of the Whisper, to find work. It also crawled with male and female prostitutes who frequently took their johns to The Den which was an Inn that was located directly across the cobble stoned street from the tavern. The tavern was filled with smoke and had a rustic vibe, but no music was allowed. It was not a place for compromise and, as simple as it seems, that very thing had triggered many brawls in the past. In the center of the room was a large circular bar with two open entrances one hundred eighty degrees from one another, aligning perfectly with the front entrance. Backless bar stools were positioned around every possible inch of the of the bar. The stools were nailed to the ground. Heavy wooden topped tables were symmetrically positioned throughout the area. Every wall except the one where the entrance was located was lined with booths which could accommodate at least six average sized people. In a booth on the wall directly across from the entrance and on the other side of the bar sat Mulati Soldaat, Bjorn Mathison, and Sampa Yambasu of the Starship Whisper. Mulati was of Evropan and Alkebulan, more specifically Scandinavian and Zulu warrior, descent. He was the leader of the crew. At 6'2" and two hundred pounds he was athletically built with a caramel complexion. His braided mohawk belied his stoic demeanor. He was a man of few words. The topic of conversation amongst the three was the amount of time they would be apart because they had, just that morning, completed one of their most lucrative missions and were looking forward to some time off. That mission was to deliver freight from Asia to Hades for the Sumner Tavern. Opiates were likely the cargo, but no one truly knew what was being transported and no one asked unnecessary questions on those missions. Either you can do it, or you cannot. The Whisper had a reputation for getting it done.

Sampa told Mulati and Bjorn that she was going to the bar for another drink and asked if either of them wanted anything while she was there.

"Of course, I do," said Bjorn in a matter of fact tone. "Always assume I do, it's easier that way. Bring me an ale."

Bjorn was a true Scandinavian tough guy in every sense. He stood on a stout 6'5" frame which was filled out with mostly fat. He had powerful forearms, a barrel chest, and a scruffy appearance. He was a physically strong individual with a very bad temper and had his twice emitter strapped to his back. The most commonly used combat weapon for deadly force in the Sapien Solar System, the twice emitter shoots a two-part projectile. The first projectile which is a fluorescent green tracer round, and the only one that needs to be aimed, simply stuns, and immobilizes its target. The second part of the projectile has to be fired within twenty seconds of the first but does not have to be aimed since it seeks the coordinates of the first projectile. The second projectile completes the work of the first, making it fatal. Neither is fatal without the other. If the first projectile hits the wrong target the shooter needs only to rack the weapon to extract the second projectile. The first projectile disintegrates, and the victim is back to normal in twenty seconds.

Mulati simply made eye contact with Sampa and waved his hand slowly with his palm down as he slightly shook his head from side to side without saying a word, an indication to her that he wanted nothing as she proceeded to the bar. Sampa had flawless black skin with a shapely 5'6" build. She was as witty and sarcastic as she was intelligent. It was rare that she was not the smartest person in any room she occupied. As she approached the bar Mulati and Bjorn turned to one another and continued their conversation. Moments later the front door to the tavern slammed open and in walked three Evropan men, the largest of whom was the first through the door. He had long, brown, matted hair that draped over his shoulders and wore a scowl which appeared more intentional than natural. He was 6'3" and overly muscled to the point that he appeared to be pharmaceutically enhanced. His companions, Louis and Eric, were of average build and were careful to walk behind him. His name was Ean. He walked directly toward the bar without saying a word, nor did he verbally acknowledge anyone who was in his path. He glared at them and they simply moved out of his way.

Bjorn, amused by what he was seeing, tapped Mulati's hand and motioned toward Ean with the same hand as if to say, "Watch this."

They both watched him as he approached the bar.

"He has no scars," said Mulati.

"Yea, I noticed that too," replied Bjorn. "Who is he trying to intimidate?"

Ean stopped short of bumping into Sampa who was standing at the bar waiting to be served. For a moment he simply glared at her expecting her to recognize the err of her ways and step aside. Sampa looked him in his eyes, deliberately scanned him from head to toe, and turned her attention back to the bar. She did not budge otherwise. That infuriated Ean. By that time Mulati, sensing an inevitable confrontation, had stood and made his way toward the bar through the dense crowd.

"Stay here," he said to Bjorn. "Hold our seats."

Meanwhile Louis said to Sampa, "Hey lady, you're in his way!"

Ever the sarcastic and fearless one, Sampa replied, "Does his mouth not work? He's a big man, I'm sure he can speak for himself."

By then, Ean's face was trembling with rage and through clenched teeth he said to Sampa in a voice that only those immediately surrounding them could hear, "Moooooovvvveeee!!!!!"

Sampa laughed to herself. Big mistake. Ean grabbed her around her neck with both hands, grasping tight enough to take her breath, and with a lunge and a thrust tossed her as far as he humanly could screaming, "I... SAID.... MOOOOVVVVEEE!!!!!"

Sampa landed on her back mere feet away from where Bjorn was sitting with her legs wide open and her arms stretched out to the side, making sure to absorb the impact with her upper back.

Completely relaxed, Bjorn began to slowly clap. "You've gone and done it now," he said with an expression that quickly went from a wry smile to a frown.

"You like that, huh?" Sampa quipped rhetorically as she picked herself up from the floor. *That wasn't very smart of me.*

"Have a seat, Sam," said Bjorn, "enjoy the show."

Suddenly a loud CLACK could be heard throughout the bar which, suddenly, fell silent. Mulati had extended his six-foot dlhá násada which was a martial arts staff made of metal that extended, with the touch of a button, three feet on both ends from a twelve-inch wand looking device that Mulati kept around his waist. Twirling it in his right hand while he had his left arm extended toward Ean with his palm facing him, and before Ean could react, Mulati took a mighty, swift swing with both hands on his weapon striking him in the midsection. WHACK!!!! Ean immediately doubled over in pain holding his stomach with both hands. Mulati was already spinning into his next move and brought his dlhá násada down on the back of Ean's neck with tremendous force. WHACK!!!!

Ean screamed out in agony, "Ohhhhhhh!!!"

Mulati in a continuous motion squatted down and executed a spinning leg sweep which left Ean supine on the floor of the tavern and dazed. His comrades, amazed, stepped back.

"Apologize to Sam," Mulati exhaled in a stern yet conversational tone.

Whether he was going to apologize or not remains a mystery. However, as he mustered what strength he had left to raise his head and open his mouth, Sampa kicked him as hard as she could on the bottom of his chin rendering him completely unconscious.

Bjorn, still sitting in his seat, yelled across the tavern floor to Mulati, "He's got a scar now!"

Not wanting to give Sampa her just due, Mulati nodded his head slightly saying, "A little one."

Sampa brushed herself off very deliberately saying, "Apology accepted."

Louis and Eric stepped toward Ean to pick him up.

"Leave him there!" yelled Bjorn. "The man needs his rest, that's probably why he's so ornery."

Mulati looked directly at one of the bartenders, known only as Scrappy, and asked him, "Can you go downstairs and get Gerald? I need to speak with him."

Without hesitation the diminutive barkeep scampered down the spiral staircase, located inside the circular bar, to retrieve Gerald, the owner. Scrappy was a 5'2," one hundred thirty pounds, thirty-five-year-old, Malaysian male who was extremely loyal to his boss, Gerald.

Scrappy returned alone and said to Mulati, "He says he'll meet you at the hangar in an hour and not to worry about your tab."

Mulati nodded, looked in Bjorn's direction, and motioned his head toward the front door. Sampa stepped over Ean's unconscious body and gave an exaggerated upper body flinch toward Louis and Eric. Frightened, they both jumped back and quickly walked away afraid to make eye contact with anyone around them. With that, Mulati, Bjorn, and Sampa exited the tavern to meet Gerald at the hangar.

Scrappy looked over at the bar goons, Rage and Chaos, and motioned toward Ean saying, "Pick up the shit before somebody steps in it!"

Within moments the two very large and heavily tattooed native New

Zealanders from planet Evropa approached. Chaos carried a large tin pail filled with water. He doused Ean with the water saying, "Get your big ugly ass up!"

They nonchalantly dragged him, coughing and barely conscious, to a booth in the far corner of the tavern where Louis and Eric scurried to join him.

Minutes later, Gerald, a 6'4," fifty-year-old, strikingly handsome, and debonair, Alkebulan man of Egyptian descent emerged from below the tavern via the spiral staircase. He said to Scrappy, "I'll return in a few hours, mind the tavern."

As Gerald walked toward the door he was approached by a small and frail American man. He had red sun-touched skin, long and silky black hair, and no facial hair. He was middle-aged and wore a deerskin shirt over his modern shirt and pants. Gerald couldn't believe that such a proper looking person was in his tavern, not to mention alone.

"Those people, the girl and the two men," inquired the American, "who are they?"

"Who's asking?" replied Gerald.

"I'm not completely at liberty to say," answered the American, "but I am interested in giving them some work for what would, most assuredly, be more DANs than they've ever dreamed of making."

Gerald was tempted to ask *why* but did not.

"What is your digital signature?" asked Gerald of the American, "I'll make sure I pass it along to them."

The American looked as if he were taking a leap of faith and said quietly, "That would be: Genesis. Please, sir, deliver my message; it is of the utmost importance."

Gerald, bewildered by the desperation on the American's face and in his voice, said, "Yea, sure. I'll make sure they get it."

"Thank you! Thank you so very much!" the American exclaimed as he quickly scurried out of the tavern.

Minutes later, twenty miles away, back at the hangar in Ciudad De Vuelo; Mulati, Sampa, and Bjorn waited in line to be granted entrance into the facility which was operated and controlled by the Debauchers of Death (DOD) gang. On Hades a place like that was absolutely necessary. Without it a ship docked in an unsecured location would surely be overrun or seized by any gangs, pirates, groups, or individuals who possessed superior manpower or superior firepower. The DOD was a ruthless, multicultural gang that consisted of a little over five thousand members. Often, they were aided by loyal wannabees. The de facto leader of the DOD was a ruthless Asian swordsman who went by the name Rokuro Onishi. Only sworn members of the DOD operated the facility. They charged a steep price but, in that environment, it was absolutely worth it. Only a fool, or someone with a death wish, would run afoul of the DOD gang or its operation.

"Step up and prepare to be scanned," said the sentry holding the scanning device called an Information Recognition Scanner (IRS) at the entrance to the hangar. Mulati stepped forward to be scanned.

"Stand still and keep 'em open," the sentry commanded.

As Mulati stood still the sentry extended a pen shaped scanning device to within five inches of Mulati's face at eye level and vertical.

"Scanning!" the sentry declared as he slowly traversed his fully extended right arm from right to left, paused slightly, and then from left to right pausing again at the end. A piercing beep signified the end of the scan. The sentry turned his attention to the IRS which was tethered to the scanner.

"Mulati...welcome back. I suppose those two are Sampa and Bjorn?" he asked.

"They are," Mulati replied.

The sentry placed his left hand into the receptacle on the wall behind him for fingerprint recognition. After a moment the double doors separated, and he looked to Mulati, Sampa, and Bjorn and said, "Proceed. You're at A-40."

They walked through the doors as ordered. As the doors closed behind them they could hear the familiar refrain, "Step up and prepare to be scanned." They stepped onto the moving walkway which was about twenty feet away from the door. The facility had four levels which were labeled A, B, C, and D with A being the bottom level and D being the top. The docking spaces for the respective ships were numeric starting from one and ascending higher. There were fifty spaces on each of the four levels.

"Is it me," asked Sampa, "or does that guy need a fun transfusion?"

Bjorn laughed, "He does, doesn't he? Either that or a trip to the Den. Corto would love that guy. You know, what amazes me is how immaculate this place always is. I mean given how bat shit crazy the DOD is you'd think this place would be a shit hole."

"True," replied Mulati, "but money is an unparalleled motivator."

Sampa's eyes widened as she looked at Bjorn and held back laughter saying, "See, I told you he wasn't getting any."

Bjorn also struggled to contain his laughter but felt it necessary to do so.

Mulati rolled his eyes and shook his head. "39...40. We're here," he said as they all exited the moving walkway together. "I hope Corto has everything ready."

As they opened the door to the massive garage, they were greeted with the angry voice of Corto Canales as quickly as they felt the backdraft of air.

"Where the fuck have you been?" yelled the 4'6" chain smoker from the Spanish Province on Evropa. "This shit has been ready to go for hours, Beth is getting on my fucking nerves, and I'm down to my last pack of smokes!"

Bjorn interrupted Corto, "Stop your crying you little..."

Abruptly, Corto cut him off, "You shut the fuck up, Bjorn! How'd I draw the short straw and have to stay back this time anyway?" Realizing what he had just said, Corto clenched his teeth together and said, "None of you say a fucking word!"

Sampa smiled and made a zipping motion over her tucked in lips with her right hand.

Bjorn reached into his satchel and tossed Corto a fresh carton of smokes. "Here, you happy fucker. Scrappy sends his regards!" said Bjorn.

With a cigarette clenched between his teeth, Corto managed to smile. He took one last drag of his smoke and plucked it away. "Good ol' Scrappy," he said, "he always pays his debts."

Bjorn and Corto were closer to one another than any of the other crew members although one would never know it by the way they talked to each other.

"Why is Mulati so happy?" asked Corto of Bjorn.

"Sam picked up another boyfriend at the Sumner and he's just jealous" replied Bjorn sarcastically.

"Did you at least get to kiss the fucker this time, Sam?" asked Corto.

"I sure did...with this boot right here," bragged Sampa as she elevated her right foot off the ground about twelve inches.

Mulati interrupted, "Unload it. Gerald will be here to get it soon."

When Mulati spoke that way they all knew that playtime was over. Quickly they all entered the cargo bay of the Whisper and began to unload their recent haul which they had acquired from Asia. Soon after, the visitor light above the entrance door started flashing.

Sampa walked over to it and viewed the monitor. "It's Gerald," she said, "I'm letting him in."

Gerald entered the garage. "Hello, Whisper!" he said acknowledging both the legendary ship and its crew at once.

The Whisper was a full capacity, medium class, heavy cargo vessel. It had ten individual sleeping quarters, a cargo bay which had a weapons locker and supply room, a galley, a dining hall, an engine room, an infirmary, a lounge, a 3-D imaging room, and a bridge. It's weapon system included two one-man assault pods called shadows. They were located on the starboard and port side of the ship and fired Steel Piercing Incendiary Missiles (SPIM). The pods either operated from a fixed position or in shadow mode causing them to detach from the Whisper completely. SPIMs could also be fired from the bridge along with Oxygen Evacuation Ammunition (OEA).

Mulati looked to Gerald and said, "It's ready for you."

Gerald walked over to the massive inventory and examined it briefly. "Good," he said as he removed his handheld electronic personal information conveyor (EPIC) from a cargo pocket, "I'll transfer the funds now."

After a moment Mulati removed his EPIC from his own pocket and after looking at it briefly he nodded to Gerald and they shook hands.

"It's always a pleasure doing business with you," said Gerald. "My men are on the way to pick this up. Until next time…" As he started walking toward the door, he suddenly stopped and turned around. "I almost forgot, you had an American admirer back at the tavern. Said he had some work for you. It's supposed to be big. Don't know who he is. Don't know what it is he wants. Says his digital signature is Genesis." Gerald shrugged his shoulders and headed toward the exit of the garage. "Listen to your conscience, Mulati," he said as he walked out.

"I will, and let yours lead the way," Mulati replied.

Earlier that morning, as he customarily did after every run the Whisper made, Bjorn had done a systematic maintenance check as soon as they arrived on Hades and checked into the hangar. He was always assisted by Corto when he performed his checks. It was either Mulati or Sampa who normally rented garage space for the Whisper while in route to the hangar. The procedure was adhered to when it was time to leave as well. Mulati pulled out his EPIC, this time to submit his payment to the DOD for the use of their hangar. He pressed send and the massive garage door behind them opened revealing the atmosphere of Iniquity. The payment was successful, and they were free to leave.

"I never like leaving this place," said Bjorn as they all ascended the rear ramp of the Whisper into the cargo area. Inside the ship was Beth who, for all intent and purposes, was the maternal influence of the crew although she was a contemporary age-wise. Beth Kirby was a thick, solidly built Irish woman with emerald green eyes and silky brown hair that draped over her shoulders.

"One of these days I'm gonna have to go out there with you. I can handle myself there too, you know," said Beth before leaning in close to Mulati, "Besides, Corto is going to drive me insane with all his cussing, smoking, and nagging."

Mulati was unmoved by the remark. He saw value in Beth that sometimes went unappreciated by other members of the crew. To him she was the glue. Despite his stoic demeanor, he cared deeply for each of them. He was loyal to them and they were loyal to him.

"Any who," continued Beth as she raised her voice back to conversational tone, "around 1800 hours the Shepherd's Pie will be ready. There's enough for everybody to have at least three bowls...that includes Bjorn."

"I love you too, Beth," Bjorn replied with a huge smile.

After they all were aboard the Whisper Bjorn yelled, "Stand clear!" as he used two hands to pull down the massive lever which initiated the raising of the long heavy ramp. Once it was closed all the way both Bjorn and Corto simultaneously turned, clockwise, two wheels which were positioned on the wall one on each side of the ramp. The cargo area was sealed. Mulati and Sampa headed directly to the bridge to prepare for departure. As he normally did,

Mulati sat in his swiveling pilot's chair and immediately adorned his headset. Sampa sat in the copilot's seat to his right and she put on her headset as well. They both paid careful attention to all the instruments displayed before them as they flipped switches to the on position initiating the launch sequence and causing the roar of the engine to overwhelme the room as the entire instrument panel lit up.

Sampa smiled as she looked over at Mulati saying, "I love that sound."

Mulati nodded, "So do I."

The massive ship began to levitate off the ground as Mulati manipulated the U-shaped steering device in front of him and rotated his ship 180 degrees clockwise until the front of the Whisper faced the sky outside.

"Engage thrusters!" commanded Mulati.

"Thrusters engaged!" replied Sampa as she pushed forward the sliding levers on the panel. The Whisper then quickly left the hangar.

"Once we've gotten past the ionosphere cut the thrusters and initiate cloak mode," commanded Mulati.

"Aye, aye," replied Sampa.

Bjorn and Corto were both in the engine room where they always were during takeoff in case they were needed to address any mechanical problems. Once they exited the atmosphere Sampa turned the thrusters off and turned on the cloaking device as Mulati had ordered. This was a practice they used to avoid detection by pirate ships that floated around the solar system looking for victims.

Upon hearing the thrusters turn off Bjorn looked at Corto and said, "That's it, another successful takeoff." He gave Corto a friendly pat on the back and they both retired to the ship's lounge which was located on the main deck near the living quarters, underneath the bridge and above the infirmary and cargo bay.

"It's almost 1800 hours," said Bjorn. "Guess I'll get ready for chow."

Meanwhile on the bridge, Mulati removed his headset, leaned back in his chair, and exhaled a deep sigh of relief. Times were always tense for him and it was at this time that he felt most at peace. He looked over to Sampa. "You can go get ready for chow if you like; Beth doesn't like it when we're late. I'm going to the communication room to make a connection. Hopefully I won't be too long."

Sampa removed her headset and, without unnecessary delay, exited the bridge. Mulati walked into the communication room which was located on the bridge and closed the door behind him. He took a seat at the Viewing Console (VC), a small round table in the room with a metallic top that was shiny.

"Communication mode: Ready to transmit," Mulati carefully enunciated. As bright lights illuminated the table before him he continued, "Contact Genesis."

Immediately a twelve-inch hologram of the American from the tavern appeared and he began to speak. "Thank you for contacting me. I will be brief as I know that your time is very valuable to you. My name is Theris Lamont and I am a Neutralian of American descent and a member of the Supreme Council thereon. I come to you with an offer for which you and your crew are uniquely qualified. Therefore, I am willing to pay you handsomely for this mission. Unfortunately, I am uncomfortable discussing the details of this endeavor through this correspondence. I would hate to be compromised by hackers. By the way, sir, what is your name?"

"My name is Mulati Soldaat. I captain the Whisper. I guess since we are talking you know what it is I do. There are five of us."

Without hesitation Theris responded, "I can pay you ten million DANs. On top of that I will provide every resource you require to complete this mission."

Mulati had never made more than fifty thousand DANs for a job before. His eyes slowly widened. "Where do we meet?" asked Mulati.

"Meet me on Neutralia," replied Theris. "A month from now there will be a convention of the Sapien Solar System on our planet. I would like for us to meet the day before."

Mulati responded, "I am interested, but I must discuss this with my crew. I will contact you again in no later than two days' time."

Theris smiled, "Thank you, Mulati. I look forward to your response. Listen to your conscience."

Mulati responded in kind, "I will, and let yours lead the way. End transmission."

With that, Theris Lamont's image disappeared. For moments that seemed like minutes, Mulati sat still at the table contemplating the ramifications of him agreeing to the offer. Until now the crew had always stuck together because they needed one another. *Is that money worth losing my chosen family? Is it fair to be offered so much money and not tell them about it?* he thought to himself. How dangerous the mission could be was never a concern that crossed his mind. They'd been in tough spots before and were adept at coming away from those unharmed. Maybe it was the lifestyle he loved so much, and he feared that getting that much money would surely be the end. However, it was Mulati's conscience that won. He could not have such an offer be presented to him and not tell them. He knew it wouldn't have been right. The conscience was the only recognized supreme being in this solar system. It was the shared belief that every living being had a conscience and it was that which they must obey. They were governed by it. It was what kept living things from killing for sport, siblings from mating with one another, and men-at-arms from murdering innocent children. Mulati was no exception to that mindset. He obeyed his conscience. His crew, they obeyed their conscience. The conscience, as varied as it may have been, controlled each one. However, it was that variance that made those in the Sapien Solar System resistant to a centralized legal system or government. From whose conscience would those laws come? No two people could agree on everything. Even the mere notion was a repulsive thought throughout the Sapien Solar System. The worlds of the solar system disagreed on many things on many levels...with the exception of that.

A soft voice coming through the intercom system in the room broke the silence. It was Beth. "Sorry to interrupt, Mulati, but your dinner is on the table. I don't want it to get cold," she paused, "or be eaten by Bjorn."

Bjorn spoke up. His voice was fainter as if he was farther away from the communicator than Beth, but he was not whispering. "Take your time," he said with a mouth full of food.

Mulati smiled and leaned his head back and spoke in a voice louder than his normal conversational tone, "I'll be right there." As if he knew that what he was about to embark on was going to be life altering, he released a long sigh and lifted himself slowly from his chair. He slowly wiped his face from his forehead to his chin with his right hand before leaving the room to join the others. As he approached the entrance to the dining room the door automatically opened before him. The aroma of Shepherd's Pie, the sound of playful banter and utensils scraping plates met him all at once. Mulati took his seat at the table, grabbed his first bowl, and began to scarf it down as if he weren't sure he'd ever eat again.

Beth looked at him with a gaze that was equally pitiful and loving. She uttered softly, as if she were saying it to herself but just loud enough for Mulati to hear, "I will never get used to the way you orphans eat."

Mulati paused briefly as if he either contemplated offering a retort or wanted to hear more from Beth. It is unclear which was the case.

Beth, noticing the slight pause, raised her voice, "There's a lot more where that came from. Eat up!"

Mulati finished his bowl of food and quickly pushed that one away as he reached for another. Just like he did with the first one, he began to scarf down the food from the second bowl. However, this time he did not finish. As if he had suddenly had enough, he leaned back and took a deep breath before taking a long drink from the goblet that was in front of him on the table. "What's more important, money or family?" he asked.

The room got silent.

"Well," said Corto, "I've never had either so I'm just as curious as you, Boss."

Sampa, knowing it wasn't just a random question, leaned back in her chair and looked directly at Mulati. "Why do you ask?" she questioned.

"I'll get to that in a moment, Sam," he replied. "Right now, I'm interested to know what you think. All of you."

Without hesitation and before anyone else could speak, Beth replied, "Family!" She began to tear up as she continued with a trembling voice, "Family is more important than anything you can ever possess, DANs included."

Bjorn joined the conversation, "Well how many DANs are we talking about?"

Aware of Beth's emotional state, Sampa angrily nudged Bjorn with her elbow.

Bjorn continued, "Well, no offense," as he nodded kindly toward Beth, "but something is clearly on his mind and it must be some decent currency for him to ask that question."

As Sampa was about to verbally reprimand Bjorn, Mulati interrupted. "Ten million." He was stone faced as he continued, "We've been offered ten million DANs for a job."

Amazed, Bjorn blurted out without thinking, "Well that's outstanding news! Why the hell are you so sad about that?"

Mulati looked at Bjorn as if he were somewhat disappointed, drank the remainder of his beverage, and stood up. "As always, Beth, your meal was delicious," he said before walking out of the dining room and into the living quarters. He never answered Bjorn's question.

As the door closed behind him, Sampa yelled at Bjorn. "Are you an idiot? We are the only family he has! If we take a job for that much then, in his mind, we won't need him anymore and he'd be all alone. Beth is right, no amount of DANs are worth that!"

"Well who said we'd have to leave?" asked Corto.

Sampa did not answer. She simply looked at Corto realizing that if he did not understand why Mulati would be concerned then it made no sense whatsoever to explain it to him. Sampa stood up, "I'm going to talk to him."

"No," said Beth, "leave him alone."

Sampa continued, "Well I'm done eating. I'm going to my sleep quarters. If you need me, I'll be there." She then angrily left the room.

Confused, Bjorn asked Beth, "So I'm the bad guy now? I never said I wouldn't be around. He asked a question and I gave my answer."

Beth sat quietly as a tear rolled down her face. "Do you know how Mulati and I met?" Before Bjorn could reply, Beth answered. "No, you don't!" She continued, "Before you two came along it was just him and Sam. This is not the life I chose. Who would choose such an existence? I had a family. I had a man and two teenage boys. We were peaceful farmers. They were murdered by the Mayhem Marauders right in front of me. As those monsters discussed amongst themselves whether they wanted to kill me or rape me and then kill me; Mulati and Sam came to my rescue. I don't know where they came from, but they came." Now with a face full of tears, she said with anger and sorrow, "They put those savages down!" She sobbed uncontrollably causing Bjorn to put his hand on her shoulder to comfort her. She continued as if she were ashamed of herself for allowing that awful memory to enter into her mind, "I would give anything to have my boys back but since I can't you all are all I have, and I'll be damned if I give that up for some DANs. It ain't worth it!" She continued to weep and neither Bjorn nor Corto had the courage to stop her, to speak, or to leave the table. They both sat quietly as she cried.

After a few minutes Mulati's somber voice interrupted the silence from the intercom. "I've plotted a course to the nearest space station. We should arrive there for supplies at 1400 hours tomorrow. Rest up."

Beth quickly dried her face. "You boys go on, I'll clear the table."

Bjorn and Corto removed themselves from the table and walked out.

Seconds later Bjorn walked back in and grabbed an uneaten roll from the table. "I don't waste food. Sorry," he said as he turned and walked back out.

Of all the things he could have done in that moment it was that which made Beth feel better. Bjorn reminded her of her oldest son who also loved her cooking. She smiled, and she cleared the table.

Chapter 2: The Onishi Empire

Location: DOD hideout, Tierra Mala, outskirts of Elba County, Zasnezene Province
2030 hours

Meanwhile in the desolate outskirts of Elba County, several miles east of Iniquity, there lied a one-story building in Tierra Mala. Its tan exterior blended seamlessly into the sandy desert scenery that surrounded it. The several thousand-square foot rectangular building was the hideout of the DOD. At nightfall the dimly lit building was difficult to see from the outside. Only someone who was looking specifically for this location would find it. That was the intent of the DOD. Three hundred yards beyond the front door the two-man Observation Post (OP) received a message via their EPIC: "We are one mile out; our ETA is two minutes." said the voice that came through.

"We copy. Stand by for authorization," replied the man holding the EPIC inside the OP. A moment later that same man spoke into his EPIC again, "All clear!"

Just then the man driving the Jagged Enhanced Durable Drivable Object (JEDDO), a heavily armored ten passenger all-terrain vehicle, turned to his only passenger, Judas Benedict, and said, "We've been given the all clear. Next stop is the DOD hideout."

"Thank you," replied the soft spoken and effeminate Benedict.

Judas was dressed in attire typical of the Albino people. His gray hooded garment resembled a sleeved blanket and covered him from head to toe. His dark goggles protected his sensitive eyes from whatever bright light might unexpectedly spring from the darkness. He carried no weapons. Moments later, the JEDDO passed the OP with which the driver had communicated before. A head nod from the driver was confirmed with a returned hand gesture from one of the men inside. The driver continued to his destination stopping just a few yards short of the front entrance.

The driver announced, "This is it. Stand by for your escort."

At that moment the side door of the JEDDO slid open from the outside. The cold wind and air rushed into the vehicle. A muffled voice emerged through the scarf worn by Francois Larue, the man standing outside the JEDDO. He wore multiple layers of clothing and carried a rifle style twice emitter strapped over his shoulder. "Step out and face away from me," he said as he motioned for Judas to step out of the JEDDO.

Judas did as he was ordered and automatically raised both of his arms to shoulder level to expedite the frisk that was sure to follow. As he stood there, he felt a hand on the small of his back as the other slowly caressed the entirety of his waistband. Then both hands massaged every inch of his left leg from his ankle all the way up to his crotch. The same was repeated for the right leg. After those same hands went from his waistline to his armpits, Francois said to Judas, "Put your arms down. What's that under your left arm?"

"That's my EPIC," Judas answered.

Satisfied with Judas' answer, Francois continued, "Follow me. He is waiting for you."

Francois marched Judas to the front door which was engraved with a large DOD emblem, a white skull impaled by a sword with the tip of the blade protruding through the crown. He inserted his hand into a portal to the right of it, and they both entered immediately after the door slid open.

Inside the building was warm and bright. Judas immediately lowered his head to minimize the amount of direct light his eyes would consume. From inside it was difficult to hear the wind that whistled on the outside of the building. No words were spoken as Francois escorted Judas through several doors, each requiring him to insert his hand into a portal for fingerprint recognition. Finally, they reached a door flanked by twin Russian brothers holding twice emitters at port arms. Their names were Alexei and Igor

Sobolevsky. Both 6 feet tall and muscular, the brothers were experts in weaponry and personal bodyguards to their DOD boss.

Francois accessed a screen on the wall and spoke into it, "Judas Benedict has arrived."

"Good, let him in," a male voice responded followed by the door sliding open.

Judas walked into the dimly lit room and was met immediately by a beautiful Ethiopian woman. "Hello, I'm Adera," she said.

"I'm Judas Benedict," he responded.

"It's a pleasure to make your acquaintance, Judas Benedict," Adera said with a smile. "Make yourself comfortable, he'll be right in."

Judas removed his hood revealing his white hair, and he also removed his goggles revealing the fire red irises of his eyes. He was impressed with Adera's beauty and in awe of her grace. To him she could not have been more perfect physically. As if he were mesmerized by her aura, he watched her intently until she exited the room. If he liked women, she would be perfect for him. Judas was in his fifties and had never been a warrior, but he should not be mistaken for a diplomat either. His battlefield was the political arena, and in that arena, he was as ruthless as he was pale. The room was comfortable and smelled of incense. Exotic tapestries from multiple cultures and worlds were strewn about the room. Clearly this was a place for relaxation. Judas sat in a very comfortable chair but looked anything but. His back was straight, and he was attentive to every sound and movement around him. This particular DOD boss's reputation preceded him. He killed at will as long as his conscience didn't hinder him. For that reason, Judas was nervous. Abruptly Rokuro Onishi, the bearded Japanese warrior, burst into the room.

"Remain seated," he said to Judas with a heavy Japanese accent. "What is it you require of the DOD, Albino?" asked Rokuro as he sat across from Judas glaring directly into his eyes. Rokuro sat on the very edge of his chair with his back straight and his hands on his knees, appearing rigid but confident. His body language demanded words that were worthy of his audience.

Judas nervously cleared his throat as he began to speak, "We share a mutual adversary. The winds of change are blowing, and the direction is favorable for neither you nor I." Judas paused as if he expected an eager question. However, Rokuro did not change his expression or move his body. He only listened. Judas, feeling the pressure now to justify his existence, continued. "Next month there will be a convention of the nine worlds on Neutralia. Businessmen and citizens from all worlds have been invited. All indications are that it will be heavily attended. The purpose of this convention is to introduce an intrasolar alliance that will essentially centralize the power in the Sapien Solar System within the Supreme Council of Neutralia, which aspires to be the Supreme Council of the Solar System."

Rokuro leaned forward, "I'm listening."

Now even more nervous, Judas continued. "The intent of Chancellor Aldrich," Judas sighed, "is to turn Hades into a penal world."

Rokuro laughed, not because it was funny but because in his mind it was an absurd notion and laughter was the most appropriate response he could render at the time for something so ridiculous.

Feeling it important to do so, Judas pressed on. "Chancellor Aldrich also has the support of Vice Chancellor Theris Lamont who happens to be a very influential man throughout this solar system. I assume you are not interested in relinquishing your hold on this region as it has proven quite lucrative for your...gang. Am I correct?"

Rokuro folded his arms, "Get to the point."

"Well," said Judas, "the consensus is that the people want to be secure in their dwellings at all times and free to participate in commerce as they see fit. As it stands, that is not where we are in the solar system, of course with the exception of Neutralia. It seems the many visits to our world have given way to the idea that security is more important than freedom. I don't share that philosophy."

Rokuro raised his chin, "You want me to do… what?"

"I want you to eliminate both the Chancellor and the Vice Chancellor," replied Judas. "I want you to preserve our way of life. I'm for changes but this much control in the hands of an unscrupulous man is dangerous."

Rokuro asked, "What do you stand to gain from this?"

"Power!" replied Judas as his entire demeanor changed from feminine and flamboyant to manly and confident, "And with that power I will wield my influence to positively affect the autonomous worlds," He raised his head and looked Rokuro Onishi directly in his eyes and continued, "And their governors! Only he who resides at the top will be exempt from taxation. Everyone else will pay a tariff which you, as governor, will disseminate as you please…if you please!"

Rokuro frowned and said, "I'm a warrior, not a politician."

Judas exploded, "You're a leader and you'll have to change nothing!"

Rokuro shook his head from side to side and said defiantly and proudly, "The DOD has no leader."

Judas immediately stood up, stepped closer to Rokuro, and pointed his index finger toward his face and whispered, "And that is why they will follow you."

As he backed away from Rokuro he allowed his finger to stay fixed in that position seconds longer as if to emphasize that point. He then sat down, crossed his legs, and, as if he were jumping back into character, he lowered his head. "One thing I know," he continued in his normal light tone of voice, "is that change is certain. The people are scared. The pendulum has swung as far as it could and now it is time for the direction to change. Either we can benefit from it or we can relegate ourselves, through inactivity, to subjects of an unjust and unworthy Chancellor. Let us, instead, be proactive and control our own destinies. Name your price."

"One hundred million DANs," Rokuro replied.

"And what of your conscience?" asked Judas.

Rokuro glared at him saying, "No man shall have his freedom to roam defined, no matter how big the cage."

"So we have a deal?" asked Judas.

"My conscience is clear," replied Rokuro.

Judas clasped his hands together in front of his own face and bowed his head slightly, a gesture of gratitude and appreciation, and said, "Thank you." He then stood and asked, "Who shall I see for passage to the Den? There's a nice young man waiting for me there."

As Rokuro stood and walked back into the room from which he originally emerged he said, "Francois awaits you just outside the door."

Judas exited the room as Adera followed Rokuro into the room, barely giving the door an opportunity to close between the transitions.

"I don't trust him!" she exclaimed. "There is something about him that unnerves me to my core."

Rokuro respected her intuition and he gazed at her as if he considered her concern. "Luckily for us, trust has no role in this agreement. His DANs will spend well," said Rokuro.

Adera came forward to embrace him. "Then I have no concern," she said as she smiled and caressed Rokuro's beard. With a gentle kiss she pulled herself away.

"Bathe with me, I need your full attention," she said softly.

Rokuro obliged her.

Meanwhile, Judas was in a JEDDO being transported to the Den in Iniquity. This time he was accompanied by two other passengers. They were men with whom Judas was unfamiliar. However, the men spoke to one another in a manner which indicated that they were very familiar with one another. Both men looked disheveled and generally unkempt. They were Evropans, but it was hard for Judas to determine their specific ethnicities. Both men were of average height, one being slightly taller than the other. Their conversation stopped abruptly. For a moment Judas enjoyed the silence but then it became awkward and uncomfortable to him as he could feel the men staring at him. Judas slowly raised his head and when he did, he made eye contact with both men. As much as he wanted to, Judas did not look away.

"Come here often, do ya?" the shorter man asked Judas.

The question did not feel like the beginning of a friendly encounter to Judas. In fact, he felt it was best at that moment to let the men know that he was familiar with this place and all of the treachery that came with it.

"Yes," replied Judas, "as a matter of fact I do."

"Funny," the man continued, "we've never seen you before. Well anyways, I'm Mitch and this here's Brady."

The driver of the JEDDO interjected, "We're coming into Iniquity, who's getting out here?"

Judas knew not to speak first...so he waited. Brady and Mitch waited as well. For a moment no one spoke, and the silent contract was signed.

Judas knew at that moment that they were up to no good. They wanted his DANs, his life, or both. "I'll be going to the Den," he said, finally, as he stared stoically at both men.

"And we're going to the Sumner Tavern," Brady gleefully uttered immediately after.

The driver replied, "Well we're about ten minutes away from the fueling depot; after that we'll be at both locations in fifteen minutes."

Judas leaned back and crossed his arms placing both of his hands in the pits of his arms. Under his left armpit and underneath his oversized garment is where he kept his EPIC. On every EPIC is a distress beacon called a snitch which, when engaged, will silently send your GPS coordinates to the last person with whom you communicated. Judas slowly caressed his EPIC for a few seconds until he found the button and he pressed it.

Brady attempted to continue the cat and mouse game with Judas, "So... what are your plans for this evening?"

Judas was having none of it. He did not answer the question and he did not take his eyes off the men.

At that point Mitch chose to dispense with the false pleasantries, "Well I guess we know what it is then."

Nothing else needed to be said. Judas's instincts told him not to trust these men. For the remainder of the ride the tension was almost tangible. As if each of them was formulating their own plan in their own mind, none of the men said a word or barely blinked.

The JEDDO came to an abrupt stop. The driver's door opened and closed and seconds later the side door slid open.

"Here we are," said the driver. "The Sumner Tavern is on the right; the Den is on your left."

In a final cry for help, Judas attempted to make eye contact with the driver who was preoccupied with his ledger. Brady, still seated, looked at Judas and slowly shook his head from side to side as if to say, *don't even try it.*

The driver, realizing that no one had moved, finally broke the silence. "Well let's go, I've got a schedule to keep!"

Judas stepped out of the warmth of the JEDDO and into the cold night of Iniquity. The Den and the Sumner Tavern were about two hundred yards away. All that separated them from both locations was two dark fields which were divided by a single cobblestone road which led to both locations. Brady and Mitch exited the JEDDO behind Judas.

"Thanks, Detlef," Mitch mistakenly uttered to the driver.

Detlef and Brady glared angrily at Mitch. Detlef got back in and almost instantly the JEDDO was driven away. They were alone.

"Unhand your trinkets, Albino gump!" demanded Brady.

Judas peered at the men with defiance. "You asked me if I came here often and I said *yes* to you. Therefore, you must know that I am not foolish enough to carry anything of value."

"Liar!" exclaimed Mitch as he rushed over to Judas frantically pushing his sleeves up his arms looking for jewelry or anything of value he could find. In his haste he stopped short of his armpits where Judas's EPIC was located and yanked the front of his garment around the neck area looking for a necklace of some sort. There was nothing.

Judas begged, "Please, I have nothing. Leave me alone."

At that moment Brady backhanded him across his face sending him flying to the ground. Without hesitation Mitch unsheathed his dagger and pierced the right side of Judas's torso between his ribs. Judas yelled in agony as he rolled over on his back. He thrusted his hands in front of him in preparation for the next cut which he received directly in the palm of his right hand. Brady repeatedly kicked Judas in his ribs right where he had been stabbed.

After what seemed to Judas like minutes, Brady looked to Mitch and said, "Kill him!"

Mitch picked Judas up by his neck and positioned himself behind him pressing his dagger's sharp edge against his throat. Before he could cut his throat, Mitch's eyes widened, and he dropped his dagger, quickly released Judas, and began to slowly back away as if he had suddenly seen a monster. Judas's badly beaten body collapsed to the ground.

"What is wrong with you? What are you afraid of, Mitch?" Brady angrily inquired.

"He is afraid that everything he has heard about the DOD is true," a familiar voice said from behind him.

A chill went through Brady's body. It was Rokuro Onishi himself! Brady slowly turned around with every intention of apologizing and pleading for his life as he dropped to his knees. With all the commotion they failed to hear the three horses approach them from behind. Rokuro was already off his horse and standing on the ground with his sword raised high, and with one precise stroke he beheaded Brady as he yelled, "Eeeyaaaaaaa!"

Rokuro maintained his finishing pose as Brady's headless body rolled over on its side and began to convulse. His head bounced a few feet away. The heavy arterial spray which gushed from his neck got weaker with each pulse. Mitch wanted to beg for his own life but knew that would only mean that he would meet his inevitable fate sooner. By that time Alexei and Igor had gotten off their horses as well. Alexei raised his twice emitter and squeezed the trigger unleashing the vibrating, muffled, low frequency, first projectile which shot Mitch in his chest. The fluorescent green tracer illuminated the immediate area as it made contact. Mitch instantly became paralyzed. Rokuro walked over to him, picked up his dagger, and stood directly in front of him. Mitch's eyes began to swell with water. He could not move, and he knew he was going to die a horrible death. With one swift slice, Rokuro opened his throat with his own dagger. Still suffering the effects of the twice emitter, he could not move as his blood streamed from his neck and soaked the entire front of the garment he was wearing. Suddenly twenty seconds had elapsed, and his motor functions returned. Instinctively he clasped his neck with both hands unsuccessfully attempting to stop the blood flow and take a deep breath. His eyes widened as he dropped to his knees trying to breathe through the gurgling blood.

Rokuro looked down at him with disgust and said disdainfully, "This is a better death than you deserve."

While Mitch writhed in agonizing pain on the ground, Igor grabbed him by his hair and with three loud grunts, "Umph...Hrrrrrr!

Umph!" he pulled his blade through his neck beheading him completely. Still holding Mitch's severed head in his hand by the hair, Igor walked over to his horse and retrieved a metal spear. He impaled the severed head with the spear and drove the other end of the spear into the ground. Alexei racked his twice emitter causing the second projectile to eject. He slung the rifle over his back and grabbed Brady's severed head and impaled it as well. As if it were a part of some ritual they had performed many times before, both Alexei and Igor grabbed folded blankets from their horses and unfurled them. Brady and Mitch's headless bodies were wrapped tightly in each blanket and bound with thick rope. They draped the lifeless bodies over the back of their respective horses. The bodies would later be given a proper burial. The impaled heads would remain as an example for all to see and as a reminder that the DOD was not to be crossed. Rokuro had already picked up Judas Benedict's body and positioned him atop his horse just forward of his saddle. Judas was badly injured but still very much alive. Rokuro hoisted himself to his saddle and with a kick his horse was at full gallop and he, along with Alexei and Igor, headed back to Tierra Mala with focused swiftness.

Chapter 3: Politics as Usual

Location: Central City, District County, Rights Province, planet Neutralia
Residential district, 0900 hours the next day

Having just completed his morning exercise regimen, Vice Chancellor Theris Lamont prepared for breakfast in his two-bedroom apartment on the second floor of a two story, eight-unit, residential apartment building in O'Neal Heights. The complex was reserved for some of Central City's more affluent and elite citizens. The living conditions in his apartment and in District County were more modern than could be found anywhere else in the solar system. The exception was the city of Sherrod, a bustling metropolis, which was in the Leanna Province on the southern continent of Neutralia. Theris Lamont's accommodations were lavish without being ornate which was exemplified by the Scandinavian design of the interior of his apartment. Upon completion of his bath Theris was alerted to his VC by the words, "Transmission incoming, Sender is Whisper."

Theris quickly adorned his robe and positioned himself in the proper proximity of his VC to receive the incoming communication.

"Receive transmission," he said.

As the holographic image appeared before him Theris was surprised to see the images of the entire five-member crew of the Whisper. "Good morning," he said. "I have been waiting for this transmission. The fact that you are all together indicates to me that you are united in your decision."

"We are" replied Mulati. "Me, Beth, Sam, Bjorn, and Corto have all agreed to accept your offer."

Theris was elated and could barely contain his happiness. "Perfect," he said. "It is a pleasure to meet all of you. I look forward to working with you. I will meet you here in District

County exactly one week before the convention like we discussed previously. I shall rendezvous with you in East City in the air field at 1900 hours. Thank you again. You have no idea how important this is...to everyone."

Mulati received the vice Chancellor's sentiment in a manner which appeared genuine but replied in a manner that was less than fervent stating, "Your payment makes it as important to us as it is to you."

Theris's response was brief, "Very well. Be safe in the meantime."

Mulati acknowledged the end of the conversation by simply waving his hand.

Corto's voice could be heard faintly in the background, "This fucker doesn't look rich to me." The rest of the crew looked at Corto with exacerbation on their faces.

"What?" replied Corto, "He can't hear me."

"I beg your pardon?" asked Theris, unable to make out what Corto had said. Hearing no other retort, he continued. "End transmission," said Theris and with that the images of the crew disappeared from his VC.

Seconds later, before Theris had an opportunity to move, the voice of the VC spoke yet again, "Transmission incoming, sender is Supreme Council."

Theris immediately responded, "Receive transmission."

The hologram that appeared before him was Chancellor Steven Aldrich.

"Good morning, Vice Chancellor Lamont. There is an urgent matter concerning Councilman Benedict that requires your presence. I expect you in the Council Chambers by no later than 1015 hours. End transmission."

Just as quickly as the Chancellor had appeared, he was gone. That Chancellor Aldrich was curt was nothing new to Theris; that was consistent with his normal behavior, but his mentioning of Judas was altogether different. That was unsettling to Theris. It was no secret that Chancellor Aldrich was not particularly fond of Judas Benedict, mostly due to his outspoken nature and their political differences. However, he respected, and was maybe even fearful of, his ability to operate in conditions less than conducive to diplomacy or personal safety. In addition to that, Judas was supposedly away for vacation on his home world, Albin. The thought of discussing another council member in his absence did not sit well with Theris. For a moment he sat in a pensive gaze before getting dressed. Theris took his time and enjoyed his breakfast which took him about fifteen minutes. The Council Chambers were only a short three blocks walk away from Theris' apartment, so he left walking as was his normal routine. As he made his way there his mind raced wondering what Chancellor Aldrich had to say or what he was up to. From time to time he was interrupted from his thoughts by the occasional, "Good morning, Vice Chancellor," from random citizens of Central City he would pass on the street. He smiled and acknowledged whoever spoke to him but would quickly return to his thoughts. After his slower than normal journey to his destination, Theris entered the Council Chambers where Chancellor Aldrich was already waiting. The vast room was characterized by simplistic elegance. Long colorful drapes bordered the large window at the end of the room overlooking Central City. They were wide open which allowed the bright sunlight to illuminate the room. A ten foot, heavily lacquered, dark, rectangular table surrounded by colorful parson's chairs with plush fabric was centered in the room. It was between the entrance and the window. The chairs surrounding the table complemented the drapes. Chancellor Aldrich was a native of the German Province on Evropa. He was a tall, stout, baritone voiced man who was relatively fit for a man of sixty years. Despite his often rude disposition he adhered to proper etiquette otherwise. Chancellor Aldrich had a thick, but well groomed, salt and pepper beard and a bald head.

"Good morning, Vice Chancellor Lamont. I have some disturbing news. Sit down."

Theris sat down slowly. "What is it?" he asked. "Is Councilman

Benedict alright?"

Chancellor Aldrich paused for a moment before continuing, "No, he is not. Right now, he is in an infirmary on a space station orbiting Albin. He, reportedly, is comatose. He was viciously attacked. By whom, I do not yet know."

Theris sat in stunned silence.

"Do you have any idea who could have done this to him?" asked Chancellor Aldrich.

"I do not," replied Theris as he continued, "but Councilman Benedict is a man of many secrets and of many alliances, some noble and some questionable. Your guess is as good as mine."

Chancellor Aldrich nodded in affirmation of Theris's last statement, "Indeed. I think it's best that we remain on Neutralia until after the convention next month. Things will have changed by then but until then we must ensure that we are safe... at least until I can find out the nature of this attack and whether or not he was targeted or if it was random."

Theris stood up. "Surely we are sending a medical team to retrieve him and bring him here?" he asked.

"Oh... yes," replied Chancellor Aldrich almost as if he had neither considered doing that nor anticipated that question from Theris. "I will dispatch a team immediately."

"Very well," said Theris as he turned to exit the room. "If you have nothing further for me I will excuse myself."

Chancellor Aldrich turned away from him and toward the large window which overlooked the Central City streets, "That is all."

Theris then left the room.

Moments later Chancellor Aldrich felt the vibration of his EPIC. He pulled it from his pocket to receive the incoming transmission. A video image of the caller appeared on the screen; it was Detlef.

"Good morning, Chancellor Aldrich. I bring you good news: Judas

Benedict is no longer your problem."

Chancellor Aldrich panicked! "It was you?" he frantically inquired.

"So... you've heard," stated Detlef confidently. "Yes, it was," he boastfully continued, "and when are you going to transmit my DANs?"

Chancellor Aldrich was incensed. "You fool," he said through clenched teeth harnessing his rage. "He is still alive!"

Detlef was incredulous. "Are you sure?" he asked, "I put my best men on that job. Brady and Mitch have never failed me! They would have told me if something went wrong."

Suddenly Chancellor Aldrich remembered that Detlef was an operative who worked in the Zasnezene Province on Hades. "Wait...where did you encounter Judas?" he asked.

"Here in Elba County," replied Detlef. "He was meeting with the DOD."

Chancellor Aldrich now had more questions than answers and, at that moment, he feared for his own safety more than ever. "I want you to contact Brady and Mitch," commanded Chancellor Aldrich. "Find out what happened or didn't happen and get back to me immediately. Do it now! End transmission!"

For the next hour Chancellor Aldrich paced around the large room waiting to hear back from Detlef. Then the call came. "Speak to me!" he commanded.

"We have a problem, Chancellor," replied Detlef. "Brady and Mitch are dead, and they were killed by the DOD!"

Chancellor Aldrich was not pleased and asked angrily, "Are you sure it was the DOD and that they are dead?"

Detlef nodded, "Regretfully, I am."

Chancellor Aldrich was more concerned now than ever that it would be revealed that he had issued a bounty for Judas Benedict's life. "Have you been compromised?" asked Chancellor Aldrich of Detlef.

"I have not," Detlef quickly replied before remembering Mitch's mistake upon leaving the JEDDO and said, "Wait... Judas Benedict may know my name."

At that point Chancellor Aldrich knew that Judas Benedict had to die before he was awakened from his coma. Surely, he would contact the DOD to inform them that there was a mole among them, and Chancellor Aldrich feared that they would torture and interrogate Detlef until they found out for whom it was he worked.

"Do not conceal the coordinates of your EPIC," commanded Chancellor Aldrich. "I'm going to evacuate you."

Detlef looked relieved, "I copy. I'll be waiting."

Chancellor Aldrich responded, "Do that. End transmission." As soon as Detlef's image disappeared Chancellor Aldrich yelled his dissatisfaction, "Noooooooo!!!"

Location: The city of Iniquity, Elba County, Zasnezene Province, planet Hades
Sumner Tavern, one hour later.

To calm his nerves Detlef resorted to what he knew would best alleviate his stress. As he entered the Sumner Tavern he couldn't help but wonder if it would be his last time there for a while. Surely, he would be forced into exile for his own protection if not for the protection of Chancellor Aldrich's identity. He walked to the bar. "Make it an ale, Scrappy" said Detlef to the always present barkeep.

"Coming up," replied Scrappy.

Within seconds Scrappy had returned with a thick glass of a foam topped, dark, alcoholic beverage.

Detlef aggressively took hold of the beverage and took a hearty swig of it. "Keep the tab running, I might be here for a while" he said.

Scrappy nodded affirmatively as he continued to handle his duties behind the bar, "Will do!"

Detlef found his way to one of the booths along the wall. He felt it was important to be able to keep his eyes on the front door and his back against the wall for safety reasons. He took his time consuming the twenty ounces of room temperature ale. He enjoyed every swallow and it seemed to relax him significantly. He threw his head all the way back as he took in the last swallow and slammed the heavy glass on the table when he was done. A scantily clad waitress quickly responded. She took away his empty glass and replaced it with another ale. "Perfect," said Detlef acknowledging the attentiveness of the waitress, "you're right on time, bitch."

Lisa, the waitress, rolled her eyes as she turned away from him to continue her rounds. Lisa was the twenty-four-year-old niece of Gerald, the tavern owner. She had seen it all before and she'd heard it all before. In this place that was not something that arose to the level of importance to require the intervention of Gerald or the tavern goons. She could handle this guy. However, something in the matter of fact way that Detlef let that word, *bitch*, roll off his tongue did not sit well with her. It was as if it were so ingrained in his personality that he was oblivious to the fact that it was rude or improper. To her it would have been more acceptable, or better, had there been some malice attached to it. Either way there was no way, in her mind, that he was a good person and she was not looking forward to serving him for the remainder of his stay.

As Detlef finished ale after ale he would periodically remove his EPIC from his pocket and gaze at the screen as if he were expecting a correspondence. There was nothing. His behavior toward Lisa never improved. In fact, it got progressively worse with him occasionally groping her perfect ass as he directed sexual innuendos toward her. After he was there for an hour, two Evropan men who were dressed in black from head to toe entered the tavern. Their attire was somewhat formal. It was definitely not the norm for the typical patrons of the Sumner Tavern. The men were known simply as One and The Other. One was holding an EPIC in his hand and he was completely consumed by what was on the screen. Lisa was directly in front of them when they entered the tavern. The Other got her attention. After a few words were said to her by One she looked to Detlef's table and pointed directly at him. She smiled as she walked away to continue her rounds, leaving the men standing there looking at Detlef. Detlef sat up in his chair. He knew what the DOD looked like and that was not them. He felt a great sense of relief. *Chancellor Aldrich was true to his word,* he thought. The men approached his table with One still holding the EPIC.

One put away his EPIC saying to The Other, "Yea, this is him." They both looked to Detlef before One spoke, "Your friend sent us for you."

Detlef smiled and stood up extending his right hand to greet the men just as The Other produced a twice emitter pistol and pointed it at Detlef's chest. He was expressionless as he pulled the trigger and that familiar sound caused a hush to come over the entire tavern. The fluorescent projectile lit up the booth. Detlef's arm remained extended from the paralysis caused by the first projectile. The Other immediately delivered the second projectile which opened a four-inch hole in Detlef's chest cavity clear through to his back. The force of the blast lifted Detlef off his feet and threw him into the wall at the back of the booth causing him to die instantly. The concussion of the round was loud and the blood splatter on the wall behind him was immense. One casually removed the EPIC from his pocket again and pointed it towards Detlef's body.

The voice on the other end of the EPIC was that of Chancellor Aldrich saying, "Good, end transmission!"

The Other slowly put the twice emitter back into his pocket without saying a word. One reached into Detlef's pocket and retrieved his EPIC. The two Mayhem Marauders then turned away from Detlef's corpse and calmly walked out of the tavern with a noticeable absence of haste.

As they exited the tavern the next voice to be heard was Scrappy's. "You know the routine," he said to the goons, "pick up the shit!"

Rage and Chaos walked swiftly over to the booth. Chaos carried two pails of water. Rage grabbed Detlef by the heels of his boots and dragged his lifeless body out of the booth. He gave little care to the fact that the back of his head banged the seat and then the ground with tremendous force. Chaos doused the blood-soaked wall with water and began to wipe it down. As they customarily did, Rage and Chaos hung Detlef's body on a meat hook in the large walk-in freezer behind the tavern. It would remain there for a week. If no one claimed it, they would burn the body in the incinerator. A few moments later and it was as if nothing ever happened; the tavern quickly reverted to its normal ambience.

Shortly thereafter, Alexei and Igor walked into the tavern with twice emitter rifles strapped to their backs. Scrappy briefly stopped what he was doing, because he recognized who they were, and said to himself, "It just keeps getting better."

Without saying a word to anyone Alexei and Igor split up and began to scan the faces of all the men in the tavern as they slowly canvassed every inch of the tavern floor. Suddenly Rage and Chaos were back inside the tavern standing at their normal post. Alexei walked over to both men. As he approached, Rage and Chaos looked at one another as if to say, *what could this guy possibly want?*

Alexei was brief as his heavy Russian accent greeted the goons, "I am looking for Detlef. He drives the JEDDO parked out front. Is he here?"

Chaos chuckled, "Oh, that guy. He's hanging out in the freezer out back."

Alexei yelled to his brother, "Igor, he's out back. Let's go get him!"

They quickly went out the back door toward the freezer. Rage just stared at Chaos. "Really?" he asked sarcastically. "You couldn't just tell them whyyyy he was in the freezer?"

Chaos answered, "They'll find out soon enough. Besides, he didn't say hello."

Seconds later Alexei and Igor returned and walked over to Rage and Chaos. "My apologies," said Alexei, "but in my haste to find this man my manners escaped me. I am Alexei, and this is my brother Igor. Greetings. Do you happen to know who it was who did this to him?"

Rage answered saying, "We have no idea who they were, but two guys came in, walked right up to him, and left his guts all over the wall without barely saying a word. They were real professional like about it too. They've been gone about thirty minutes or so now."

Alexei nodded to both men, "Thank you very much."

He and Igor turned and walked out of the tavern.

Once they were outside the tavern, Alexei used his EPIC to contact Rokuro Onishi.

"Did you find him?" inquired Rokuro.

Alexei's reply was to the point, "He is dead. Two men arrived and killed him before we arrived. His JEDDO remains parked outside of the tavern."

"I understand," said Rokuro. "Bring it here."

As they ended their transmission, Igor mounted his horse while grabbing the reins of Alexei's horse and slowly pulling it along as he began his journey back to Tierra Mala. Alexei drove the JEDDO following closely behind Igor. For the next thirty minutes they traveled at a methodical pace making sure that they weren't being followed. They reached the DOD hideout shortly thereafter. As they approached the front entrance a lone sturdy figure was there waiting for them to approach. Rokuro Onishi stood firm amidst the strong and cold wind as his clothing fluttered accordingly.

As Alexei prepared to exit the JEDDO Rokuro looked to him and said, "Alexei, download the memory from the onboard computer and bring it in with you."

Alexei did as he was ordered. While that was going on, Igor walked both horses into the nearby stable. The brothers both knew that Rokuro was extremely angry that their gang could be so easily infiltrated, and so were they. Alexei joined Rokuro near the front door and they both waited for Igor to join them. Once Igor returned from the stable, they all turned and entered the hideout together.

"This is very bad," said Rokuro. "He who has committed this act must pay with his life."

Nothing else was said as they made their way to Rokuro's living quarters. As they entered the room Adera stood from her chaise to greet Alexei and Igor, kissing them both on both sides of their face. She returned to her chaise and her wine while seductively staring at Rokuro as if she wanted him right then and there. As he briefly returned the affectionate gaze, she slowly diverted her attention to her glass of red wine and spoke softly but clearly, "I will be patiently waiting for you." She looked directly at him and smiled.

Rokuro simply turned his attention to the other room as he and the twins walked in toward the VC. Alexei inserted the memory from the JEDDO into the VC.

"Playback mode, three days back" enunciated Rokuro.

For three hours they carefully examined the footage looking for any contact Detlef may have had with a DOD member until they finally found what they were looking for.

"There!" stated an excited Igor. "I recognize that place; that's Valle Sin Retorno, it's a few kilometers beyond the OP."

The footage showed that the JEDDO was stationary in the valley.

Igor continued, "He has stopped and is clearly waiting to meet with someone."

Igor was right. The image of a man on a horse could be seen passing in front of the JEDDO. However, the image was not clear, and they could not make out the identity of the person with whom

Detlef was meeting.

"Traitor," whispered Rokuro. "Show us your face."

The rogue DOD member did not make that mistake. He kept his back to the JEDDO's camera the entire time. As he spoke to Detlef his voice never rose above a whisper. Whoever he was he was smart.

"He will give us nothing," inserted a defeated Alexei.

Just then the man, ever so gently and briefly, laid his hand on the front of the JEDDO for a fleeting moment.

Rokuro's eyes widened. "He just gave us his life. He may as well have touched his own mortality. Go put the JEDDO into the garage. I will meet you there shortly. Be careful not to touch the front of it."

Alexei and Igor did as they were told. Moments later Rokuro joined Alexei and Igor in the garage. He carried an IRS with him as he walked in. He quickly walked over to the front of the JEDDO and waved the scanning wand of the IRS over the spot where they had observed the rogue DOD member place his hand. All three men diverted their attention to the screen portion of the IRS and gasped as the identity of the owner of the fingerprints was revealed.

Rokuro stepped away in disbelief. "Francois is one of our most loyal members, why would he place us in such jeopardy?"

Igor quickly moved past his shock and asked Rokuro, "What will we do? What is your plan?"

Rokuro thought for a moment. He meditated on the true depth of the offense and he concluded that Francois should be immediately locked out of and denied access to all DOD facilities and technology.

"Block him from our database," commanded Rokuro. "He will come to us."

Alexei nodded and said, "Consider it done."

Rokuro returned to his quarters. His one weakness was his undying attraction to, and love for, Adera. He was anxious to feel her embrace and to kiss her full lips. She fully appreciated his masculinity which, ironically, made it easier for him to show his affectionate side to her. She sat up on the chaise and sat her glass of wine down on the table beside her as he entered the room. There was a look of consternation on his face.

"Tell me," she said, "were you thinking of making love to me while you talked your strategy of debauchery with Alexei and Igor?"

Rokuro glared at her in a way that indicated he was more confused by the question than anything. "No," he replied.

Adera continued, "Good. Do not allow thoughts of evil men to consume your mind while you are here with me."

Although he was reluctant to obey Adera's request, Rokuro could see her logic in making it. In his mind, if he had more energy to give to the situation then that's what he would do. "Why are you still clothed?" he asked.

She smiled as she softly and seductively whispered her reply, "The very same thing should be asked of you."

Almost as if he were attacking her, he lunged toward her while she reclined on her chaise and aggressively grabbed her lower jaw with one hand while he passionately kissed her. She offered no resistance and seemed to wilt from the passion of his kiss. She enjoyed it. In fact, there was nothing more that she loved than the thought that a man so rigid, so disciplined, and so calculated was anything but around her. He entered her body right there on her velvet chaise.

While Rokuro, Alexei, and Igor were at the DOD hideout making their discovery; Francois was in Ciudad De Vuelo attempting to enter the hanger to finalize repairs on his personal craft. He had been working on a vintage, one-man traveler which was a personal craft designed to travel long distances without the need for a crew. Because access to the back entrance was not busy and could only be accessed by DOD members, that was the entrance Francois liked to use. He placed his hand into the portal, removed it quickly, and stepped into the door which, he assumed, should have opened by that time. It did not open, and his face and body slammed forcefully into it. Somewhat confused, he stepped back, and he put his hand into the portal again. This time he waited for the readout on the screen. ACCESS DENIED it read. Francois' eyes widened as he stepped away. As a veteran of the DOD this was a protocol with which he was all too familiar. As his mind raced he began to calculate the amount of time he thought he had. *Think, Francois, think! You've gotten out of worse before.* Mere minutes ago, he was just inside the hangar so whatever triggered the lockout was discovered very recently. Francois mounted his horse and headed for a village of gypsies who were just beyond the facility. He knew he needed to get rid of his EPIC. It was unlike the DOD to contact their enemies that way; they preferred the element of surprise. However, he knew that they were aware of his familiarity with their tactics and would likely do something different this time. He needed to know how much time he had so he decided, in the meantime, to contact one of his closest longtime DOD associates, Roderick. "Contact Roderick," he spoke into his EPIC.

Roderick, a black haired Scottish man from Evropa, answered immediately with a smile and his usual greeting, "Francois, my boy."

Francois felt relieved. He was aware of Roderick's schedule and lifestyle and knew that he was never available during this time of day. "I was wondering if you would join me for an ale in Iniquity at the Sumner in about an hour?" he asked.

The question seemed odd to Roderick, but he declined the offer saying, "I'm busy, you know that."

Francois feigned disappointment as he nodded to Roderick, "I understand. I will speak with you later. End transmission." *Good! Not everyone is aware. I have time.* Francois kicked his horse into a full gallop as he hurried toward the gypsy village. The gypsies were very familiar with Francois as he often availed himself of their prostitutes and traded goods with them. This time he sought bandages as he arrived. What he offered in return was his EPIC. Sure, that the gypsies knew nothing about the more complex features of the EPIC, Francois decided that he would not immediately wipe his personal information from its software. After acquiring the bandages, he returned to the hangar, this time to the dense tree line leading up to the busy front entrance. Francois was a prominent member of the DOD and was very well known. He pointed his horse in the direction opposite the hangar and sent it galloping away by slapping its hindquarters. He wrapped both of his hands with the bandages prior to approaching the low-level DOD sentry holding the IRS near the front of the line.

"Francois, what happened to your hands?" inquired the young warrior.

"It's a very long story," Francois replied. "Obviously I can't access the portal right now," he said as he held both hands up to show the sentry. "Could you give me a little help?"

Without hesitation the sentry turned and placed his own hand into the portal granting Francois access into the hangar. As Francois quickly walked into the hangar he could hear the sentry speaking to the next person in line, "Step up and prepare to be scanned."

Up the elevator Francois went to the D level of the facility. That's where the DOD stored their personal crafts whenever they felt the need to use the hangar, which was normally for a brief period of time while they made repairs. Once on D level, Francois quickly entered hangar D-1. He immediately closed the door behind him and locked it. Just as quickly he removed the bandages from his hands and got busy preparing his vessel for flight. His final repairs would take him no more than thirty minutes.

Meanwhile at the DOD hideout, Alexei and Igor assembled their vast array of weaponry for target practice. As Alexei raised his twice emitter to sight in, he lowered it slowly as if something altogether unrelated had entered his mind.

"What is it?" asked Igor.

Alexei replied as if they had made a catastrophic oversight, "We need to send a mass communication to all of our members to let them know that Francois is a wanted man."

"You're right," replied Igor, "it was careless of us not to have done so already."

They sent out the mass message and within seconds they received an incoming transmission from Roderick.

"Speak to us," said Alexei.

Roderick frantically replied, "Francois contacted me an hour ago wanting to meet at the Sumner Tavern for an ale. He said he wanted to meet me around this time. What has he done?"

"We will release that information on a need to know basis," replied Alexei. "Thank you for responding, what you have given us is very helpful. End transmission."

Alexei spoke into his EPIC once again, "Locate Francois."

Immediately the GPS coordinates of his EPIC appeared on the screen.

"Rokuro will want to know this information," Igor said to his brother, "and without delay."

Within minutes Rokuro Onishi, Alexei, and Igor were on horseback and headed toward the GPS coordinates. They led them to the outskirts of Ciudad De Vuelo. They chose their horses because they would be able to negotiate a wider variety of terrain and reach Francois more quickly. Also, the JEDDO was a very noisy vehicle and they did not want him to hear them coming. As they rode they were armed with their usual weapons of choice. Rokuro wore his sword attached to his waist. Alexei and Igor had their twice emitters strapped across their backs. They were prepared, and determined, to kill Francois for his betrayal. This time they were prepared for what would surely be an intense battle as they were sure that Francois would have recruited allies to help him fight.

Meanwhile Francois' vessel departed D-1 without further incident. He was careful to shield his coordinates from all inquiries and decided to fly blind. He was familiar with the space immediately surrounding Hades, so he did not have a problem negotiating his way through that portion of the solar system. For him it was a clean getaway.

Rokuro arrived at the gypsy village with the twins shortly thereafter. He traced the EPIC to one of the elders.

"Where did you get that, and where is Francois?" demanded Rokuro.

The elder, speaking in a barely decipherable dialect, indicated that it was given to him in exchange for bandages. He handed the EPIC to Alexei who gave him a deleted one in exchange.

"He knew we were coming; this was a stalling tactic!" exclaimed Igor. "He has a vessel at the hangar; we must go!"

All three men raced to the hangar's entrance where they quickly encountered the sentry as they dismounted their horses.

"Have you seen Francois?" asked Rokuro.

The sentry replied without hesitation, "Yes, of course. He came here a while ago."

"Was he allowed entrance into the hangar?" Rokuro continued.

The sentry answered, "Yes." This time there was a hint of hesitance in his voice as he realized that Francois had possibly fooled him.

Rokuro unsheathed his sword. "How...did he get into the hangar?"

The sentry stood silent as he was paralyzed with fear.

Rokuro asked the question again. "How did he get inside?

"H-H-His hands were wrapped and..."

"You fool!" interrupted Rokuro.

The sentry attempted to continue, "And I thought..."

SCHLIIIIIIIIINNNNGGGG....was the next sound heard as Rokuro had swung a mighty swing with his sword with great precision removing the sentry's head from his body. His head landed upright between Rokuro's feet with its mouth wide open and its eyes closed. The headless body fell to its knees after a momentary delay and collapsed backwards. Rokuro carefully aligned the tip of his sword with the opening of its scabbard and, with a confident thrust, he returned it to its place as he uttered the words, "Death embraces you."

Igor picked up the now discarded IRS that had been held by the sentry. "According to this he's docked in D-1," he said. "He never checked out."

Rokuro stepped over the sentry's lifeless body and inserted his own hand into the portal on the wall. The doors opened immediately. They reached D-1 only to find that the door had been locked from the inside. Igor quickly input an override code into the keypad and the door slid open to reveal an open garage door on the other side but no vessel and no Francois. Only the bandages remained. He was gone.

Upon exiting the hangar Alexei motioned to the backup sentry to pick up the IRS. "That's your job now," he said. "Be better than your predecessor."

"I will," replied the nervous sentry.

Igor removed a metal spear from his horse and forced the dead sentry's decapitated head down onto it. Groans could be heard coming from the line of onlookers as most of them turned away from the sight of the severed head being impaled, some from fear, the others from disgust. He drove the other end of the spear into the ground. Alexei then rolled the sentry's body up into a heavy blanket and hoisted it atop the back of his horse situating it behind the saddle.

As they turned and started their journey back to Tierra Mala that familiar refrain could be heard in the background.

"Step up and prepare to be scanned," said the sentry.

Chapter 4: Just in Time

Location: Atmosphere of Hades
Aboard the Whisper

The crew of the Whisper, with the exception of Mulati, were in the lounge area of the ship having a discussion. As usual Corto, Bjorn, and Sampa were the most vocal participants in the debate.

"Why would someone want such a barbaric and irresponsible weapon?" asked Sampa. She had already grown tired of the debate but Bjorn and Corto, who shared the same opinion, were just getting warmed up.

"I beg to differ," replied Bjorn. "First of all, it's an inanimate object so it can't be irresponsible or responsible for that matter. That burden lies with the individual who wields it! Secondly, it would be the ultimate weapon. It would be efficient. In most cases it would either wound or incapacitate as opposed to killing, and it allows you to acquire more targets in half the time. If you want to kill someone you simply aim for the head, the heart, or a major artery. It's just that simple!"

Sampa rolled her eyes. "What if you happen to hit the wrong person? I've seen you with your twice emitter and you're not the most accurate person I've ever seen with that thing."

Bjorn raised his voice, "That child ran into my line of sight at the last moment, there was no way for me to avoid him!"

Sampa and Corto laughed as they remembered the incident together. Bjorn was always embarrassed when that particular incident was brought up and he became very defensive about what happened.

"Don't worry," interjected Corto, "you didn't kill the little fucker! I've had worse things happen to me than being paralyzed for twenty fucking seconds I'll tell you that much."

By that time Bjorn was seething. All he could do was shake his head as he reflected on the incident that occurred on India during one of their spice runs.

"All kidding aside," continued Corto, "there's mucho black powder on Asia. We have all seen it. Bjorn and I have done the specs for the projectile and casing already. It's a simple machine to put together and would definitely help us out."

"I strongly disagree," said Sampa. "Clearly you two don't follow your conscience as much as you claim. I'm glad no one else has thought of something so stupid."

Finally seeing an opportunity to get back into the verbal fray, Bjorn spoke up. "You know, Sam, that's the problem with you sometimes. If it's not your idea, then it's a stupid one. This solar system somehow managed to function before you were born into it and I, somehow, believe that it'll be just fine after you've left it." Realizing his last statement sounded a bit harsh, he paused before adding an addendum. "Not that I want you out of here prematurely or anything like that."

The whole room got quiet. Sampa was done with the debate but she was not angry. She knew she couldn't change their minds and it frustrated her. What frustrated her most, however, was not their lack of acceptance of her point of view but her inability to convey it on a level that would appeal to their simple minds.

"That's it, we win again!" exclaimed an exalted Corto as he sprang from his seat clapping his hands together once in a display of artificial joy intended to make light of the situation.

Just then Mulati walked into the room. "What's all the commotion about down here?" he asked.

"We're just down here proving Brain Almighty wrong again," teased Corto as he pointed in Sampa's direction.

Immediately Mulati was brought up to speed with what was being discussed. "Oh.... you three are arguing about those once emitters again? If you ever manage to make one it's not welcome on the

Whisper, it's too irresponsible."

Bjorn and Corto gave one another a quick glare that was half disappointment that Mulati had unwittingly given credence to Sampa's argument and half frustration that they did not seem to have a majority with their opinion. They looked at Sampa who was waiting for them to do so. She smiled and nodded because her ally in this argument, Mulati, had the only opinion that truly mattered. As Mulati sat down, Bjorn stood and got ready to speak. At that moment the lights inside the lounge dimmed and then flashed rapidly five times before coming back on. Beth was startled as the crew began to scurry to their predetermined emergency stations.

"What's going on?" asked Beth in a panicked voice.

Sampa answered immediately before heading to the bridge. "It's either a mechanical malfunction or a distress signal, we'll know shortly."

Beth went to her living quarters while the rest of the crew went to diagnose the problem. Bjorn and Corto went to the engineering room as Mulati and Sampa made their way to the bridge. Bjorn and Corto frantically scanned every switch and light on the control panels and switchboards in the room. Nothing seemed to be out of place or malfunctioning. Moments later Mulati's voice could be heard through the intercom.

"It's a distress signal. It's coming from just outside the atmosphere of Hades. Grab your twice emitters and meet me down below at the rescue hatch."

Mulati got up from his pilot's chair and prepared himself for the unknown.

"Sam, continue to go toward the distress beacon and alert us when you're in position."

"Will do, Mulati," replied Sampa. "Be careful down there."

Mulati didn't say another word as he left the bridge and headed below to join Corto and Bjorn at the rescue hatch.

Meanwhile Sampa could see the disabled vessel on her monitors and was able to calculate that they would reach it in approximately five minutes. "It's small. It's one of those livable long-range vessels. According to the life scan there's only one man aboard it," said Sampa's voice through the intercom.

Corto and Bjorn both looked up at the speaker as Sampa's voice came through. They readied themselves for the unknown. Moments later Mulati entered the room and grabbed his rifle style twice emitter from the weapons locker.

Bjorn asked of him half-jokingly, "You sure you know how to use that thing?"

Corto, slightly amused, chuckled to himself, but Mulati's expression never changed.

"Yes," replied Mulati, "you squeeze the trigger twice... unless it's aimed at an unarmed child."

Bjorn rolled his eyes as Corto laughed even harder.

"He ran in front of me at the last...Oh, forget it! I'm done explaining myself," shouted a visibly irritated Bjorn.

Mulati looked to Bjorn with a seldom seen wry smile on his face. Bjorn dropped his head and shook it from side to side as he laughed realizing, in that instant, that Mulati had only done to him what he had attempted to do to Mulati, poke fun.

"Get into position," ordered Mulati as he refocused on the matter at hand.

The rescue hatch was a circle on the floor, large enough for three people to fit through at the same time. It was positioned three feet away from one of the walls which served as a blast wall.

Sampa's voice came over the intercom again. "Its weapons have been disabled. I'm going to align the hatches now," she said.

Sampa began the process of aligning the hatches of both ships with one another, a maneuver that required her to relinquish controls of the Whisper to the ship's computer while it hovered over and magnetically engaged the hatch of the vessel below. Once both ships were in position, a tubular electromagnetic field connected both vessels. Oxygen was pumped into the tube from the Whisper followed by the rescue hatch sliding open and the metal ladder above it extending downward and into the tube. Mulati, Bjorn, and Corto, while taking cover, trained their twice emitters on the hatch. Seconds later the ladder reversed direction and the extraction began. Francois was pulled into the Whisper through the rescue hatch. He was completely naked which was protocol for individuals being rescued in that situation to show that they were unarmed and not a threat to their rescuers. Once he was fully inside the bowels of the Whisper, the hatch closed below him and jumped down from the ladder as it fully retracted into the ceiling.

"My name is Francois Larue. I am alone. My ship is moments away from exploding and we must get away from it now!"

"Watch him," said Mulati as he hurried over to the intercom on the wall. "Sam, cut bait and fly! This is a hot one!"

"Aye aye, Mulati," replied Sampa as she reacquired control of the Whisper and released the crippled vessel. As it floated away from them, Sampa engaged the Whisper's thrusters.

The Whisper quickly flew away from the disabled vessel along the trajectory it was already set. Since they weren't certain how long it would take the disabled vessel to blow up, Sampa did not want to waste time. She tried to cover as much distance as she could by travelling in a straight line. Meanwhile Francois was taken from the cargo bay to the ship's infirmary where Beth could scan him for any harmful sickness he might have or viruses he might be carrying.

"Francois, is it?" asked Beth.

"Yes," replied Francois.

Beth continued. "Go ahead and stretch out on this table. Let's have a look at 'cha, shall we?"

Francois did as he was told with no delay. Beth reached down and grabbed his hand with her gloved hands. She pricked his finger and deposited the droplet of blood onto a small, thin slither of metal. She immediately inserted the blood sample into a slot connected to a computer behind her. Seconds later she had her data. *Hmmm...interesting.* She grabbed Francois's left arm and promptly administered a heavy dose of antibiotics in the form of a high-powered injection.

"If I were you, I'd stay away from prostitutes. You should be disease free by 1500 hours tomorrow," said Beth. "Other than that, he's clean," she concluded as she removed her gloves while Mulati looked on.

"Here, put this on for now," said Bjorn as he handed Francois a clean, cotton parka.

"Good," replied Mulati to Beth before looking to Bjorn and Corto saying, "You two, take him to the multidimensional imager and generate him some clothing."

Corto motioned to Francois, "Come with us, Nature Boy, let's go and get you some ropa!"

As they exited the infirmary, the entire Whisper shook as the vessel from which Francois was rescued exploded. Fortunately, Sampa had gotten them far enough away in time.

"You people saved my life," said Francois.

Bjorn replied, "Thank Mulati when you see him again, he makes the decisions around here."

As they entered the room where the multidimensional imager was located, Corto strapped his twice emitter across his back and started pushing buttons on the machine.

Corto started asking Francois questions. "How tall are you?"

"1.83 meters," replied Francois.

"How much do you weigh?" asked Corto.

"13 stone 3 lb.," replied Francois.

"What's your shoe size?" asked Corto.

"25.4 centimeters," answered Francois.

Corto busied himself with inputting those figures into the multidimensional imager. The imager, when prompted by Corto, started constructing the garments and shoes.

"So, what the fuck did you do to your space house out there, Frenchie?" sniped Corto.

"It's Francois, and there was a problem with the dualonic dalfilator. It caused the system to overheat; one thing led to the next, and here I am."

"Was the smoke white or black?" asked Bjorn.

"It was white. Why do you ask?" replied Francois.

"I asked," said Bjorn, "because every experience is one from which we can learn, and I like to know how things work in case I need to fix them. White smoke means something in your engine wasn't sealed properly. Your fluids got all mixed up. Since you mentioned the dualonic dalfilator I assume you installed it wrong. Although it looks like it goes over, it actually goes under the leaf spring. That, my friend, is what caused you to have a bad seal and to lose coolant. You're lucky to be alive."

"Under?" asked Francois.

"Under," replied Bjorn and Corto simultaneously.

Bjorn gave Francois a pat on his shoulder before going to take a seat in a chair in the corner of the room. For a moment Francois stared blankly in disbelief that he had made such a foolish mistake.

"That's a beginner's mistake. Stick with me and Corto and you won't make mistakes like that anymore. Is there anything you do well?"

"I'm an expert with the twice emitter," replied Francois.

Bjorn rolled his eyes dramatically and sighed heavily saying, "Forget I asked! Everybody's an expert with twice emitters!" Again, he was angry. His face turned red as he sat in the chair with his arms folded.

Corto fought to contain his laughter as he paid close attention to the imager.

Francois stood confused as he looked back and forth from Bjorn to Corto wondering what he had missed.

Meanwhile Mulati was back at the controls in his pilot's seat beside Sampa. "I think now would be a good time for us to go back to cloak mode," he said to Sampa.

"Aye aye," she replied, "doing it now."

Moments later a red light on the control panel positioned between the two seats began to flash. It was the proximity alarm which indicated that another life sustaining ship was close. Sampa looked over to Mulati as if she was concerned.

"I see it," said Mulati.

They both turned their attention to the 360-degree radar which showed a ship larger than theirs approaching the area they had just left.

"It's a pirate cruiser! I think the explosion must have gotten their attention," said Mulati.

"I'm sure that's true," said Sampa, "but a ship that big is bound to have a proximity alarm as well, and a ship that size won't have a problem catching up to us. So, do we power down to hide our signal or do we stay in cloak mode and hope they don't see us?"

Mulati thought for a moment. "Cloak mode. That way if we're discovered we won't waste precious time trying to power up. Now we wait. Hopefully they won't see us."

Just then a startled Sampa shouted, "They're moving our way! They're coming fast, they definitely saw us!"

"Drop cloak mode," said Mulati. *We need the energy.* "Engage thrusters. We have to outrun them!"

Mulati pressed the intercom, "Bring Francois to the bridge and man the guns, we have pirates on our tail."

Sampa reached up to the control panel and pushed the levers up all at once. The rear thrusters fired and with a jolt the Whisper accelerated to full unassisted speed.

Moments later Corto appeared on the bridge with Francois, left him there with Sampa and Mulati, and immediately left to man one of the guns, positioned on the port side and the starboard side of the Whisper.

"Have a seat back there and don't move," said Mulati to Francois. "And strap yourself in, this is definitely going to be rough."

"We're not going to outrun them," said Sampa, "that ship is too powerful."

Mulati started hitting different switches on the panel.

"Prepare to jump to maximum celerity," he ordered.

Sampa paused as she looked at him with bewilderment. "We were headed for Neutrailia's orbit. If we jump to max cel we'll be forced to overshoot it and end up near Evropa…"

"I'm well aware of that, Sam," interrupted Mulati, "just do as I say!"

"They're almost close enough to touch us with their missiles," said Sampa, "if we don't hurry we will be caught."

"I'm almost done with the coordinates," replied Mulati. "Just a few more seconds."

Francois sat quietly in the seat behind them. He threw his head back and closed his eyes. He did not want to panic and make an already stressful situation even worse.

Mulati blurted out, "Now! Full forward capability!"

"Aye aye," shouted Sampa as she initiated the jump to maximum celerity.

Moments later the Whisper came out of maximum celerity into the orbit of Evropa and, as Sampa suspected it would be, it was littered with unfriendly space cruisers which were floating around the perimeter of Evropa's atmosphere. In addition to that, the pirate ship that was following them had engaged celerity at the same time they did and drafted directly into their coordinates.

"We might be in trouble now," said Mulati. "We're trapped!"

"Our best chance might be to fight the Evropans along with the pirate ship, maybe one of us can escape. Hopefully it will be us," said Sampa.

"No!" shouted Francois. "That's suicide! Most likely the Evropans are operating off instruments and not by sight. That world is 70% ocean. Go full speed ahead until you reach their atmosphere and cut your engines. They'll assume you've had a system failure and will go after the larger vessel."

Sampa looked at Francois and then looked at Mulati. "That might work! We could manually control the outboard and inboard flaps and…"

"And glide right in," said Mulati as he finished Sampa's sentence. "Full unassisted speed ahead, it's the best chance we have at this point!"

The pirate ship again began to close the distance between them as the Whisper sped toward the atmosphere of Evropa. As predicted, the Evropan starships started to move toward them from their front. The Whisper quickly approached the outer layer of Evropa's atmosphere. As soon as they were in it, Mulati shouted to Sampa, "Now!"

"Aye aye!" replied an excited Sampa as she cut the power.

The entire ship went dark as Mulati and Sampa forcefully grabbed hold of the controls which controlled the inboard and outboard flaps.

"Este que mal!" shouted Corto from his port side gunner position. "We are fucked, amigo! Where are the lights? Where are our fucking lights?"

Seconds later, as Francois suggested they might, the Evropan space cruisers diverted their attention away from the Whisper and began to fire on the pirate ship.

"Yes!" shouted Sampa. "It worked!"

Francois breathed a huge sigh of relief.

"That's the Macabre Sea, we can make it," said Mulati calmly as they emerged from the clouds. "When we are close we will initiate hovercraft mode."

The Whisper continued to descend at a furious rate as the Evropan ships engaged the pirate ship in combat. The percussion from the bombastic confrontation behind them could be felt throughout the Whisper as they continued to glide toward the sea.

Bjorn spoke to Corto using their headsets which are designed to work in the event of power outages. "You ok over there, buddy?" he asked.

"Fuck no," screamed Corto, "we are about to die!"

"Calm down," said Bjorn, "I think I know what they're doing up there. We should be ok." Bjorn released the communicate button on his headset. *I hope we'll be alright.*

"We're over the sea, go to hovercraft mode now, Sam," said Mulati.

With less than 5,000 feet to go before impact, she restarted the engines and quickly switched to hovercraft mode. The lights turned back on and the roar of the engine could be heard and felt throughout the Whisper.

Corto was overjoyed. "Haaaa! I knew they could do it! I never doubted them for a second!"

"We need to steer toward the darkest portion, that's where it's deepest," said Sampa to Mulati.

"I copy," replied Mulati. He pressed the intercom and spoke to the crew, "We're moments away from impact, brace yourselves."

Sampa and Mulati positioned the Whisper so that it would hit the water nose first at a 45-degree angle. Everyone, including Corto, remained silent as they all prepared for the impact. It came with a tremendous jolt. Suddenly the entire ship was submerged and going deeper into the blue abyss.

"Reverse propellers," yelled Mulati.

"Already on it," said Sampa, "I don't wanna crash into the bottom of this sea either!"

The Whisper slowed to a momentary stop, leveled itself, and, as it was programmed to do, captured its buoyancy. As soon as it did, it quickly began its ascension to the surface.

As the Whisper breached the sea's top, Bjorn ran over to the wall, pressed the intercom, and gleefully screamed into it, "Wooooooooo...Yeaaa!"

They all laughed, Francois included. They were relieved. They were alive. Mulati put his face in both hands, leaned back, and exhaled a huge sigh of relief. He swiveled around in his chair to thank Francois. He pointed at him and said, "You...," as he suddenly looked upon him with more scrutiny, "nice clothes."

Sampa turned around to look at Francois too, "Those are nice. Did Corto pick those out?"

"The midget? Yea, he picked them out," replied Francois.

"Great advice a while ago," said Mulati, "but, if you wanna live, don't ever let Corto hear you say that word."

Sampa looked back at Francois, grinned without showing her teeth, and nodded in agreement with what Mulati was saying about Corto. Mulati reached over to the control panel and flipped a switch releasing the ship's anchor.

"Destiny has guided us here, this is where we will remain until we can figure out our next move," said Mulati. He then switched the Whisper to low power mode.

Bjorn made his way from the starboard side gun to the gun on the port side of the ship looking for his buddy, Corto. He wasn't there so Bjorn went to the bridge looking for him.

"Great job, Mulati and Sam," said Bjorn as he entered the bridge.

"Thank Francois too, he helped out a lot," said Sampa.

Bjorn looked to Francois and nodded, "Yea. Where's Corto?"

"I don't know, he hasn't come here," replied Mulati.

Bjorn walked over to the intercom and pressed the button, "Corto, where are you buddy? Answer up."

For about thirty seconds there was no reply. Then the static of the open microphone could be heard as someone on the other side clumsily fumbled around with the button. The next voice heard was Beth's. "He's in the shower," she said.

Sampa's mouth opened wide with shock and so did her eyes. She had to cover her mouth with both hands to stop her laughter.

Bjorn wasn't so nice. He began to laugh hysterically. "The fucker shit himself," said Bjorn through his laughter. "That is awesome!"

Mulati was in no mood for games at that time although he was relieved. "Bjorn, as soon as Corto gets himself together I want you two to perform a systematic analysis on all the onboard computers and engines and function checks for all the weapons. We need to make proper use of this down time."

"Right away," said Bjorn. "Do you want me to take Francois with me?"

"No," replied Mulati, "he's had enough excitement for now."

Mulati wasn't actually concerned that Francois would be overwhelmed. In fact, he could care less about his mental well-being at that time. What was more important to him was for them to find out who he was and if he was potentially dangerous to them. Before Francois had the freedom to roam about the Whisper as he pleased, he had to be properly vetted.

Sampa had leaned back in her chair, her eyes were closed, and her long fingers were clasped together across her flat stomach. She was tired; they all were. However, her mind was never one to rest. While her eyes were still closed she spoke, "You know if the Evropans came out on the lucky side of that battle they'll be sending someone to look for our wreckage, right?"

"I'm aware of that," replied Mulati. "I've been thinking about that since we first cut the engines. This is a big body of water and an even bigger planet. Plus, by us being in low power mode we'll be difficult to pick up on their radars."

"True," said Sampa. As she continued to speak her voice tapered to a whisper, "That's very true."

Francois leaned forward in his seat as he undid his harness, "Looks like she's asleep."

"She is," replied Mulati. "It might be a good idea for you to do the same thing while you can. Things tend to change fast out here."

"I've noticed," said Francois. As he continued to talk, Mulati reached up and hit a switch which dimmed the lights inside the bridge. His only concern at that moment was Sampa's comfort. Moments later he covered her with a light blanket and she adjusted her body position slightly as she drifted further into her slumber. Francois got the message and stopped talking. Mulati paid close attention to the ship's radar and saw an island about thirty miles from their present location. The Whisper has extensive maps of every planet in the solar system programmed into its computer, but this particular land mass was uncharted. He programmed the coordinates of the island into the Whisper's navigation as he awaited the results of the system analysis from Bjorn and Corto. He finally sat back in his chair and tried to relax as much as he could. However, his eyes remained open as thoughts of being in uncharted territory continued to run through his mind. He turned to ask Francois a question, but he was also sound asleep in his chair. That everyone was fatigued was not an unusual occurrence after entering the atmosphere of a planet that was closer to the sun. The fatigue was a side effect of the increased gravity. Mulati turned his attention to the horizon and stayed focused on it for minutes. His gaze was interrupted by the sound of the Whisper's intercom coming on.

"Everything is functioning properly with the exception of a torque converter which is about to go," said Bjorn's voice through the speaker. "We're gonna go ahead and replace it. That's if we have time?"

Mulati pressed the intercom button to reply, "That should take about an hour, correct?"

"You guessed it," replied Bjorn.

"Fine," said Mulati, "go ahead and take care of it. Let me know when you're done."

"Will do," replied Bjorn. "Talk to ya in a few."

Mulati looked to Sam and Francois hoping that they had not been awakened by his conversation with Bjorn but they were both still asleep. Mulati turned his focus back to the horizon as he had become consumed by thoughts of the uncharted island that lay just beyond it.

Maybe because the bridge was so quiet the hour seemed to pass slower than usual, but it was almost exactly an hour when Corto's voice blared through the intercom.

"We're done, Mulati," he bellowed, "she's ready to go!"

Sampa's eyes instantly opened. She almost slid out of her chair because of the intense and exaggerated stretch that quickly followed. "I needed that," she said. "How long was I out?"

"About an hour," replied Mulati. "There's an uncharted island out there about thirty clicks, I think we should check it out."

"Uncharted? Really?" asked Sampa. "That's really strange because I personally updated our maps. If that's not in there, someone left it out intentionally."

"Then I'm absolutely sure I want to check it out," said Mulati.

"I agree," interrupted a curious Francois.

Both Mulati and Sampa swiveled around in their chairs to look at him at the same time. Apparently Corto's voice had awakened him as well.

"I appreciate your enthusiasm," said Mulati, "but your opinion, on matters such as this, has a few obstacles to overcome before it can register as valid."

Francois tilted his head to the side and showed the palms of both of his hands to Mulati and Sampa, acquiescing to their authority and showing humility all at once. He knew from that moment on that, unless it was an emergency, it was best that he would speak only when spoken to. Mulati hailed Beth's chambers over the intercom.

"How are you, Beth?" he asked.

"I'm fine now," she replied. "That was almost a little too much excitement for me but I'm alright."

"Good," said Mulati as he released the button and turned his attention back to Sampa. "We've got to get into those hyperbaric chambers before this gravity drains us all."

"Absolutely," replied Sampa. "I think I'll head down there right now."

"Perfect," said Mulati, "get Bjorn and Corto in theirs too. I'll jump in when you're done."

"Aye aye," said Sampa as she stood up and exited the bridge.

Mulati turned to address Francois. "We've got some things to discuss; I like to know who it is I'm dealing with, but that can wait until the rest of my crew is available."

Francois nodded in agreement as he replied, "Whenever you're ready, Mulati. Hopefully I pronounced that correctly?"

"You did," replied Mulati. "Come on, let's go to the lounge area, it's more comfortable there."

Francois followed Mulati from the bridge to the ship's lounge. Mulati wasn't, necessarily, interested in making things comfortable for Francois. He was more concerned with the thought of someone with whom he was so unfamiliar getting too acquainted with the inner workings of the Whisper. Therefore, to Mulati, the safest place for Francois to be was in the ship's lounge where there was no important information about the Whisper to be discovered.

Beth was already in the lounge when they got there.

"Has he eaten anything today?" she asked Mulati referring to Francois.

Mulati said nothing. He simply looked at Francois which was a signal to him to go ahead and speak for himself.

"I have not eaten today," replied Francois, "and I'm starving."

"Let's get you fed then," said Beth as she exited the lounge and headed toward the ship's galley. Moments later Sampa, Bjorn, and Corto walked into the lounge having spent that time in their hyperbaric chambers. Sampa's new found energy level was readily apparent as her entire demeanor had changed. "I feel soooo much better. That thing is amazing," she said.

"Yea, I'm feeling pretty good too," said Corto. "I'm also hungry. It's time to eat!"

"Beth is in the galley right now getting something for Francois to eat, so you're in luck," said Mulati.

He looked to Francois and said, "While she prepares something to eat we may as well get into the chambers ourselves. Let's go."

Francois stood and followed Mulati out of the room. "Ok," he said before leaving. His body language suggested that he was not completely enthusiastic about the culture in which he was now immersed, but he had no choice but to go along with their program.

After they left the room Corto began to chime in on the obvious saying, "Frenchie doesn't like to take orders, does he?"

"I think it's the structure that bothers him. The whole chain of command thing may be a bit much for him," said Sampa.

"Or maybe," said Bjorn, "where he came from he was in charge. Kinda hard to humble yourself when you're used to being the leader of the pack."

"Or a lobo solitario," added Corto.

"Good point," said Bjorn, "he was alone out there when we encountered him."

Sampa thought for a moment as she listened intently. "Actually, he encountered us. If he hadn't sent out that distress we'd have never known, he was out there. Secondly, he overworked that vessel..."

"So?" questioned Bjorn.

"So," continued Sampa, "he could've been running from someone or something. Who knows? For all we know he could be a good guy who just had a rough few hours."

"Rough for who?" asked an incredulous Corto. "That fucker was floating around in a vast sea of nothingness outside of, of all places, Hades; sent out a distress signal which could have been picked up by any number of pirates out there, gets plucked off of that piece of shit you call a vessel right before it blows into a million pieces, and is about to eat probably the best meal of his life from Beth. I'd say he's having a pretty damn good day."

Bjorn folded his arms and looked at Sampa. "He's got you there."

Sampa capitulated with a smile saying, "I see your point."

As the aroma of Beth's cooking started to creep into the lounge from the galley, the trio continued to talk about various things. Sampa, as intellectual as she was, did enjoy the banter she was often confronted with from Bjorn and Corto. She felt it gave her balance. For Bjorn and Corto those interactions were mutually beneficial. Sampa kept them mentally sharp while allowing them to be the men they were without reservation. There was no pressure from either side and that's the way they all liked it.

After some time Mulati and Francois re-entered the lounge. Bjorn, Corto, and Sampa continued to converse as Mulati and Francois sat down to join them. Mulati was constantly trying to balance duty with positive morale aboard the Whisper so, despite his eagerness to discuss Francois with the crew, he waited for a natural lull in their conversation to bring him up.

Beth walked into the lounge with her proclamation that their late afternoon meal was almost done. "I have stew simmering in the galley, it won't be long now," she said.

"Beth, you're right on time," said Mulati, "I wanted everyone to be present while Francois told us about himself."

As everyone looked to Francois, he started to speak, "There's really nothing to tell. I guess if I had to describe myself I'd have to say I was somewhat of a drifter. I'm skilled at quite a few things and I'm pretty good with my hands."

Bjorn interrupted him with a question that seemed more skeptical than inquisitive, "What were you doing on Hades?"

"Well, how'd you know I was on Hades?" asked Francois.

"Given the size of your vessel, I don't think you were long on supplies," continued Bjorn. "That ship is incapable of more than one celerity unit, so you were either coming from Hades or from the space station. My guess is that you were trying to make it to the space station."

That explanation sounded better to Francois than what was actually true, so he agreed with Bjorn. "You're right," he said.

"About which part?" asked Corto.

"Both," answered Francois. "I was on my way from Hades to the space station for supplies."

"Do you have a family?" asked Beth.

"The only family I had was my grandfather who raised me in a whorehouse in the Zasnesene Province," replied Francois. This time he was telling the truth. His body language changed because he was not proud of his upbringing. He had no siblings that he knew of and he was taken to Hades by his paternal grandfather, who was his only remaining grandparent, after the untimely deaths of his mother and father at the hands of pillaging Mayhem Marauders. He was ten years old when the murders occurred.

Beth recognized the subtle shift in his demeanor. "I believe him," she said. "Besides, judging from his lab results, he goes home a lot."

Francois was slightly amused by Beth's comment. He wasn't offended by it in the least. The lightheartedness of her statement was a welcome interruption to the rigid structure he had perceived to that point. He instantly took a liking to Beth that was no different than the affection she received from the rest of the crew. She had that effect on people. As she turned and left the lounge to head back to the galley he watched her intently as if the feeling she had just injected into the room was going to leave with her.

"A whorehouse, huh?" asked Corto abruptly as he broke Francois' gaze. "Care to elaborate on that?"

"Well..." said Francois, "it was fun for a while, especially during my adolescent years, but as I grew older I started to see the long term emotional damage that was being done to those people. It got depressing after a while."

Sampa was surprised by his confession. She expected him to say that he had gotten tired of using the prostitutes sexually but was pleasantly surprised by the notion that he had gotten emotionally attached to those people. In that instant she gained a modicum of respect for him.

Of course, Corto was quick to bring things back to reality.

"Only a madman would be uncomfortable with those arrangements, Frenchie! That's about as close to perfect as life can be," he said.

"You would definitely have loved it," replied Francois with a straight face, "all of the prostitutes were male."

Corto was not amused. "What the fuck is that supposed to mean?" he demanded.

Francois winked his eye at Sampa who was suddenly in on the joke and could not control her laughter. Bjorn found it hard to contain his laughter as well. Francois stayed in character and did not smile once. He felt he had gotten his revenge on Corto for him calling him Frenchie again.

Corto sprang from his seat and headed toward the lounge exit. "I'm going for a smoke," he declared. "Let me know when the food is ready!"

After Corto left the room Bjorn looked at Francois and said jokingly, "He is really going to kill you if you keep that up."

Francois feigned solace with the statement saying, "Nobody lives forever."

Chapter 5: What's Out There?

Location: Evropa
Aboard the Whisper in the Macabre Sea

Beth's meal was devoured completely by the crew and, as usual, they all enjoyed it. One hour after eating, Mulati and Sampa were on the bridge seated in their pilot and copilot chairs respectively. They were alone.

"I want to see what's on that island, Sam," said Mulati.

"Me too," said Sampa, "I'm very curious to see what's there and why it's not on any maps."

"Right," replied Mulati, "we'll start to ferry to that location soon."

Mulati pressed the intercom and spoke into it, "All hands on deck. Meet Sam and me on the bridge in fifteen minutes."

Immediately Bjorn's voice could be heard responding through the speakers, "Me, Corto, and French...um Francois copy, we'll be right there."

Moments later the air of the open microphone could be heard along with the sound of someone clearly fumbling around with the button. Sampa glanced over at Mulati with a look of pity because she knew it was Beth, who was as technologically challenged as they come, trying to figure it out yet again.

"I...c-copy. I'll be up there too," said Beth's soft voice. After another five seconds of dead air the microphone went silent.

In exactly fifteen minutes the entire crew was on the bridge, some seated and some standing, and they focused their attention on Mulati as he began to speak.

"There's an uncharted island about thirty clicks east of our location. We are going to check it out. Francois, you will join myself, Bjorn, and Corto on this expedition to the island. This is a reconnaissance mission. I anticipate this taking us twenty-four hours maximum. If we haven't seen or discovered anything significant by then we will pull out."

"Can we hunt?" asked Bjorn. "There's sure to be some tenderloin running around out there somewhere. It'd be nice to be able to carve up something fresh for a change."

"Absolutely," replied Mulati, "I wouldn't have it any other way." He looked to Beth and smiled at her saying, "You'll get your chance one day. This time we need you to stay back to keep Sam safe."

Beth returned Mulati's playful smile. Although she was anxious to go on some of the adventures with the crew she knew that this was neither the time nor the place. She didn't want to slow them down. However, she wondered if they truly knew how much she worried about them each time they were away.

"Sam, go ahead and pull anchor and start your ferry. Set your speed at thirty knots, that should give us time to get ready," ordered Mulati. "I want you to drop anchor about a half click out, we'll raft the rest of the way in."

"Aye aye," replied Sampa as she assumed the pilot's seat normally occupied by Mulati and began the process of retracting the ship's anchor.

"Let's go, you three," said Mulati to Bjorn, Corto, and Francois as he walked toward the exit of the bridge.

"Mulati, listen to your conscience," said Sampa.

"I will, and let yours lead the way," he replied.

They headed to the cargo bay of the Whisper to stage their gear for inspection and to mentally prepare for the task at hand. This was not the first time they'd gone on one of these missions and the one thing that was consistently true about them was that they were unpredictable. Mulati, Bjorn, and Francois arrived at the cargo bay together. Corto had taken a detour to his living quarters to retrieve his tactical knife vest which was equipped with thirty perfectly balanced daggers made specifically for throwing. Corto was extremely accurate with throwing the razor sharp, four inch, daggers which were attached, blades down, to his vest with velcro so that they could be quickly removed. Moments later Corto joined the other three men in the cargo bay. Mulati and Bjorn had their equipment already laid out on the floor in front of them and were carefully inspecting each individual piece. In front of Mulati was his twice emitter, twice emitter ammunition, some rope, a dagger, a canteen, and a small amount of rations; all laid out on an olive drab poncho liner. Bjorn had the same items laid out before him. Corto immediately unfurled a poncho liner in front of him and he began to retrieve those same items from the supply locker which was also located in the cargo area.

"Francois, go over there with Corto, grab your supplies, and lay them out over here just like we have done. He'll make sure you get what you need," said Mulati.

Francois did as he was told. Shortly thereafter he returned with both arms full of the items that were issued to him by Corto. Like Bjorn and Mulati, he laid the items out before him on the floor. Soon all four men had their equipment laid out.

"When I call it out, hold it up," ordered Mulati. He then began to call each item out one by one pausing after each to give each person enough time find it and hold it up.

"Twice emitter...ok. Twice emitter ammunition...alright.

Rope. He looked around to make sure they all had it. Got it. Dagger...good. Canteen? Good. Poncho? Good. And rations?" He looked around again. "Good, we're ready," he said as they all commenced to collect their items from the floor and place them into dark satchels.

"Let's get the Rapid Arachnids ready, I think we should use them here since we are unfamiliar with this terrain," said Mulati.

"Will do," replied Bjorn as he and Corto walked across the vast floor of the cargo bay to unlock four of the mechanized, spider-like, modes of transportation which are equipped to handle a rider and one passenger. If necessary, the passenger could ride directly behind the driver. The eight-legged machine was designed to negotiate hazardous terrain very quickly with minimal disturbance to its rider. It had a narrow leather seat and handlebars. A fully charged rapid arachnid could run continuously for forty-eight hours. The Rapid Arachnids were stored in coiled mode mainly to maximize space. Moments later they returned to the staging area with four of the Rapid Arachnids on top of a wheeled flat surface that was just long enough to carry all four of them. Bjorn was in front pulling and guiding them by the chain to which they were tethered, and Corto was pushing from the rear. They appeared to be heavy and hard to move. Francois immediately ran over to assist. He joined Corto at the rear and helped push which increased their speed immediately. Corto pushed as hard as he could and, without looking up, said, "Thanks, Francois."

Francois immediately looked at Corto but resisted the temptation to reply more than the simple, "You're welcome," that he uttered. He didn't know if Corto had simply forgotten to call him Frenchie or if he was making progress with the crew. Either way it was positive to him and he was not going to question it.

"That's fine right there," said Mulati as he motioned for them to stop where they were. "We'll leave them there until we have deployed the boat."

Suddenly Sampa's voice came through the intercom, "We are ten minutes out. Ten minutes. Start your final checks now."

Mulati had already gotten them ready. Now it was time for them to mentally prepare themselves. Corto lit another cigarette, put it to his lips, and took a long drag. Mulati found an empty space away from the others and dropped to his knees and closed his eyes. He had his hands on his knees, got completely quiet, and remained still.

"What's he doing?" asked Francois.

"Shhh...he's meditating," whispered Bjorn.

Francois matched Bjorn's tone asking, "How long does he normally do that for?"

"As long as it takes," answered Bjorn.

Corto adorned his knife vest and busied himself with tightening the straps and securing the daggers to it while his cigarette dangled from the corner of his mouth. He was quiet as he worked, and, in his own way, he was meditating as well. Moments later Mulati sprang to his feet and crossed both his arms in front of him. Without hesitation Bjorn and Corto did the exact same thing. They executed five synchronized, aggressive, ritualistic, and exaggerated, boot high stomps which started with the left foot and alternated left to right followed by them thrusting their clenched fists downward while throwing their heads back, sticking out their chests, and exhaling a primal yell on the fifth stomp. "AAAAAHHHHHHHH!!!!" they yelled in unison.

Each stomp represented a member of the crew of the Whisper, thus there were five.

Bjorn pounded his own chest and yelled, "Let's go," as his eyes widened, and his nostrils flared. They were ready.

Sampa was watching the surveillance monitor of the cargo bay from the bridge along with Beth who had joined her there.

"I get chills whenever that's done," said Beth, "I hope they're careful out there."

Sampa smiled, "That Whisper Yell gets me going too. They're ready now!" She pressed the intercom button and spoke, "Dropping anchor now, Mulati. Go get 'em boys!"

As the massive back hatch was being lowered, Francois stood silently and, although he was impressed, was somewhat confused as he could not put his finger on the pulse of this crew. The Rapid Arachnids and the rest of their equipment, to include hunting bows, were loaded onto the boat. They all got in as it slid down the ramp and into the green-blue water. Corto and Bjorn were on one side of the boat and Mulati and Francois were on the other. Bjorn and Mulati were up front. They used oars to paddle toward the shore instead of the motor because they wanted to get there as stealthily as possible. Once she was sure that they were clear of the ramp,

Sampa initiated the sequence to close it. The ramp slowly lifted back into the ship.

"What are they going to find out there?" asked Beth.

"Hard to say," replied Sampa, "but they will find something, they won't stop until they do. If this place is anything like the rest of Evropa there's sure to be an abundance of reptiles, primates, and wild pigs out there. Bjorn will like that last one."

"I'm sure he will," replied Beth. "How long will it take them to reach shore?"

"Not long," answered Sampa, "maybe fifteen minutes. They'll take their time."

"Why didn't we just take them all the way up to the shore?" Beth asked.

Sampa looked over at Beth fondly. Beth was now seated in the copilot chair. That she was so interested in this information demonstrated to Sampa that she was willing to step outside of her comfort zone to learn something new. "Since we don't know anything about this island we can't take the chance that we'd damage our intake or our hull on a sandbar or reef. It's safer for us in the deeper water. Also, there's nothing for us to run into out here should we need to get away fast."

"Oh," replied Beth, "I see. Well let's hope that's not the case."

"If it is, we're ready," replied Sampa as she smiled and reached over and gently patted the back of Beth's left hand. Don't worry."

Beth put her hands together in her lap and smiled nervously. She tried to pretend as if Sampa's answer had satisfied her, but she was not put at ease. She was never relieved until the crew returned from their mission intact.

"It's getting dark," said Beth.

It is, isn't it?" replied Sampa. "Most likely they'll camp out somewhere near the shore tonight and explore at dawn."

"Why'd they leave you behind this time?" asked Beth. "You can handle yourself out there."

"Oh, that's not the issue," replied Sampa. "Besides Mulati, I'm the best at piloting the Whisper. I'm here for their safety."

"Oh," said Beth as she was apparently surprised by the frankness of Sampa's answer, "I see. Very good."

Seconds later, almost without warning, rain began to pour. In fact, it was a thunderstorm. The rain was heavy, and it made the island difficult to see from the Whisper. Sampa reached up to the control panel and hit a switch turning on the night vision. "There they are," said Sampa as she pointed to the crew's boat through the windshield of the Whisper. She leaned forward in her chair and squinted her eyes as if she had seen something.

"What is it?" asked Beth.

"I'm sure it's nothing," replied Sam while reaching up to a keyboard on the control panel and sending Mulati a direct message to his EPIC which read, *There are heat signatures on the island beyond the shore about one hundred fifty meters into the woodline. Could be animals. Not sure.* Sampa looked over to Beth and said, "Relax, everything is ok. I'm going to lay back in this seat and rest for a few. You're welcome to stay and do the same."

Beth didn't respond. She was worried, and it showed.

Sensing her concern, Sam said to Beth, "Trust me, they won't hesitate to contact us if something is wrong."

"Ok," replied Beth as she got up from her seat to exit the bridge. "If you'll excuse me, I'm going to go down to my quarters, it's a little less nerve-racking down there."

Meanwhile Mulati, Bjorn, Corto, and Francois were one hundred yards from shore and moving at a constant speed with synchronized paddle strokes. Mulati had felt the vibration of his EPIC when Sampa messaged him but he did not want to interrupt their progress or pace to answer it. By this time, they were so soaked from the constant downpour of the rain that being wet no longer bothered them. They were focused on the task at hand which was to get to the island and set up their bivouac. Suddenly they were there. The front of their boat crashed the jagged shoreline of the rocky white sand beach as Mulati and Bjorn jumped out before it stopped. They grabbed their respective sides of the boat and dragged it along with them. As the back portion of the boat hit the sand Corto and Francois did the same thing, running alongside the boat and maximizing the momentum gained by the tide and their strokes. Mulati quickly tied one end of his rope to the front of the boat and allowed the rolled-up rope to unfurl as he ran the other end to the dense wood line which was twenty-five yards away from that particular portion of the beach. He tied that end around the base of a sturdy redwood tree making sure to keep the white rope as close to the ground as possible. All four men put the dark satchels of supplies on their backs and moved with speed and silence saying as little as possible. They also grabbed a piece of the first rapid arachnid and moved it from the boat to the beach. They did the same for the others as well. Within five minutes, all four were in the sand. Mulati grabbed a handful of the white sand and placed it into the chameleon port of the boat. Almost instantly the boat, from front to back, began to change to the color of the beach. It was perfectly camouflaged.

"Turn them on," said Mulati to the others as he pointed to the Rapid Arachnids.

They all reached underneath the coiled-up metal to the center and pushed a button on their respective machines. Five seconds later the Rapid Arachnids unfurled into seated, eight legged, modes of transportation. The handlebars were the last to unfold coming from inward to an upright position. They mounted the mechanical spider-like vehicles and headed to the woodline. Approximately fifty yards into the thick woodline they found a clearing big enough for their bivouac.

"This is it, we'll place our camp here," said Mulati as he waved his arm over a portion of the clearing.

They dismounted the Rapid Arachnids and placed them back into coil mode. Shortly thereafter they got busy constructing their lean-tos with their ponchos, poncho liners, and rope. The open-ended shelter would be enough to at least shield them from the pouring rain. While the others worked on their makeshift shelter, Mulati reached into his pocket and retrieved his EPIC. He sent a simple message back to Sampa, *Copy*.

Sampa received the message she had been waiting for and rerouted all incoming transmissions for the Whisper to her own EPIC before retiring to her personal living quarters.

An hour later all the lean-to shelters had been constructed. Each lean-to was within two feet of the next in a semicircle. Mulati and Bjorn were positioned to the outside, Corto and Francois had the two inside positions. Francois was in between Corto and Mulati. Within the next hour the rain slowed to a drizzle before it eventually stopped.

"Gather around," said Mulati as he exited his lean-to. "I received a message from Sam that she was picking up heat signatures about one hundred fifty meters into the woodline. It's heavily vegetated here so there's a good chance it's only wildlife. We can't be too careful though, just in case. We need to exercise noise discipline tonight. Also, we need to set up firewatch. Corto, congratulations, you have first watch. I'll take the last watch. You can figure out the middle shifts amongst yourselves. You see that high rock about twenty-five meters out, Corto?"

Corto turned around to look where Mulati was pointing, "Yea, I see it."

Mulati continued, "That's our observation post, take the night vision goggles with you. We move at dawn, gentlemen. Get as much rest as you can; you will need it."

Corto grabbed his twice emitter and started toward the rock.

"Bjorn you're up next," he said as he walked away.

Bjorn, who was already laying down in his lean-to simply put his thumb in the air to acknowledge that he had heard Corto. Corto continued on his way placing the goggles over his eyes as he walked to the rock. Bjorn quickly drifted off to sleep. Francois found it difficult to rest at first but was able to force himself to sleep about a half an hour after Bjorn. Mulati, purposely, was the last to drift off.

Chapter 6: Mystery Lady

Location: Evropa
Uncharted Island, 0500 hours

At dawn Francois, Bjorn, and Corto were awakened by Mulati gently kicking the soles of their feet. "Get up, we move in thirty minutes," he said.

All three men, upon waking up, immediately grabbed their boots, turned them upside down, and shook them before putting them on.

"How'd you sleep?" Bjorn asked Corto.

"Like a drunk in a whorehouse on payday," replied Corto.

"What about you, Francois?" asked Bjorn.

"Eh...," replied Francois as he shrugged his shoulders while he laced his boots. He didn't sleep well. He had not yet gotten accustomed to his predicament even though he tried desperately to fit in.

"I advise you to go ahead and scarf down your chow now, it might be the only chance you'll have to eat," said Bjorn to Francois. "Mulati doesn't like to slow down once he gets moving."

Francois heeded Bjorn's advice and dug into his rations. Within minutes they were all done eating and all their gear was placed back into their respective satchels.

"Corto, give it a once over and make sure we haven't left anything behind," ordered Mulati.

"Will do," said Corto as he immediately got up to visually inspect the areas where they had eaten and slept. "We're good to go," he said moments later.

"Good," said Mulati, "let's move out."

They all placed the satchels on their backs and walked over to turn on their Rapid Arachnids. They attached the hunting bows to the rear of the Rapid Arachnids and laid their twice emitters, which were slung over their shoulders, across their laps.

"We'll travel in a diamond formation. Corto, you've got the point. Bjorn, you'll bring up the rear. Francois, you stay abreast of me. We'll move out eastbound in ten-meter intervals."

"Moving," said Corto as he set out toward the sun through the rugged forest.

As soon as Corto was ten meters ahead, Mulati started moving and he motioned to Francois to do the same. Staying abreast of one another, Mulati and Francois put approximately ten meters across between themselves while staying ten meters behind Corto. Once Mulati and Francois were ten meters ahead, Bjorn moved out as well. Periodically, Corto would put his right hand in the air with his open palm facing forward as he stopped to survey the landscape. When he stopped they would stop. After he determined it was safe to proceed he would wave his hand forward indicating it was time to move. Mulati relayed every hand signal to Bjorn so that they would maintain the integrity of the formation as they continued their trek. As the brush got thicker the formation moved slower. Finally, it got so thick that it was too dense for the Rapid Arachnids to get through. Again, Corto put his right hand up and the formation stopped. This time he put both hands out to the side and brought his palms together in front of him indicating he wanted the rest of the men to come up to him, and so that's what they did.

Once they were all together Corto spoke: "It's too thick for the Arachnids, we have to continue on foot."

"I agree," said Mulati. "We'll stage our gear here and travel light from this point on. I'll leave a tracker on my arachnid, so we'll know how to find them."

They turned off the Rapid Arachnids and staged their satchels beside them at the base of a very large tree which was surrounded by thick brush. They took small pieces of the plants and stuffed them into the chameleon ports. Within seconds the Rapid Arachnids were perfectly blended into the scenery. Equipped only with their twice emitters and canteens, they moved out on foot. Corto was still wearing his vest. They switched from a diamond formation to a column and stayed within three meters of one another. Corto still had the point and Bjorn still brought up the rear. Francois was third. After another hour of moving slowly through the brush, Corto stopped abruptly and put his right hand in the air. This time he closed his fist, which meant that he wanted them to be completely still and remain silent. As they stood silent for about a minute, a faint voice could be heard in the distance. It sounded like a scream and it sounded like a woman. After hearing the sound Corto turned to make eye contact with Mulati who nodded his head up and down acknowledging that he had heard it too. Corto waved his hand forward and started to walk toward the sound. Mulati turned to look at Francois and Bjorn with his right index finger vertically touching his closed lips before waving them forward and moving out. They continued to walk in a column. This time they walked slower and listened more carefully. Suddenly, Corto stopped again. He immediately thrusted his closed fist into the air. They all stopped. Corto put his arm out to the side palm down and lowered his hand to his side. Simultaneously they all kneeled.

Corto turned to Mulati while pointing his index finger and middle finger toward his own eyes and mouthing the words, "Enemy in sight."

Mulati turned to relay the message to Francois and Bjorn. Again, the screaming female voice could be heard. This time it was louder and more agonizing. Each of them moved their twice emitters to port arms. Mulati whispered to Francois and Bjorn to standfast as he low crawled to Corto's position.

"We gotta act now," said Corto, "or else they're going to kill her."

Mulati pulled out his binoculars and looked for the woman to whom the voice belonged. Within seconds he found her and gave the binoculars to Corto.

"There she is, right there about one hundred meters out tied to that tree," said Mulati. "She looks bad, they've probably been beating her all night."

"I see her," said Corto. He started counting, "One, two, three, four, five, six. I see six men so far. The fat balding one with the eye patch looks like he's in charge, he must be pretty important."

The woman was tied to the sturdy tree by three ropes, one around her ankles, another tightly around her waist, and one loosely around her neck which allowed her head to dangle forward slightly.

Mulati low crawled back to Bjorn and Francois to relay to them what he had seen and what he and Corto had discussed. They all low crawled up to Corto's position. For a few minutes everything got quiet. Neither the men nor the woman made a sound.

"What are they doing now?" whispered Bjorn.

"I don't know, it's hard to see through this brush," replied Corto. "I need to stand up and look."

"I don't know if that's a good idea," said Bjorn, "you might expose yourself."

Corto brought the binoculars down from his eyes and gave Bjorn a stone-faced glare.

"Then again, maybe not," replied Bjorn. "Go ahead."

"Slowly," said Mulati. "Be careful."

Corto slowly stood for a clearer line of sight but as soon as he cleared the brush and got a better view he said, "Uh oh!"

No sooner than those words left his mouth there was a low frequency, vibrating, hum in the distance and just like that he was paralyzed. The fluorescent green projectile sliced through the air and made contact with his chest. Thinking quickly, Francois tackled him and draped his entire body over him. "He's been emitted," yelled Francois. A moment later the second projectile sliced through the air and bounced harmlessly off Francois' back.

"Everybody stay down!" yelled Mulati. "We don't know where else they could be!"

Corto was still on the ground with the binoculars up to his eyes. He could not move.

"Fan out! Protect our flanks," yelled Mulati.

Twenty seconds passed and Corto regained his motor functions.

"Hhhaaaaooooppp…," he inhaled as his body violently contorted upon regaining its ability to move voluntarily. "Those fucking dogs! They tried to kill me," he screamed with wild eyes while hyperventilating.

"Keep it down or you'll get us all killed," pleaded Bjorn through clenched teeth.

"I just got emitted, they know where we are!" screamed Corto.

"He's right, we've got to move out and advance on them," said Mulati. "Francois, you ready?"

"You're damn right I am," replied Francois.

Seconds later a canister of white phosphorous bounced off a tree right next them. Dense white smoke quickly filled the air and there was no visibility.

"We need to get out of this," screamed Francois through his coughs.

"Run!" yelled Mulati.

The first to emerge from the smoke was Corto. He was so far ahead that it was as if they had given him a ten-yard head start. He was followed by Mulati who was closely followed by Francois. Finally, Bjorn came lumbering out of the smoke as he attempted, unsuccessfully, to keep pace. As they exited the smoke cloud through the dense bush a hail of arrows poured into the heart of the smoke from higher ground.

"There's an opening up ahead," yelled Corto. "I'm going there!"

Francois knew it was a trap, but he felt he had no time to explain. Instead he just ran harder, passed Mulati, and was able to catch up to and tackle Corto just prior to him exiting the thick brush and entering the clearing. Corto swung wildly after he was tackled by Francois as he tried to escape his grasp.

"What are you doing?" complained Corto. "You're going to get us killed!"

"It's a trap," said Francois as he panted heavily. "They're trying to flush us out into the clear, so they can get a better shot."

A second later Mulati caught up to them and dove onto the ground right next to them. "What's going on?" he asked. "Why'd you stop here?"

Before Francois could explain, Bjorn, who did not see them lying on the ground and assumed he was very far behind, ran past them and was headed toward the clearing. Francois quickly sprang from the ground and hustled to catch up to Bjorn. Just as the front of Bjorn's body exited the wood line and entered the clearing Francois was able to grab a handful of his belt from behind and, with all his might, he pulled him back into the thicker brush.

Bjorn was startled. "What the…" said Bjorn as he started to speak while being pulled backward.

However, he was quickly interrupted by the arrows that flooded the spot in the clearing for which he was headed. Two more steps and he would surely have been killed. He and Francois both rolled over onto their backs from pure exhaustion. Bjorn looked over to Francois and wanted to thank him, but he was breathing too heavily to utter a coherent sentence. Francois was hyperventilating as well. Seconds later Mulati and Corto had caught up to them. They both grabbed Francois and together they dragged him deeper into the woodline away from the clearing. They then went back for Bjorn.

"You gotta help us out, big fella," said Corto as he and Mulati struggled to pull Bjorn deeper into the brush.

Bjorn used his legs to help as much as he could. Soon they were several feet into the bush and away from the clearing.

"We're surrounded," said Mulati while still breathing heavily. "We need to find out where they are and exactly how many they number. Fan out. We need to set up a perimeter."

"I'll hold south and watch the clearing," said Corto.

"I have north," said Bjorn after finally catching his breath.

"I guess Francois and I will cover the other two directions then," said Mulati. "I have east and Francois you have west. Keep it tight. Let's stay within twenty meters of one another."

All four men fanned out to their chosen positions. With their twice emitters at port arms they crept quietly until there was twenty meters between them. Corto was less than three meters from the clearing. They all kneeled to one knee as they scanned their respective areas of responsibility. For the next twenty minutes they remained still and completely silent.

Finally, Mulati turned to face the rest of them. "We can't stay here forever, they'll be coming for us soon," he said.

"Which way are we moving?" asked Francois.

"We're going this way," said Mulati as he pointed the way with a head nod. "Let's go get the woman. They've all left her now. Let's go."

The others immediately began to duck walk toward Mulati's location keeping their twice emitters at the ready. The woman was several meters away from them in a small clearing at the foot of the hill that they were presently atop. This time Mulati took the lead as they descended the steep hill. He was followed by Corto, then Francois, and finally Bjorn who brought up the rear. While making their way down the hill, silence was sacrificed for the ability to stay upright and not come down the hill too quickly for their own safety. They were moving so fast, it was almost as if they were sliding downward. The brush remained thick throughout their descent down the hill and they also struggled to keep branches from smacking them in their faces. To slow their descent and maintain some semblance of control, they all grabbed a fist full of the belt of the person in front of them. That proved to be effective. Finally, they safely reached the base of the hill. Aware that it could be a trap, they did not immediately move in. As they waited they all visually scanned the immediate area and readied themselves to free the woman from captivity. The woman had long black hair and was only clothed on the bottom half of her body. Her upper body was badly bruised. Her head was hanging, and it appeared as if the ropes were the only thing keeping her from collapsing completely.

"Get those twice emitters ready," said Mulati. "Corto, you approach first and cut her loose. We'll cover you from here. Bjorn, it looks like you're going to be the mule this time. She doesn't look fit to walk."

"Got it," said Corto.

"No problem," said Bjorn.

"Francois, you stay with Bjorn, he'll need you to cover him," continued Mulati. "Alright? Go, Corto!"

Corto unsheathed his dagger from his thigh holster and quickly duck walked his way over to the woman. As soon as he reached her, he pressed his hand against her stomach to keep her upright as he began to cut the ropes. He stopped when he heard the woman trying to speak.

"They are behind me," she whispered.

"What?" said Corto. "Say it again, I didn't hear you!"

She spoke again, this time a little louder and with all the force she could muster. "They are behind me!"

Corto immediately stepped back and stood up to get a broader view of the bush behind her. "It's a trap, they're behind her!" he yelled.

Immediately five men emerged from the bush behind the woman. Corto quickly backpedaled to create space between himself and the advancing men. As he did he sheathed the larger dagger back into his leg holster and removed two throwing daggers from his vest. Two of the men who advanced on them were immediately paralyzed as the simultaneous hum of the three twice emitters behind him could be heard. The fluorescent tracers sliced through the air. One of the men continued to advance toward them because Bjorn had missed his target entirely. The other two men who were emitted had, by this time, received their second shot and were blown back into the woodline. They died instantly. With no time to spare, Bjorn immediately slung his twice emitter around to his back and delivered a mighty punch directly to the advancing man's chin stopping him in his tracks. The man staggered backward before being punched again by Bjorn and knocked completely unconscious. As Corto planted his back foot, he tossed with his right hand the first dagger which severed the carotid artery of the man who approached his front left. The man immediately collapsed to his knees as blood sprayed from the soon to be fatal wound. With one continuous motion Corto tossed his left dagger to the femoral artery of the second man who approached his front right causing him to slow down significantly as blood spurted from his thigh. Corto advanced on the man who received his second dagger, unsheathed his thigh dagger, and he stabbed him directly in his heart. The man attempted to grab the dagger with both hands as Corto ripped it out of his chest and immediately plunged it into the chest of the man whose carotid artery he had already severed. Within a matter of seconds four of them were dead. Corto removed his dagger from the chest of his second victim and went back to cut the woman down. Bjorn violently and repeatedly stomped on the face of the unconscious man until his skull was shattered to a mushy mesh and he was dead.

"Stand down, Bjorn," said Mulati calmly as he scanned left to right with his twice emitter still aimed at the woodline behind the woman.

Bjorn slowly slid his bloodied boot from the dead man's face as his massive chest rapidly expanded and collapsed from the quick deep breaths he took. His eyes were wide open, and his nostrils flared. Over the next minute his breaths began to slow as his heart rate returned to normal.

"Easy, big fella. Breathe," said Mulati to Bjorn as he continued his efforts to calm him down.

"She's Asian," said a surprised Corto. "What's an Asian woman doing here on Evropa? There's another one of those guys down here somewhere too, we gotta be careful. I counted six earlier!"

"That's right," confirmed Mulati, "there were six, the one with the eye patch isn't here. Stay alert!"

As Corto sliced the ropes, the woman collapsed into the waiting arms of Bjorn who quickly tossed her tiny limp body over his shoulder and turned back toward the hill. Francois kept his twice emitter at the ready with his right hand and placed his other hand in the small of Bjorn's back. Corto ran around Bjorn to lead the way back up the hill. Francois started up the hill with his back to Bjorn and Corto so that he could provide proper rear security. Mulati stayed near the tree for a few moments as he continued to scan the area for any other hostiles. He did not want them to be attacked from behind while they were so vulnerable. He thought of having Sampa fly in to get them with the Whisper but there was not an area large enough for her to land it. The forest was simply too dense. He continued to wait anxiously as the crew aggressively attacked the hill. Once they got halfway up, he followed them leaving the five dead bodies in his wake. He caught up to Bjorn and Francois three quarters of the way up the hill. Corto had already reached the summit and was securing the area while he waited. Minutes later they caught up to Corto at the top of the hill.

"We can't go south to the clearing," whispered Mulati, "we know they're there already."

"Surely you don't think we should go back to where they smoked us out?" asked Corto.

"That's exactly what I'm thinking," replied Mulati. "If you don't think we should go back, chances are they won't think so either. We're going north."

"I don't care which way we go," said Bjorn, "but we need to keep moving. I'm carrying extra weight here."

"Is she still alive?" asked Mulati.

"Far as I can tell, yes," said Bjorn. "She's still warm and I think I feel her breathing. She's definitely out cold though."

"Good!" said Mulati. "Go back the way we came, and I'll stay back to protect our rear."

The three of them headed back into the bush and as Francois, who brought up the rear, disappeared into the woodline, Mulati removed his EPIC and messaged Sampa. *We have trouble, stay woke*, was the message he sent her.

As soon as he put his EPIC away, he heard voices coming through the bush from the clearing. He immediately crouched down to conceal himself. He saw them, but they did not see him. All three had bows draped over their backs and were chopping through the brush with machetes as they walked single file. Mulati slowly removed his twice emitter from his back and gently placed it on the ground beside him. Given the proximity of the men he did not want to take the chance that he'd miss any of them. As soon as they were close enough, Mulati sprang to his feet while opening his dlhá násada in one motion. Before they could react, Mulati had plunged the end of the staff into the solar plexus of the first man and immediately delivered a vertical stroke to his chin with the other end knocking him out instantly. He followed with an extended high block as the second man swung his machete in a downward motion. A front kick from Mulati to his midsection knocked him back into the third man. Without hesitation Mulati assaulted both of his knees with his dlhá násada side stepping and advancing on the third as the second man fell to the ground in agony. Mulati quickly ducked out of the way of a wild overhead swing from the third man and immediately jumped backward as his next swing was a desperate attempt to slice Mulati's midsection open. He missed badly both times. Mulati plunged the end of the dlhá násada through the throat of the supine second man and left it there before side kicking the third backward. He assumed a fighting stance as the second man gasped for the last three or four breaths of his life. The third man charged Mulati once more in an attempt to cut him with the razor-sharp machete. Again, he missed and with his next move, Mulati disarmed him. From that point on the third man's hand to hand combat skills were no match for Mulati's wing chun kung fu style. He was left unconscious in a matter of seconds. Mulati walked over to the now deceased body of the second man and grabbed the center of his dlhá násada which was still wobbling from the force with which it was thrusted downward into his throat. As he pressed the button it snapped back to its original closed form. Mulati kept his arm extended with the closed dlhá násada in his clenched fist as he visually surveyed the area. Moments later he reattached it to his belt. He reached down, picked up his twice emitter, strapped it over his back, and ran swiftly through the bush to catch up to the others.

Minutes later he had caught up to the other three. They were still moving fast through the brush as they tried desperately to make it back to their Rapid Arachnids.

"Everything alright?" asked Francois. "You were back there awhile."

"My conscience is clear," replied Mulati.

"What's that supposed to mean?" asked a confused Francois as he maintained his pace.

"It means somebody's dead," replied Corto as he continued to lead the way through the brush.

"You mean someone else besides the five we just slaughtered?" asked an incredulous Francois.

"Yep," replied Bjorn.

For a moment Francois entertained the thought that they were joking until he looked back at Mulati and realized his facial expression had not changed. For the next few steps as they ran no one spoke. Francois was in stunned disbelief as questions about Mulati's mental makeup ran through his mind. Clearly, he had underestimated the abilities of the crew of the Whisper.

"Hold the rear," said Mulati to Francois as he hustled to the front to catch Corto with his EPIC in hand.

"The Rapid Arachnids are west of here. Keep moving," said Mulati.

For approximately ten more minutes they moved as fast as they could through the dense terrain. Finally, Bjorn had to stop. He gently laid the woman down in the grass and reached around for his canteen to take a giant swig of water. The others took advantage of the break as well. Mulati walked over to the woman and depressed her carotid artery with his index and middle fingers. "She has a pulse but it's very faint," he said. "She's in very bad shape."

"We gotta move," said Corto. "There's no telling where the rest of those guys are."

Bjorn carefully hoisted the woman back onto his broad shoulders and they continued on their way. As they force marched through the bush for the next twenty minutes familiar landmarks reassured them that they were headed in right direction.

"We should be coming up on the Arachnids at any time now," said Mulati as he studied his EPIC.

Corto ran right into one of the Rapid Arachnids almost knocking the wind out of himself.

"Found them!" he said as he briefly doubled over in pain.

Mulati and Francois reached underneath all four and activated them. Five seconds later they were completely uncoiled and ready to ride as the natural metallic color returned to each of them. Bjorn positioned the woman across his lap as they moved out. He gave his twice emitter to Francois to hold. This time they rode the Rapid Arachnids in a single file line and doubled their speed. They knew they didn't have much time. The woman was badly beaten, and she was unresponsive. After twenty more minutes of nonstop movement they were back at the beach. Mulati went to the tree where the rope was tethered while the others followed the rope across the beach to the camouflaged boat. Bjorn immediately laid the body of the unconscious woman in the center of the boat and then they loaded the Rapid Arachnids into it. Mulati gathered the rope as he marched his rapid arachnid toward the boat. Once he got to the boat they all worked together to load his rapid arachnid onto the vessel. Once they were all on the boat, Mulati removed his

EPIC.

"Contact Whisper," he said.

Sampa's image appeared on the screen. "Speak to me, Mulati," she said.

"We're coming in hot. Tell Beth to get ready in the infirmary, we have something for her, and drop the rear hatch."

"Aye aye," replied Sampa. Sampa immediately did as she was told. She also switched the Whisper from low power mode to full energy as she prepared them for a quick getaway.

As Corto, Francois, and Mulati started to push the boat from the beach into the water, Bjorn got in and positioned himself beside the woman. He was exhausted. Just as he was about to lay back, he received an arrow to his left shoulder.

"Aaarrrggghhh!!!" Bjorn cried out as the arrow remained lodged in his shoulder. Six inches of the arrow had passed through his flesh and the arrowhead protruded from the back. Several more arrows began to fall into the boat and onto the beach around the boat. Mulati quickly turned on the motor and immediately began to steer the boat toward the Whisper as soon as they were all in it. The arrows were coming from the woodline. Francois draped his body over the unconscious woman to protect her from the incoming arrows as the boat sped away from the beach. Corto positioned himself near Mulati at the back with his twice emitter so that he could emit any hostiles who emerged from the tree line. Suddenly a man with a bow and arrow emerged from the tree line and went to one knee while drawing his bow. Corto took aim at him with his twice emitter and he shot. As Corto shot, the man released his arrow. The man was instantly paralyzed as he was struck by the first projectile. As the incoming arrow struck the inside wall of the boat behind Mulati, Corto released the second projectile. The man was killed instantly as a four-inch hole was opened in his chest as two of his comrades were attempting to pull him back into the woodline. Once they were out of the reach of the arrows, Francois made his way over to Bjorn and unscrewed the arrowhead from the metal shaft of the arrow.

"Corto, give me your dagger," said Francois. Corto hurried over to him and handed him the dagger from his thigh holster. Francois took the dagger and shaved the fletching from the shaft of the arrow. "Brace yourself, big fella, this is going to hurt a little," Francois said to Bjorn as he quickly snatched the shaft of the arrow out of his shoulder. Bjorn again screamed in agony as the shaft was removed.

Minutes later the Whisper was in sight. The boat was headed directly toward the nose of the massive Whisper. Mulati altered the path of the boat to take a more circuitous route so that they could enter the Whisper through the rear hatch. Moments later they were approaching the massive ramp that led into the cargo area. As they neared the ramp, Mulati cut the power to the boat's engine to minimize the impact as they entered the cargo area. Once inside Mulati sprang from the boat and sprinted over to the intercom.

"We're in, Sam, close it," he said.

"I'm on it, Mulati, I was watching you on the monitor," replied Sampa.

Francois and Corto also exited the boat quickly. Bjorn gingerly helped himself out of the boat. By this time Beth had entered the cargo area of the ship. "I heard we have company again," she said. "How is she?"

"She's alive, that's all we know," said Mulati. "Hopefully you can tell us the rest. Bjorn took an arrow to the shoulder too. You might wanna take a look at him as well."

"OK," said Beth, "Let's get them into the infirmary right away."

Corto quickly returned with a stretcher and unrolled it to quickly, yet gently, place the woman on. Corto and Francois lifted her up and followed Beth into the infirmary.

"Put her down there," said Beth as she pointed toward the

examining table. Beth quickly put an oxygen mask over the unnamed woman's nose and mouth to help her breathe. She inserted an intravenous needle into her arm and a pulse reader onto the tip of her index finger. She also slid a thin sheet over her bare-naked top in an attempt to preserve what little dignity she could salvage for the woman. After taking a small sample of blood from her and inserting it into the computer behind her, she summoned Bjorn over to her location. "Come here, big guy," said Beth, "let momma fix it for ya." She gave him a shot to stop infection and another dose to dull the pain. She waited a few minutes for the medicine to take effect and began to stitch Bjorn's wound. "They got you pretty good this time, didn't they?" she asked.

"Sure did," replied Bjorn. "Things got pretty hairy out there."

"Well you all made it back. That's what counts," said Beth. She turned to remove the blood sample from the computer and studied the woman's results carefully on the screen. "Get Mulati in here," she said to Corto.

"Ok," replied Corto as he quickly left the room.

Less than a minute later Corto returned to the infirmary with Mulati.

"What's going on?" asked Mulati.

"She's dying, and she can't be saved," said Beth.

"Those rotten fuckers beat her that bad?" asked an angry Bjorn.

"No," answered Beth. "I mean, yes, they put a beating on her but that's not what's killing her. What's killing her is this mix of sodium thiopental, pancuronium bromide, and potassium chloride that they injected into her bloodstream."

Bjorn, Corto, Mulati, and Francois simply stared at Beth as if she were speaking a language they didn't understand.

After it quickly registered to her that they had no clue what she was talking about, Beth went on to explain.

"Well," she said, "the first drug does two things, it completely relaxes you and makes you tell the truth. The second one is the stuff they put in those twice emitter things y'all like so much that stops you from moving. The third drug stops your heart. According to her results they gave her a very small dosage of the last one. They wanted to keep her alive for a while at least. Looks like they were interrogating her. She's one tough woman."

"How much time does she have left?" asked Mulati.

"She'll be lucky to make it through the night," replied Beth. "Poor girl, that's no way for a person to go."

"Make her as comfortable as possible," replied Mulati. "I'm going to the bridge. Alert me when her condition has changed."

Bjorn looked especially somber as Beth spoke those words. After carrying the woman for so long and risking so much to get her to the Whisper, he was heartbroken that her prognosis was so bleak.

"You ok?" said Beth to Bjorn.

"I don't know," replied Bjorn. "I really don't know how I feel right now. It's strange. It really is strange. These last hours have been filled with nothing but us missing death by seconds yet we are too late to save this woman's life. That doesn't sit well with me." Bjorn got up from the stool he was sitting on and left the infirmary with his head down, slowly shaking it from side to side. Beth looked to Corto and was about to speak.

"I know," said Corto, "I'm on it. Let's go, Frenchie."

He and Francois followed Bjorn out of the infirmary. Beth was now alone with the suffering woman. She removed the remaining garments from her body so that she could examine her more thoroughly. She paid close attention to and carefully scrutinized every inch of her body. On the inside of her right ankle Beth noticed what looked like a word. Further inspection revealed that it read G/5W2. Beth had no way of knowing what it meant but she felt it was significant enough to include it in her notes and to photograph it, and so she did. She focused her EPIC on the inscription and she snapped and saved the photo. Over the next hour she carefully monitored the woman's vital statistics until she finally died on the examining table.

Meanwhile Mulati sat quietly in his pilot's seat on the bridge watching the instruments on the control panel and paying close attention to the ocean. He replayed the events of the recent hours in his mind. Suddenly the open microphone of the intercom could be heard, and as the person on the other end fumbled with the buttons he realized it was Beth.

Her message was brief, "This is Beth, she's gone."

"I copy," said Mulati, "I'll be down in a few."

Beth removed the IV from her arm, the oxygen mask from her face, and the pulse monitor from her finger. She began the process of cleaning her body to prepare it for a proper burial. As she was doing that, Mulati rose from his seat and started toward the bridge door.

"Stay on these monitors, Sam. I suspect we might have company once they have regrouped out there; I think we caught them off guard."

Meanwhile in the lounge Bjorn, Francois, and Corto discussed what they had just gone through.

"That's really weird," said Bjorn. "I wonder what they were doing with her. Who are they? Are there other victims?"

"Who knows?" replied Corto. "They know we've been there, that's for sure! They'll think twice before messing with us."

"Who? Those guys?" asked Francois. "You think those guys were warriors? I don't think so."

Bjorn and Corto looked confused.

"What makes you say that?" asked Bjorn.

"Maybe they were, maybe they weren't. My guess is they were mostly hunters. There was no way they were expecting to encounter other humans."

"What about the six who had the lady?" asked Corto. "Who the fuck were they?"

"I don't know," answered Francois. "What I do know is that they weren't armed. I guess everybody else was too busy killing to notice that though."

"Are you implying that they didn't need to die?" asked Bjorn as he rose to his feet.

"Calm down, big fella," said Francois, "that's not what I'm saying at all."

"Then what are you saying?" asked Bjorn.

"I'm saying that right now some heads are rolling on that island. That's how we handle things in the D..."

Francois caught himself. *That was close! Don't forget where you are, Francois.* He got too comfortable and almost made the grave mistake of exposing his true past. He quickly continued. "I mean there is clearly some type of covert operation going on there and we weren't supposed to see what we just saw. For that someone will surely pay."

"I suppose you're right," said Bjorn. "That certainly seems logical."

"Well whoever they are, they had it coming," stated Corto emphatically. "You can't just torture a woman and not expect something to happen to you in return."

Mulati walked into the room along with Beth.

"She's dead," said Mulati to the rest of the men. "Beth did all she could to save her but was unsuccessful."

Bjorn looked over to Francois and said, "They were just hunters alright. Unbelievable."

"I was just pointing out that tactically...oh, forget it," replied Francois. "It is what it is. She's dead."

"Beth has cleaned and prepared her body already," said Mulati, "we'll give her a respectful ceremony."

An hour later the entire crew was in the cargo bay of the Whisper with the ramp down. The deceased woman was dressed completely in white and floating on a makeshift raft at the end of the ramp. Her delicate hands were overlapped across her waist as she lay supine in the center of the raft. Beth had placed a small white flower in her hair.

Mulati spoke:

"What do we remember most, a whisper or a yell? The answer lies in the heart of he who has made the cry and not in the ears of those who have heard it. For the whisper and the yell are only significant to their source. The perception of power lies within the yell. The perception of strength and wisdom lie within a whisper. However profound those words may appear, reality has taught us that the opposite is often true. As children we introduce ourselves to the world with a yell when we are at our weakest. Death is the only thing more silent than a whisper, yet the whisper of death, as sudden as it may be, represents the power of knowledge obtained throughout a lifetime. A tornado, though it may yell, is only powerful if it can demonstrate its strength against something weaker. The whisper is measured against all other whispers throughout time and has the ability to be as weak as a lamb or as mighty as that tornado against a twig. When your story is told, I hope it is done so with a mighty whisper."

Mulati looked to Bjorn and nodded. Bjorn slowly walked to the end of the ramp carrying a container filled with a flammable liquid and he stepped onto the raft. He doused the woman's body and the raft with the liquid. Afterward he placed the container on its side at the edge of the raft, so the remaining contents would leak into the sea. He removed the rope that attached the raft to the Whisper and he set the raft adrift with a hard push from his large foot. For minutes they watched in silence as the raft became more distant. Corto walked to the edge of the ramp and tossed a fiery cloth into the water. The fire followed the trail of flammable liquid across the sea to the raft and within seconds the raft was fully engulfed in flames. Mulati put his left fist across his chest and his right fist across that fist, and, without hesitation, they all, with the exception of Francois, went into their five stomp Whisper Yell. Afterward they simply turned and walked into the cargo area of the ship together and they pulled up the ramp.

Chapter 7: Goodbye, Evropa; Hello, Nasty

Location: Macabre Sea, Evropa
Aboard the Whisper, 1500 hours

Mulati and Sampa walked slowly into the bridge and assumed their normal seat positions. As they looked out of the windshield, their eyes fixed on the black smoke that rose from the now distant raft carrying the body of the deceased Asian woman. They both sat silent and motionless as they watched the fiery raft and quietly reflected on what had just occurred.

"Will we be back?" asked Sampa.

Mulati looked to his right and into Sampa's eyes as if he searched his own mind for an answer to that question. He knew exactly why she asked. She, like he, wanted to know if there were others on the island who needed help. He also thought, from what they had just endured, that they did not have enough crew members or weaponry to safely accomplish such a mission. He broke eye contact with Sampa and he slowly looked forward and exhaled a long breath. He quickly sprang to his feet and slammed both hands on the control panel in front of him as he glared through the windshield. He slammed his hand down on the emergency button on the panel causing the interior lights to dim and then flash five times before coming back on. With his right hand he pointed out to the many approaching boats in the Macabre Sea.

"We're surrounded," said Mulati to Sampa.

"I see them," she replied.

Bjorn's voice came through the intercom. "What's going on?" he asked.

"We're surrounded," said Mulati. "Grab Corto and man the guns!"

"I'm on it," replied Bjorn.

"Do you see what I see?" asked Sampa.

"No," replied Mulati. "What do you see?"

Sampa pointed to the horizon where there were three aircrafts approaching from the front.

"Those are short range fighters!" said Mulati. "There's definitely a base around here somewhere. We've got to go!"

"They'll be on us too fast," replied Sampa. "We have to submerge!"

Mulati shook his head from side to side as if he did not want to do that but he knew it was what had to be done.

"Seal it up and prepare to dive," said Mulati.

Mulati pressed the intercom and communicated with the rest of the crew. "We're going down, prepare yourselves!" he said.

"They'll have divers on those boats," said Sampa.

"I know," replied Mulati. "We have to hit them with the electromagnetic pulse."

"Tell me when," replied Sampa.

"When you're ready," replied Mulati. "Just make sure those boats are close enough for it to be effective."

"Aye aye," said Sampa as she uncovered the button for the EMP and they waited for the right moment as the boats sped toward them. The short-range aircrafts were still in the distance but approaching fast. Moments later Sampa pressed the button sending the jolting electric current across and through the sea. The boats were all short circuited instantly and those who were aboard them were stunned to unconsciousness.

"Submerge!" ordered Mulati.

"Submerging," replied Sampa.

As the Whisper lowered itself below the surface of the Macabre Sea Francois and Beth entered the bridge and belted themselves into the seats behind Mulati and Sampa.

"Why are we going under?" asked Francois.

"We have attackers coming by air and sea," replied Sampa.

"I see," said a now understanding Francois. "We pulsed the sea goers and are hiding from the air raid?"

"Exactly," replied Mulati.

"Initiating cloak mode," said Sampa calmly as the Whisper slowly sank deeper toward the bottom of the sea.

"Would it be poor timing if I mentioned how pretty and peaceful looking it is down here?" asked Beth.

The entire bridge remained silent as they stared out into the blue-green water. They were all in awe of the aquatic scenery. As they stared they were interrupted by munitions which suddenly descended into the water from above and exploded around them but not close enough to damage the Whisper.

"It's the air fighters, they're concussion probing our last location," said Mulati.

"Should we move?" asked Sampa.

"No," answered Mulati. "They've already missed. They'll probably aim where they are guessing we might go next. Our best bet is to stay here."

Moments later another round of munitions entered the sea from above. This time they were further away in all directions.

"You were right," said Francois. "They're firing blind and trying to get lucky. It's a good thing we didn't move."

Moments later a third round of munitions entered the sea at an even greater distance away. The air fighters were systematically concussion probing the water in hopes that they would contact the Whisper. Within minutes the Whisper had reached the sea floor. No more probes entered the water. All was quiet until Francois could be heard snoring from his back seat. Mulati and

Sampa both looked back at Francois who was sound asleep.

"I don't know what it says about a person who finds solace in trouble," said Beth, "but I have never seen a man sleep so peacefully amid so much chaos."

"That is strange," said Sampa.

"Or maybe he's just tired," added Mulati. "He…"

"What's that noise?" asked a frightened Beth.

"What noise?" asked Sampa as she suddenly began to concentrate.

They all heard the moaning cries coming from the sea.

"Leviathans!" shouted an excited Mulati. "We have to move!"

"They can't see us, can they?" asked a worried Beth.

"They don't need to," replied Sam, "they have built in sonic abilities."

"Meaning?" Beth further inquired.

"Meaning they can find us without looking," said Mulati. "They make contact through sound".

"Mulati's right, we have to go," said Sampa.

"Stand by for ascension," said Mulati as he pressed the intercom.

"We copy," answered Bjorn.

"I see them," said Sampa.

"Oh my, they are huge!" said Beth. "There must be five of them."

Beth looked worried as the gigantic sea creatures approached together. They were each almost the size of the Whisper. The black-eyed creatures each had a large tail, four short legs and two long tentacles on each side toward the head of their bodies. Razor sharp teeth lined their mouths. They looked menacing. As was typical for them, the leviathans were hunting in a pack of five. Two younger, slightly smaller males usually attacked while the larger, older leviathans, two females and one male, followed closely behind.

"The ship is not food, they won't attack us, will they?" asked Beth.

"They won't know the Whisper isn't food until they've tasted it. Then it may be too late," answered Sam.

"It's our vibrations and frequency that are attracting them," said Mulati. "Turn the cloaking device off, Sam, it's time to fly."

"Done!" said Sampa.

"Full power now!" said Mulati.

As the Whisper roared to full unassisted power, Francois awoke from his slumber only to see the leviathans approaching quickly.

"Incredible," said Francois as he stared into the sea shaking his head slowly from side to side in stunned disbelief. "One problem to the next."

"Hang on, we're moving," said Sampa while engaging the thrusters to full power with Mulati pulling back on the throttle to lift the nose of the Whisper upward. As they accelerated up, the closest leviathan reached out and wrapped its long tentacles around the nose of the Whisper.

"It has us!" screamed Sampa.

"Hang on," said Mulati as he steered the Whisper into a spiral as they continued to travel upward ripping two of the tentacles from the body of the aggressive young leviathan. As blood poured from the beast and into the sea, the Whisper broke free and continued to travel toward the light of the sky. The other four leviathans turned on the severely injured leviathan and began to frenzy as they mauled and devoured it. Moments later the Whisper erupted from the surface of the sea still traveling in a spiral as it headed toward the sky. Two air fighters scrambled to the location of the Whisper. As Mulati came out of the spiral and righted the Whisper he observed the air fighters approaching. He took evasive action to narrowly avoid being hit by a missile shot from one of the air fighters. Bjorn and Corto each rotated their cannons toward the air fighters and began to fire. Corto scored a hit with his first shot breaching the hull of one of the air fighters with a SPIM sending it spiraling downward toward the sea with smoke billowing from it.

"I can't hit him, he's too fast," shouted Bjorn to Corto through his headset. "See if you can pick him off from your side."

"I'll try!" said Corto.

As the air fighter came into Corto's sights he pulled the trigger releasing another SPIM which was a direct hit that disabled the second air fighter.

"Two shots, two kills!" yelled an excited Corto. "We're clear!"

Bjorn removed his headgear. "That's just great," he said with a frown on his face. He was disappointed in himself for not being able to make contact with either of the air fighters. Meanwhile on the bridge, Mulati and Sampa prepared to exit the atmosphere of Evropa.

"As soon as we get into space, I'll prepare us for maximum celerity," said Mulati. "Hopefully those Evropan battle cruisers aren't waiting on us out there."

"Who is that on the port side gun?" asked Francois. "He can shoot!"

"Corto," replied Mulati and Sampa in unison.

As the Whisper sped to and through the outer layer of Evropa's atmosphere Mulati busied himself with inputting the coordinates of Neutralia's orbit into the Whisper's navigation system. Everyone else on the bridge remained quiet. They were all concerned about what awaited them in space. As they entered space they were taken aback by what they saw before them. Floating out there alone was the pirate ship that had pursued them from the orbit of Hades. It was completely disabled and had sustained several breaches to its hull. Sampa studied the instruments on the control panel as she scanned the massive ship for life. There was none.

"They're all dead," said Sampa. "Not one single person on that ship survived. That could've been us."

"It could have, but it's not," said Mulati.

Mulati made eye contact with Sampa and pointed to the ship's radar discreetly with his index finger. Sampa glanced at the radar and instantly contorted her face as if she had seen something that was very interesting to her.

"The coordinates are in. Full forward capability, make the jump to maximum celerity, Sam," ordered Mulati.

"Aye aye," replied Sampa as she initiated the sequence to make the jump.

"Anybody else, besides me, suspicious that those Evropan ships are nowhere to be found?" asked Francois.

"No," said Mulati.

Francois thought the one-word answer was somewhat cold, but he dared not ask Mulati to elaborate. One thing he had learned in his short time with the crew of the Whisper was that Mulati was a calculated individual who never acted without purpose and to question his actions would be unwise. The Whisper made the leap to maximum celerity.

Location: Albin Space Station, hospital quadrant
Orbiting Albin, 1800 hours

Nastasia Rodmanovic, the tall, young, athletically built, brown haired, chief assistant to Chancellor Aldrich who was of Romanian descent, arrived at the Albin space station with a three-person entourage consisting of her pilot, Friedrich, and her two assistants, Erwin and Arianna. They were there to check on the welfare of Judas Benedict. As they waited in their skiff to be granted admittance, she was finishing up her conversation with Chancellor Aldrich via her EPIC.

"The last update on his condition that I received was that he was still not conscious and in very bad shape," said Chancellor Aldrich. "I want him brought here to our facilities so that we can better care for him."

"I will see to it, Chancellor," replied Nastasia with her heavy Romanian accent.

"End transmission," said Chancellor Aldrich and with that his image disappeared.

"Why is it taking them so long to let us through?" asked an impatient Nastasia of Chancellor Aldrich's personal pilot, Friedrich.

"There are protocols that must be adhered to even in this cold place, Nastasia," replied Friedrich.

Nastasia said nothing more and simply waited as patiently as she could for the door to their passenger ship to slide open. She was dressed in her usual sartorial splendor with not a thread out of place. Her posture was emblematic of the elegance, class, and proper emissary etiquette she sought to portray at all times. Despite her penchant for protocol and commiserate diplomacy in regard to her duties, she had the reputation of an individual who was driven to a fault and lacked empathy. That bothered her, so she worked very hard to disguise that aspect of her personality, but not to change it. "Raise them again, this is ridiculous!" she blurted out. "This is no way for me to be treated."

Friedrich did as he was told. Moments later the door to their skiff slid open revealing two middle aged Albino women.

"Nastasia Rodmanovic?" one of the women asked.

"Yes, I am she," replied Nastasia coldly. "I have a schedule to keep so delay your pleasantries. Where is Judas Benedict?"

"Very well," replied the very pleasant Albino. "Follow us."

Nastasia exited her vessel into the dimly lit and cold space station. Friedrich, Erwin, and Arianna stayed behind. The dark gray hallways of the hospital quadrant in the space station were filled with Albino nurses, doctors, and technicians. After a short walk through the busy hallways they came to an elevator where they waited for a short period of time. Nastasia was flanked by the two Albinos as they waited. She sighed heavily as she focused her eyes toward the ceiling in an obvious display of impatience as the elevator took what seemed like forever, to her, to arrive. As the door opened, Nastasia quickly stepped toward the opening only to be pushed back by three male Albino technicians who were exiting the elevator and almost ran her over completely. The two Albino women who were escorting her had not moved. As she was being pushed backward and nearly knocked off balance, Nastasia quickly shook her head from side to side as if that would help to silence the vitriol she was tempted to spew toward everyone around her at that moment. Suddenly there were no more people exiting the elevator and her escorts entered. Nastasia followed. As the elevator ascended she was careful not to touch any of the others inside. She stood with her hands clasped together in front of her. They quickly reached the third floor and the door slid open revealing people standing outside of the elevator who were waiting to get on.

"This is our floor," said one of the escorts as they both exited the elevator.

Nastasia followed them.

"He is here in room 323," said the woman as they arrived at Judas's suite. "We will wait for you out here."

Nastasia entered the room without knocking only to find Judas staring out of a porthole into the darkness of space. *He's awake!*

Without turning around, Judas started to speak. "There had better be a good explanation for this unannounced intrusion," he complained.

Nastasia was taken aback by the sight of him awake and standing. "My apologies," said Nastasia, "I assumed you were still…"

"Oh…it's you, Nasty," said Judas bitterly.

"My name is Nastasia," she replied defiantly. "I loathe that word, it feels derogatory when you speak it."

"That's interesting. How can a word with no history have a connotation?" asked Judas. "Steven invented it and we've only used it in reference to you," he said while still looking out the window.

"The Chancellor doesn't call me that!" said Nastasia angrily.

Suddenly Judas turned to face the now seething emissary. He was pleased that he had gotten under her skin. "I was unaware that Chancellor Aldrich only called you that name in your absence," he said. "How naive of me. Nevertheless, why are you here instead of him? What has he to do that is so important that he could not come here himself?"

"He wanted to be here," replied Nastasia, "but given the circumstances of your attack he had cause to be concerned that both he and the Vice Chancellor would be targets as well. Therefore, I was sent in his stead."

"Tell me...Nastasia," said Judas while slowly cutting his eyes toward her, "were you transported here by covert means or by normal transportation?"

"Quite normally actually," replied Nastasia.

"Then how were these alleged assassins supposed to know that neither he nor Theris were aboard?" asked Judas suspiciously.

"I don't know," said Nastasia. "Maybe you should ask the Chancellor that yourself."

"Maybe I should, Nasty," sniped Judas. "I would very much like to know his answer to that one! One more thing, child... I care not what you loathe. I don't care one infinitesimal percentage of a skosh about what upsets you. If your opinion is required, it will be requested. Until then, keep it to yourself. Now fetch my things!"

Nastasia quickly turned away from Judas and exited the room. Upon doing so she immediately directed her ire toward the escorts. "Go to my transport vehicle and retrieve my assistants. Do it now!" Nastasia demanded.

Once the escorts were out of her sight, Nastasia removed her EPIC from her pocket and contacted her assistants. "Stand by to be escorted to the councilman's suite and be prepared to collect his things," she ordered. "End transmission," she said before they could respond. As she waited for the escorts to return, Nastasia paced back and forth outside of Judas's suite with her arms folded. She was furious. *He is impossible to deal with. I do not like to be treated as a child.* She never understood why Judas was so dismissive of her. Having to constantly submit to his authority was a pain for which she was not prepared.

Inside his suite Judas moved gingerly about as he prepared himself to leave. The very thought of Nastasia Rodmanovic repulsed him. In a way, however, he admired her toughness. That she was not afraid of her obvious lofty ambitions was a reminder to Judas that he needed to be at his sharpest whenever she was around. By default, she made him better. His ribs were broken so he found it difficult at times to breathe. After his rant toward Nastasia, he was coping with shortness of breath. As he slowly walked around the room he kept his right armed pinned closely to his side to ensure that nothing made contact with his badly bruised and heavily bandaged sore ribs. His right hand was also bandaged due to the stab wound he had received to it during his attack from Brady and Mitch. A loud knock came at the door to his suite.

Judas took a painful deep breath. "Who's there?" he asked.

"Nastasia," replied the voice from the other side of the door.

Judas rolled his eyes. *Goodness, is she back already?* Although he was ready to leave he was not anxious to interact with Nastasia yet again. "Come in! I guess I'm ready," he barked.

Nastasia re-entered the suite this time with her two assistants, Erwin and Arianna. "Gather the councilman's things quickly, we haven't a moment to spare," she ordered.

As her assistants busied themselves with the task of gathering Judas's belongings, Nastasia stood in a corner of the room watching their every move but saying nothing. Judas followed them around as much as he could making sure that they left nothing behind. Moments later two duffel bags were filled with personal effects belonging to Judas.

"My goggles," said Judas to the assistants, "make sure you have my goggles."

"They're here," replied Erwin as he held them up to show Judas prior to putting them into one of the bags.

"Give them to me," said Judas. "I'll be needing them soon." Judas reached out to receive the goggles with his left hand and proceeded to place them on top of his head. He stopped short of covering his eyes with them. "I'm ready," he said to Nastasia without looking her way.

"Move," said Nastasia to her assistants. "Get his things to the skiff."

As they exited the room, Nastasia led the way walking quickly and confidently toward the elevator. The escorts walked with Judas who methodically made his way to the elevator as well. Erwin and Arianna followed closely behind Judas carrying his personal belongings. Nastasia entered the empty elevator and waited for the door to close.

"Hold it for me!" yelled Judas as he flashed an evil grin.

He wasn't even halfway down the hallway and did not speed up his pace to get to the elevator. Sighing heavily, Nastasia reached out to press the hold button. She glared at Judas every step of the way. It seemed, to her, that he was purposely walking even slower. Finally, he was there in the elevator with Nastasia. Not that she expected him to, but he did not thank her for holding the elevator for him.

"Has Steven been apprised of my condition?" he asked of Nastasia.

"No, he has not," she replied. "I will do so once we are aboard our skiff."

"That won't be necessary," said Judas, "I'll contact him myself. I want to see, first hand, his glee when he understands that I am still very much among the living. I'm sure he will be pleased."

Nastasia held her tongue. She did not want to engage in any type of inflammatory dialogue with Judas in front of strangers or in front of her assistants. Besides, she was not sure of the sincerity in his last statement.

Once they were aboard their transport vessel and preparing for their voyage back to Neutralia, Judas thought it was a good time to contact Chancellor Aldrich.

"Nastasia, contact Chancellor Aldrich," he said.

For a moment Nastasia contemplated suggesting that Judas use his own EPIC to contact Chancellor Aldrich, but she quickly resisted the urge to be combative and simply complied with his command. "As you wish, Councilman," she said and focused her attention on her EPIC. "Contact the Chancellor," she spoke into the device before passing it to Judas.

Chancellor Aldrich's image quickly appeared on the screen and without hesitation he began to speak.

"How bad off is he?" asked Chancellor Aldrich.

"What do your eyes tell you?" asked Judas as he positioned his face in front of the EPIC as soon as he received it from Nastasia.

"Judas! You're... I don't understand!" replied a stunned Chancellor Aldrich.

"I'm alive, what more is there to understand?" asked Judas.

"It's not that," replied Chancellor Aldrich. "In fact, I expected a full recovery. However, I left strict orders for that staff to notify me as soon as your condition changed. I see now that those orders were not obeyed."

"An order such as that transforms into a mere suggestion once the individual who is infirmed becomes capable of speaking for himself, especially when he is amongst his people. They followed the orders that mattered most," quipped Judas.

"Very well," said Chancellor Aldrich. "You will meet with Vice Chancellor Lamont and I the morning after your return. Safe travels. End transmission."

Judas immediately tossed the EPIC to Nastasia who was not expecting him to do that and almost dropped it.

"You're welcome," said Nastasia sarcastically.

Judas did not reply. He simply sat back, belted himself into the seat, and waited for their skiff to be cleared for departure.

Chapter 8: It's All Clear Now

Location: Orbit of Neutralia
Above the Whisper

In the ship's lounge Francois and Corto discussed their escape from Evropa. They were alone. As Francois praised Corto for his shooting display, Beth walked into the room.

"Where's Bjorn?" asked Beth as she searched the room with her beautiful green eyes.

Both Francois and Corto looked around as if they expected him to be in the room with them.

"I guess he walked out," answered Corto. "He was just here. He could be anywhere. I'd check the cargo area or engine room first if I were you. Is everything ok?"

"I hope so," replied Beth. "I just think it's odd that he isn't in here. You two are usually inseparable."

"Why don't you just raise him on the intercom?" asked Francois.

"It's not that urgent," said Beth. "Besides, he could be in the head. I'll just look for him."

"Have it your way," said Corto as he turned to continue his conversation with Francois. "What I usually do is aim just beyond the nose on those fast movers. The same sight alignment and sight picture principles apply after that. That usually puts my rounds right there in the cockpit or the fuselage."

"Well, it certainly works for you. That was some fantastic shooting," said Francois. He leaned back in his chair looking over his shoulder for Beth but she was no longer in the room. "I didn't even hear her leave," he said. "Why do you think she wants Bjorn?"

Corto was reluctant to answer at first feeling that he'd somehow betray his friend by telling the truth, but he decided it was ok to let Francois know what was going on. "Bjorn gets a little sensitive about his shooting," said Corto. "If he doesn't perform well he sulks. More than likely he's somewhere getting it out of his system."

"He's crying?" asked Francois.

"No, not at all," replied Corto. "He's angry though. He gets lost so he won't hurt any of us. His temper is fucking bad."

"Wow...interesting," said Francois. "That's good to know, I wouldn't want to end up like that guy on the island."

"He's capable of much worse than that, trust me," replied Corto.

As Beth searched the ship for Bjorn, she looked in the engine room but could not find him there. Next was the cargo area of the ship. Again, he was nowhere to be found. She went to the bridge to see if he had gone up there to be with Mulati and Sampa. As she walked through the door, she observed Mulati and Sampa in their respective seats deeply immersed in a conversation about what had occurred on Evropa.

"Sorry to interrupt," said Beth as she entered the room, "but have either of you seen Bjorn?"

"No, we haven't," replied Sampa, "but I'm sure he and Corto are somewhere together. I'd check the lounge or the engineering room."

"I've done both," said Beth. "He's not there. As a matter of fact, Corto and Francois are in the lounge, but he isn't."

Mulati reached up to engage the intercom.

"That won't be necessary," said Beth. "It's really not that important. I'll check his suite; he's probably there."

Beth turned and left the bridge.

"What's that about, Sam?" asked Mulati.

"Beth has good intuition," replied Sampa. "Bjorn's been quiet since we left Evropa. She's probably concerned about him."

Mulati continued the conversation they were having before Beth entered the room.

"The radar showed that those ships were directly above the island we explored. What I don't understand is why they chose to go there instead of leaving a ship out there in case we made it out," said Mulati.

"They scrambled those air fighters to our location. They also attacked us by sea. Normally that's enough to eliminate someone," replied Sampa. "I'm sure they were confident they'd gotten it done. By the time they would have realized that they were unsuccessful we were gone."

"That makes sense," said Mulati, "but I'm still confused as to why the whole entire fleet needed to amass over that island. I wish we could have gone deeper and found out what's really happening there. Nevertheless, we have the coordinates and we can always go back."

Speaking of which, what do we want to call that place?" asked Sampa.

"Whisper Island...what else?" replied Mulati with a smile.

"Whisper Island it is then," said Sampa as she attached the name to those coordinates on the ship's map.

Meanwhile in Bjorn's suite he laid supine in his bed with his fingers interlaced behind his head and his ankles crossed as Beth spoke to him.

"I understand it's hard," she said. "You worked really hard to save that woman's life. We all did. It just wasn't meant to be, Bjorn. She was, for all intent and purposes, dead already. There was absolutely nothing we could have done for her."

Bjorn absorbed her words as he glared at the ceiling. He paused a long time before responding. Beth waited patiently for him to do so. She wanted badly for him to feel better. "Did you stop by the lounge first?" he asked.

"I did. Why?" she asked.

"What were they talking about in there?" he continued.

Beth thought it strange that Bjorn would be concerned about that. "They were talking about Corto shootin' those things out of the sky when I left out of there," she said. "They seemed to be pretty interested in that."

Bjorn immediately grimaced but did not reply. Suddenly Beth had a clue as to the source of Bjorn's frustration.

"Sit up for me," she requested.

Bjorn thought that the request was odd, but he did as he was asked. He immediately repositioned his body and sat on the side of the bed facing Beth. She grabbed his face with both hands and studied his eyes intently from arm's length away.

"Can you see my pupils?" she asked.

"Clearly," replied Bjorn.

"Good," said Beth before walking over to the entrance of his suite which was about twenty feet away and turned to face him. "Look at my face and tell me what I'm doing, ok?" she said.

"Whatever you want, Beth," said Bjorn.

She moved her head from left to right and up and down.

"You moved your head all around".

"Good," replied Beth.

Next, she opened her mouth wide and closed it.

"You just opened and shut your mouth," said Bjorn. "What's this about, Beth?" asked a confused Bjorn.

"I'm almost done," said Beth. "You're doing fine." She then closed her left eye for a few moments. Bjorn said nothing. "You still paying attention?" she asked.

"Yea, go ahead," replied Bjorn.

Beth, again, closed her left eye and kept it closed for about ten seconds.

"I'm waiting," said Bjorn.

"That's fine," said Beth. "I've seen enough. Thank you. Lay back down and get you some rest."

Bjorn simply shrugged his shoulders and laid back down. As Beth turned to leave his suite he crossed his ankles and put his hands back behind his head.

Ten minutes later Beth's voice came through the intercom in Bjorn's suite. "Hey, big guy, it's me again. Can you come down to the infirmary for a few, please?"

"Sure," replied Bjorn, "I'll be right there."

Moments later Bjorn walked into the infirmary where Beth was waiting. The room was dim, and Beth was gathering slides to show to Bjorn. She had him take a seat as she projected images on the wall about twenty feet or so in front of him. She showed him images of varying sizes with both eyes open, with his left eye open only, and with his right eye open only. After each image she questioned him about its clarity. After about twenty minutes she was done.

"That's all I need, you may leave now," she said with a smile.

Bjorn left the infirmary and went back to his quarters. Beth remained focused on what she was doing. An hour later Beth went to Bjorn's suite and asked to be granted entrance.

"Just a minute," replied Bjorn.

Seconds later the door slid open and Beth stepped in with her hands behind her back. Bjorn was sitting on the edge of his bed with his arms folded.

"Yes?" he said.

"I need you to have an open mind," said Beth nervously. "Promise me you will."

"Alright, I will," said Bjorn. "What you got?"

Just then Beth walked over to Bjorn and handed him a pair of silver framed eyeglasses with round lenses and temples that were designed to curve around the back of his ears. Bjorn immediately frowned upon seeing the eyeglasses.

Beth quickly went back to the entrance of his suite.

"Before you put those on I want you to look at my face," she said as she closed her left eye.

"I'm looking," said Bjorn. "Go ahead and do something."

"I'm not going to move a muscle," said Beth. "Put those on and look at me."

Bjorn did as he was told. "Wow!" said an amazed Bjorn. "Did you have your left eye closed the whole time?"

"Yes, I did," answered Beth as she opened her eye and smiled.

Bjorn stood up and immediately took the glasses off, attempted to focus on Beth with his naked eyes, and then put them back on. "I can't believe this," he said. "This is amazing!" He turned around in a circle, then stood still and quickly turned his head from left to right as he visually scanned every inch of the room. He ran over to Beth, gave her a big bear hug, picked her up off her feet, and kissed her on her cheek.

"How'd you know?" he asked. "I had no idea I couldn't see."

"I had a hunch," said Beth. "That should solve a few problems for ya, big fella. Dinner is in an hour. See you then." Beth left the room as Bjorn continued to look around in amazement.

One hour later Bjorn walked into the dining hall wearing his new eyeglasses. He was the last person to arrive. Beth had already told the rest of the crew about his new accessory and they were already seated at the table. They were almost more anxious for Bjorn's arrival than they were for the food itself. As he walked in, silence befell the room. It was awkward. Everyone was already seated at the long rectangular table and they were looking directly at Bjorn and waiting for him to speak.

"There's a problem with these things, Beth," said Bjorn in a serious voice.

"What's that, big guy?" asked a concerned Beth.

"Everybody is uglier!" he replied as he burst into loud obnoxious laughter.

Everyone else at the table joined in and started to laugh as well. Bjorn took his normal seat at the table between Corto and Sampa and started stacking his plate with food.

"Well, I think you look just fine, Bjorn," said Beth.

"I wouldn't go that far," replied Corto.

"He looks professorial if you ask me," said Sampa.

"Profess what?" asked Corto.

"He looks smart," replied Sampa. "Forgot who my audience was."

Corto turned to Bjorn holding up three fingers.

"How many fingers am I holding up?" he asked.

"One and a half," replied Bjorn.

As the joke quickly registered to everyone else they began to laugh at Corto.

"Fuck you, Bjorn," said a stone faced Corto.

The crew went on to enjoy Beth's meal as usual, occasionally teasing Bjorn about his new eye wear as they ate. Afterward they all retired to their respective suites. Bjorn napped for about an hour and when he woke up he could not find his glasses. As he searched for them, he stopped immediately realizing that he had not misplaced them. They were likely hidden from him by Corto. He left his suite in search of Corto and eventually found him standing at the multi-dimensional imager. Corto turned around when he heard Bjorn enter the room.

"Here, try these out," said Corto as he handed Bjorn a more stylish piece of eyewear.

"What did you do with my eyeglasses?" asked Bjorn.

"Nothing really," replied Corto. "Well... your old lenses are in these new ones. I made some upgrades. Put them on, I think you'll like what I've done."

Bjorn put the goggle like glasses on and looked around.

"Besides looking more stylish and feeling more durable, I don't see a difference," said Bjorn.

"Wait one second," said Corto as he walked over to the wall and turned down the lights.

"No way!" said Bjorn. "How'd you get infrared vision in here?"

"Reach up and hit that small button on the side," said Corto.

Bjorn pushed the button and immediately a digital readout appeared in the lenses which gave the exact distance in meters to whatever object Bjorn focused on.

"This changes everything," said Bjorn. "I'm amazed."

"There's more," said Corto. "Once those nose pads are depressed everything is recorded to a memory card I have inserted in them. The information stays for thirty days."

"Wow, that's unbelievable," said Bjorn.

"One more thing," said Corto. "Those lenses will automatically darken to protect your eyes in the sunlight. If you miss another target from this point on it's all on you, you blind fucker."

Corto retired to his suite to rest up for the night. Bjorn went to the cargo bay to target practice for the remainder of the night. He fired inert rounds from his twice emitter onto targets he had positioned against the blast wall. He immediately noticed that his marksmanship was markedly better. As each hour passed his confidence in his shooting ability grew. He was beyond pleased. *This changes everything. I can't believe my eyes were so damn bad all this time.* At approximately 0200 hours he was done practicing and slowly walked through the darkness of the quiet Whisper all the way to his suite taking in every detail as if he was seeing them for the first time. The hum of the ship's engine was the only sound being made besides him walking. As he entered his suite he took a moment to appreciate the fact that for the first time in the last couple of days there was absolutely no drama. Not long after that he was asleep and so was the rest of the crew.

Chapter 9: Eye for an Eye

Location: Central City, District County, Rights Province, planet Neutralia
Council Chambers 0900 hours

Chancellor Aldrich paced in front of the large window as the bright sunlight cast his shadow across the room. He awaited the arrivals of Theris Lamont and Judas Benedict. Many questions ran through his mind as he paced back and forth. *What was Judas doing with the DOD on Hades? What is going to happen after the convention? Will we be prepared for the convention?* He also could not help but smile when he thought of the power that he would soon have after his plans have been unveiled. As he stepped toward the large window and looked onto the streets of Central City, he could see Theris Lamont walking up to the building. He turned and walked toward the door to the Council Chambers and opened it. To his surprise, there stood Judas Benedict.

"Hello, Steven," said Judas.

"Welcome, Councilman Benedict," said a startled Chancellor Aldrich. It's good to have you back. Come in, your seat awaits you. Vice Chancellor Lamont is on his way up now."

Judas walked into the room and took his normal seat on the darker side of the table. Because the room was still too bright for him he wore his goggles to protect his sensitive eyes. He also pulled his hood over his head. Upon sitting down, he immediately lowered his head to further minimize the effects of the sunlight. Seconds later Theris Lamont entered the room.

"Greetings, Councilman Benedict," said Theris. "It's really good to have you back here with us. I'm sorry to hear about what happened to you on Albin."

Without saying a word, Chancellor Aldrich cut his eyes toward Judas to capture his visceral response to Theris Lamont's statement.

Judas did not flinch. He remained stoic as he uttered his response. "I truly appreciate your concern, Vice Chancellor Lamont," he replied without looking up. "They'll have to bring more than that if they wish to kill me."

"Have you any idea who they were?" asked Chancellor Aldrich.

"I don't," replied Judas. "Have you any idea who they might have been, Chancellor Aldrich?"

Chancellor Aldrich quickly looked in Judas's direction with a scowl. He was shocked by the boldness of the question. Theris was confused by the question and simply stood in stunned silence as the tension grew in the room.

"My investigations have yielded nothing thus far," replied Chancellor Aldrich. "Perhaps I should extend my search beyond the borders of Albin. Maybe Hades would be a good place to start."

"That you have not done so already comes as a surprise to me," said Judas.

Both men stared at one another for a few seconds with Judas wondering if Chancellor Aldrich was lying about not knowing more details of his assault. Chancellor Aldrich knew that Judas was lying about where he was when the assault occurred. Theris Lamont had no clue what was going on.

Chancellor Aldrich was the first to break his gaze. "The convention is less than fifteen days away. I have taken measures to ensure that we will be secure, but we must remain here in Central City until then. We have to make sure that this was not a planned attempt on your life. Did it seem planned to you, Councilman Benedict?"

"I don't know," replied Judas as he casually looked away from Chancellor Aldrich, "it all happened so fast. I was attacked from behind and never saw their faces."

"Well, rest assured that we will do our best to find out who they were. An attack on one of us is a threat to us all," said Chancellor Aldrich.

Theris had taken his seat at the table across from Judas. The sun shined brightly on his face as he eagerly awaited the start of business.

"I officially call this meeting to order," said Chancellor Aldrich. "Before us we have the birth of a new horizon. It is no secret that Neutralia has given hope to the hopeless by being an example of what a civilized society has to offer. However, the solar system cannot be brought here, so we will bring our system to Sapien. Nastasia has assured me that merchants from every planet will be here to hear our plan. I have also taken the liberty to implement things that I will unveil on that special day. We are on the precipice of peace."

"Has Nastasia told these merchants about the taxation you wish to implement for all of this peace you boast about?" asked Judas.

"Nothing good comes without a price, everyone knows that, Judas," replied Chancellor Aldrich.

"So, she hasn't told them then?" asked Judas rhetorically. "Interesting."

"We haven't told them yet," replied Chancellor Aldrich.

"Taxation is the only way," said Theris. "Once they have reaped the benefits for that which they have paid they will come to embrace the idea."

"How naive are we to believe that you can take a system that is already perfect and make it better?" asked Judas.

"Perfect?" asked Theris. "You were just beaten to within a breath of your life for nothing. People have to know that that is not acceptable behavior. There has to be some consequences for those actions."

"I fail to see how paying taxes would have stopped those thugs from accosting me," snapped Judas.

"Proactive patrol!" replied Chancellor Aldrich. "In every dark corner of the solar system there will be well trained protectors who will ensure the safety of all law abiding Sapiens."

"And what of your book of laws? Has it been completed yet?" asked Judas.

"We are further along than you could ever imagine," replied Chancellor Aldrich. "In fact, next week we will convene to review those very laws."

"Whose conscience is the barometer for these laws? Or are they as arbitrary as I fear them to be?" asked Judas.

"Save those questions until after you have read them," replied Chancellor Aldrich.

"The only thing, so far, that gives me pause is the lack of input from the people to the process," said Theris.

"The people have no idea what's good for them," said Chancellor Aldrich.

"That may be true," replied Theris, "but I believe they should at least have the right to vote for their leaders. That way they are assured that they have representation from a like-minded person who understands their needs."

"Never!" said Chancellor Aldrich. "They would make a mockery of the entire process. Something so important cannot be subject to the whims of the uneducated majority."

Judas began to laugh. Both Chancellor Aldrich and Theris looked at him as if they were confused by that.

"Already he is drunk with power," said Judas matter of factly. "What is your contingency plan, Chancellor Aldrich? What happens if this plan of yours is rejected by the uneducated majority? What will you do then?"

"If it is rejected, which I highly doubt, then things will go back to the way they are now," replied Chancellor Aldrich.

"Once you have instilled fear in the people they can never be the same," said Judas. "Remember that."

"Fear of what?" asked Chancellor Aldrich.

"Right now, those people have no idea how much freedom you wish to take away from them," replied Judas, "but once you have placed it in their minds that you want it, they will always fear that you will not rest until you have it. Once you have gotten it, Chancellor Aldrich, where will you stop?"

Theris thought that Judas posed an excellent question and he looked to Chancellor Aldrich for his answer.

"You worry too much, Judas," said Chancellor Aldrich. "Look past your goggles from time to time and you will see that the people enjoy the safety of Neutralia when they are here. Rules are necessary for peace. To gain that peace some liberties have to be sacrificed."

"They always go home though, don't they, Steven?" asked Judas. "They always go home."

Chancellor Aldrich did not reply to that. He knew that Judas had a point. The unanswered question that bothered Chancellor Aldrich was would they stay if they were given the opportunity to do so?

"So, each world will be appointed a governor?" asked Theris attempting to break the tension.

"Yes, we have gone over this before. That is the plan," replied Chancellor Aldrich. "We will run the government from here, Central City. The solar alliance will be regulated and governed by the Supreme Council."

"Chancellor Aldrich, ruler of the Sapien Solar System," proclaimed Judas sarcastically. "I hope you realize what it is you're asking for."

"It is not the power that I covet, it's peace," replied Chancellor Aldrich. "I guess there is no secret which you would enjoy were you in my position."

"If I were in your position a great many things would be different, Chancellor Aldrich," replied Judas. "Alas it appears your conscience is more forgiving than mine."

Nastasia entered the room and when she did they all stopped talking and watched her. As she walked toward Chancellor Aldrich the only sound in the room was the cadence of her heels striking the marble floor. "Please pardon me for the interruption, gentlemen," she said before she addressed Chancellor Aldrich. "You have a communication from General Branimir. He said to summon you immediately."

"Thank you, Nastasia," replied Chancellor Aldrich.

Nastasia nodded to him, turned around, and walked out the same way she came in. After she was gone Chancellor Aldrich ended the meeting.

"Excuse me, gentlemen. Duty calls. I will see you again at next week's meeting. This meeting is adjourned," he said. He exited the Council Chambers to meet with Nastasia. Judas and Theris both remained seated.

"Why must you challenge him at every phase?" asked Theris of Judas.

"Were it not for my opposition to his antics thus far we'd all be slaves to him and those Mayhem Marauders by now," replied Judas. "You would be wise to temper your loyalty to him, Theris."

"My loyalty is to this council and to the people it represents. If within that allegiance loyalty must be shown to its leader then I will do as I must," replied Theris.

"You have the faith of a child who has yet to see his father falter and believes him to be perfect," said Judas.

"And you possess the cynicism of a man who doesn't know his father," replied Theris.

"Oh...I knew my father," replied Judas "but not as well as the prostitutes, opium dealers, and other malefactors of our world. The anniversary of his demise is a holiday in my heart, but his ways showed me the true nature of men."

"It's too bad you didn't have a father that you can consider a good person," replied Theris.

"Good?" asked Judas incredulously. He chuckled at the naivety of that statement. "There are no good people. There are no bad people. You're either better or worse and that is only relative to those to whom you are compared."

Realizing that it would be impossible to further the discussion cordially, Theris got up from his seat, walked around to Judas's side of the table, and gently put his hand on his shoulder. "Enjoy the remainder of your day, Councilman Benedict. I'm happy that you're alive," he said. He left the room and started his walk home through the streets of Central City.

Meanwhile, Chancellor Aldrich sat at the VC in his office conversing with the hologram of General Branimir, the balding, eye patch wearing, leader of the intelligence division of the Mayhem Marauders.

"I don't know who they were," said General Branimir. "We were only alerted to their presence once they were upon us. They savagely murdered five of my men before escaping and killing more. I barely escaped with my own life. They took the woman."

"Was she alive?" asked Chancellor Aldrich.

"Barely," replied General Branimir. "However, there was no way she could have made it through the night considering what we injected into her. I have transmitted to your EPIC a full report regarding the incident. Also, the evacuation of that base is complete. We are presently attempting to find another location suitable for our operation."

"Very good," replied Chancellor Aldrich. "Keep me apprised of all significant occurrences. End transmission."

As General Branimir's image disappeared into thin air, Chancellor Aldrich rose from his seat. He summoned Nastasia back into his office. "Make sure Councilman Benedict gets home safely," he ordered as she walked through the door.

"Friedrich is already waiting for him outside," Nastasia replied.

"Good, you may go now," said Chancellor Aldrich.

Nastasia backed out of the room giving a slight bow to Chancellor Aldrich and pulling the large wooden door closed as she exited.

Moments later Judas was in the passenger compartment of Friedrich's JEDDO being driven home. As they entered the O'neal Heights community, where Judas resided, he prepared himself for the sunlight by adjusting his goggles and pulling his hood over his head.

"We're here, councilman," said Friedrich as he slowed his JEDDO to a stop.

Moments later the side door slid open and Judas lowered his head as the sunlight filled the passenger compartment of the JEDDO. Judas extended his left hand and Friedrich took it as he assisted him out of the JEDDO. Once his feet were firmly on the ground, Judas visually scanned the area, looking from side to side, as Friedrich walked around to the driver seat. Judas's heart began to race. Suddenly, he was afraid.

"Will you stay until I've reached my dwelling?" asked Judas.

Friedrich stopped in his tracks and came back around to where Judas was standing. "Yes, councilman, I'll wait right here," he said.

"Thank you," replied Judas as he started the short walk to his first-floor apartment. Once Judas was inside, he walked over to the window and waved to Friedrich. Friedrich climbed into his JEDDO and drove away. Judas's apartment was dimly lit and very cold, just the way he, and most Albinos, liked it. He removed his goggles and pulled back his hood. Shortly thereafter he removed his gray outer garment all together. As much as he tried to maintain his composure, Judas was terrified. The fear he felt upon exiting the JEDDO had now manifested itself in the form of a strong hunch that Chancellor Aldrich had something to do with his attack on Hades. In fact, he was now almost certain of it. He attempted to calm his nerves by sitting but was unsuccessful. However, that fear and anxiety slowly turned into rage the more he thought of how close he came to death. *He tried to have me killed. It was him.* He now wanted Chancellor Aldrich dead more than ever. This time, in his mind, he had a legitimate reason. As his heart rate began to return to normal, he slowly made his way to his VC. "Contact Rokuro Onishi," he whispered.

"Unable to process request. Speak louder," was the audio message returned by the VC.

Judas took a deep breath and as he exhaled he said, "Contact Rokuro Onishi!"

Rokuro's face then appeared in the form of a hologram. There was a lot of noise behind him. He was in Iniquity at the Den. Judas instantly became frustrated because he knew it would be difficult for him to raise his voice to a level that Rokuro could hear over the noise.

"What do you want?" slurred Rokuro.

"I want you to come to Neutralia earlier than we planned," said Judas.

Rokuro could barely hear Judas's voice and did not understand what he had said. "Repeat your message," he said now concentrating even more.

Judas made a throat slashing gesture with his left hand and said, "End transmission."

Rokuro's image disappeared. Judas sent him a message via his EPIC which read, *I wish to start earlier than planned. Contact me later today or tomorrow when you are in a quieter environment.*

Rokuro read the message and typed his response, *I will contact you tomorrow.* He pocketed his EPIC and continued to wait in the lounge of the Den for Alexei and Igor to finish their visits with their favorite prostitutes. The three DOD members were at the Den to celebrate the memory of Rokuro's top assassin, Bahadur, who never returned from a mission on his home planet of Akkadian Arabu two years prior to this very day. The Persian assassin was also Rokuro's best friend and he missed him. Rokuro assumed Bahadur had to be dead. He had many enemies because he was feared by many. Bahadur had the conscience of a blind snake and he would strike anyone he perceived to be a threat. That was his reputation and he was known as Bad Bahadur because of it. After Alexei and Igor were done with their prostitutes, they joined Rokuro in the common area of The Den. They continued to celebrate until the early evening. When they were done they stumbled out to the JEDDO that was waiting for them and made their way back to their hideout in Tierra Mala.

Location: DOD hideout, Tierra Mala, outskirts of Elba County, Zasnezene Province
Rokuro Onishi's bedroom, 0900 hours the next day

As Rokuro slept Adera moved freely about their bedroom giving little care to the amount of noise she made. In fact, she wanted him to wake up. Within minutes Rokuro began to stir and slowly woke. As his eyes came into focus, he saw her beautiful naked body standing beside the bed.

"It lives," said Adera sarcastically.

Rokuro slowly sat on the edge of his bed. He was tired and hungover from his day of celebrating and drinking. Adera sat closely beside him on the bed and rested her head on his shoulder. Normally she would want all of Rokuro's time and attention, but she made exceptions when he set aside time to devote to his deceased friend, Bahadur.

"It hardly seems like two years have passed," said Adera.

"To me it feels exactly like two years," replied Rokuro. "I have felt every excruciating second of that time. I don't know what's more painful, his absence or my inability to avenge him. Those who are responsible for his absence will suffer like no others have before them." Suddenly he remembered that he said he would contact Judas. "I have to make a call. It will be brief," he said to Adera.

She removed her head from his shoulder and flopped backward on the bed with her arms stretched out to the side.

Rokuro got up and walked over to his VC. "Contact Judas," he said into his VC.

Moments later a hologram of Judas appeared before him and Judas began to speak. "Greetings, Rokuro. First of all, thank you, again, for saving my life and delivering me safely to my home infirmary. I won't take much of your time. There have been some developments with my situation and I believe my nemesis, Chancellor Aldrich, is responsible for my attack."

Rokuro's eyes widened. "Surely you want the same result then?" he asked.

"Yes!" replied Judas. "Only I want it faster! Now that I feel he wants me dead as much as I want him dead, there is no time to waste. If you could be here a week prior to the convention, then surely, we can get things done cleaner and more efficiently. I meet with the council a week from today to discuss the book of laws. I shall meet with you in Westborough afterward."

"No problem. Consider it done," said Rokuro. "I will await your signal and respond at that time."

"Good enough," said Judas. "End transmission."

After Judas's image disappeared Rokuro disrobed and got back into bed with Adera.

Chapter 10: The Calm Before the Storm

Location: Orbiting Neutralia
Aboard the Whisper, Six days later, 1400 hours

As Bjorn, Corto, and Francois target practiced in the cargo bay of the ship, Mulati seized the opportunity to speak with Sampa and Beth on the bridge about Francois' status among the crew.

"In all honesty, he's been nothing but helpful since we picked him up," said Sampa.

"I should hope so," replied Mulati, "it was because of him that we got into all of that trouble in the first place."

Sampa thought for a moment as she replayed the previous events in her mind. "True," she replied.

"Besides you two," Beth chimed in, "we all got here under less than favorable circumstances. His arrival was really not that much different."

"I understand that, Beth," replied Mulati. "I just don't feel that we've fully vetted him. He knows too much about some of everything to be some hapless drifter."

"You don't trust him," declared Beth.

"Trust is earned," replied Sampa. "He hasn't been with us long enough for that to happen."

"You said yourself, Mulati, that he was integral in getting you boys off that island," said Beth.

"And he did save our butts running from those pirates," added Sampa.

"That was self-preservation at work," replied Mulati. "If we died, he died. I can think of no greater incentive for a stranger to be helpful than that. Where in any of these events has his conscience been tested? We've only witnessed his resolve and fortitude. At some point we have to say that enough is enough. We get everything we need out of who we have. His only actual purpose going forward would be to divide our profits by another person."

"The Whisper can accommodate ten people comfortably," said Beth succinctly. "He'd be number six. Bjorn and Corto seem to like him a lot as well."

"What about you, Beth?" asked Mulati. "What do you think of him? Do you trust him? Right now, if he drew the short straw on a mission and had to stay aboard the Whisper with you, would you be completely comfortable?"

Beth had never thought about it that way. "I don't know," she said honestly. "I do like him, but, I guess you're right, trust is altogether different. I probably feel sorry for him more than anything. What are his plans? Does he even want to stay with us? We could be assuming too much ourselves."

"Since he's been here, Mulati, would you count him as an asset or a hindrance?" asked Sampa.

Mulati pondered the question momentarily as if he were trying to talk himself out of what he knew to be true. "He has been an asset," he conceded.

"I have an idea," said Sampa. "We have that meeting with the American next week. Why don't we use that mission as a trial run for him? If he performs to our satisfaction, he stays. In the meantime, his pay will be the food, lodging, and security we have and will provide for him. After this mission he gets an equal cut of whatever we do from then on."

"That sounds like a heck of a deal to me," said Beth.

"I agree," said Mulati. "Great idea, Sam."

Meanwhile in the cargo bay, Corto, Bjorn, and Francois continued to practice. They were focused as they took turns firing upon the target with their twice emitters. Despite the usual jocularity among each other, Corto and Bjorn took their shooting very seriously. The intensity with which they trained caused each of them to work up a sweat. Putting rounds on the bullseye of the stationary target wasn't a problem for any of them, Francois included. During this session they worked on rapid target acquisition. As Francois quickly raised his weapon, got stockweld, and aimed his twice emitter; Corto reassured him.

"That's it, the quicker you get there the more time you have on the sights and the trigger. Slow, steady pressure to the rear. Let it surprise you," said Corto.

Francois' round, again, impacted the bullseye. "Just like that," said Corto. "Good!"

They all paused momentarily to acknowledge Mulati as he walked into the cargo bay. With no hesitation Mulati retrieved his own twice emitter from the weapon locker and joined them. Although he was not quite as good as Corto, Mulati was also a capable marksman. As he aimed his twice emitter, he took that opportunity to probe Francois about his intentions. "How long are you planning on staying with us?" he asked.

Francois was caught off guard by the question. He knew it would come eventually, and he had thought about it, but he wasn't expecting it at that time. "I-I don't know," stammered Francois. "Am I being asked to leave?"

"You're being asked your intentions, Francois," replied Mulati as he eschewed the shot he was about to take and lowered his twice emitter to make eye contact with him. Suddenly everyone in the room was quiet as they focused on Francois. Bjorn and Corto wanted to know his answer as well.

Francois rotated his twice emitter around to his back, letting it hang there by its sling so that he could use hand gestures as he spoke and to appear non-threatening. After a slight delay he spoke. "I'd very much like to stay. I have nowhere else to go. That ship was all I had." He looked to the faces of Bjorn and Corto who looked to

Mulati. Undaunted, he continued. "I know you guys are a family here and I look like another mouth to feed, but I know my way around places. I know how to do things. I know my place and I won't make trouble with the crew. I promise you that."

"Here's your deal, Francois, and tell me if you two disagree," said Mulati as he acknowledged Bjorn and Corto. "We have a new mission we're about to embark on next week. The terms have already been negotiated and you won't be paid. However, if you continue to do what you have done thus far you will have a place here. Equal split from there on out. If for some reason you don't meet our expectations, we drop you off wherever it is you want to go and we part ways."

"I have no issue with that," replied Bjorn.

"Neither do I," said Corto.

"That's fair enough," said Francois. "I accept."

"Good," said Mulati, "we have a deal." Mulati reacquired his target and fired a round directly into the bullseye. He placed his twice emitter back into the weapon locker and left the cargo area.

"Welcome to the Whisper, Frenchie!" said Corto with a smile.

"Thanks," said Francois as he raised his twice emitter to the target, sighted in, and took a shot. He missed the bullseye completely.

Location: Central City, District County, Rights Province, Planet Neutralia
1100 hours the next day, Council Chambers

Seated at their normal positions around the long rectangular table were Chancellor Aldrich, Judas Benedict, and Theris Lamont. Joining them were the intelligence director, General Branimir; the law enforcement director, General Tolliver; and Nastasia Rodmanovic. The meeting had been going on for two hours already and it was contentious. They had openly discussed the proposed laws which had been made up by the two generals and Nastasia. The merits of each law had been debated, and either ratified or vetoed, by the triumvirate of Chancellor Aldrich, Judas Benedict, and Theris Lamont. Most of the queries or critiques of the laws being debated were directed toward Nastasia. Much to the chagrin of Judas, Nastasia was well prepared and had an answer for every question posed by the council. They were almost done and, although it was difficult, the majority of the laws they discussed had been ratified, which only required a two thirds majority vote. Chancellor Aldrich voted *yes* each time which meant that a law only failed when both Judas and Theris agreed to veto it. There were very few laws that Judas actually agreed to. In most cases he was a lone dissenter. Theris seldomly used his veto but did carefully scrutinize each law put before him based on its fairness to the citizenry, its appropriateness for the time and culture, and, most importantly, whether or not it satisfied his conscience. Judas was not pleased and had already counted this event as a lost battle. Nastasia, on the other hand, was silently ecstatic. She knew that she was an integral part of something truly historic and the gravity of the event was not lost on her. Her body language, however, gave no such indication. Likewise, Judas remained stone faced throughout. He did not want to give Nastasia the slightest impression that she had in any way bested him. The generals were mostly silent except for the occasional technical expertise they would provide to Nastasia when it was asked of them. Finally, after three hours of reviewing laws, they were done.

"Next week at this time we will usher in a new era," proclaimed Chancellor Aldrich as he stood up from his seat at the table. "The anarchy with which this solar system is beset will soon be a distant memory, and we have the people in this room to thank for that."

Nastasia began to clap and, not long after, the generals joined her. Within seconds everyone in the room, except for Judas, was standing and applauding. For once Judas was happy that his hand was injured because it gave him a convenient excuse not to clap. Chancellor Aldrich nodded in appreciation of the gesture and waited patiently for the applause to stop.

"We are adjourned," he said proudly.

Judas slowly hoisted himself up from his chair, bracing himself on the solid table with his healthy hand. He carefully positioned his goggles over his eyes and made his way to the door after excusing himself. As he walked out onto the streets of Central City toward the waiting JEDDO he pulled his hood over his head and lowered his eyes toward the ground. His mind was on the meeting that had just occurred and also on the upcoming meeting with the DOD which was to take place in Westborough later that night. "Good afternoon, Friedrich. I'll be headed home," he said as he entered the JEDDO.

"Good afternoon, councilman," replied Friedrich. "As you wish, sir. Productive meeting today?" he asked.

"Only time will tell," replied Judas. "However, I suspect that it was not. I wish that I could tell you more about it, but I like you and would rather you bask in the bliss of your ignorance as long as you can."

Friedrich received the comment appropriately and laughed accordingly. He liked and respected Judas for his strength and his willingness to stand strong in his convictions against sometimes seemingly insurmountable odds. Friedrich's laughter forced a smile out of Judas, which was a very rare sight. Judas was able, now, to talk for extended periods of time without losing his breath because his ribs were finally healing, and it didn't hurt him to breathe. Throughout their journey to his apartment, they continued to converse about different topics but nothing in particular. Before long they arrived at Judas's home and, like he did after the last council meeting, Friedrich stood and watched him until he disappeared into his apartment. Upon entering his apartment, Judas felt the same anxiety as the last time but this time it wasn't as intense. It bothered Judas that he had obvious psychological scars from being attacked. He had contacted Rokuro Onishi an hour before the meeting and they decided they would meet in Westborough at 2100 hours. By that time the sun would have gone down which would be better for Judas because he was more comfortable in darkness. He ate a healthy lunch and he laid down for a nap.

Location: Southtown, District County, Rights Province, Planet Neutralia
The Hidden Bastille, 1400 hours

Chancellor Aldrich arrived at the secret facility with General Tolliver and General Branimir to make sure all was going well. Unbeknownst to Judas Benedict and Theris Lamont, Chancellor Aldrich, with the help of the Mayhem Marauders, had secretly overseen the construction of the prison for three years and it housed some of the most dangerous men and women in the Sapien Solar System. The big surprise, to which Chancellor Aldrich had previously referred, was to be the unveiling of the existence of this facility at the conclusion of his speech during the convention. Housed in the facility were twenty of the most dangerous criminals in the Sapien Solar System. The Hidden Bastille was located beneath the mountainous outskirts of Southtown. Chancellor Aldrich was able to hide the construction of the facility by camouflaging it as a mining operation. No one had reason to suspect that it was anything other than that. General Tolliver and an intermediate level Mayhem Marauder guard, Klaus Moken, led the way as both Chancellor Aldrich and General Branimir were given a tour of the now completed facility. The spacious one-man cells were all identical to one another and looked relatively comfortable. Highly glossed cement floors ran throughout the well-lit facility. As they slowly passed by the cells, General Tolliver gave detailed background information on each occupant and how long they had been there. Finally, they made it to the second to last cell. Inside the cell was a young Albino man. His cell was darker than the others and Chancellor Aldrich was shocked to find him already peering out of his cell as they looked inside. He had the look of a man who would kill without thought or fear of repercussion, and he was uncharacteristically strong looking for an

Albino. He was not wearing a shirt and his upper body was chiseled, hard, and vascular. His hair was short, and he wore a long mustache and goatee. His thumb nails were an inch long, sharpened, and dirty.

"That's Onin Gesh, the pale terror," said General Tolliver. "He has killed over fifty people. His hands are his weapons of choice, and he's known to torture his victims before killing them. He is unbelievably strong despite being Albino. He has promised that he will kill every one of us on several occasions."

"Let's hope he never gets that opportunity," said Chancellor Aldrich.

"He won't," General Tolliver responded confidently as he continued to the next cell. "This man, as you may already know, is the Persian, Bahadur. He's a member of the DOD and is known as Bad Bahadur. He has personally killed over one hundred men. His weapons of choice are swords, short spears, daggers, and bow and arrows. We have chosen these two men as your examples for your demonstration."

As they looked into his cell, Bahadur paced from wall to wall never taking his eyes off them. He was heavily bearded, heavily muscled, tall, and angry.

"Both men have subcutaneous electrodes inserted into every quadrant of their bodies, both pectoral muscles and the front of each quadricep," stated General Tolliver. "We don't want to have them shackled in public because of the negative image it will present, so this is our way of controlling them."

"How does it work?" asked Chancellor Aldrich.

"Like this," answered General Tolliver as he directed Klaus to flip the switch on his troll, the palm sized electronic device he was holding, sending both men to their knees screaming in agony.

"That's enough!" said Chancellor Aldrich after five seconds. He was satisfied that they could be controlled so easily but dissatisfied with the malice with which General Tolliver had deployed the device.

As Klaus switched his troll to the off-position Bahadur immediately jumped up and ran toward the cell door yelling as loud as he could. Chancellor Aldrich and General Branimir instinctively jumped back as his body slammed into the door.

"You do that all the time, but you have never budged that door," taunted Klaus.

Bahadur spat on the glass that separated them, and he simply went back to pacing in his cell and staring at the four men until they walked away. The fact that Bahadur and Onin Gesh appeared to kill indiscriminately, and without constraints of a reasonable conscience, made them prime candidates to exemplify the effectiveness of Chancellor Aldrich's pilot prison and law enforcement program. They were both notorious killers.

As they walked back past his cell, Onin Gesh yelled his promise, "I! Will! Kill! Yoouuuuu!!!" His voice was raspy and had the timbre of the growl of a large beast. The very sound of it sent chills through the spines of Chancellor Aldrich and the generals.

"Has anyone ever escaped?" asked Chancellor Aldrich nervously.

"No," replied General Tolliver. "In fact, that's virtually impossible. These cells are airtight and have one point of entry. The air vents are six inches, so no man can fit through them. All of the cells are opened and closed electronically from the main control room."

"What happens in the event of a power outage?" asked Chancellor Aldrich.

"I'm glad you asked that," replied General Tolliver. "Should that occur, the cells would open automatically. However, the backup generators will automatically kick in which will prevent that. There are four of them. They are sequenced so if one goes down then the next one would automatically and immediately engage."

"Where are they located?" asked Chancellor Aldrich.

"They're all outside of the facility positioned on the north, south, east, and west boundaries of the facility," replied General Tolliver. "We have covered every aspect and considered every potential problem. We are prepared. In addition to the engineers and fixed posts, we have one guard assigned to every two prisoners for three separate shifts a day. That is why Klaus is so familiar with Bahadur and Onin Gesh."

"It looks like you have things under control," said Chancellor Aldrich. "Let's keep it that way."

"We will," replied General Tolliver.

"One more question," said Chancellor Aldrich. "What is the maximum range for that shock apparatus that Klaus has?"

"That would be twenty meters," replied General Tolliver.

The tour concluded at that point. After escorting Chancellor Aldrich and General Branimir to the exit, General Tolliver remained there to continue his work. Chancellor Aldrich and General Branimir returned to Central City by JEDDO.

Chapter 11: Deception All Around

Location: East City, District County, Rights Province, Planet Neutralia
Airfield, 1845 hours

As Mulati and Sampa placed the Whisper into low power mode, Corto and Bjorn performed their customary total system analysis of the ship. Francois was with them taking the opportunity to learn more about the inner workings of the Whisper. Beth was in the galley putting the finishing touches on another of her fantastic meals. As usual, she made more than enough food for the crew. She always thought having too much was better than having just enough. The crew confirmed her belief because they usually finished whatever she prepared for them. She had, once, half-heartedly asked Sampa for her assistance in the past, but Sampa was not at all interested in helping in the galley. That didn't bother Beth in the least because she considered the galley her domain and didn't really like anyone else to be in there anyway. She had only asked Sampa to join her because she felt it was both proper and polite to do so. She would often joke that Mulati was the head of the Whisper, but its heart belonged to her. In a lot of ways, she was right. If anyone was the glue to the crew, it would be her. Sensitivity was her duty, she felt, and it came naturally to her. Her meal was, for all intent and purposes, complete so she left the galley and went to relax in the ship's lounge. Bjorn, Corto, and Francois were already there.

"Everything ok with this ship?" she asked to no one in particular.

"We're good," replied Bjorn. "She's running clean; no issues whatsoever."

"We're just waiting on the American now," said Corto.

"Anybody else nervous about this besides me?" asked Beth.

"Not really," replied Bjorn. "In fact, I'm looking forward to it."

Mulati's voice came through the intercom and said that a JEDDO was approaching from the west. He ordered everyone to the back hatch in the cargo bay of the Whisper. They all got up and made their way down as ordered. Moments later the entire crew was standing in the cargo bay as Bjorn lowered the ramp. By the time the JEDDO reached them, the ramp had been fully lowered and they all stood together at the top of it and at the entrance to the cargo bay. Bjorn, Sampa, and Francois were armed with their twice emitters. Corto wore his dagger vest. Mulati was two steps in front of everyone else.

"According to the life scan there are four occupants including the driver," said Sampa.

"I copy," said Mulati.

The JEDDO slowly came to a stop about twenty yards short of the Whisper's ramp. The driver got out, walked around, opened the side door, and stood there. The first to exit was Theris Lamont. Next to exit were Louis and Eric.

"Those two look familiar to me," whispered Sampa referring to Louis and Eric. "I've seen them somewhere."

"So, have I," said Bjorn. "I just can't place it."

"I've never seen them a day in my life," said Corto, "I'm sure of it."

Mulati felt the same as Sampa and Bjorn. It bothered him that he could not remember who they were. Both men stood behind Theris Lamont.

"Welcome to Neutralia," said Theris. "These are my assistants, Louis and Eric." Before anyone could say anything else, Ean walked out of the JEDDO. Mulati instantly opened his dlhá násada and scurried down the ramp with it in attack position. Sampa and Bjorn ran behind him bringing their twice emitters up to the ready. Realizing what was about to happen, Ean did not take another step forward. Corto was confused and drew his dagger from his leg holster but stayed where he was. Mulati stopped a few feet short of them and took up an offensive stance with his dlhá násada at the ready. Bjorn and Sampa positioned themselves where they faced Ean at forty-five degrees. With their twice emitters trained on him, they stayed abreast of Mulati. Suddenly it dawned on Theris that he had forgotten to mention to the crew of the Whisper that Louis, Eric, and Ean all worked for him.

"Wait!" yelled Theris.

"What is this, a trap?" asked an angry Mulati as he peered at a nervous Theris.

"No!" replied Theris desperately. "They're with me. Louis and Eric here are my assistants and Ean is my personal bodyguard. We mean you no harm!"

For a moment Mulati maintained his offensive stance. He then stood straight up and closed his dlhá násada. "You need a better bodyguard," he said to Theris.

"He does what I ask him to do, and he does it well," replied Theris. "I apologize for the confusion, I should have told you about him sooner."

"Bjorn, Corto, check them out," said Mulati as he motioned them over to Theris's entourage with two nods of his head. Bjorn and Corto walked over and thoroughly searched each one of them for weapons while Sampa covered them. Afterward, Corto went onto the JEDDO and searched it as well.

"All clear!" said Corto as he reappeared from the JEDDO.

"I knew I recognized those two guys from somewhere," said Sampa as she lowered her twice emitter.

"We can talk inside," said Mulati. "If any one of you causes trouble on my ship, we'll kill you all without hesitation."

"Understood," said Theris. "I assure you, there are no more surprises."

"Anybody care to tell me how you know that guy?" asked a confused Corto.

"That's Sam's boyfriend from the Sumner Tavern," said Bjorn

sarcastically.

"Ha ha," said Sampa as she offered a fake smile to Bjorn.

"Looks like his chin healed up pretty good," said Bjorn. "So much for that love tap you gave him, Sam."

Sampa took a long hard look at Ean's chin and was disappointed to find there was no scar there. Without saying a word, she simply shook her head, slightly disgusted with herself.

"Follow me," said Mulati to Theris and his entourage as he walked up the ramp and into the cargo bay of the Whisper. Beth turned to walk with him as he reached her at the top of the ramp. Theris' entourage followed closely behind him. Francois, Sampa, Corto, and Bjorn followed behind them.

"You're gonna have to recalibrate that life scanner, Sam," said Francois, "because it only accounted for four people."

"I'll check it later," said Sampa, "it's probably just a glitch."

"Alright then," said Francois as he decided to change the subject. "Maybe you can tell me the story about how you met these guys, sounds like I missed a good one."

"That's an understatement," said Sampa as she rolled her eyes.

Mulati stopped suddenly as it dawned on him that he wasn't sure of what they were going to be asked to do or if he was comfortable with Francois knowing the full details. "Francois, stay back and guard the rear hatch. We'll be busy discussing the mission and won't have time to monitor our surroundings."

Without hesitation, Francois agreed. He viewed the request as a step in the right direction. This was an opportunity to further gain the trust of the crew by demonstrating his trustworthiness. It also afforded all the other members of the crew the ability to sit in on the meeting with Theris without being concerned with their security. The pride he felt in the responsibility he was given outweighed his curiosity about what was going to be discussed in the meeting. Also, he was fairly certain that Bjorn and Corto would later tell him what they could about it.

Mulati led Theris and his entourage to the ship's lounge where they could discuss the mission in comfort. After they all entered the lounge, Theris, Louis, and Eric sat. Ean stood closely behind Theris with his chin up and his hands overlapped together in front of him. He had yet to say a word.

"What went on out there?" asked Beth.

"Theris is about to tell us about that," said Mulati as he gave a suspicious glare toward Theris.

"Absolutely," replied Theris. "I had to be assured that the crew I hired possessed a few necessary traits which, I feel, will be required to accomplish this mission. Courage was demonstrated by Sam when she stood up to Ean in that tavern on Hades. Bravery was displayed by Mulati when he immediately confronted him, but most important to me was the conscience you displayed," said Theris as he looked up at Mulati.

"My conscience?" asked Mulati.

"Yes, your conscience," replied Theris. "You could have attempted to kill Ean, but you didn't. You did only what was necessary to stop the threat. That was the most important test of them all. I didn't go there looking for just a mercenary, any of them could have done that. I went there looking for a mercenary with a conscience, and there you were full of courage."

"I would've killed him," said a tight-lipped Bjorn.

"You would have tried," whispered Ean.

"That is enough!" snapped Theris to Ean. "That is not why we are here. Please forgive him."

Bjorn and Ean both stared menacingly at one another as Theris spoke those words. Bjorn was serious about what he had said and everyone in the room knew it.

"What your crew demonstrated in that tavern that night," Theris continued, "is exactly what I have been searching for. You have what it takes to get it done."

"So, what is this mission that is so important?" asked Mulati.

Theris took a deep breath and exhaled an exaggerated sigh before he spoke. "As you already know, there is a very important convention here in District County next week. Without giving away too many details, I feel that we are headed down a dangerous path. The way we are going, there is only one logical conclusion to our existence that I can foresee, and that's total annihilation. The division caused by the separation of our cultures is a poison. There is no love or appreciation for the differences of others. What we can learn from one another is overshadowed by our desperation to hold on to what is uniquely our own to the detriment of us all. My time here on Neutralia has shown me that. Nothing bad has ever come from sharing. The same cannot be said for withholding from others what ultimately makes us all human. This solar system may never be the same after next week and I fear it is too late for any of us to do anything about that. Some time ago I started the Genesis plan. That plan is a multicultural expedition consisting of farmers, scientists, doctors, blacksmiths, carpenters, pilots, and a few other professions necessary to successfully start a new civilization. Four couples from each planet were recruited. The purpose of the expedition is to find one life sustaining planet on which all races and cultures could peacefully coexist. One day before they were to meet me here in this very airfield, they all vanished. I have not heard a word from any of them since that day. That was a year ago."

"So, your plan is to force different cultures to live together?" asked Sampa.

"I would not say *force*," said Theris. "This mission is completely voluntary."

"I don't know about that," said Sampa. "Neutralia only works as a society because that is where everyone goes to get away from it all. If you force, excuse me, *put* everyone together for good it stands to reason, by that logic, that people will want to gravitate inward to their own kind whenever a respite is needed. If that is not an option, then what will you have?"

"A society where people will learn to live together despite their differences, unlike Sapien," replied Theris.

Sampa was not satisfied with the answer, but she knew that arguing with Theris about it at that time would not be smart. She decided it would be best to wait to talk to Mulati about it later.

"How will we know who we are looking for?" asked Mulati.

"Hopefully they are all still together somewhere," said Theris. "In the event that you happen to find any, or all, of them, there should be markings on the inside of their right ankles. Those markings are codes that tell us who they are."

"On my conscience!" gasped Beth to herself as her eyes widened and she covered her mouth with her hand.

"What is it, Beth?" asked Mulati.

"The Asian woman we got from Evropa had that!" replied Beth.

Theris immediately stood up. "What did the markings say? Where is she? Were there others?" he asked.

"She's dead," replied Mulati. "We tried to save her but could not. The island was uncharted. We stumbled upon it by accident and we believe it was hidden purposely."

Beth had left the lounge while Mulati was talking and returned a short time later with her medical notes in her hand. "G/5W2," she read as she slowly walked back into the room.

Theris fell back into his chair with a blank look on his face. He softly mouthed the words that coincided with the inscription. "Genesis, 5th world, woman 2. You found them. They are there. You have to go back to get them."

"Not without reinforcements," said Mulati. "They have it too well protected. We have to have a plan."

"As I have already indicated you will have vast resources at your disposal. Whatever you need, just ask," said Theris.

"Understood," said Mulati. After pausing to think for a moment, he spoke. "I do have one question. Why is this mission a secret at all? Why do you have to hide it?"

Theris methodically studied the faces of each person in the room before answering. "The people with whom I govern lack the ability to think as I do. They fail to see the advantages, as I do, of integrating the people of our worlds for a greater cause. As I look around this room, I see the future. Your crew embodies what I have envisioned long before now. Even you, Mulati, are a product of what I believe to be a better existence. Here you are an outcast, a man without a home, and not for what you have done in this solar system but for the way that you came into it. Your birth was something over which you had absolutely no control, however a union of races is a beautiful thing. You are ostracized for that. That is most unfortunate. So now is the time. I have been forced to suppress my true feelings because my comrades are beholden to tradition, nostalgia, and other intangible things that could just as easily be inscribed in the scrolls of history. Whereas they feel it is important to advance each race of people individually, I hope to advance us all collectively as one, in harmony. My plan contradicts everything they have openly endeavored to do with my reluctant support. I do not enjoy the bitter taste of reticence. Any challenge to the ideals of small minded men who possess infinite power is tantamount to a declaration of war. As popular as I am, I lack the political clout to fight that battle. This mission, done covertly, hurts no one. However, the mere mention of it publicly would shake our entire government to its core. That is why it is a secret. That is why I hide it. That is why you must succeed."

Mulati looked to Sampa who barely accepted his eye contact before looking away. The rest of the crew was more accepting of his gaze and seemed to be satisfied with the explanation given by Theris. He cared about what Sampa thought and appreciated her point of view, but this time he disagreed with her. He liked what Theris had to say and so did his conscience. "I will contact you soon with a list of everything we will need to accomplish this mission. I have to discuss this further with my crew. We will get your people if they are still alive."

"Good enough," replied Theris. "I will be waiting."

Mulati looked over to Sampa and said, "I'll see you on the bridge now," and walked out of the lounge. Sampa immediately followed. Beth rolled her lips inward and widened her eyes as she looked around, sure that Mulati and Sampa were about to engage in a heated debate. She said nothing, however, and simply left the lounge for the galley to put the final touches on her meal.

As Theris, Louis, Eric, and Ean prepared to leave the Whisper; Bjorn and Corto rose to escort them back to the cargo bay. Ean was careful to walk in front of Theris wherever they went, but he also kept his distance from Bjorn. Louis and Eric followed closely behind Theris. A couple of minutes later, they were at the exit to the cargo bay where Francois was attentively standing guard.

"What was her name?" asked Bjorn of Theris before they stepped on the ramp to exit.

Theris suddenly stopped, turned to look Bjorn in his eyes, and said, "Her name was Lihua. It means beautiful and elegant. She was both. She was a historian. She was loved." He turned, continued down the ramp with his entourage, and they got into their JEDDO headed to Central City. As Bjorn stood atop the ramp watching them drive away, his mind went back to Lihua and what she had gone through. He felt the anger beginning to swell in his body. Francois and Corto noticed it too. Whoever was responsible for her death was going to pay, of that they were certain.

"Let's close her up," said Corto as he gave Bjorn a friendly slap on his back and disappeared into the cargo bay. Bjorn said nothing and simply turned to follow him inside, clearly still consumed by thoughts of Lihua. Francois had already gone in as well. They sealed the cargo bay and headed to the lounge to wait for Beth to give the go ahead for evening chow.

Meanwhile, Sampa and Mulati were in their normal seats at the control panel on the bridge.

"As Alkebulans, my people know who they are," said Sampa, "and I'm fine with that. I have chosen this life. It works for me. As much as I love this life, though, I am not naive enough to believe that what is good for me is great for my people. In fact, I'm in the minority when it comes to that. There is nothing wrong with my people wanting to be with their own."

"It is the exclusion of others that makes that way of thinking somewhat problematic, Sam," replied Mulati. "I have never thought it to be a bad idea for people to want to be with people who are like them. It's the shunning of those who are different that bothers me. You have never been called a half-breed."

"You have the benefit of both cultures, Mulati," said Sampa immediately and sharply.

"Physically, I do," replied Mulati. "Culturally I am an outcast. I'm too Evropan for Alkebulans and I'm too Alkebulan for Evropans. I'm a man of two worlds without a world to call my own."

Suddenly the open mic of the intercom could be heard. They both paused knowing it was Beth.

"Sorry to break up your party," she said, "but chow is ready. We're waiting on you two."

"We copy, Beth," replied Mulati, "we're on our way." He waited for the intercom to go completely silent before he spoke to Sampa again. "I know you value the traditions of your people, Sam, but I am a real person. I'm flesh and blood. Your people is a construct of your mind. You say you want your people's identity to be preserved. What I hear is you don't want your people to become our people."

"We'll agree to disagree," said Sampa as they both stood up from their seats. Instinctively they embraced then left the bridge and headed for the dining room.

Chapter 12: The Francois Faux Pas

Location: Westborough, District County, Rights Province, Planet Neutralia
2100 hours

Because he was away from Hades, Rokuro Onishi felt he was out of his element but he was not uncomfortable. He, along with Alexei and Igor, had already disembarked their transport vessel, the Iron Raven. It was a mile behind them and they were on horseback awaiting Judas's arrival. His JEDDO arrived on time and his Albino driver slid his door open for him. Judas emerged from the darkened interior of the transport vehicle into the night of Westborough to meet with Rokuro, Alexei, and Igor. He was wearing neither his hood nor his goggles.

As he got within speaking distance of the three men, Judas got right to business. "He tried to have me killed, I'm almost certain of it. Every instinct I have tells me that he was behind my attack. His smugness reeks of guilt. He has stated that he will not be leaving Neutralia for the foreseeable future, therefore you will have to kill him here. Anyone who meets their demise because of their acquaintance with him... I will consider collateral damage."

"Where will he be exactly?" asked Rokuro.

"Most times he is in his office in the Council Chambers in Central City. However, my sources tell me that he has spent a considerable amount of time at a mining facility in Southtown as of late. I would prefer that you kill him there because Southtown is sparsely populated. The news of a murder on Neutralia will be bad enough, we don't need witnesses to further exacerbate the hysteria that is sure to follow."

"We will kill him when the opportunity presents itself," said Rokuro. "I am not concerned with the weak stomachs of Neutralians."

"Fair enough," sighed a somewhat frustrated Judas. "I must warn you, however, that he is sure to be accompanied by those Mayhem Marauders."

Upon hearing Judas's warning Alexei and Igor both looked inward at Rokuro, smirking as if they were unbothered.

"If they are who he has chosen for protection, then he is dead already," said Rokuro confidently.

Judas produced his EPIC which was set to an image of Chancellor Aldrich. From atop his horse, Rokuro leaned over to take a long hard look at it. He waited patiently while Alexei and Igor took time to examine the image for themselves.

"Send it to my EPIC, Judas," said Rokuro referring to the image of Chancellor Aldrich.

"I will," said Judas. "I will also include his schedule. Underestimate those Mayhem Marauders at your own peril. They are not the hapless barbarians they used to be."

"It was only their barbarism that made the Marauders formidable," said Alexei in a matter of fact tone. "Without that they are nothing. There is no room for a conscience in the heart of a savage."

Satisfied with Alexei's retort, Rokuro abruptly yanked the reins of his horse turning it one hundred eighty degrees. Alexei and Igor did the same. They slowly made their way back to the Iron Raven.

Judas stood and watched as the distance between them slowly increased before he turned and got back into his JEDDO. Suddenly he felt a tremendous sense of calm. He rested his head against the wall behind him and breathed a huge sigh of relief. "Take me home," said Judas to his driver from his comfortable seat in the passenger compartment. His body rocked forward ever so slightly as the JEDDO was shifted into gear and was driven away.

Location: Southtown, District County, Rights Province, Planet Neutralia
The Hidden Bastille, 2130 hours

Klaus made his way to the cells of Onin Gesh and Bahadur to deliver to them their dinner. On the wheeled cart he pushed were two covered dinner trays and two sealed beverages. He got to Onin Gesh first and, as usual, he was already standing and peering out at Klaus from his dark abode. His white body was luminous against the black backdrop of his personal dwelling. Klaus spoke into his EPIC, "Feeding Onin Gesh." Almost immediately the slot on his cell door slid open. Klaus grabbed Onin Gesh's tray and began to slide it toward the opening. Suddenly he stopped and pulled the tray back. "I almost forgot your gravy," said Klaus as he removed the lid from Onin Gesh's food. He loudly gathered as much saliva as he could in his own mouth and forcefully spat it onto the tray contaminating all of the food. "Enjoy your meal, Onin Gesh," he said as he cut his eyes wickedly toward him and continued to Bahadur's cell. Bahadur was sound asleep on his bed. Smiling, Klaus removed his troll from his pocket and pressed the button for an instant delivering an electric jolt to Bahadur's body. Bahadur screamed in agony as he immediately sprang from his bed and ran full speed into the door with a force so great that he knocked himself unconscious. Klaus laughed obnoxiously before delivering yet another half second jolt to Bahadur as he laid unconscious on the floor. Bahadur's eyes opened immediately as his body convulsed from the jolt of electricity. Slowly he rose to his feet hyperventilating with rage. "Feeding Bahadur," said Klaus into his EPIC as he extended Bahadur's meal and sealed beverage through the feeding slot. Klaus jumped as he heard the crash of Onin Gesh's metal tray against the cell door next to him. He grinned an evil grin because he knew that Onin Gesh had completed his meal. He always threw his tray at the door disdainfully when he was done.

Bahadur looked at the wall that separated his cell from Onin Gesh's as if he could see through it to Onin Gesh himself. He walked over to the slot to retrieve his meal and while at the door he looked Klaus directly in his eyes and said in a measured tone, "You are a coward." He walked over to his bed, sat down, and removed his food tray cover to reveal a dead and rotting snake. Bahadur raised his head and looked out of his cell door just in time to see Klaus laughing as he walked away. He also heard the raspy voice of Onin Gesh saying, "I will kill yooouuu," as Klaus passed by his cell. Bahadur calmly walked back to the cell door and deposited the tray back into the food slot. In one large gulp he consumed the nutrient rich beverage that accompanied what was supposed to have been his meal and he deposited the empty container into the slot as well. Afterward he returned to his bed and he went back to sleep.

Location: Wilderness between East City and Northland Township, District County, Rights Province, Neutralia
0900 hours the next morning

As he traveled on his rapid arachnid to Northland Township through what, to him, was very familiar territory, Mulati was in deep thought about what had recently transpired with his crew, what he needed to do, and what was yet to come. He needed a respite. He left the Whisper in the care of the capable hands and mind of Sampa as he always did. He had full confidence in her abilities as a leader. As a boy Mulati roamed these woods while learning lessons about life. Often times he was under the guidance of the headmaster of the Northland Orphanage, Yeung Chow Lo, who was also responsible for Mulati's mastery of the Wing Chun kung-fu style. As he grew into his teenage years, Mulati often explored these woods alone whenever he sought the peace and solitude they provided. Whatever questions about life he had difficulty answering himself, he would pose to Yeung Chow Lo who never really gave him direct answers, but, instead, phrased his responses in ways that made him look within himself for the truth. As a child that frustrated Mulati but as a teenager and young adult he relished those opportunities to learn and to be challenged. More than a mentor,

Yeung Chow Lo was a patriarch to him since Mulati never had a relationship with either of his biological parents. As Mulati got closer to Northland Township, thoughts of his crew gave way to nostalgia as familiar landmarks brought a sense of calm to him. He was home. Everything was familiar and had some sort of significance to him. As he exited the woodline into acres of green grass he could see it in the distance. As if he could not wait to lay his eyes upon it, he looked through his binoculars at the Northland Orphanage. He savored the view of the large farm momentarily before putting his binoculars away and heading toward the front gate.

Minutes later Mulati reached the front entrance. He dismounted his rapid arachnid and entered his code on the keypad. The large wrought iron gate slowly opened, and he continued through on foot. As he came into their sight, the children, of varying ages and ethnicities, stopped their chores and rushed to his direction. One after the other they latched onto him screaming his name with glee until they eventually overwhelmed him, and he fell to his back under the weight of thirty or more of them. They were happy to see him, and he was happy to see them. Finally, he was able to rise to his feet and, when he did, he saw Yeung Chow Lo standing near the front door of the orphanage. The headmaster had heard the commotion and came outside to investigate.

A man of small stature, the clean shaven, black haired, Yeung Chow Lo stood proudly with his chin level, chest out, and his hands behind his back. He was twenty years older than Mulati and dressed in his usual black Tang suit with a white shirt underneath. "It is good to see you, Mulati. Welcome home. The children have missed you. I have missed you," he said proudly.

"And I have missed this place," replied Mulati as the student and teacher stepped toward one another. Mulati kneeled and bowed to Yeung Chow Lo who then removed one hand from behind his back and placed it on his shoulder to acknowledge the gesture of respect.

Mulati stood. "We have some catching up to do," he said.

"That we do," replied Yeung Chow Lo as he gestured for Mulati to follow him inside. "Have you given your skills the time they require?" he asked referring to Mulati's martial arts abilities.

"I have," replied Mulati knowing full well what was coming next. "Do I get to rest first this time?"

"Yes, of course," replied Yeung Chow Lo. "I will meet you in the dojo at 1400 hours. Your things are where you left them last."

At 1400 hours Mulati walked into the dojo dressed in his white karate gi and black belt to find Yeung Chow Lo already stretching and sweating. All the orphans were seated Indian style around the walls of the dojo as they eagerly awaited the demonstration. The floor was clear. Upon seeing Mulati enter the room, Yeung Chow Lo stopped stretching and stood erect with his hands by his side. Mulati walked to within three feet of him and did the same. They both bowed slightly to one another. Afterward Mulati sprang into his combat stance demonstrating a form that indicated his mode of attack would be tiger style. Upon seeing that, Yeung Chow Lo smiled before slowly placing his hands behind his back. Mulati launched a ferocious attack, the viciousness of which surprised Yeung Chow Lo and forced him to quickly retreat three or four steps before regaining his balance. He never removed his hands from behind his back during the initial offensive onslaught from Mulati. Minutes went by and Mulati had still failed to force Yeung Chow Lo to use his hands. Undeterred, Mulati intensified his attack. Finally, after some time Yeung Chow Lo had to remove one of his hands from behind his back to block some of Mulati's strikes. An audible gasp could be heard from the orphans sitting around the room. None of them had ever forced him to use his hands before. The sight of him having to do so was truly incredible. The combat remained intense and highly skillful. Mulati was unrelenting in his assault until finally it happened. To thwart Mulati's assault, Yeung Chow Lo had to deliver an offensive strike. Mulati was knocked to the floor. Silence befell the dojo. Yeung Chow Lo still held his hand in the position of the strike he delivered with his other hand still behind his back. He slowly stood erect placing both hands back behind his back. As Mulati stood, the orphans sprang to their feet and applauded loudly. They were impressed. To anyone else what they just witnessed would have been a defeat. However, the significance of what had just occurred was not lost on any of them, Yeung Chow Lo included. He and Mulati bowed to one another and ended their session.

"Either I am getting too old, or you have gotten better," said Yeung Chow Lo with a smile. "Tomorrow we finish and bring your dlhá násada."

Two hours later Mulati joined Yeung Chow Lo for rice and sushi in the courtyard. They sat together on a wooden bench using chopsticks to eat their food from porcelain bowls. The open area was peaceful and green.

With their earlier demonstration in mind, Yeung Chow Lo spoke. "One does not acquire that level of skill without having killed a man. I know that you are a capable warrior and can handle yourself, Mulati, but you belong here," he said as he waved his hand symbolically over the land. "Therefore, we belong to you. Be careful that your worlds never mix," he said as he interlocked his fingers in front of him to emphasize the point.

"I understand," said Mulati. "I love this place more than anything and I will protect it with my life."

"My wish," replied Yeung Chow Lo, "is that you never have to do that." Observing that there was no reply from Mulati, he looked over to see him in deep thought. "What troubles you, Mulati?" he asked.

Appreciative of the fact that Yeung Chow Lo was in tune to his emotional state, Mulati didn't hesitate to answer his question. "I don't know if I should trust someone, Master Lo," he replied. "I have taken on a new crew member and I am unsure of his true intentions."

"Do you need to trust him?" asked Yeung Chow Lo.

The fact that Yeung Chow Lo asked Mulati that question made him certain that it required more than a simple yes or no answer. After some thought he said, "Yes, he would be living with us, so I have to."

"Does he provide benefit to you?" asked Yeung Chow Lo.

"What good is help if you cannot trust the one who provides it, Master Lo?" he asked.

Yeung Chow Lo thought for a moment and then he replied. "Without benefit of history, trust is only an instinct. A child, for example, will see a snake, and almost every time his instinct will be to run from it or to kill it, because he automatically assumes it is dangerous. We know that is not true. We trust the ones we know are harmless, but we should not trust the ones that are poisonous. On the other hand, a child will always attempt to capture a bird because they do not fear them and, therefore, trust them automatically. It is only when the bird has plucked the eye of the child that he realizes that his trust is misplaced. Trust is an unreliable barometer for usefulness. A more dependable lesson is the plight of the aged leviathan and the symbiotic relationship it shares with the white sea scout."

Mulati looked confused but did not interrupt.

Half expecting a question, Yeung Chow Lo paused briefly. "Let me explain. The aged leviathan has a blowhole on its dorsal side that accumulates sea growth. When it surfaces for air, the white sea scout lands on it to eat that sea growth, thereby keeping the blowhole clean and clear of debris. Once the leviathan has aged too much to keep up with the younger leviathans or to hunt for itself, it begins to attack the white sea scouts for food. As a result, the white sea scout starts to see an over accumulation of sea growth as a warning sign instead of a meal. It stays away from the leviathan. Eventually that same sea growth starts to suffocate the leviathan. The leviathan realizes that it needs the white sea scout to keep its blowhole clean so that it may breathe and it, therefore, no longer desires to attack the white sea scout. But it is too late. Eventually the aged leviathan beaches itself because it can no longer breathe on its own, and it dies. There is a price to be paid, Mulati, for attacking one who provides you a service when it is not in your best interest to do so."

"I see," said Mulati as he focused on shoveling the remainder of his food into his mouth with his chopsticks. He spent the next thirty minutes drinking tea with Yeung Chow Lo and reminiscing about times past.

Location: Central City, District County, Neutralia
All Worlds Eatery, 1900 hours

Sampa, Beth, Corto, and Francois sat together at a table near the center of the restaurant dining on entrees from their respective worlds. It was Bjorn's turn to stay with the ship, so he remained aboard the Whisper. Aside from Corto, who had several daggers concealed all over his body, none of them brought weapons with them. Openly carrying weapons was frowned upon on Neutralia, especially in Central City. Most visitors respected that unwritten rule. The eatery was filled with people from all ethnic backgrounds. The vast variety of colors and styles of clothing worn by the different people was representative of their diversity. It was a large restaurant with ornate fixtures. It overflowed with decadence and could easily accommodate many more patrons than were there at that moment, although it was very busy. The well-lit restaurant was also noisy, and the decibel level raised slightly above the already constant murmur when Chancellor Aldrich walked in accompanied by Nastasia Rodmanovic. As he made his way through the dining room floor, patron after patron stood to shake his hand and acknowledge him. He greeted each of them warmly with a firm handshake and his baritone voice. Nastasia made sure to stay behind him, responding appropriately whenever she was acknowledged. His walk was full of confidence and he looked self-assured. Before long, an Albino maître d' approached Chancellor Aldrich and greeted him and Nastasia before leading them to a closed room near the back of the restaurant. Once they were inside, One and The Other took their places outside the door, one on each side.

The maître d' continued to make his way around the floor greeting people and making sure their meals were satisfactory. Before long he arrived at the table where the crew of the Whisper sat. "How is everything?" he asked with a genuine smile on his face.

For a moment there was awkward silence as they all looked to Beth who suddenly realized that she could probably best answer that question. "Everything is great," she replied with an embarrassed chuckle. "Your chefs are amazing. Everything tastes so authentic."

"We pride ourselves with that," replied the maître d.' "We only allow our chefs to prepare foods from their home worlds."

"Makes sense," said Beth. "That way you'll always get it right."

Sampa, not one to be shy, asked, "Who are the man and woman you took to that back room?"

"Oh, them?" replied the maître d,' "He is the Supreme Chancellor Steven Aldrich. The woman accompanying him is Nastasia Rodmanovic. She is his chief assistant. They, along with Vice Chancellor Lamont and Councilman Benedict, run Neutralia. They are very important people."

Francois leaned back in his chair and folded his arms. Hearing those names together made him nervous. He remembered Judas Benedict and he had heard Chancellor Aldrich's name from Rokuro Onishi. It suddenly dawned on him that just as easily as Chancellor Aldrich walked through that door, so could have Judas Benedict. He wasn't sure if Judas would remember him or not, but that was a chance he was not willing to take. He got nervous and his palms began to sweat.

Beth, Corto, and Sampa all glanced at one another acknowledging that they now knew who Theris Lamont's superior was. Neither of them said a word about it however. They knew better than to reveal the fact that they had met with him already to the maître d,' or to anyone outside of their circle for that matter.

"What's with the two guys standing by the door?" asked Corto.

"I really don't know," replied the maître d.' "All I know is that they call themselves One and The Other. The strange thing is it's never the same two but always the same names. As far as I can tell they're some sort of security detail, not that they would ever need that here. Well," he concluded, "please enjoy your stay with us. If you need anything, don't hesitate to ask."

"So that's the leader, huh?" asked Sampa rhetorically after the maître d' walked away. "He certainly looks the part, I'll give him that."

"You ok, Frenchie?" asked a suddenly concerned Corto. "You don't look good."

"It's nothing," replied Francois trying to conceal his angst. "Maybe I ate a little too fast for my own good. This food is delicious," he said with a nervous chuckle, "but not as good as yours, Beth."

"Why thank you, Francois," Beth replied smiling. "There's no need to butter me up, sweetheart, I'm gonna keep feedin' ya anyway."

They all laughed and just as Francois started to feel comfortable again, he saw Alexei and Igor walk through the front door of the restaurant. "Shit!" he said under his breath as he instantly turned his back toward the door and put his elbow on the table. He tried not to look like he was intentionally covering his face with his hand. *I need to get out of this place.*

Sampa paid closer attention to Francois as he transitioned both elbows to his thighs and clasped his hands together over his nose and mouth and began to rock back and forth. Clearly, he was worried. "Are you ok, Francois?" she asked as she watched him with a great deal of scrutiny.

"I need to make a head call," replied Francois. "I'll be right back." He quickly got up and walked away in the opposite direction of Alexei and Igor with his head down.

As he got to the bathroom door, he looked back to see where Alexei and Igor were. They were being seated on the opposite side of the restaurant and had their backs to him. He also noticed that Sampa was still watching him. He smiled at her and gave a simple hand wave and nod trying to convince her that he'd be alright. Once he was inside the large, twenty stall, bathroom he searched frantically for a way out. He checked each stall to verify the bathroom was empty. Just beyond the last stall was a rectangular window which was about two feet wide and approximately one foot away from the ceiling. He quickly placed a metal trash can under the window, stood on top of it, and he pushed the window open. He hoisted himself up to and through the window and jumped out to the paved alley in the back of the one-story building. About twenty feet away near the back door of the restaurant were several busboys and dishwashers who were sitting down and taking a smoke break. Thinking that Francois was possibly attempting to avoid paying his bill, one of them stood and yelled out, "Hey, stop right there!"

Francois didn't bother to look back as he quickly ran out of the alley. No one pursued him, and as he ran away he could hear the men laughing as one of them called him a cheap asshole. He thought that they must be quite accustomed to people skipping out on their bills as he heard that. He slowed to a walk as he neared the front of the restaurant and tried to act as normal as possible as he walked past those who were dining outside. He was careful not to walk past the front entrance as he continued on his way.

As she waited longer and longer for Francois to return, an uneasy feeling came over Sampa. She no longer enjoyed her meal and focused her attention on why he had not returned. She tuned out the conversation that Beth and Corto were having as she tried to quell that uneasy feeling she had. *Something isn't right. Francois is acting really weird right n...*

"Do you agree, Sam?" asked Beth.

Hearing her name snapped Sampa out of the trance that she was in, but she had not heard the statement that preceded Beth's question. "I'm sorry, Beth, I was just...what did you say?"

"Never mind that, Sam, why don't you and Corto just go in there and check on him?" said Beth.

"That's a good idea," said Sampa, "I think I'll do that. Let's go, Corto."

Somewhat exasperated, Corto tossed his napkin on his plate as he shoved the remainder of his food into his mouth. He quickly washed it down with the remainder of his sangria. "He can handle himself; I'm sure he's just taking a good shit to calm his stomach. Either that or he's puking his insides out."

"Just come on," replied Sampa as she got up from the table rolling her eyes.

As they walked into the bathroom, they both immediately noticed how quiet it was inside.

"Sounds empty in here to me," said Corto.

"You're right, Corto, it does sound empty," replied Sampa as her demeanor suddenly shifted from concerned to suspicious.

Corto pushed each stall door open one by one until he got to the end. "Hmm...this is interesting," he said as he stood near the metal trash can looking up at the open window. "Unless there's another head in this restaurant, I think he left out of this window."

"There may be another head," replied Sampa, "but this is definitely the one he entered. He never came back out that door. I watched it the whole time."

As they were talking the door to the bathroom opened and Igor entered. He walked into the first stall and closed the door behind him.

Satisfied that Francois was not in there, Sampa decided it was a good time to go back to the table to get Beth. "Let's go, Corto. Francois had better have a damn good explanation for disappearing like that. That's really strange."

"The man was raised in a whorehouse on Hades," said Corto, "he's bound to do weird shit from time to time. Let's get outta here, I need a smoke anyway."

Igor's ears perked up upon hearing those words from Sampa and Corto. There was no doubt in his mind that the Francois they spoke of was the rogue member of the DOD who had eluded them previously in Ciudad De Vuelo on Hades. He waited until they were all the way out of the bathroom before he exited the stall. As he left the bathroom, Igor paused momentarily to scan the restaurant until he saw where Sampa, Beth, and Corto were seated. He casually walked back to his table to join his brother, Alexei. "I think I have found Francois," he said as he sat down.

"Really? Where is he?" asked an excited Alexei as he slowly raised up from his seat scanning from side to side.

"He's not here," said Igor. "I heard those people over there talking about him in the head. He came here with them but left through the window. Apparently, he has double crossed them too."

"We have to contact Rokuro, he will want to know this immediately," said Alexei.

"You are right," said Igor.

Beth got up from the table and walked toward the bathroom with both Alexei and Igor watching, they knew that it probably meant the group was about to leave.

"Get the host," said Alexei as he got up from the table, "I will be right back." He walked out of the restaurant as Igor went to get the maître d.' When Alexei returned the maître d' was already at the table with Igor. "We are leaving," he said to the maître d,' "could you please give this to the people at that table over there. Their companion dropped it as he was leaving. I have gone through it for identification purposes and his name is Francois." He and Igor turned and left the restaurant.

With Francois' EPIC in hand, the maître d' walked over to the table where Sampa and Corto were seated. "Excuse me, but this was given to me by someone who saw your companion drop it as he was leaving. They said it belonged to a Francois."

"Thank you," replied Sampa as she extended her hand to receive the EPIC. She looked more confused than ever.

"That was pretty careless of him," said an oblivious Corto.

"Careless?" asked Sampa rhetorically. "Unless I missed something, he was naked when he came aboard the Whisper, right? That's unless you guys dropped protocol. Where would he have gotten this?"

"I don't know," replied a suddenly perplexed Corto. "He was definitely naked, and empty handed when he came aboard. Turn it on. Let's check it out."

Sampa did just that. After studying the screen for a few seconds, she was convinced that it did indeed belong to Francois. "I don't know what to say," she said as she handed the EPIC to Corto. "Keep that in your pocket. We'll ask him about it later. That's if we see him again. This is weird."

Beth returned from the bathroom refreshed. She pulled her chair and sat back down.

"You're not ready to leave?" asked Sampa. "I think we should get back to the Whisper, I wanna know what's going on with Francois."

"Oooooh NO!" replied Beth. "There's no guarantee he's coming back tonight. You know he likes brothels, and I haven't been off that ship in weeks. I need a break from that thing."

"I'm with Beth," said Corto. "Let's stay out and have some fun. He'll pop up sooner or later."

Reluctantly, Sampa agreed. "Waiter…," she said as she raised her hand and made eye contact with a nearby server, "another round of drinks, please." She turned her attention back to the table where she found both Corto and Beth as happy as they could be. The three of them drank for hours. They also laughed, joked, and generally had a good time. After a while the restaurant patrons had thinned out and they were one of three or four groups of diners who remained. At 2230 hours Chancellor Aldrich and Nastasia

Rodmanovic emerged from the back room, quickly exited the restaurant, and got into Friedrich's JEDDO which was waiting outside. Corto and Beth were drunk. Sampa was tipsy but in control of her faculties. The restaurant was closing, and it was time for them to go. Sampa paid their bill with her EPIC. As she got up to leave the restaurant, Corto and Beth stumbled behind her. Sampa had remembered to order some food for Bjorn and she grabbed it before she walked out.

Location: East City, District County, Rights Province, Planet Neutralia
The Whisper, 2330 hours

As the JEDDO they were riding in pulled up to the Whisper, Sampa was the only one who was awake. Beth's head was all the way back with her mouth wide open as her body shook side to side from the bumpy ride. Corto was lying on his back and stretched out across two seats as one of his arms dangled off the edge. Sampa asked the JEDDO driver to wait a few minutes while she went inside to get help for Beth and Corto who she had already tried unsuccessfully to wake. Moments later she returned with Bjorn who was instantly amused by the sight of Beth and Corto passed out. Without hesitation he walked into the JEDDO, picked Corto up, tossed him over his shoulder, and walked him up the ramp into the cargo bay. He returned for Beth. Placing one arm through her arms and under her back, and the other arm under the bend of her knees, he picked her up, and he carried her from the JEDDO all the way to her sleeping quarters. He gently laid her on her bed. As he came back to the cargo bay to get Corto, Sampa was slowly, and carefully, walking up the ramp carrying Bjorn's food with her.

"We lost Francois tonight," she said as if it almost drained the last of her energy to say it. She was tired and also feeling the effects of all the wine she had drank.

"What do you mean you lost Francois?" asked Bjorn. "He's up there in his living quarters sound asleep. He came back around 2100 hours."

"Hmph, that's interesting," said Sampa. "Did he say why he left the rest of us at the restaurant without saying anything?"

Bjorn laughed. "He sure did. He said he tried to make it to the head but couldn't. He messed his pants up pretty bad, so he didn't want to walk back through the restaurant floor. He came here, took a shower, and went to sleep."

"Poor guy," said Sampa with a chuckle, "that makes sense. I should've checked on him sooner."

Bjorn and Sampa raised the ramp and sealed the cargo bay before he scooped Corto up and took him to his sleeping quarters. Like he did Beth, Bjorn laid Corto on his bed and he left out.

Sampa was exhausted and had already stripped down to nothing as she prepared for her shower. She laid back on her bed and took a moment to appreciate how good the satin sheets felt against her soft skin. She ran her hands up and down the sheets and before long those same hands found their way to her own soft, toned body. She arched her back and clenched her knees together as her hand made its way to her crotch. It was warm there and she could not resist exploring herself with her middle finger as she squeezed her breasts and played with her nipples with her other hand. She continued until she had satisfied herself. When she was done she removed her finger, and she tasted it. She smiled to herself. It was a good ending to a great night for her. After a very quick shower she got back into bed and she quickly fell asleep.

Bjorn devoured the food that Sampa had brought back for him in a matter of minutes. It was very good to him and he wanted more. He had already done his target practice for the night and he was tired as well. The entire Whisper was quiet and before long everyone onboard was asleep.

Chapter 13: Bjorn To Be Mad

Location: Northland Township, District County, Rights Province, Neutralia
Northland Orphanage, 0400 hours

Emboldened by his performance on the previous day, a shirtless Mulati had already been practicing with his dlhá násada for fifteen minutes when Yeung Chow Lo joined him in the dojo. Mulati stopped momentarily to acknowledge him. "Good morning, Master Lo," he said as he stood erect and bowed his head slightly. The gesture was acknowledged by Yeung Chow Lo with a simple head nod. Mulati returned to his intense training, but the sound of Yeung Chow Lo's dlhá násada opening let him know that it was time for combat. This time there were no children to witness what was about to transpire. The older ones had already started their morning chores and the younger ones were still asleep. Mulati's skills with the dlhá násada were legendarily formidable, but he learned them from Yeung Chow Lo. For minutes they sparred with precision and skill, neither man capitulating to the other. Yeung Chow Lo was effortlessly thwarting Mulati's attacks as if he was thinking three moves ahead at all times. Mulati remained focused and determined as he attacked with vigor.

"Stop!" said Yeung Chow Lo suddenly as he stepped back and closed his dlhá násada. "Very good, Mulati," he said as he calmly slid his hands behind his back. "Your dedication to your craft is undeniable. I think you should take on an apprentice soon. I have taught you all that you need to know. All that remains for you is mastery through repetition."

Pleased to have heard those words, Mulati closed his dlhá násada and bowed his head slightly saying, "Thank you, Master Lo." He walked over to the corner of the dojo to pick up his shirt. As he was doing so he received an incoming transmission on his EPIC from Sampa. "Receive transmission," he enunciated carefully. "Good morning, Sam," he said as her image appeared.

"Good morning, Mulati," she replied. "All is well here, I hope that you are enjoying your visit. When should we expect you back?"

"I'll begin my journey back to East City at 0600 hours," said Mulati. "You look tired, it must have been a long night."

"Long, but not bad. I'll tell you about it when you get here," replied Sampa.

"Good enough, I will see you soon," replied Mulati. "End transmission." Sampa's image faded away and Mulati looked to Yeung Chow Lo who was already staring at him like a proud father watching his fully matured son.

"She is loyal to you, do not lose her," said Yeung Chow Lo. "Hopefully you will eat and say goodbye to the children before you leave?"

"I will," replied Mulati as he placed his hand on the shoulder of Yeung Chow Lo and they walked out of the dojo together.

After eating a light breakfast consisting largely of fruit, Mulati said his goodbyes to Yeung Chow Lo and the children. He exited the main gate and activated his rapid arachnid. With his twice emitter strapped to his back and his canteen full of water, he started his journey back to East City through that same familiar wilderness. Because he wanted to use the travel time to meditate, Mulati switched his EPIC to the off position. Yeung Chow Lo and the orphans stood at the gate watching him as he crossed the field and disappeared into the woodline.

Location: East City, District County, Rights Province, Neutralia
The Whisper, 0600 hours

After finding it difficult to sleep through the night, Francois sat alone in the lounge drinking coffee in the dark. His close encounter with Alexei and Igor left him unnerved. The last people he expected to see at an upscale eatery in Central City were high ranking DOD members. As his mind raced, Bjorn walked in and flicked on the lights.

"Morning, Frenchie," said Bjorn as he noticed him sitting there as the room lit up. "If you're waiting on breakfast, it's gonna be a bit. Beth got three sheets in the wind last night and I don't think she'll be up for a while. And Sam was none too pleased that you skipped out on 'em last night; not as much angry as she was worried though."

"I'll have to make it up to her," said Francois as he tried to act normal through his worry and concern. "Question... when will it get to the point where I'm allowed to be on the Whisper by myself? I mean, it's not fair that you didn't get a chance to go out to enjoy Central City with the crew last night."

"You know that's not my call," replied Bjorn, "but you gotta see it from Mulati's point of view. This ship is pretty much all he has. It's a lot, but that's it. He's just making sure, ya know?"

"I guess," said Francois. "I just didn't feel right having fun while you were stuck here. Next time I'll just stay back with whoever pulls duty. I think that's only fair."

"If you say so," said Bjorn. "I don't think that's really necessary, but whatever makes you feel better." He rubbed his stomach as he looked toward the galley. "If I didn't think Beth would kill me, I'd be in that galley messin up some grub right about now; I'm starving." Bjorn poured himself a cup of coffee and sat across from Francois. "You miss your ship?" he asked.

"I did at first, but I've kinda gotten used to the amenities around here," he replied as he nodded and raised his cup. "Tell me, what exactly is max cel for the Whisper? Full forward capability felt a bit strong for a ship this size when we ran from those pirates."

"Maximum celerity for the Whisper is four," replied Bjorn. "It's supposed to be three but Corto and I made some mods and boosted the full forward capability."

"This thing goes one and one third times the speed of light?" asked an amazed Francois. "That's incredible! That's what the top tier medium class fighters do!"

"That's right," said Bjorn, "the Whisper is a one of kind deal. You won't find many like it in the solar system."

"I was working on getting one cel out of my one man but couldn't quite get it figured out," said Francois. "It's a moot point now though."

"I think one third the speed of light would have been pushing it for something so small," said Bjorn. "That works for single man fighters but not for passenger vessels. One jump probably would've torn your hull to shreds; you'd be space dust right now."

Francois chuckled. "You're probably right. Maybe it's a good thing I didn't get it installed."

Sampa slowly walked into the lounge with her hand on her forehead and flopped down on the couch beside Bjorn. "Good morning, guys," she said, "I feel like I've been hit by a JEDDO."

"Here, this should take the edge off," said Bjorn as he handed her his cup of coffee.

Sampa cradled it with both hands as she slowly took a sip. "Ahh that's good. Thanks, Bjorn," she said.

"Not a problem," said Bjorn as he got up to pour himself another cup.

Looking up from her cup at Francois, Sampa said, "I heard you pulled a Corto and crapped your pants last night. Next time just call one of us in there and let us know. That way we won't have to worry if something happened to you or not. We had no idea where you were."

"I apologize, Sam," said Francois. "I know better than that, and I'll do better."

"Good, as long as we have an understanding," said Sampa as she went for another sip of the hot coffee. "I talked to Mulati this morning, Bjorn," she said as she brought her cup back down. "He plans to be back here from Northland Township around 0800 hours."

Bjorn nodded. "I'll be glad when he starts letting at least one of us make those trips with him," he said. "There's too many things that can go wrong when you're out there alone."

"I don't think he wants those children exposed to too much too soon," said Sampa. "Corto and children are not a good mix." They all laughed as they imagined him interacting with them.

"You hear that?" asked Bjorn with a smile. "Beth is in the galley. Not a moment too soon either."

They continued to talk among each other as the lounge slowly began to fill with the aroma of breakfast coming from the galley.

Not long after, Beth walked into the lounge. "Good morning, everyone, breakfast is ready," she said. "You guys can head on over to the dining room right now if you like."

"I like!" said Bjorn as he quickly got up from the couch. He extended his hand down toward Sampa and pulled her up carefully because she was still holding her cup of coffee.

As they all sat around the table having breakfast, Corto stormed into the dining room. "Somebody had better have a damn good explanation for how I got to my sleep quarters last night!" he said angrily.

Bjorn rolled his eyes. "It's way too early for this, Corto. Sit down and have some breakfast. You walked. You just don't remember because you were so trashed." Bjorn sheepishly glanced across the table at Sampa who saw him but acted as if she had not.

Suspiciously looking at them both, Corto took his normal seat at the table beside Bjorn and started filling his plate with food.

"I'd take it easy on the carbohydrates, buddy, you're starting to get a little heavy," said Bjorn as he burst into uncontrollable laughter.

Sampa dropped her head as she laughed to herself. She had hoped that Bjorn would refrain from taking that verbal jab at Corto.

"Oh hush, Bjorn," said Beth. "Leave him alone. For what it's worth, Corto, I think he carried me too."

"I don't care how drunk I get, you ass," yelled Corto as he jumped down from his chair and pointed his finger in Bjorn's face, "You just leave me outside in the dirt until I wake the fuck up and can walk in myself! Do not carry me!" He got back into his chair and, when he did, he felt something hard poking him in his thigh. He reached into his pocket and pulled out Francois' EPIC. "Hey, Frenchie, is this yours? Some guy said you dropped it when you left last night."

As Corto held the EPIC in his hand, Francois just stared at it. A look of terror instantly came over his face as everyone at the table got quiet. He slowly reached up to receive the device from Corto and, upon looking at it, immediately dropped his head.

"Is it yours?" asked Sampa.

"Yes," said Francois. "We're dead."

"What do you mean *we're dead*?" asked Bjorn angrily.

"I'll explain it later. I promise," said Francois. "Right now, we've got to move." He got up and quickly left the dining table.

"Follow him and get the intel!" said Sampa to Bjorn and Corto. They both instantly got up and exited the dining room behind him.

"What is going on?" asked a concerned Beth.

"I'm not sure," said Sampa, "but I don't have a good feeling about this at all." She got up from the table and made her way to the bridge.

Bjorn and Corto finally caught up to Francois in the cargo bay. He was headed toward the weapon locker for a twice emitter and he was moving at a frenetic pace. "What are you doing?" yelled Bjorn. "You can't just say something like that and run out like we're not gonna wanna know what's going on! Are you crazy?"

As if he hadn't heard a word Bjorn said, Francois stayed focused on what he was doing. "Open the gate back there, I need a rapid arachnid. Hurry! And what's the code to this weapon locker?"

Frustrated, Bjorn grabbed Francois by his shoulders and slammed his back to the nearest wall. "Snap out of it, you asshole!" yelled Bjorn. "If you don't tell us what's going on right now I will break your fucking neck!"

For a moment Francois stared through Bjorn with an empty look on his face. He was incapable of speaking.

Bjorn pulled his body away from the wall and slammed him back into it again with even greater force and yelled, "Speak!"

Francois' stiff body wilted as he started to cry and said, "I messed up. They're going to kill me. I need to go now."

"Who?" asked Bjorn.

Francois just shook his head from side to side as the tears streamed down his face, but he did not answer Bjorn's question.

"Then go!" said Born angrily as he snatched him away from the wall almost tossing him to the ground. "Get your ass out of here, and you're not taking one single piece of equipment off this ship! Let him out, Corto!"

Corto started the process to open the rear hatch and lower the ramp as Francois stood near the opening with his head down waiting to exit. As the ramp was fully lowered, the sunlight rushed into the cargo bay, but Francois stood there afraid to take a step.

Bjorn stomped over to where he was, put his foot on the small of Francois' back and gave a mighty shove. "Move!" he said and watched as Francois tumbled down the ramp.

Once he was on the ground, and back on his feet, Francois quickly looked around the immediate area only to have his worst fears confirmed. On a rocky hill in the distance he saw three horse-mounted men. Although he could not make out any distinguishing characteristics or features, he knew full well who they were, Alexei, Igor, and Rokuro Onishi.

Sampa came running into the cargo bay seconds later. "I did a life scan and they are everywhere! All over the place! Whoever they are, they've got us surrounded, and I cannot reach Mulati. He'll walk into an ambush if he comes back this way. Get Francois back in here so he can tell us what's going on!"

"He won't talk," said Bjorn.

"Well make him talk!" said Sampa. "These are our lives he's playing with!"

After a loud and frustrated sigh, Bjorn immediately walked down the ramp to get Francois. Once he got to him he forcefully reached out to him grabbing a handful of his shirt and pulling him closer. "You've got one chance to make this right, Frenchie, and I mean that!" he said as he suddenly released him and pushed him toward the ramp.

"I'll talk," replied Francois. "I have to; I have no choice at this point." He slowly walked back up the ramp and into the cargo bay with Bjorn following closely behind.

Sampa was inside the cargo bay waiting with her arms folded as she glared into Francois' eyes. He could barely look in her direction, but she did not break her gaze. "Your selfishness has put us in a bad spot here, Francois. Who are those people and what are we up against?"

Francois inhaled deeply and let out a loud and long sigh before speaking. "They're DOD. I was running away from them when I saw your ship in the orbit of Hades. My vessel didn't malfunction. I destroyed it."

Corto stepped closer to Francois. "What could you have done to them that was so bad? Why would they travel so far to kill you?"

"He probably owes them money," Bjorn chimed in.

"I was a member," said Francois nervously. "I mean, I am a member. I... I... I really don't know what my standing is with them. I'm pretty sure they want to kill me for betraying them. I just couldn't take the chance. They're not known for their mercy."

"They just saw you with us!" yelled Sampa. "They probably think we're your new gang!" She walked closer to him and got within an inch of his face. Through clenched teeth she said with a low but angry voice, "You're going to go up there and you're going to make it right. Or you're going to go up there and die. At this point, I don't care. They have to know that we are not harboring you from them. Do you understand me?"

"You ask the impossible of me," replied Francois. "If I go up there, I'm a dead man."

"If you stay on this ship, we're all dead," replied Sampa. "Me, Bjorn, Corto, and Beth! Why should we have to die because of you?" she yelled as she pushed him in his chest with both hands.

Francois looked at Bjorn hoping he would attempt to convince Sampa to reconsider.

"Sam's right, Frenchie," said Bjorn. "This is your fuck up; you gotta fix it. Good luck."

"Can't we just fly out of here?" begged Francois. "You can drop me off anywhere in the solar system. Let me fend for myself!"

"No!" said Sampa. "Mulati's out there and expects us to be here! And here is where we're going to be! Either you go up there and face those men, or we'll kill you and deliver you to them. Either way you're leaving the Whisper now! The choice is yours!"

As Francois desperately studied each of their faces, Corto unsheathed his dagger. "I'll go," he said. "Fuck! I'll face them. I'm a dead man, Sam. You just killed me."

"You killed yourself, Frenchie," replied Bjorn. "Sam's doing exactly what she has to do. I'd do the same myself. Now get the fuck out!" he said as he balled his fists.

Francois turned and walked back toward the ramp. As he got to it he paused and turned back to look at Corto, Sampa, and Bjorn. He wanted to speak, but he did not. He turned and continued down the ramp.

As he got halfway down, Corto caught up to him. He extended the handle end of his dagger to Francois. "You ain't got much of a shot at living, amigo, but at least this gives you a chance."

Francois accepted the blade from Corto. As he somberly nodded his head, he hid the dagger on the inside of his pants near the waistline. He turned and started slowly walking toward Alexei, Igor, and Rokuro.

Corto was visibly upset as he walked back into the cargo bay and Sampa could tell. As he walked over to the lever that controlled the ramp, he looked over to Sampa.

"Leave it open," said Sampa. "When they're done with him, we'll go get his body. He'll get a proper burial. That's the best we can do."

Corto nodded and he walked away from the controls. Bjorn gave him a tap on his back in an attempt to comfort him.

From the dirty flat surface atop the hill, Rokuro, Alexei, and Igor watched as Francois approached.

"Look at him," said Alexei. "He knows he's about to die."

"Tell the others to hold their positions," said Rokuro, "I don't trust that ship."

Igor pulled out his EPIC and sent the message to rest of the DOD members who surrounded the Whisper. Minutes later, Francois finally made it to the top of the hill. He was now face to face with Rokuro Onishi, Alexei, and Igor. The clearing was defined by boulders and an outline of thick brush and sturdy pine trees.

"I won't insult you with an explanation," said Francois, "and I will not beg you for my life. All I ask is that you send my body home to France."

Rokuro dismounted his horse and started walking toward Francois. "On your knees, traitor," he said as he unsheathed his sword.

Francois slowly got down on both knees and he closed his eyes. The last thing he saw was Rokuro raising his sword. He tensed his entire body as he heard Rokuro yell. The next thing he heard was the loud ping of metal on metal. He felt nothing, so he opened his eyes immediately. When he did he saw Mulati with his dlhá násada fully extended and blocking the swing of Rokuro's sword. Rokuro fell backward into the dirt from the power of the block. Alexei and Igor immediately dismounted their horses and began to attack Mulati. He engaged both men with his dlhá násada as Rokuro searched for his sword which had fallen out of his hand.

Francois saw that Mulati's rapid arachnid was a few feet away and had his twice emitter attached to it. He ran toward it and removed the weapon. As he turned to take aim, he saw that Rokuro Onishi had recovered his sword. As Mulati battled Alexei and Igor, his back was toward Rokuro Onishi. As he crept up behind Mulati, he noticed that Francois had his twice emitter trained on him. Francois and Rokuro Onishi locked eyes with one another. Francois lowered his twice emitter and when he did, Rokuro Onishi lowered his sword. Francois got on Mulati's rapid arachnid and he left.

The moment Francois was out of sight, Rokuro Onishi yelled to Alexei and Igor, "Stop!" He walked around to face Mulati with his sword drawn as Alexei and Igor backed away. "Prepare yourself for combat, half breed."

"You will respect me," said Mulati as he moved his dlhá násada into position.

"I will never give what should be earned," replied Rokuro Onishi.

Mulati removed his EPIC, depressed his snitch, and tossed it to the side. Rokuro Onishi advanced on him and began his attack. The sound of Rokuro's sword striking Mulati's dlhá násada echoed throughout the valley and all around. Their battle was intense, but what resembled a sparring session for Mulati was a frustrating war for Rokuro Onishi. Nothing came easy. Mulati's skill level was not something for which he was mentally prepared. Occasionally Mulati would strike his exposed body part whenever Rokuro Onishi overextended himself or somehow got off balance. That caused Rokuro Onishi to be more cautious with his attack and, therefore, more predictable. Before long, Mulati began to toy with him. He struck him at will. Rokuro Onishi was beginning to weaken physically and it was showing. The more they fought the more abuse he endured. That he would be defeated was, by now a foregone conclusion. Both sensing Rokuro's eminent demise, Alexei and Igor joined in on the attack. Because he considered the sword wielding Rokuro a bigger threat, Mulati chose to focus his attention on him. That left him open to being struck on several occasions by Alexei and Igor. Mulati started to weaken. An energized Rokuro Onishi intensified his attack.

At that moment, three Rapid Arachnids crested the top of the hill where they were fighting. Bjorn, Corto, and Sampa had arrived. Without hesitation Bjorn jumped down and joined the fight. He punched Alexei right between the eyes knocking him flat on his back. He mounted him and began to pummel his face with elbow strikes and closed fists. Alexei quickly brought his forearms up to cover and shield his face from Bjorn's vicious attack. Sampa and Corto attacked Igor. After regaining his composure, Alexei was able to roll Bjorn over to his back, but he failed to disengage from him. He was trapped in Bjorn's guard. Pulling him closer, Bjorn wrapped his arm around Alexei's neck forcing the top of his head into the dirt. Alexei was unable to escape the inverted guillotine headlock and before long his body went limp and he was unconscious. Exhausted, Bjorn pushed Alexei's heavy body off him and he slowly got up. As soon as he did, Sampa landed on her back right near his feet. Igor was attempting to choke Corto with one hand as he drew his fist back to punch him. Sampa scrambled to her feet and ran back over to help Corto. Igor had his hands full. Bjorn went to help Mulati but was denied.

"Don't help me, help them!" said Mulati to Bjorn.

Bjorn ran over to Igor, picked him up, and scoop slammed him onto his back.

"Find Francois," yelled Mulati as he continued to battle Rokuro Onishi. "He has my arachnid!"

Corto and Sampa mounted their Rapid Arachnids and went looking for Francois. As they searched for Francois, Sampa and Corto began to encounter corpses of some of the DOD members who had come with Rokuro Onishi, Alexei, and Igor.

"These men were ambushed, they were all emitted from behind," said Sampa.

"You're right," said Corto. "Stay alert."

Meanwhile, as Mulati and Rokuro Onishi continued to battle, so did Bjorn and Igor. The dynamic action of the combat between Mulati and Rokuro Onishi forced them to gravitate to a lower elevation away from the top of the hill. They could no longer see Bjorn and Igor from their lowered position. As they battled one another, Mulati and Rokuro Onishi both gained respect for the skill level of the other. The fight between Bjorn and Igor, however, was brutal. Both men were bloodied, beaten, and completely exhausted. Eventually Igor disengaged and staggered toward his horse to get his twice emitter. Upon seeing that, Bjorn ran to his rapid arachnid to get his twice emitter as well. After retrieving their weapons, both men turned and fired simultaneously striking one another with their first projectile. They were both paralyzed instantly. The green glow of the projectiles could be seen by Mulati and Rokuro Onishi from the lower elevation. Both men continued to fight. Almost immediately afterward, Francois returned to their location at the top of the hill. Both men were at his mercy.

Mulati and Rokuro Onishi abruptly stopped fighting each other after hearing the familiar sound of the second projectile from a twice emitter which came from the top of the hill. As they stared menacingly at one another, breathing heavily, they wondered who had been killed. Just then Francois came running down the hill past both men making eye contact with neither. They both instinctively ran toward the top of the hill. They were side by side. As they neared the top of the hill a rapid arachnid came down toward them. It was Bjorn. As he continued down after Francois, Mulati ran past him to survey the scene and to retrieve his rapid arachnid. Rokuro Onishi was expressionless as he slowed to an ominous jog and then to a walk.

As he reached the top of the hill, Mulati casually strolled past him on his rapid arachnid going in the other direction with Corto and Sampa following closely behind. They were headed toward the Whisper.

Mulati looked him directly in his eyes and said, "My name is Mulati Soldaat" and he continued on his way.

Igor was dead.

Rokuro dropped to his knees with his head in both hands. He began to pound the ground with alternating fists as he screamed, "No, no, nooooo!" Then, almost as if he had told himself that his time to grieve was over, he hoisted himself up from the ground, walked over to Igor's horse and grabbed his blanket. "Death embraces you, my friend," he said to Igor's corpse in a somber voice as he reached down and touched his hand. With great care, he wrapped Igor's body and hoisted it atop the very horse on which he had arrived. He sat and waited for Alexei to regain consciousness.

Before long Alexei began to stir. Rokuro Onishi stood as he slowly awakened. As Alexei stood, he squinted his eyes and he steadied himself. He didn't say a word as he looked around. He froze as his eyes found Igor's horse. He immediately feared the worst. He looked over to Rokuro Onishi, and when his leader dropped his head and looked at the ground, he knew his brother, Igor, was gone. Alexei ran over to Igor's horse and yanked the body down. After it hit the ground he rapidly unfurled it. The hole through Igor's chest cavity was immense. Alexei closed Igor's eyes and fell to his own back, sobbing like a child. Rokuro Onishi turned and walked toward the path that the crew of the Whisper used to make their escape. He watched as the Whisper lit up, lifted off the ground, and flew away. Not even the sound of a medium class, heavy-duty, cargo vessel lifting off could drown out the cries of a man who had just lost his twin brother. After the Whisper was out of sight, Rokuro Onishi walked over to Alexei and kneeled beside him. He pulled his friend up to a seated position and he hugged him, placing his hand behind his head as Alexei continued to cry on his chest.

Chapter 14: Bird of Prey

*Location: East City, District County, Rights Province, Neutralia
Aboard the Whisper*

As Mulati and Sampa piloted the Whisper to an altitude above and beyond the clouds, the rest of the crew, including Francois, were strapped into the seats behind them on the bridge.

"Take the controls, Sam, put her just beyond the atmosphere," said Mulati as he removed his headset and swiveled around in his chair to look at the rest of the crew. "Not everyone at once," he said sternly as he stared into their eyes.

"Francois belonged to them," said Bjorn. "He was DOD. They were chasing him when we picked him up. He had us fooled. We sent him up that hill to fix whatever issue he had with them and the next thing we knew we got your snitch beacon. Tell you the truth, I never thought we'd see him alive again."

"Mulati, I tried to contact you to warn you that you'd be coming right through their perimeter, but your EPIC was powered down," said Sampa.

"Francois?" said Mulati as he stared at him expecting a reasonable explanation for what he had just heard.

Francois nodded his head and said, "He's telling the truth. It wasn't my intention to have things go down the way they did. I was looking to get dropped off at the next space station. One thing led to another. There were pirates, and then Evropa, and all that other stuff. Before I knew it, I was stuck. Using you was not my intention."

Mulati stood up from his seat. "What are your intentions then, Francois?"

"My desire...," replied Francois, "is to live to be an old man. It would please me if I could do that with present company. Somewhere along the line I started to feel something here that I've never felt before. Everyone is here, pretty much, because they want to be, not because they need to be. Until this week I only needed to be here. Now I can't see myself anywhere else."

"Why?" asked Sampa without taking her attention away from the sky ahead of her.

"I belong," said Francois succinctly. "That's the best I have for you, Sam. I care for each one of you in ways I can't explain."

"You care so much you left me to fight three men by myself after I saved your life," quipped Mulati.

"I'm a lot of bad things, Mulati," said Francois, "but a coward ain't one. The DOD are masters of deception. For every man you see there are two more in reserve. Had I stayed and fought them with you the others would have come to their aid, overwhelmed us, and slaughtered us both. I went after the support while you fought with them. I've seen you in action before; I knew you could survive."

"He's right, Mulati," said Sampa. "When Corto and I went looking for him we saw the dead bodies of three men. He took them out with your twice emitter."

"Not all of them," said Francois. "I got the first one with this," he continued as he pulled Corto's bloodied dagger from his belt line and handed it back to him. "Thanks, buddy," he said with a nod as he did so.

As Corto received the dagger by its handle he said, "I could have used this up there myself. At least you didn't let it go to waste." He then wiped the blood off the dagger on his pants leg before returning it to its sheath.

"There's nowhere else I can go now," said Francois. "I'm a marked man now for sure because of what just happened."

"And we're a marked crew because we were with you," said Bjorn.

"That I cannot deny," replied Francois, "but whether I'm with you or not, they'll still be coming for ya. I think we're all better off together."

Silence befell the bridge as they all waited for a response from Mulati. They remained stone faced as they continued their bumpy ascent to the orbit of Neutralia. Francois' face was finally beginning to show the stress of all that he had been through. He was defeated and out of rope. Beth clasped her hands together in front of her face as she held her breath. Bjorn folded his massive arms and waited while Corto nervously caressed the sheath that contained the dagger he had just received from Francois.

"The leviathan needs the white sea scout," said Mulati. "Welcome to the crew."

Relieved, Francois let out a long exhale saying, "Thank you, Mulati. You will not regret this decision. I won't let you down."

"Yes!" said Beth with a pleased look on her face. She reached over and squeezed the back of Francois' hand and smiled at him as her eyes sparkled with moisture. "On my conscience, this gets to be a bit much for me at times."

Choked up, Francois replied, "Stop it before you make me cry, Beth."

Bjorn slapped Francois' shoulder hard and said, "It's official, Frenchie. You made it."

As they made their way beyond Neutralia's atmosphere, the morning light gave way to the darkness of space. What was a bumpy climb was now a smooth orbit. Suddenly everything was peaceful and calm. Beth was the first to undo her safety belt and get up. She made her way off the bridge to her personal quarters. Next to leave were Bjorn and Corto as they made their way to the engine room.

Francois stayed on the bridge with Mulati and Sampa. "I think there's something else I may need to mention," he said with trepidation.

Mulati and Sampa both looked inward over their inside shoulder toward Francois.

"What is it now, Francois?" asked Mulati as he and Sampa both removed their headsets.

"It's about the American," said Francois. "I think they want to kill him."

"Who wants to kill him? The DOD?" asked Sampa. "How do they even know who he is?"

"There's another councilman... an Albino," replied Francois. "His name is Judas Benedict. He came to the DOD hideout in the Tierra Mala to put a bounty on the American and the leader, Chancellor Aldrich."

"The guy who came into the eatery?" asked Sampa.

"Yes, that's the one," answered Francois. "He wants them both dead. Apparently, they intend to turn Hades into some sort of penal colony."

"A penal colony?" asked Mulati. "What's that?"

"I had the same question," replied Francois. "It's a place where they would keep people they deem too dangerous to dwell among the rest of the population."

"For how long?" asked Mulati as he swiveled his chair completely around to face Francois.

"For as long as they see fit, from what I gathered," replied Francois.

"Who else knows about this?" asked Mulati.

"About what?" asked Francois. "The penal colony or the plot to kill those two men?"

"The plot to kill," replied Mulati.

"Everybody who is anybody within the DOD knows about it," replied Francois. "That could be up to one thousand or so people. They don't tell the underlings or also-rans anything."

Mulati turned to face Sampa. "We have to warn Theris, Sam."

"I agree," replied Sampa. "He could be in a lot of trouble."

Suddenly the red light on the control panel began to flash. It was the proximity beacon. Upon seeing it, Francois instantly panicked. "Shit, it's the DOD!" he shouted as he grabbed his head with both hands.

"How do you know it's them?" asked Sampa.

"Because I forgot to disable that freakin EPIC!" said Francois as he got up from his seat and searched frantically for the personal information conveyor. "Here it is. It's still enabled. Fuck!" he said as he removed it from a pocket on the jacket he was wearing. He switched it off, placed it on the floor of the bridge, and stomped on it until it was completely destroyed. He quickly moved up and between Mulati and Sampa to get a better look at the control panel's radar. "They're in cloak mode! They won't reveal until it's time to fire."

"Full forward capability?" Sampa asked Mulati.

"No! We can't risk it. We could run right into them and we'll all be dead," Mulati replied. He pressed the emergency button on the control panel. The interior lights of the entire ship dimmed and flashed rapidly five times before coming back on.

Bjorn's voice immediately came through the intercom. "What've you got, Mulati?" he asked.

"Trouble!" said Mulati. "We believe the DOD was able to track us. Grab Corto and man the guns!"

"I'm on it!" said Bjorn.

Francois continued to lean in with his left hand on the back of Mulati's seat and his right hand on the back of Sampa's seat as he watched the stars and the panel. "That's them!" he said as he pointed at the suddenly visible medium class fighter. "That's the Iron Raven! They're preparing to attack!" Francois lightly placed his left hand on Mulati's right shoulder. "Can I make a suggestion?" he asked.

"Go ahead," said Mulati appreciative of the fact that Francois was now fully aware of the crew's pecking order, chain of command, and protocol.

"They have a SPIM launcher located just below the nose of their bridge. Once they've locked onto their target they have to stay engaged until they've fired the missile. There's a light that is situated on the weapon. Prior to each shot it will flash. Once you see that light you should make evasive moves. Not sooner."

"There's a light," said Sampa as she immediately looked left to Mulati.

"That's it!" said Francois.

Without hesitation, Mulati took evasive action and, just like Francois said it would, the SPIM came from the Iron Raven following the trajectory of their previous location. It missed.

After they were out of the way, Bjorn's voice came through the intercom. "Guns up, Mulati, get us into position and we'll do the rest!" he said.

"Copy," said Mulati. "Standby!"

"We won't be able to out maneuver them for long, Mulati, we're not built for that," advised Sampa.

"I'm aware of that, Sam. As soon as we get the chance we're going to one cel, that should be enough to put us on the back side of Neutralia."

"I copy," said Sampa.

Meanwhile, Corto was manning the port side gun as Bjorn took up his usual position in the starboard side gunner's pod.

"We're in position, big guy. Let's work!" shouted Corto through his headset.

"I'm on it," said Bjorn as he paid close attention to the distance readouts displayed inside his goggles. As he aligned the sights with his target, the hull of the Iron Raven, he squeezed the butterfly trigger launching one SPIM in their direction. It was a direct hit but appeared to cause minimal damage to the vessel. The Iron Raven quickly moved out of the way.

"Great shot, big fella!" said Corto to Bjorn. "Let's keep pounding 'em!"

On the bridge, Sampa was somewhat dismayed and confused at the lack of damage caused by the direct hit. "That should have taken them out!" she said. "What happened?"

"The Iron Raven has a multi-layered exoskeleton. Each layer is filled with coolant. It's designed to absorb lower calibered SPIMS," explained Francois.

"Then how do we defeat it?" asked Mulati.

"You can't," replied Francois. "Not with what you have here."

"Looks like they're locking in on us again," said Sampa. "There's that light again."

"Gotcha," said Mulati as he, again, maneuvered out of the way of the incoming SPIM. "We're gonna have to get out of here soon," he said. "We can't do this all day."

"I don't know if you can outrun them," said Francois.

"We're going to have to try," said Mulati. "Sam, the next time they light up we're making the jump to one cel. Set the coordinates for the southern continent."

"Aye-aye," said Sampa as she began to input the coordinates into the navigation system of the Whisper.

Aboard the Iron Raven the captain, Sunday Okonjo, made the decision to scramble three one-man fighters, called Sparrows, from inside the Iron Raven's hangar. "They are anticipating our attacks," he said to his co-pilot. "Let our Sparrows pick them apart." He sounded the alert from the bridge which sent three pilots to their Sparrows. In a matter of seconds, they were launching from the bowels of the Iron Raven and starting their mission to destroy the Whisper.

Rokuro Onishi and Alexei stood near the back wall of the bridge looking out of the large panoramic windshield at the battle as Sunday Okonjo and his crew executed their attack.

Aboard the Whisper Mulati, Francois, and Sampa observed the Iron Raven's counterpunch and were forced to act quickly.

"Those are Sparrows," said Francois. "They have three SPIMS each. They're very fast and they have excellent pilots. Unless you have some sort of answer to that we're in trouble here."

"We do," said Mulati as he engaged the intercom. "Go to shadow mode, Bjorn, they've scrambled some one-man fighters."

"We see them, Mulati," said Bjorn. "Standby!"

Bjorn and Corto quickly secured themselves inside their pods, donned their oxygen masks, and activated detached mode converting their gunner pods into shadow fighters. Metal clamps used to attach the pods to the Whisper detached and the connecting surface was demagnetized. Once that happened, both shadow fighters commenced to free fall away from the Whisper. As soon as they were clear, wings extended out of both sides of each shadow fighter and their rear thrusters engaged.

"Shadow one away!" communicated Corto to the bridge.

"Shadow two away!" said Bjorn as he and Corto sped in opposite directions away from the Whisper.

Once the shadow fighters were away, Mulati initiated cloak mode and the Whisper disappeared. He moved the Whisper away from its last location, so they wouldn't fall victim to a lucky shot from the Iron Raven or any of the three Sparrows.

Quickness and clever flight maneuvers that they had practiced on many occasions in the past helped Bjorn and Corto to befuddle the Sparrows with their shadow fighters. The Sparrows attacked in a tight V formation with two fighters up front and one in the rear.

"Shadow one and two, according to Francois, the fighter on the front right is the leader. Take him out and the others will retreat," Mulati could be heard saying in the headsets of Bjorn and Corto.

"Shadow one, we copy!" replied Corto. "In that case, Bjorn, I'll be the rabbit. Follow them on the starboard side after they get behind me. Once you give the signal I'll bank hard right to my starboard side. They should follow. Once they do that, take out the leader. You should have a clear shot at his flank."

"Copy!" said Bjorn. "Go get 'em!"

Listening from the bridge of the Whisper, Francois liked Bjorn and Corto's plan. "Mulati, let them know that once they've done that the other Sparrows will immediately return to the Iron Raven. According to protocol, they always return to its port side bay. If the shadow fighters rendezvous with us on their starboard side, we'll be safe. Their choice will be to get their pilots first instead of coming after us."

"I copy that," said Mulati. He verbally relayed the message to Bjorn and Corto through their headsets.

As the Sparrows got behind Corto and gave chase to him, Bjorn's shadow fighter flew in the opposite direction and out of sight. Watching from the bridge of the Iron Raven, Sunday Okonjo stated plainly, "They have realized already that they are no match for the Sparrows. It was wise of that one to flee."

"Don't mistake them for cowards," interjected Rokuro Onishi from his position at the back of the bridge.

"Fish swim in water, wolves hunt on land, and birds fly. We are in the sky," said Sunday Okonjo. "This is my domain."

"My domain is battle," snapped Rokuro Onishi, "and I know warriors when I see them!"

"Then what do you suggest?" asked Sunday Okonjo.

"I suggest you take them seriously," replied Rokuro Onishi.

"I always do," said Sunday Okonjo.

They continued to watch as the Sparrows closed in on Corto who, all of sudden, started to fly in a straight line.

"They have him now," Sunday Okonjo stated with confidence. "He is almost within their range. Like I said, this is my domain."

At that moment, Bjorn's shadow fighter returned and got behind the Sparrows. As soon as he did, and before Sunday Okonjo was able to warn them from the bridge, Corto turned his shadow fighter hard to the right. The Sparrows followed, as predicted, and Bjorn quickly sighted in and fired his SPIM to the broad side of the leader. It was a direct hit. The inside of the leader's sparrow filled with flames killing the pilot instantly. Sunday Okonjo instantly stood up, amazed by what he had just witnessed. As Francois foretold they would, the two remaining Sparrows broke formation and headed back to the port side of the Iron Raven.

Sunday Okonjo, in stunned disbelief, sat down and pressed the intercom. "Maintenance control, we have incoming; open the hangar." He swiveled around in his chair just in time to see Rokuro Onishi and Alexei storm out of the bridge without saying a word.

"Yes!" erupted a jubilant Francois from behind Sampa and Mulati.

Mulati smiled as he looked at Francois. "Let's go get our men, Sam," he said as he removed the Whisper from cloak mode and rushed to rally with Bjorn and Corto.

Upon making contact with the Whisper, Bjorn and Corto quickly realigned their shadow fighters under their connection points.

"Shadow one, prepared for reattachment," said Corto.

"Shadow two, prepared for reattachment," said Bjorn.

"Re-attachment sequence initiated," said Mulati. He hit the switch activating the heavily magnetized connection points as Bjorn and Corto both retracted their wings. The shadow fighters were pulled up and attached. Large metal clamps completed the seal as the shadow fighters and the Whisper were reunited.

"Shadow one, attached," said Corto.

"Shadow two, attached," said Bjorn.

"Good job, guys," said Sampa. "Now prepare yourselves for celerity."

The Whisper jumped to one cel, headed for the southern continent of Neutralia and left the Iron Raven far behind.

Chapter 15: The Eve of Eternity

Location: Dana Province, Southern continent, Neutralia
Aboard the Whisper

As the Whisper descended through the clouds over the west coast of the southern continent of Neutralia, Mulati and Sampa searched for a suitable surface to land the legendary spacecraft. It was winter on that side of the world. The glare of the sun bouncing off the snowy wilderness landscape was almost blinding. Sampa dimmed the Whisper's windshield to dull the brightness as Mulati activated the ship's defrost.

"There, just over those mountains," said Sampa as she pointed to the beyond. "We can sit her down on that plateau."

"I see it," said Mulati. "Head that way. That'll be perfect, those trees surrounding it will give us cover while we run our systems analysis. Where exactly are we, Sam?"

"According to this," said Sampa as she looked at the ship's map, "we're in the Dana Province. It happens to be very sparsely populated. Only a few wilderness people and nomads live here."

"Nearest metropolis?" asked Mulati.

"That would be Leanna, the province that borders this one on the east," replied Sampa.

"Why does that sound familiar to me?" asked Mulati.

"Well..." said Sampa sarcastically, "it's only the technological epicenter of the solar system. It's most likely where the Whisper's engine was made. It's also where we met." She playfully rolled her eyes.

"Oh," said Mulati as he shook his head as though it would release the stupidity that made him ask such a question. *How could I have forgotten that?*

He and Sampa skillfully piloted the Whisper to the center of the snowy plateau. As they sat it down on the surface, a white wall of snowy haze loosened by the ship's thrusters rose up all around them before eventually settling back down to the ground. It was a smooth landing.

"It's beautiful here," said Sampa. "You don't get to see this on Alkebulan."

"I agree," said Mulati. "It is beautiful."

For a moment they both stared out of the windshield marveling at the majesty before them. They finally enjoyed a peaceful moment with no immediate responsibility.

Bjorn's voice came through the intercom breaking the silence. "Hey, is it ok if we look around out there for a couple hours after we've done our systems analysis?"

Mulati looked over to Sampa before answering the question. She simply shrugged her shoulders as if she was indifferent to the request. "Sure, you can, Bjorn. I have no problem with that," replied Mulati. He released the handheld mic as he turned to address Sampa. "Sam, we need to call Theris and tell him about what Francois told us."

"That we do," she replied. "I agree wholeheartedly."

Mulati and Sampa went to the communication room and stood in front of the VC. "Contact Genesis," enunciated Mulati carefully.

Theris Lamont's hologram appeared before them. "Good morning, Mulati. Good morning, Sam," he said making sure to address them both individually. "Have you finalized your list of needs and supplies?"

"We are working on that still," replied Mulati. "That is not why we are contacting you."

A look of concern came over Theris's face. "Is something wrong?" he asked.

"Yes," replied Mulati. "We have heard from a reliable source that a Judas Benedict has placed a bounty on the lives of you and

Chancellor Aldrich."

"That's impossible! How can this information be confirmed?" asked Theris Lamont anxiously.

"Supposedly he met with the DOD on Hades," replied Sampa. "If that is true, the location history on his EPIC should be able to confirm that."

"Also," Mulati added, "the DOD are presently on Neutralia. I can't think of any other reason for them to be here. They normally do their work in Elba County of the Zasnezene Province on Hades."

"This is very disturbing," replied Theris, "and I must admit that I find it very hard to believe. If I am to present this news to Chancellor Aldrich, I'm going to need more proof."

"I understand," said Mulati. "Stand by." He looked to Sampa. "Go get Francois and tell him to come in here."

"Right away," said Sampa as she left the communication room.

"I'm going to bring you the source," said Mulati. "I trust him."

"For goodness sake, I hope he is mistaken," said Theris. "I consider Judas Benedict a friend."

Moments later Sampa returned to the communication room accompanied by Francois.

"This is Francois," said Mulati. "He is a former member of the DOD."

"What have you to say about what I have just heard?" asked Theris of Francois.

Francois replied quickly and confidently saying, "I personally escorted an Albino who called himself Judas Benedict to one of the DOD leaders at our hideout in Tierra Mala. Once their meeting was over, we were all told of a plan to kill two politicians, the Chancellor and you. He, himself, was also nearly killed in Iniquity later that day. Rokuro Onishi saved his life. That's how I know."

Theris seemed stunned by the accuracy of the information given to him by Francois. No one outside of the council, the people of Albin, or the people on the infirmary should have known about Judas being attacked. "Thank you for telling me this," said a now sullen Theris. "I will get back to you. End transmission." The holograms of Mulati, Sampa, and Francois faded away. Theris knew that the information he had just received would forever alter the paradigm of the council consisting of him, Judas, and Chancellor Aldrich. The ramifications would surely be far reaching and that filled him with fear of the potentially volatile unknown. His instincts told him that what he was just told by the crew of the Whisper was true. His heart longed for the opposite to be fact. He had to reconcile the two for the edification of the council. He was already scheduled to meet with his assistants, Louis and Eric, and his bodyguard, Ean, at 1600 hours that day. They could spy on the DOD for him to find out their true intentions while he went about the business of being the Vice Chancellor. Theris walked out onto the balcony of his apartment and stood there just beyond the threshold of his door watching the city. Somehow, he felt that it was his last time viewing it in its innocence. That made him sad.

Location: Dana Province, Southern Continent, Neutralia
Aboard the Whisper

Roughly an hour later, Mulati and Sampa both sat quietly in their respective seats drifting in and out of consciousness. The morning had proven to be an eventful one and the rest was just what they both needed. The dimmed windshield darkened the entire bridge since Mulati had also gone to low power mode to conserve energy and turned down the interior lights. He had also retracted the four panels atop the Whisper revealing the shiny, copper colored solar panels so that they could recharge the ship and store the energy from the sun. The bridge was warm which was the way Sampa liked it.

Sampa looked over at Mulati, noticing that he was still half awake, and she asked, "Do you think you could live out here?"

"You mean in all of this snow?" he asked barely bringing his voice above a whisper.

"In this wilderness," replied Sampa. "Do you think that you could live off the land? Is that something that appeals to you?"

"I could, I suppose," he replied, "but I'd prefer not to. It has its advantages, but nature is as formidable a foe as it is a friend. Growing old here would be a chore, I fear. Excitement and adventure are fun when you're a young man..." he said as he paused to look at Sampa, "but old men tell stories. Young men live. Right now, I want to live, and I'm not sure this is the place for me."

"Then where?" asked Sampa.

Mulati paused as he pondered the question. "I belong to Sapien. My nature is to roam. There's so much to see out there. So much to do. There's..." He paused. "Why do you ask, Sam?"

"I don't know," she replied. "I like places like this; I thought maybe you would too."

Mulati said nothing but looked forward and beyond the windshield. *I've never thought about where I would live. The Whisper is my home.* He could feel Sampa looking at him from the right. He also felt it when she looked away. Looking back at her he observed that her facial expression was somewhat different. For the first time that he could remember, she looked empty.

"What do you think of me, Mulati?" she asked with a sharpness of tongue that he rarely heard from her.

Without flinching he asked, "What do you think of yourself?"

"I mean..." she started.

"I know what you mean, Sam. I respect you, but my opinion of you personally is irrelevant."

"How so?" she responded determined to get her answer.

He looked her directly in her eyes and then looked back toward the outside before speaking. "You know what I think is the worst invention ever, Sam?" he asked rhetorically. "It's the mirror," he said before she could respond.

Sampa sat up in her seat and swiveled to face Mulati making sure that he knew she was looking directly at him. *This should be good.*

"I say that," he continued, "because that one thing has done more to erode humility, morality, and conscience than anything in this solar system."

"How so?" she asked.

Mulati sighed before speaking. "The ability to perceive oneself is nearly impossible and remains, in my mind, a frontier that needs not be explored. The inability to do that one thing keeps us humble and helps us to maintain the natural order of things through our deeds and accountability to one another, nothing more. For that reason, I feel it's best that personal perspective remains a mystery. That is, and always will be, my answer."

"Did Yeung Chow Lo teach you that?" she asked.

"No," he replied. "Life has taught me that." Again, he rested his eyes.

"All systems go!" said Bjorn's voice through the intercom. "Me, Francois, and Corto are going huntin' for a few."

"That's fine," said Mulati as he opened his eyes and reached up to press the intercom talk button. "You know, Sam..." he said as he swiveled back around to face her. To his surprise she had gotten up and left the bridge just that fast. He was now alone. He couldn't help but think back to what Yeung Chow Lo had said to him about Sampa. *She is loyal to you, do not lose her.* Those words were so clear to him it was as if his teacher were in the room with him saying them aloud. "I won't, Master Lo. I won't," he said to himself as he angrily pounded his fist into the palm of his other hand. He shook his head feeling that in a rare moment he had failed to see the big picture and did not do what was proper. *That was very selfish of me.*

As Sampa walked into the cargo bay a few minutes later wearing her winter gear, Bjorn, Francois, and Corto all turned around surprised that she was there.

"You huntin with us?" asked Bjorn. "It's a little cold out there. I don't know if your Alkebulan blood can take it."

"It's not as cold out there as it is on the bridge," she replied with a straight face.

Bjorn and Corto glanced at one another quickly but said nothing. Francois was about to speak but got the message when he made eye contact with Corto who was shaking his head.

"Here take this, Sam," said Bjorn as he handed her a high-powered bow and a quiver full of arrows. The bow was complete with a bow sight, stabilizer, and grip. "You think you can handle one of those?"

Sampa smirked. "Somehow, I don't think this is what the Americans had in mind when they first made these," she said referring to the gadgets with which the bow was equipped. "I think I can get by with this."

"Good enough," said Bjorn, "let's head out."

Corto and Bjorn lowered the ramp and once it was down, the cold air rushed in and took over the cargo bay. The air was visible as they all breathed through their noses. Bjorn's goggles went from clear to dark as he faced the sunlight. He balled his fists and slammed them both across his chest making an X. Knowing what was coming next, Corto and Sampa did the same. Without hesitation they went into their customary Whisper Yell. "Aaaahhhh," they all yelled in unison as they all thrusted their chest forward and pulled their shoulders back to end it.

"Five stomps only, huh?" said Francois sarcastically.

"Well maybe if you participate next time, Frenchie, we'll remember to do six," said Corto.

"Good point," said Francois. "I'll take that."

"I'm sealing off the rest of the ship," said Bjorn as he walked over to the door Sampa entered through. "We're going to leave this back hatch open."

"Sounds good to me," said Sampa. "Let's go."

Mulati watched the monitor with great interest from the bridge as all four exited the Whisper's cargo bay headed for the wilderness. *Sam must really be angry with me; she's never gone hunting with them before.* He looked away from the monitor when he heard the door to the bridge open. "Hey, Beth," he said as she walked over and took a seat in Sampa's chair.

"Hey, Mulati," she replied. "Think they'll come back with something this time? The last two times they went out they came back empty. I think Bjorn's ready for some meat and, to tell you the truth, I think I am too. You know they'll be out there showing off for Francois; they can't help themselves. Bjorn and Corto are like children sometimes. I worry about them so much it..."

"What's the matter, Beth?" Mulati interrupted anticipating a problem.

Being overly chatty was Beth's way of breaking the ice when she had something on her mind and needed to vent.

"You owe Sam an apology," she said getting straight to the point. "I think you sometimes forget, because she knows her way around these gadgets so well, that she's a woman. I know it sounds strange and it makes you a little uncomfortable, but sometimes we need to be reassured. She only wanted your honest opinion, that's all. Now if she can't get that from you, our leader, then she may seek it elsewhere. I'm gonna leave you with that." She got up from Sampa's chair, leaned over and kissed Mulati on the cheek, and headed toward the bridge exit.

"Beth..." said Mulati just before she got to the door.

Beth stopped and turned to face him.

"Your eyes are pretty," he said in a feeble attempt to make a good faith down payment with his wit.

Beth smiled. "Nice try, but I'll let you know when it's my turn. You ain't gotta tell her everything but tell her something. She deserves that." She walked out of the bridge.

Mulati slowly ran his hand over his face as he sighed heavily and leaned back in his chair. Minutes later he was asleep.

Bjorn led the way followed by Francois, Sampa, and finally Corto as they trudged single file through the snow and woods looking for something to kill. Somehow, they managed to find a natural path to walk on, although it was narrow. Bjorn paid careful attention to the fresh snow as he looked for animal tracks or any sign that something was in the area. Even though they were the only things moving for the most part, the four of them were very quiet as they made their way. After about thirty minutes or so, Bjorn raised a closed fist in the air. They all stood still. He turned his upper torso around to face the others pointing his index and middle fingers toward his own eyes. The rest of them instantly understood that to mean he had something in sight. He put both hands on top of his head with his index fingers pointed toward the sky. That was his informal way of letting them know that he had seen some deer. They all understood what he meant, so it worked. Bjorn put his arm straight out to his side with his palm facing down and lowered it to his side. They quietly crouched down at the same time and waited. Before long a herd consisting of three bucks and four does walked into the clearing. It was still snowing, and the crew were starting to blend into the scenery as it covered them. They all readied their bows and arrows as they waited for one of the four legged animals to present its broad side to them. The largest of the bucks momentarily stood tall as it presented its flank to the crew. Bjorn drew his bow and sighted in. The digital readout for distance in his goggles settled on forty meters. He steadied himself and finally let an arrow fly. The vibrato of the string was complemented by the sound of the arrow quickly slicing through the wind. It was a hit. His arrow lodged into the torso of the large deer just behind the front leg causing it to take off running through the woods. The rest of the herd immediately dispersed.

"Let's go, I got him!" yelled Bjorn as he sprang to his feet and ran to the area where the buck was impacted.

After a short sprint, they were there.

"That's his blood right there," said Corto. "Looks like he went that way," he continued as he pointed in the direction of the blood droplets.

After following the trail of scarlet for about two hundred yards, they located the lifeless buck nestled up to some brush.

"He looks like he's sleeping," said Sampa.

"Well, he ain't waking up that's for sure," said Bjorn. "This your first time, Sam?"

"Yes, it is actually," she replied.

"No offense," said Francois, "but I find that hard to believe."

That pleased Sampa. "Why thank you, Francois, I'll take that as a compliment," she said smiling. Thoughts of her conversation with Mulati were long gone. Despite it being too cold for her comfort, she was thoroughly enjoying herself and was glad that she had come along with the guys.

"Come here, Sam," said Corto as he stood by the dead buck holding a blood-soaked cloth. "Initiation time!"

"Is this necessary?" Sampa sighed playfully as she walked over to Corto and lowered her face.

He dabbed both of her cheeks with the cloth and then crammed it into his pocket. "You're official now!" he said as the rest of them shook hands proud of what they had done.

"Let's get him back to the Whisper," said Bjorn.

Location: Southtown, District County, Rights Province, Neutralia
The Hidden Bastille, 1400 hours

Klaus centered himself between the cells of Bahadur and Onin Gesh peering at both of them as he slowly and repeatedly slapped the troll in the palm of his hand like a metronome. The sound echoed through the otherwise quiet facility. This was his preferred method of torture. Some days he would shock them and some days he would not. It wasn't the physical pain that bothered either of the two men and Klaus knew it. They were long past that. His pleasure was derived from the fact that the device rendered them unable to control their muscles while he seasoned them with pain. It was all about control. He was trying to break them mentally. Bahadur slowly paced from wall to wall never taking his eyes off Klaus. If he could kill him with his eyes he would have died ten horrible deaths by now. Onin Gesh refused to look at Klaus. He learned to play the game with him and would not give him the satisfaction of seeing him squirm. He stood with his back to the cell door, his feet shoulder width apart, and his arms folded as he stared at the back wall. He did not move. He had long ago figured out that it mattered not what he did or did not do. Whether they were shocked or not depended solely on how evil Klaus was feeling at the moment.

With every slap of the troll, Klaus calmly repeated Onin Gesh's name barely above a whisper as if it could cut him each time he said it. The impact of the troll and the word Gesh were perfectly synchronized as Klaus raised his voice ever so slightly whenever he said it. "Onin Gesh... Onin Gesh... Onin Gesh... Onin Gesh... Onin Gesh... Onin Gesh," he said it so many times on rhythm that it only registered as ambient noise to both men. "Turn and face me and I won't shock you, Onin Gesh. Turn and look me in my eyes like a man, Onin Gesh. Turn and beg me for mercy, Onin Gesh. Onin Gesh... Onin Gesh... Onin Gesh."

Outside the rain was pouring. Rights Province was known for heavy thunderstorms and this particular one did nothing to tarnish the reputation it had long established. As Klaus continued his childish taunts, the facility sustained a direct hit from a lightning strike. The lights momentarily shut off and when they did, both cell doors quickly opened about six inches. Onin Gesh immediately turned and faced the door. Upon seeing it open he ran swiftly toward it. Klaus was terrified. Both cells were sliding open and the two prisoners were furiously approaching. In his panicked state, he dropped his troll and ran away. Within seconds the generators kicked in repowering the facility. The lights turned on and the doors slammed shut before either of them could get out. For Klaus it was three seconds of sheer horror.

Bahadur began to laugh as loudly and obnoxiously as he could. "Klaus! Come back! You have survived another day to continue your cowardice, Klaus. Klaus, come back! Klaus... Klaus... Klaus... Klaus," he yelled while slamming the palms of his hands on his cell door with each mention of the name.

Before long Onin Gesh joined him and they chanted in unison, "Klaus... Klaus... Klaus... Klaus..."

Finally, Klaus returned, full of anger, rage, and shame. He slowly crouched down and retrieved his troll from the floor.

As he raised his troll to deliver what would surely be an extended shock to both of them, Bahadur tried to pierce his brain with his cold stare. "Fear is your master. You are nothing more than a servant. Without that device you are nothing."

Onin Gesh looked Klaus in his eyes with a sinister gaze and smiled but said nothing. Incensed, Klaus pressed the button on his troll and held it down, shocking them both for the maximum time possible, fifteen seconds. To him it was as if they forced him to shock them. He was no longer the one in control. For the first time ever, he felt no satisfaction in shocking the men and it showed on his conquered visage. They both fell to the floor screaming and writhing in pain. Before they could recover, Klaus was gone.

As Onin Gesh laid down on the floor looking up at the ceiling of his cell, he smiled to himself. *I'm going to enjoy killing you,*

Klaus. Through pain they had achieved a small, but crucial, victory.

Location: Dana Province, Southern Continent, Neutralia
Cargo bay of the Whisper

Corto stood facing Sampa, attempting to hand her his dagger, as Francois and Bjorn prepared the buck to be butchered. "Here you go, Sam. There's nothing to it."

"No way," she replied. "I've done enough for today. We'll save that for another time. I need to get warm and get this blood off me."

"Now that's more like what I expected," said Francois with a chuckle.

"That's more like what I expected ha ha ha," Sampa whined sarcastically while closing her eyes and making a funny face at Francois.

They all laughed together.

"Well at least I tried," said Corto as he skillfully flipped his dagger around in the palm of his hand and thrust it into its sheath in one motion. "Are you going to bring us some coffee at least?"

"Now that I can do," said Sampa as she left the cargo bay headed to her quarters.

As the door closed behind her, she nearly bumped into Mulati who was about to enter the cargo bay. Without saying a word, she sidestepped him, took a quick glance into his eyes, lowered her head, and continued on her way. Mulati kept his eyes locked on her and turned to watch her as she continued into the elevator. As Sampa turned around inside the elevator she made eye contact with Mulati once again. This time neither of them looked away and their gaze was interrupted by the closing elevator door.

When Sampa exited the elevator on the main deck, she saw Beth exiting her suite.

"How'd it go out there?" asked Beth.

"Like this," Sampa replied pointing with pride to her blood-stained cheeks.

"Oh congratulations! You got your first kill!" Beth said with a huge smile.

"Let's not get carried away, Beth, they did the killing. I got this because I was there. Bjorn got him."

Beth smiled. *He's really making good use of those lenses I made for him.* "Well, that's good, Sam. At least you had fun out there."

"That I did, Beth. It was incredible. By the way," she paused just short of entering her own suite, "the guys said for you to bring them coffee." *I know they didn't really expect me to make it.*

"It's already brewing," said Beth as Sampa disappeared into her suite.

In the cargo bay Bjorn, Corto, and Francois busied themselves removing the hide from the large buck.

"How'd Sam do out there in the cold?" asked Mulati.

"Just fine," answered Bjorn as he tugged hard at the deer skin. "In fact, she was amazing; she's a natural."

"Is this your kill, Corto?" Mulati asked.

"No, not this time," Corto replied pointing to Bjorn. "There's your man right there."

Mulati walked over to examine the buck. "One shot? I'm impressed, Bjorn."

"Thanks, it was easy," replied Bjorn. "We made a good team out there. Frenchie fit right in too."

"And what'd you do, Francois?" Mulati asked lightheartedly.

"Besides get cold and follow them?" said Francois. "Absolutely nothing. I enjoyed the hunt though. You should go sometime."

"What makes you think I don't?" asked Mulati in tone that seemed to say *how dare you.*

"You're right, I should've known you had," replied Francois.

They all stood and watched as Bjorn masterfully butchered the buck, assisting whenever needed. Most of the assisting was done by Corto as he seemed to instinctively know which part to hold in position to be cut before Bjorn got to it. They had done this as a team many times before. When a piece of unusable tissue was cut off, Corto would toss it to Francois to be disposed of. Mulati rarely touched anything while they butchered the animal. The conversation remained light hearted in nature as they worked.

Francois seamlessly fit in with the crew and Mulati was pleased with the way they all interacted with one another. *I'm glad I made the decision to keep Francois. There's something about him that makes things a little more cohesive with Bjorn and Corto. They like him.* "Make sure we get this deck power washed when you're done. I'm headed back to the upper deck, I'll be there if you need me." He walked out of the cargo bay and headed toward the elevator.

"The power washer's over there, Frenchie," said Corto as he pointed with a head nod because his hands were occupied.

"I'm on it," said Francois. As he walked over to gather the hose and bring it to their carving area, he thought back to his earlier question. "Hey Corto, earlier I was about to ask Sam what she meant about it being colder on the bridge and you shook me off. Is there something I should be aware of?"

Corto momentarily stopped working as he looked up from his kneeling position, apparently thinking of the proper way to phrase what it was he was going to say. "Sometimes... not always but sometimes, there's a weird energy between those two. Bjorn and I have noticed it but I'm not sure if they're even aware of it. It's like the old leviathan in a pond thing. We see it, and they might feel it, but no one says anything."

"You think they might've gotten it on at some point?" asked Francois.

"Who knows?" said Bjorn as he continued to focus on butchering the buck. "They were a team for a while before they got Beth on board. Anything could've happened during that time. Personally, I think that's the way you act when nothing has happened but will. You know what I mean?"

"Yeah, I do," said Francois, "but I usually get rid of that feeling fast!"

They all laughed.

"Well, that should do it," said Bjorn as he stood up. "Let's get this meat to the freezer in the galley."

After Corto and Bjorn gathered all the meat, Francois turned on the power washer and used it to push all the blood and animal remains toward a grate in the middle of the floor. Before long the wet floor was so clean it was as if nothing had ever been there. After a few trips back and forth to the galley, they were done and each of them retired to their respective suites.

On the upper deck Mulati sat in his captain's chair on the bridge. Leaning forward he paid close attention to the ship's map, scanning the area surrounding the Whisper. As Sampa walked in he stopped what he was doing, sat back, and swiveled around in his chair to face her. "Welcome back, Sam. I heard you performed well out there."

"I did alright," she replied. "Bjorn was the one who did all the work. It was definitely good to be out there though."

"I'm sure it was," he replied as she made herself comfortable in the co-captain's chair.

"You see anything interesting on those monitors?" she asked.

"Nothing to report," he answered playfully with the inflection of a subordinate answering to a superior. He smiled as he did so.

Sampa returned his smile.

"Sam, I owe you an apology."

Sampa sat erect in her seat. "Oh?"

"Yes, I do," he continued. "This operation cannot run without you. I think, in fact I know, that you're the smartest person on this ship. That makes me pretty smart because I recognized that and brought you on."

Sampa turned her head slightly to the left looking down her nose at Mulati. *Really?*

Mulati chuckled. "I know what you're thinking, Sam. The fact of the matter is you're irreplaceable. If something happened to me right now, I'm confident that you would lead them where they need to go. Wherever that might be. I really don't know what to say except that I appreciate you. You…"

Sampa reached over and grabbed the back of Mulati's right hand and squeezed it tight. She gave it a firm shake as she looked him in his eyes. As her own eyes swelled with moisture, she said, "Thanks, that's all I needed."

"So, you're not leaving me?" Mulati asked with a smile.

"No," she replied with a chuckle. "You're stuck with me. Besides, my conscience would eat me alive if something happened to you or the crew."

"Great," he said with a subdued fist pump.

As Mulati returned his attention to the instrument panel, Sampa interlaced her fingers across her stomach as she leaned back and closed her eyes. She remained that way for a few minutes. "That big convention is tomorrow, are we going?" she asked when she opened her eyes.

"We're going back to Rights Province, but not until that's over," he replied. "I would actually like to spend the first half of tomorrow in the Leanna Province. I'd like to see what new technology they have there."

"Sounds good to me," she replied. "In fact, I like that idea a lot." As

Sampa got up from her seat, she turned to face Mulati, lightly crossed both of her fists over her chest giving a modified Whisper salute. Mulati, from his seat, returned the gesture. Sampa walked out of the bridge lethargically as she headed for her suite.

Mulati turned his attention to the Whisper's monitors. As he scanned the common areas of the ship the only activity he observed was Beth preparing food in the galley. No one was in the lounge, the cargo bay, or the engine room. *I guess I should get some rest too.* Since the proximity beacon was primarily responsible for picking up vessels of all sizes, Mulati activated the motion detectors for the ship in case any animals or humans approached it. He left the bridge headed for his suite.

Chapter 16: The Dangerous Duo

Location: Southtown, District County, Rights Province, Planet Neutralia
The Hidden Bastille, 0830 hours

Having already eaten their breakfast, both prisoners positioned themselves in their usual places within their cells. Onin Gesh stood peering out of his darkened cell into the corridor just beyond its door. Bahadur paced from wall to wall scowling as his body language reflected the rage he felt inside. Their breakfast had been served to them by someone other than Klaus. The new Mayhem Marauder guard had comported himself professionally. The men within the Mayhem Marauder ranks who were usually strapped with menial tasks such as this were referred to as squaddies and Klaus was ranked one step above that.

General Tolliver positioned himself in the center of both cells in the outside corridor so that he could personally observe both men. He was accompanied by two subordinate Mayhem Marauders, a captain and a lieutenant. For the first time ever all, of the Mayhem Marauders were dressed uniformly. They wore form fitting dark green uniforms that had long sleeved shirts. They wore black boots that stopped just below the calf muscle. Their trousers were tucked into their shined black boots. Underneath their green shirts was a dark blue crew neck shirt. Their blue belt matched the color of the blue shirt.

"Are we sure that they have a healthy enough respect for the control device?" General Tolliver asked of his subordinates.

"They do," the captain replied.

"Then proceed as planned," ordered General Tolliver.

The captain nodded to the lieutenant who radioed to the control tower through his EPIC. "Fill it up."

At that moment the cells decompressed. Bahadur stopped pacing and began to look around suspiciously noticing that all vents had been sealed. Onin Gesh also suspected something was wrong. He walked all the way up to the cell door, close enough for his nose to touch the glass. He looked at the Mayhem Marauders to see if their body language would foreshadow what was to come. Suddenly both cells began to fill with gas. Bahadur immediately grabbed the sheet from his bed, wrapped it around his face, and crouched down face forward into an empty corner. Onin Gesh stepped back to his original place in the darkness and he started taking deep breaths filling his lungs with the gas. He made sure that the Mayhem Marauders knew he was looking at them as long as there was visibility. After a while his stance began to soften as the white gas filled the room. He struggled to stand. Eventually he collapsed hitting the floor face first with a thud. Bahadur fell backwards to a supine position after being fully affected by the gas. His body was completely relaxed. Five minutes later both men were unconscious.

"They're out," the lieutenant said to the tower through his EPIC.

Two minutes later Klaus joined the three men outside of the cells. They all donned gas masks as the remaining gas was sucked out of the cells through the same vent through which it entered.

"Let's get those cells open," said the captain to the lieutenant.

"Wait!" said Klaus as he reached over and grabbed the lieutenant's hand preventing him from speaking into his EPIC. "Are we sure that they're out? We have to be completely sure."

"Why wouldn't they be?" asked the captain. "Do as you were told and open those cells now!"

As the lieutenant communicated to the tower, Klaus caressed his troll. The doors slid open quickly and simultaneously. There was nothing separating the notorious killers from the Mayhem Marauders. General Tolliver stepped behind the others and folded his arms.

Klaus walked up to the threshold of Bahadur's cell. "Bahadur!" he yelled at the top of his lungs while looking for any sign that the

Persian assassin might have been awake. He did not move. "Ba-ha-dur!" Klaus repeated cupping his hands over his mouth to amplify the sound as he continued to linger around the doorway.

"Get your ass in there, Klaus!" commanded the impatient captain.

Klaus took a deep breath inside his gas mask, removed the troll from his pocket, and he entered Bahadur's cell. Making sure to keep himself between the cell door and Bahadur, Klaus bent over enough to touch his shoulder with his empty hand. He gently tapped him. No response. He gave him a slight nudge. Again, there was no response. He then firmly grasped Bahadur's shoulder and shook it causing Bahadur's entire body to move. Nothing happened. Satisfied that Bahadur was indeed unconscious, Klaus turned and gave a thumbs up to the lieutenant. He walked out of the cell as two more squaddies entered carrying a stretcher with restraints. As the men secured Bahadur to the stretcher, the lieutenant radioed to the tower for them to turn on the lights in Onin Gesh's cell. As the cell lit up, Klaus watched Onin Gesh's face closely to see if there would be a reaction to the bright light. There was none. With extreme trepidation, Klaus entered the cell. "Onin Gesh!" he yelled from the doorway. Hearing and seeing no response, he made his approach. He quickly confirmed that Onin Gesh was knocked out and, just as quickly, he exited the cell. Immediately two more squaddies entered Onin Gesh's cell carrying a stretcher. Klaus stood behind the captain and the lieutenant as the men were removed from the cells.

General Tolliver walked over to look at Onin Gesh's face. He wanted to make sure that he didn't have any bruises resulting from his fall. He did not. "Take them away."

Klaus's face dripped with perspiration as the lieutenant turned to address him. "Make sure they are secured in the JEDDO, we have an hour to get them to Central City."

Klaus nodded his head nervously before turning to address the four squaddies who were carrying the men. "Be careful with them. Make sure you don't bump into anything and hurry up! We don't want them waking up before we reach the JEDDO." He walked away headed to the Hidden Bastille's garage as the men wheeled the assassins behind them.

Location: Leanna Province, Southern continent, planet Neutralia Aboard the Whisper, 0900 hours

The crew of the Whisper had been up and moving since 0400 hours. They had already eaten breakfast and completed the short flight from the snowy plateau in the Dana Province to a state of the art airfield in the Leanna Province. They were excited because they were looking forward to seeing what new technological advances the brilliant minds of the Leanna Province had come up with. The best scientists and engineers from every planet made their living there as a part of the Collective Alliance, commonly referred to as the CA, which was created to benefit all worlds equally. The CA was headed by Director Ryan Rand who was a native of Evropa. Because the technicians, CATs, tended to be singular in their mental approach to things, the position of the director was always filled by a non-scientist. A well-rounded citizen proved to be a better liaison between the CA and the Sapiens they served. His two deputy directors, however, were scientists and served as his technical advisors. The prevailing motivating factor for the birth of the CA was the idea that no culture or world should be able to outpace the others technologically. *All worlds equal* was the mantra of the CA. If it had any type of mechanical function, it was likely created in the Leanna Province by the CA. To eliminate the possibility of any one inventor gaining more notoriety than the others, all credit for anything created was attributed to the alliance as a whole. Regardless of tenure or experience all technicians were paid 150,000 DANs yearly, which was nearly two thirds above the median income of Sapien. To be a technician carried a great deal of prestige. In fact, no one under the age of twenty-four years of age was allowed to be a technician. Sampa was a CAT when she met Mulati. The fact that she found it to be boring and felt unfulfilled working within that environment proved to be of great benefit to the Whisper.

The airfield was busy. Ships were separated not only by their size, but by their intended function as well. Other crafts arrived and departed on an almost constant basis. The Whisper was parked among the other medium class cargo vessels. It, no doubt, was the only one in that class capable of reaching four celerity units. Mulati had requested that they all meet in the cargo bay on the lower deck at 0930 hours. To blend in with the people of Leanna they would need to eschew their normal utilitarian clothing for something more fashionable.

Mulati buzzed Francois' suite. "Meet me on the bridge in two minutes, Francois."

"I copy," he replied, "I'm on my way."

As Francois walked into the bridge two minutes later Mulati swiveled around in his captain's chair to address him. "I'll be brief. You got the short straw this time. You'll be staying behind while the rest of us are out there in Leanna."

Francois clasped both of his hands together in front of his face and closed his eyes in an obvious display of gratitude. *Yes!* "I really appreciate this, Mulati. Thanks!"

"I'll have my EPIC open, so if anything happens, anything at all, contact me or Sam. Keep that rear hatch sealed. I've already gone to low power mode as you can see. If for some reason you need to get out of here fast, you do it from this seat. You can fly it without help if you enable the virtual co-pilot with that switch right there. You got it?"

"Got it."

Mulati nodded his head. "That's all, you can go now."

As Francois exited the bridge, Mulati could hear his voice from beyond the closed door. "Yes! Finally!"

Francois walked into the ship's lounge on the main deck and started a pot of coffee for himself. He sat on the couch and made himself comfortable. Like a person does when they spend their first night alone in a new home, he looked around taking it all in slowly. *I finally have a real family. It feels like home already. I'm not gonna mess this one up.*

Bjorn walked into the lounge and instantly noticed that Francois hadn't changed into fancier clothes. "Hey, when are you gonna get dressed?"

"I'm not," he replied waiting for Bjorn to ask him why.

"You know," said Bjorn, "we're a tight team here. You don't wanna seem like you're not with the program."

"Oh, I'm with the program alright," Francois replied while placing his hands behind his head as he leaned back and crossed his feet on the ottoman.

"Then why are you not dressed?" Bjorn asked.

"Because I got the short straw," Francois replied with pride.

"Really?" asked Bjorn with a look that was equal parts amusement and approval. "That's very interesting. Normally I'd feel sorry for someone in that situation, but in your case... congratulations!"

"Thank you very much," said Francois as he playfully tilted his head from side to side with each word.

"Well we'll make sure to bring you back a souvenir, Frenchie."

"I'd appreciate that, Bjorn."

Corto walked into the lounge moving quickly. "Hey guys, we've gotta get down to the lower deck; can't keep the boss waiting."

"Go on and tell 'em, Frenchie," said Bjorn.

"Tell me what?" asked a somewhat confused Corto.

"I'm staying behind," said Francois.

"No way!" said Corto. "Really?"

"That's what I said," Bjorn added.

"Yes really!" said Francois. "I get to watch the Whisper."

Sampa stepped halfway into the doorway of the lounge.

"Guess what, Sam?" said Corto and Bjorn together as Francois sat on the couch smiling with his arms folded in front of him.

"Mulati told me already," she said in a dry tone knowing she was stealing their thunder. "Congratulations, Francois. Let's go, you two, Mulati and Beth are waiting for us on the lower deck." She gave an insincere smile before exiting.

"See you guys when you get back. Have fun!" said Francois as Bjorn and Corto followed Sampa out of the lounge. *You gotta love Sam. At least she's consistent.*

As Sampa, Bjorn, and Corto walked into the cargo bay Mulati and Beth turned to face them.

"Looking good, everybody," said Beth.

"Not too bad yourself, Beth," said Sampa as she nodded with approval.

"Listen up, everybody," said Mulati as he commanded the attention of the room. "Francois is staying behind this time. He has his orders, he knows what to do. We should be gone for only a few hours. This is strictly for pleasure. Enjoy yourselves. Make sure your EPICs are open. That way if we get split up, or if I need to get you, there won't be any issues communicating. Alright? Let's go have some fun."

As they lowered the massive ramp to the busy airfield outside, Francois entered the cargo bay to see them off. "Have fun, guys. I got it!"

As they walked down the ramp onto the tarmac, the smell of heavy machinery and mechanized vehicles filled the air. Service vehicles and workers in overalls were all over the place. The sounds of heavy equipment being worked on, vehicles moving, and a thousand conversations let them know that they were surely in a place that was full of life and fast paced. As they looked around, it was apparent that no one outside of their circle cared for or concerned themselves with what anyone else was doing. Neither of them bothered to speak while they walked because they wouldn't be heard over the noise anyway. They all just focused on getting away from the Whisper and enjoying themselves. Mulati led the way as they negotiated their way through the dense crowd making sure that they stayed close together. Before long they came to the rear of a large one-story building that separated the airfield from the city of Sherrod which was just beyond its front doors. As they entered the well-lit building the first thing they noticed was the quiet, although it was still very busy inside.

"I could barely hear myself think out there!" said Corto as soon as they got into the building.

"When can you hear yourself think is the question?" quipped Sampa.

"Ha ha she got you there, buddy," said Bjorn as he gave Corto a friendly tap on the back.

"Don't laugh too hard, Bjorn, I'm pretty sure we're in the same boat there," said Corto.

They continued to talk to and laugh amongst each other until they made it to the front of the building. Outside were lines and lines of JEDDOs waiting to pick up passengers and take them to their desired destinations.

"Let's meet back here at 1600 hours," said Mulati. "Don't steal anything, Corto! I'd like to be able to come back here someday."

"I won't, I promise," he said shrugging his shoulders and showing the palms of his hands.

"Good, I have your word," said Mulati. "You will NOT bring me back a new case for my EPIC?"

"That's right, Boss," he replied. "Anything else you don't want me to steal?"

Beth leaned over and whispered in Mulati's ear, "You know that pretty much guarantees he is stealing something, right?"

"Yea," replied Mulati, "I'm counting on it."

They hugged one another and then went their separate ways. Bjorn and Corto got into a JEDDO together. Everyone else split up and went by themselves, each one getting into a different JEDDO.

Location: Central City, District County, Rights Province, Neutralia
The Grand Amphitheater of Central City, 1000 hours

At the rear of the Grand Amphitheater of Central City, and under the watchful eyes of the Mayhem Marauders, was the JEDDO in which Onin Gesh and Bahadur were brought to the venue. They had been parked there for approximately thirty minutes. Inside the JEDDO both men were awake and sitting across from one another. They were restrained to their seats at four points by both ankles and both wrists. They were both still groggy from the sleeping gas that was used to subdue them earlier. Standing inside the JEDDO with them were two unarmed squaddies. They were under orders to keep them there until they were summoned to the inside by General Tolliver. Neither Onin Gesh nor Bahadur knew what was going on. General Tolliver made the decision to keep them in the dark about what was going to happen because he felt that tactic would rob them of the opportunity to devise a plan. They were both warned not to speak to one another as soon as they were coherent enough to comprehend.

Bahadur looked down at both hands upon realizing that he was strapped into his seat after he could not scratch his nose. He studied the squaddies and he looked at Onin Gesh wondering if he was thinking the same about their current predicament. *Before today none of them wore uniforms. Now they do. They also have a clearly defined chain of command. They are trying to send a message to someone. This is a clear show of strength. The Marauders have changed.*

As he got stronger and more lucid, Onin Gesh began to violently yank at his restraints trying to rip his arms away from the chair. His muscles rippled with every tug. He grunted and exhaled each time determined to break free.

"Hey, stop that," said the squaddie closest to him. "Those restraints are too strong, you can't break them."

"Shut up, bitch!" Onin Gesh replied with a menacing look on his face. He resumed yanking his body around so violently that it actually shook the JEDDO.

The squaddie stepped closer and repeated his command. "I said stop that."

"Make me!" screamed Onin Gesh as he stopped moving to look the squaddie in his eyes. As the squaddie backed away saying nothing, Onin Gesh deliberately made eye contact with Bahadur. *Am I alone?*

Bahadur noticed Onin Gesh looking at him and started flexing his arms trying to break his restraints as well. When the squaddie closest to him closed the distance, Bahadur spat in his face. The stunned Mayhem Marauder immediately retreated wiping the slimy expectorant away. *They won't touch us. Whatever it is they have planned, they want us in good condition for it. Now is not the time for us to fight them.*

Onin Gesh again yanked around in his seat. This time he pulled his butt away from the chair while releasing a primal yell. The restraints were the only thing that prevented him from standing all the way up.

"Don't tire yourself, young warrior. Our time is coming, and they know it," said Bahadur. "These men are under orders not to strike us."

Onin Gesh was never one to take orders, or suggestions for that matter, from anyone, but the certainty with which Bahadur spoke led him to believe that he had something in mind that was beneficial to the both of them. He complied.

"Shut your mouth, Persian!" said the squaddie as he quickly stepped to Bahadur with the back of his hand raised.

"Hit me!" said Bahadur as he raised his chin in clear defiance of the squaddie.

Slowly the squaddie lowered his hand and went back to his original position. Both squaddies were clearly frustrated with Bahadur and Onin Gesh but could not do anything about it.

"That's what I thought," said Bahadur in a tone that seemed to signify that he was in control.

Although he was seething, Onin Gesh managed to remain calm.

The side door of the JEDDO slid open. In walked two more Mayhem Marauders carrying twice emitters, a sergeant and a corporal. As Bahadur turned his head to say something to them he was immediately emitted by the sergeant. Almost simultaneously Onin Gesh was emitted by the corporal. Both men were temporarily paralyzed.

"You've got twenty seconds," said the sergeant. "Unstrap their hands and secure them behind their backs."

Without hesitation the two squaddies quickly unstrapped both hands of Onin Gesh and Bahadur. Bahadur's hands were quickly secured behind his back. However, the squaddie who was working on Onin Gesh had taken too long undoing the straps and was quickly running out of time.

"I need help!" he yelled as he realized that he was not going to make it.

The corporal raised his twice emitter and aimed it at Onin Gesh. "Stay calm, you can do it."

Time ran out.

Onin Gesh regained his motor functions. Immediately he grabbed the squaddie by his neck with both hands, thrusted his thumbs into his trachea, and pulled him into a headbutt leaving him bleeding from the nose and unconscious. All in one motion he had moved the squaddie between himself and the corporal, so he couldn't be emitted again. Knowing he was not supposed to kill Onin Gesh, the corporal racked his twice emitter which caused the second projectile to eject. It was now ready to fire another paralyzing round but it was too late. Onin Gesh pushed the squaddie away and immediately put both hands in the air. Bright red blood dripped from the palms of his hands to his elbows. Unable to breathe, the unconscious squaddie fell backward to the floor and immediately started to turn blue.

"You can shoot me again, or you can help him," said Onin Gesh.

For a moment the sergeant, the corporal, and the other guard stood motionless, astonished by what had just occurred.

"He's dying," said Onin Gesh without emotion.

The sound of the unconscious squaddie's aspirated breathing and the sight of his punctured trachea unnerved the men.

"Place your hands behind your back!" commanded the very tense corporal.

Onin Gesh leaned forward and slowly placed his hands behind his back.

"If you do anything other than allow yourself to be restrained we will kill you! Do you understand?" said the sergeant. "They only need one of you for the demonstration."

Bahadur raised an eyebrow. *That's what it is. We're their spoils of war. They just made a terrible mistake.*

"I'm done killing for the day," said Onin Gesh as he stared at the sergeant the entire time the squaddie nervously fastened his hands together.

"Get him out of here now," said the sergeant referring to the unconscious squaddie.

The corporal and the other squaddie picked up the gravely wounded man's limp body by his arms and legs and carried him out of the JEDDO.

Onin Gesh and Bahadur sat quietly and motionless while the sergeant watched them closely. Moments later the corporal returned. "He's dead. That fucking Albino killed him!"

Instinctively the sergeant turned his twice emitter to Onin Gesh.

Onin Gesh briefly turned and looked him in the eyes, looked at his twice emitter, and then he nonchalantly looked away. "I told you he was dying, why do you look surprised?"

"They were right," said the sergeant, "you don't have a fucking conscience. They should've killed you both."

The other squaddie returned to the JEDDO accompanied by a new Mayhem Marauder. He was also a squaddie.

The sergeant walked over to Onin Gesh and placed the barrel of his twice emitter against his temple.

The corporal walked over to Bahadur aiming his twice emitter and covered him as well.

"Undo their leg restraints," said the sergeant to the two squaddies. "Any sudden moves and one of you dies."

The squaddies both loosened the leg shackles of Bahadur and Onin Gesh and quickly stepped away.

"Stand...both of you!" said the sergeant.

Onin Gesh and Bahadur did as they were told.

'When I give you the word," said the sergeant, "you're going to walk out of this JEDDO and toward the back entrance of this Grand Amphitheater. Anything other than a direct route to that red door where that squaddie is standing gets you emitted. Walk!"

The first to step out of the JEDDO was Bahadur. As he did so, he paused for a moment realizing that it had been two years since he had seen the blue sky, green grass, trees, or smelled fresh air.

The corporal gave him a slight nudge with his twice emitter. "Keep moving, you."

Slightly annoyed, Bahadur continued to walk. "Gesh is going to need goggles, it's too bright out here for him."

"He ain't got far to go," said the corporal, "he'll be alright."

As Onin Gesh emerged from the JEDDO, he immediately lowered his head and clamped his eyes shut. His body almost collapsed from the intensity of the sun burrowing into his head through his eyes.

"Grab him," said the sergeant.

The two squaddies each grabbed an arm and assisted Onin Gesh all the way to the door as the sergeant kept his twice emitter pointed at him.

From the brightness of the morning sun they stepped into the relative darkness of the inside of the building. No longer feeling the glare of the sun, Onin Gesh opened his eyes to see General Tolliver and several other high-ranking Mayhem Marauders standing before him.

"Put these on him," said the captain from the Hidden Bastille as he handed a pair of dark goggles to the sergeant.

It became apparent to Onin Gesh at that moment that they wanted him to be exposed to the sun as he walked to the building. He had already killed one of their men and they didn't want to give him an opportunity to make an example of another one.

Bahadur was the biggest man in the room. His herculean physique drew a lot of attention from the Mayhem Marauders. As if it somehow made them safer, they now had three men surrounding him. More than likely their primary objective was to keep both men away from General Tolliver.

"Your actions this morning completely justify your confinement, Onin Gesh," said General Tolliver. "That was a good young man you killed."

"Not good enough," replied Onin Gesh unapologetically. He was able to focus on General Tolliver now that he was wearing goggles.

General Tolliver stared back at him. *This man is pure evil.* "Very well then. There is an important ceremony today. For a very brief period of time you will both be unshackled and in front of thousands of people. I am sure the temptation for you to act out will be irresistible. I assure you that that would be a grave error on your behalf. These men are under orders to kill you if you act out."

"There are no such orders," said Bahadur in a matter of fact tone, "but we will participate in this charade. A battle lost does not a war end."

General Tolliver simply stared at Bahadur unable to formulate a believable retort as quickly as he desired. Frustrated, he walked away leaving Onin Gesh and Bahadur with the Mayhem Marauders.

At that point the captain took over. "Get them into the holding cell now."

Onin Gesh and Bahadur were whisked away by six Mayhem Marauders and led into a nearby holding cell... together. Save for two very comfortable chairs, the cell was nearly empty. It was rudimentary at best having only a water fountain and an open toilet. Two squaddies posted outside of the cell. The other Mayhem Marauders left. As he was summoned to the cell door, Bahadur approached and turned his back to the door placing his shackled hands into the waist high slot. His hands were freed by the squaddie. Onin Gesh stepped to the door and had his hands freed as well. Then slot was closed. Confident that they could not get out, the squaddies turned their backs to Onin Gesh and Bahadur while they talked to one another.

Bahadur took that opportunity to get close to Onin Gesh. "I think I know what they are doing, Gesh. All we need to do, when the time is right, is provoke them to shock us. An attempt to escape would not be wise at this time."

"How will I know when?" he asked.

"There's no need to be covert at this point," said Bahadur. "I'll just say go and you do what comes natural. They're scared to death. They'll shock us both. From there we can count the hours until our freedom. I guarantee it."

"Done," said Onin Gesh.

Bahadur ran as fast as he could and kicked the cell door. "Hey!"

Startled, both squaddies immediately turned around bringing their twice emitters to the ready.

"Don't get comfortable, that's disrespectful," said Bahadur as he walked away from the door and sat in the comfortable chair. He leaned back and closed his eyes.

Onin Gesh sat down and he did the same.

The squaddies would not take their eyes off them again.

Inside the auditorium of the Grand Amphitheater the staff worked at a feverish pace to finalize things in preparation for the event. The stage on which the dais would be was wide and deep and had highly glossed hardwood flooring. The backdrop was a wall of long blue curtains. The stage opened to a semicircular seating arrangement. Immediately in front of the stage was twenty rows of floor seating. All the seating behind the floor gradually rose in elevation. Each elevation consisted of five rows. A second-floor balcony hung over the last ten rows all the way around. The fabric on the seats and backs of the plush chairs matched perfectly the color of the curtains on the stage. The maximum capacity of the building was three thousand people. General Tolliver stood in the center of the stage overlooking the progress as the staff worked. Behind him on stage were six empty chairs. From time to time he would check his time piece to make sure that they were on schedule.

Finally, the event organizer approached him from the floor. "Everything is ready, sir. We can bring them in whenever you're ready."

"Good," said General Tolliver, "open the doors."

"Right away," said the event organizer as she turned and gave the order to her assistants.

General Tolliver walked out of the auditorium and headed backstage to the lounge where the dignitaries were waiting. In the lounge were Chancellor Aldrich, Vice Chancellor Theris Lamont, Councilman Judas Benedict, General Branimir, and Nastasia Rodmanovic. Chancellor Aldrich was the only one standing as they all casually conversed among themselves while they enjoyed refreshments.

"We are filling the auditorium now," said General Tolliver when he walked into the room.

"Very good," said Chancellor Aldrich as he looked up from his watch pleased that they were on schedule. "Anything else to report?"

"No, sir. Nothing at all." General Tolliver made his way over to General Branimir who happened to be sitting alone. "Gesh has killed this morning," he whispered to him as he sat down beside him.

"Killed who?" asked General Branimir matching General Tolliver's whisper.

"A squaddie. He was a nobody. It only took him ten seconds, Branimir. Ten seconds!"

"Don't you think we should tell the Chancellor, Tolliver?"

"No need. We won't let either of them get close enough to harm anyone else. They'll die first." General Tolliver received a message on his EPIC. "We're at five percent capacity already," he announced as he looked up.

"Very good," said Chancellor Aldrich as he continued his conversation with Nastasia Rodmanovic.

Theris Lamont conversed with Judas Benedict in an opposite corner of the room. Given what he had previously been told about Judas, Theris wanted to be alone. Judas, however, had sought his company. Theris did not want to raise any suspicion by acting strange in any way. He paused as he received an incoming message on his EPIC. The message was from Ean. *It's true* the message read. Theris's face instantly became flush. As much as he tried, it was hard for him to hide the turmoil that he was feeling. "Excuse me, Councilman Benedict," he said as he got up from his seat, "I have to use the head. I will return shortly."

"Hurry back," replied Judas, "you're the only one I can trust in here."

Interesting choice of words Theris thought to himself as he got up to leave the room.

"Don't get lost out there, Vice Chancellor," said Chancellor Aldrich, "I don't want to have to look for anyone when it's time for us to make our grand entrance."

Theris paused at the door. *Should I tell him now? No, now is not the time.* "I'm not going far, nature calls." As he exited the waiting room he felt the need to get some fresh air. As he walked toward the back door he saw the two squaddies standing up ahead of him and to his right. They were still watching Onin Gesh and Bahadur. *I wonder what it is they're so interested in over there.* Everything else seemed to fade away as he started walking toward them.

"I'll have to ask you to stop right there, Vice Chancellor," said the captain who had suddenly stepped into his path. "I'm sorry, sir, but no one is allowed beyond this point until the ceremony is over. I do apologize."

Why would that be? "Yes of course. I understand," said Theris. "I'll just make my way to the head. Thank you, Captain." Theris found his way to the backstage bathroom. It was empty. He couldn't decide whether to contact Ean for details on what he had uncovered or to wait until later to talk to him. He trusted Ean completely and had no doubt that what he told him was true. Judas Benedict was a traitor. *Pull yourself together, Standing Wolf, Comanche are strong.* He always thought of himself as an American first. He had taken on the name of Theris Lamont sometime after he committed to being a Neutralian. He also wished to conceal the true gravity of what his name represented on his home world. He was once a feared warrior. After briefly looking at himself in the mirror, he left the bathroom and went back into the waiting room to join the others.

"We are now at fifty percent capacity," said General Tolliver.

Chancellor Aldrich nodded. "Now is the time, Nastasia. Make the notification."

"Right away, Chancellor," she replied before leaving the room and calling Director Rand of the CA in the city of Sherrod. Their plan was to broadcast the convention live to every VC in the solar system since a great deal of interest had been generated from the moment of its inception. She successfully made her contact and came back into the waiting room. "Everything is online, Chancellor," she said as she walked back into the room. "Sapien is waiting on us."

"Good," he replied. "We will make our entrance at noon as scheduled. Continue to keep me updated on the status of the crowd, General Tolliver."

"I will, Chancellor," General Tolliver replied as he paused his chat with General Branimir to reply.

Chapter 17: Unconventional

Location: Central City, District County, Rights Province, Planet Neutralia
The Grand Amphitheater, 1100 hours

On every world of the Sapien Solar System, they gathered around their VC tables to view the ceremony and to bear witness to a historic event. On Alkebulan, America, Akkadian Arabu, India, Asia, Evropa, Neutralia, on Hades, and on Albin they all waited with great anticipation. A better life was promised for all, and they all looked forward to it. All eyes were on the Grand Amphitheater of Central City. The signal sent by the CA was strong and the three-dimensional images of the stage and auditorium were clear. The crowd inside the amphitheater was restless but remained orderly. The nervous energy, the rumble of conversation, and the chatter made the room electric. In attendance were Sapiens from all walks of life from warriors of the legendary One Forty-Four of Alkebulan, to the dairy farmers of Evropa, to the quasi cosmopolitan citizens of Neutralia; they were all present. The One Forty-Four were the only warrior faction from any planet represented. Their name was derived from the fact that there were only one hundred forty-four members at any given time. To join, a yearlong trial was required with the candidates starting at the age of twenty-four and being at least six feet tall. Twelve Alkebulan countries would send five of their best warriors to compete for twelve available slots. One warrior was selected from each country at the end of the process. At the age of twenty-five they were neophyte warriors. The elders were thirty-six years of age. Upon retirement from the One Forty-Four the elders would return to the Alkebulan proving grounds to train the candidates. From the ages of twenty-five to thirty-six, every age was represented by twelve warriors hailing from twelve different Alkebulan countries. The top warrior from each age group was tabbed an elite. He was recognized by his age followed by the word *elite*. The primary mission of the One Forty-Four was preservation of the Alkebulan way of life. They were also fierce defenders of its borders and were renowned for being the most lethal and prolific fighting force in the Sapien Solar System.

The venue quickly rose above one hundred percent capacity. Sapiens who weren't there in time to find a seat stood shoulder to shoulder along the back wall, down the side walls, and in the aisles. The diversity of the solar system was on full display as it was reflected by the audience. Uninfluenced by worlds other than their own, the natives of each planet dressed in accordance with the traditions of their worlds and their respective cultures. Albino men and women in dark gray oversized parkas brought a palatable contrast to the colorful attire of the people from Alkebulan, India, and Asia. For the most part, Sapiens sat with people from their home world which made them easily identifiable by culture and ethnic background. Never before had one singular event, not entertainment related, drawn so many Sapiens together. However, the future of the solar system was an important thing and the attendance reflected that.

Location: City of Sherrod, Leanna Province, Southern Continent, Neutralia

Walking through the downtown streets of the city of Sherrod, Mulati found it to be eerily calm. The activity on the streets juxtaposed to what he had just experienced at the airfield was strange to say the least. The few people who were still on the streets paid close attention to their EPICs. Curious, he stopped at a bakery to ask what was going on. As he walked in the first thing he noticed was the delightful smell of French pastries in the air. The second thing he noticed was that there was no one behind the service counter. Then he saw everyone in a corner of the bakery surrounding a VC. As he walked over and looked for himself he saw the clearly projected three-dimensional image of the inside of the Grand Amphitheater rising from the table. *Oh, that's what it is...*

that convention. I had no idea it had generated this much interest. I wonder if it's like this everywhere.

"This is very exciting isn't it?" asked, Laurent, the short and overweight pastry shop owner who happened to be standing beside Mulati. "I heard that after today we'll be able to go wherever we want to go in this solar system. I can set up shop on every planet! Can you imagine that?"

"Yea, I guess that's a good thing," Mulati replied as it suddenly dawned on him that open borders would be a threat to his livelihood. "Excuse me, sir," he said as he stepped away from the VC and walked out of the bakery and onto the street. He pulled his EPIC from his pocket. "Contact Sampa."

As her image appeared she confirmed that she was as confused about everything as he was. "Have you seen what's going on out here?" she asked. "The whole city has stopped for this convention."

"That's what I was calling you about," he replied. "This might be something we need to pay closer attention to, Sam. I'm going back to the Whisper to watch it there."

"That's not a bad idea, Mulati, I think I'll join you," she replied. "This seems pretty important."

"Right. End transmission." He got into the nearest JEDDO and headed back to the airfield.

Minutes later Mulati stood near the rear of the Whisper as Francois lowered the massive ramp to grant him entrance into the cargo bay. What had been a bustling tarmac earlier that morning was now relatively calm and empty, further serving notice that what was about to occur was of great importance.

"You're back early," said Francois from inside the cargo bay. "Don't trust me?" he asked with a chuckle and a hint of playful sarcasm.

Mulati smiled. "It's not that. Sam's on her way back too. We're going to watch the convention from here." He walked up the ramp and into the cargo bay. "Leave it open for Sam."

No sooner than those words were spoken, Sampa appeared at the foot of the ramp and ran up into the cargo bay. "Close her up and let's get to the bridge," she said. "I don't wanna miss anything."

"Right away," said Francois as he got busy closing the ramp.

They left the cargo bay and rode the elevator to the upper deck together. Immediately they walked into the communication room.

"Entertainment mode: Sapien convention," enunciated Mulati.

The VC powered on and the three-dimensional projection of the Grand Amphitheater appeared before them. The stage was still empty but Mulati, Sampa, and Francois all sat and waited for the event to begin.

At Bell Square, in the entertainment district of the city of Sherrod, Bjorn and Corto stood just beyond the perimeter of a large crowd as they all circled around and focused on an outdoor VC that was positioned between a few prominent buildings. They watched not because they were interested, but because it drew the interest of such a vast array of people that they did not want to miss out on something potentially important. Also, because almost everyone in the city of Sherrod was watching, it left them with no one they could interact socially. The three-dimensional image was projected high above the crowd with great clarity and definition. Unlike the people inside the Grand Amphitheater, the people watching outside in the city of Sherrod were quiet and patient.

"What do you think about this?" asked Bjorn.

"I really don't know," replied Corto. "Hopefully nothing that affects us comes out of this shit. We really ought to get off that ship more and interact with people; everyone seems to know a bit more about what's about to happen than we do."

"That's the fucking truth there," said Bjorn. "Think we should contact Mulati and Sam?"

"No need to bother them right now," said Corto. "We can fill them in if something important happens."

*Location: Westborough, District County, Rights Province, Neutralia
Aboard the Iron Raven*

Still mourning the loss of Igor and seething from their inability to exact revenge on the Whisper, Rokuro Onishi paid close attention to the VC in the communication room of the Iron Raven. By his side were Alexei and Sunday Okonjo. Rokuro Onishi's purpose for watching the event was to gather as much information about Chancellor Aldrich and Vice Chancellor Theris Lamont as possible. They sat in comfortable chairs spaced evenly around the room. The main VC was in the center. For a while no one spoke. The pain was still very evident on Alexei's face as he focused on what was in front of him.

Sunday Okonjo rubbed his chin as he replayed the events surrounding the Whisper's escape in his mind. "If we see that ship again, I will defeat it. Of that I am certain. They apparently used inside information to their advantage. Whether I underestimated them or not, the outcome would likely have been the same."

"Your cockiness made you overzealous," replied Rokuro. "I advised you they were capable warriors. You were only interested in victory. You gave no thought to learning your adversary."

"And I advised you that the air and space are my domain," snapped Sunday Okonjo. "Never have I told you how to wield that sword and, if I'm not mistaken, the half breed survived combat with you. Maybe we both need to learn to respect our opponents a little more. Or maybe he was just better than you!"

"Silence, Okonjo!"

"This is my ship! It is you who should mind his tongue, Rokuro Onishi!" he replied as he sprang from his seat.

"It begins," said Alexei in a slightly elevated but not excited tone of voice.

"We will finish this discussion later," said Rokuro Onishi.

"I look forward to it," replied Sunday Okonjo while slowly sitting.

They stopped their bickering and focused on the VC.

Location: Central City, District County, Rights Province, Neutralia
The Grand Amphitheater, 1200 hours

The entire audience rose to their feet and began to applaud as General Tolliver, General Branimir, and Nastasia Rodmanovic walked onto the stage. Next to make his way to the stage was Judas Benedict. Theris Lamont had lingered behind to discuss an important matter with Chancellor Aldrich. The generals stood in front of both end chairs. General Branimir stood in front of the last chair stage right. Nastasia Rodmanovic stood in front of the chair beside him. Judas Benedict stood in front of the chair next to General Tolliver. Two open seats remained in the center. The applause slowly subsided as they all stood there silently. Another minute passed before Chancellor Aldrich and Vice Chancellor Theris Lamont walked onto the stage. Again, the audience started to applaud. Theris Lamont walked over to the chair beside Judas Benedict. Theris avoided eye contact with Judas which Judas thought was very strange. Chancellor Aldrich walked to the front of the stage with his arms raised in a triumphant fashion. After absorbing the applause for a few moments, he slowly fanned his extended arms to the side with his palms facing downward requesting that everyone be seated. After the council, generals, and Nastasia sat, the crowd sat too. Chancellor Aldrich looked to the left at a stagehand who was just off stage and gave a nod for the stage to be amplified. Everything said on stage from that point on would be heard throughout the amphitheater and on every VC in the solar system. Even the slightest whisper would be heard.

Chancellor Aldrich began to speak. "Fellow Sapiens, greetings!"

Again, the audience roared.

Chancellor Aldrich nodded in approval until the cheers finally ceased. "We have heard your voices. We have seen your needs. We have felt your pain. We know your fears. With great consideration, we have put our minds together for the betterment of our people as a whole. No more will Sapiens be hungry, cold, or afraid. Our intrasolar alliance will bring all homes, neighborhoods, communities, towns, hamlets, cities, counties, provinces, countries, continents, and worlds to a level that meets at least the minimal standards of comfortable life. Our proposed system allows for subsidies for the needy whenever appropriate with a minimal contribution from us all."

The audience groaned.

The elder elite who sat amongst the other eleven elite members of the One Forty-Four voiced his displeasure to his men. "Alkebulans have those assurances already." His men agreed.

Chancellor Aldrich raised his hand and the small rebellion was quelled. "In exchange you will receive safe passage to each world. You will enjoy the protection of a newly formed and capable force intended to keep you safe and to maintain order."

A small percentage of the audience applauded briefly. The One Forty-Four did not.

Chancellor Aldrich scanned the audience momentarily. "Nothing worth having comes without sacrifice," he said in a softer and more measured tone. "The DANs you will pay will be a mere pittance compared to what you will receive in return."

"I have heard enough, Alkebulans don't need more protection," said the elder elite to his men. With a wave of his hand the other eleven members of the One Forty-Four got up to leave. "You would be wise to follow us," said the elder elite to the other audience members who sat close to them as they walked out. No one else moved.

Location: City of Sherrod, Leanna Province, Southern Continent, Neutralia
Airfield aboard the Whisper.

Mulati, Sampa, and Francois listened with great interest to Chancellor Aldrich's speech. They were all quiet as they were not sure what to make of what they were hearing. Suddenly Mulati got up from his chair and walked closer.

"What is it, Mulati?" asked Sampa.

"I'm not sure, but I think that's..." He paused. "Isolate image. Male, far left," he carefully enunciated.

General Branimir's image became enlarged. "That's him!" Mulati continued. "That's the man who got away from us on the island on Evropa."

"Are you sure?" asked Francois.

"I'm beyond sure!" replied Mulati.

Mulati's EPIC signaled an incoming call from Corto. "Receive transmission!"

"Are you seeing this shit?" asked Corto. "That's that fat one-eyed fucker from the island! What's he doing there?"

"I don't know, Corto. Thanks, you just confirmed my suspicion. You two grab Beth and get back here right now!"

"On our way, Boss! End transmission."

As Corto's image faded away, Mulati instantly became concerned that Theris Lamont was in even more trouble than they had previously thought. "Full image," he said in the direction of his VC. The original image then returned. They continued to watch as Chancellor Aldrich continued his speech.

Location: Central City, District County, Rights Province, Neutralia The Grand Amphitheater

Chancellor Aldrich had reached a fever pitch with his speech. "Those who prey on the helpless will be hunted down like the dogs they are! If you do not have a conscience, then you will answer to the conscience of the Intrasolar Alliance!"

Again, the audience roared.

Chancellor Aldrich paused as they took time to quiet down. He continued. "Every ship will be given a serial number which will be kept in a CA database. We will track down and eliminate the pirates that roam the open space between our planets. No longer will they be able to pillage with impunity."

Again, there was loud applause and cheers.

"There will be no twice emitters sold without a name and a face to account for it!" he continued.

The audience again began to rumble and groan with disapproval. Instantly debates about whether or not twice emitters should be logged started between members of the audience. Debates grew to disagreements which turned into arguments. Something that the Chancellor himself considered to be no big deal ended up being a sticking point for the audience. This time they did not quiet down when he raised his hands.

Judas Benedict leaned back and crossed his arms. *Once you have threatened their freedom, they will always fear that you have a thirst for it. I told you so, fool* he thought to himself. His thoughts harkened back to the disagreement about that very subject that he and the Chancellor had in the Council Chambers previously.

"Listen! Please listen to me," said Chancellor Aldrich as he tried to continue over what now was an uproar. He tried and tried to no avail to get the audience to quiet down. Again, he looked to the left and signaled to the stage hand. Seconds later a long line of Mayhem Marauders armed with twice emitters walked onto the amphitheater floor between the stage and the first row of Sapiens. After coming to a synchronized halt, they all executed a left face with their twice emitters at port arms. They were face to face with the audience. A hush came over the crowd. The amphitheater got completely quiet. No one in the Sapien Solar System had ever seen a uniformed army before. None of them knew what to expect. With his confidence restored, Chancellor

Aldrich continued. "For two years we have operated a hidden bastille which we are unveiling today. Right there in Southtown we have housed some of the most notorious killers and thieves ever known to Sapien."

Judas Benedict's mouth fell open. He was shocked. He had no idea. Neither did Theris Lamont. They both looked at one another in disbelief.

Judas leaned to his right and whispered into Theris's ear. "It appears that I am not the only one the Chancellor does not trust. He could have told you at least."

Keeping in mind the power of the amplification device on the stage, Theris did not respond. However, he thought that Judas was right. There was no reason for him not to be informed of the bastille.

As he looked out into the audience, Chancellor Aldrich saw looks of astonishment, fear, and disappointment which was a far cry from the feeling of appreciation he had anticipated. Surely his one last surprise would win them over. "Bring them out!" he commanded with a wave of his arm.

At that moment, Onin Gesh and Bahadur were brought out onto the stage. Both men were unrestrained.

"I present to you the Persian assassin, Bad Bahadur, and the pale terror of Albin, Onin Gesh. Together they are responsible for the deaths of over one hundred fifty Sapiens. They have been locked away for more than two years, and in that time, they haven't killed anyone. This is the kind of safety we will provide for you!"

General Tolliver cringed as those words were spoken knowing that just that morning Onin Gesh had killed again. A collective gasp could be heard from the crowd as many of them stood to get a better look at the prisoners.

Location: Westborough, District County, Rights Province, Neutralia Aboard the Iron Raven

Rokuro Onishi, Alexei, and Sunday Okonjo all sprang from their seats.

"How can this be? Bahadur's alive!" yelled Rokuro Onishi. "Prepare our things, we are going to get him now! Send out a mass transmission, we need all hands to District County. Prepare for war. No Marauder will be safe."

Full of rage, motivated by revenge, and eager to rescue Bahadur, the powerful DOD members quickly left their communication room. The convention continued to play on the unattended VC as the room emptied.

Location: City of Sherrod, Leanna Province, Southern Continent, Neutralia
Airfield aboard the Whisper.

Francois shared Rokuro Onishi's surprise. "Oh shit, there's going to be trouble now!"

"Why? Who are they?" asked Sampa.

"The Persian is DOD, Rokuro Onishi's best friend and right-hand man. We thought he was dead all this time. This is not good. There is going to be trouble in District County. They have no idea what they are in for. He will not stop until they have Bahadur and those men are all dead."

Location: Central City, District County, Rights Province, Neutralia
The Grand Amphitheater

"This is the last time you will see either of these monsters not in captivity," continued Chancellor Aldrich.

"Release them now!" a voice from the audience could be heard saying.

"No Sapien should be caged like an animal!" said another.

With each outburst the outraged crowd voiced their support for the notorious captives.

Bahadur had heard enough and felt the time was right. "Now, Gesh!" he said as he braced himself for the high voltage that would soon be surging through his body.

Hearing Bahadur say those words made Chancellor Aldrich look directly at him. *Has he no fear of us?* he thought as he stared at the Persian.

General Tolliver immediately stood up and said, "Oh no!"

By that time, it was too late. Onin Gesh had taken a running start and leaped from the stage. All eyes were fixed on him as he gracefully glided through the air with his right knee forward. His arms were flared out to the side like a landing eagle accepting the wind into its wings. His fingers were spread like talons, putting his long dark nails on full display. He completely cleared the row of Mayhem Marauders who were standing on the floor. He landed between the uniformed men and the front row of Sapiens. As he hit the ground he kept running toward the people, bent on destruction. The red irises of his eyes were like fire as he charged.

"What are you waiting for? Shock his ass!" yelled General Tolliver.

Klaus emerged from backstage and pressed his troll. The audience, still standing, gasped as Onin Gesh's stiff body fell to the ground and continued to slide from the momentum he had gained while running. Bahadur collapsed to the ground in agonizing pain. Both men were piled on by multiple Mayhem Marauders. They kicked, punched, and beat both men viciously in full view of the now disgusted Sapiens. Eventually they placed them back into restraints. Pandemonium ensued. The now raucous crowd became violent and aggressive. Instead of being happy that Onin Gesh and Bahadur were no longer a threat to them, they rushed the stage and attempted to free them both. Startled Mayhem Marauders circled around Bahadur and Onin Gesh in an attempt to maintain control of their prisoners. What was intended to be a coming out party for the Mayhem Marauders was now a full-on fight for their lives.

General Tolliver took control and started giving orders. "Get them to the JEDDO!" he commanded. They extracted Onin Gesh and Bahadur without either of them putting up a fight. The damage was done. Bahadur had achieved his objective. General Tolliver had everyone who was on stage moved backstage as several Mayhem Marauders provided security. While General Tolliver moved the dignitaries to the waiting room, Onin Gesh and Bahadur were rushed into the JEDDO parked at the rear of the building.

"Stay calm, Gesh, now is not the time to fight," said Bahadur as they were both being strapped to their seats.

As soon as they were secure in their seats, the JEDDO started to move and headed back to the Hidden Bastille. On board with them were Klaus and three squaddies armed with twice emitters.

Overwhelmed, the Mayhem Marauders who were left inside the amphitheater started emitting overly aggressive audience members who continued to attempt to get past them to free the brutalized captives. The entire first row dripped with blood as the vanquished bodies fell by the dozens. All of the Sapien Solar System bore witness to the slaughter of unarmed men and women. It wasn't long before the Mayhem Marauders resorted to that which they were known best, unbridled barbarism. Not only did they kill the violent audience members, but they also went after and killed innocent people who were attempting to flee. A mass exodus from the Grand Amphitheater was underway. Soon more than three thousand angry people filled the streets of Central City.

Location: City of Sherrod, Leanna Province, Southern Continent, Neutralia
Bell Square

The citizens watched in stunned disbelief as the slaughter unfolded before their eyes. No one walked away from the circle surrounding the outdoor VC. They were all silent. Until that very moment,

Neutralia was the one planet on which they all felt safe. With one failed event that completely changed. It was as if the realization that they were all vulnerable to the whims of an unhinged council had completely paralyzed them.

Bjorn and Corto had left Bell Square the moment Mulati summoned them back to the Whisper. As they exited their JEDDO with Beth, they quickly made their way through the building and to the Whisper which was waiting for them on the airfield. Because they were in transit back to the ship, they were unaware of the massacre that had taken place at the Grand Amphitheater in Central City. The ramp to the cargo bay was closed.

Bjorn pulled out his EPIC to call the ship. "Contact Whisper," he said.

Instantly, Mulati's image appeared. "Francois is on his way down to let you in. End transmission."

"Something must've happened," said Bjorn. "He wasn't fooling around just now."

"Hopefully everything is ok," said a clearly worried Beth.

They all waited as they heard the ramp unlock.

As it lowered Francois stood dead center of the entrance to the cargo bay. As soon as the ramp was flush with the ground he waved them in. "Let's go! There's no time to waste!"

"That bad, huh?" said Corto as they all hurried up the ramp.

"What's going on?" asked Bjorn as they all stepped inside.

"The Marauders, that's what," replied Francois.

Beth froze. The memories of what they had done to her family immediately returned. "What have those monsters done now?" she asked.

"Still doing," Francois replied. "The convention went bad," he said as they raised the ramp. "They brought out a DOD lieutenant named Bahadur and a crazy Albino and it all went downhill from there."

"Did they do something to them?" she asked.

Francois stopped what he was doing and looked Beth in her eyes. "Beth, innocent people are being slaughtered by the hundreds as we speak."

Unable to speak, she placed her hand over her mouth. Her eyes began to water.

"She has bad history with those assholes," said Bjorn. "Come on, everybody. Let's get up there to the upper deck. You gonna be alright, Beth?"

"Don't worry about me, Bjorn," she replied. "I'll be just fine. Let's go."

As they walked into the communication room they could feel the tension as Sampa and Mulati stood watching the Mayhem Marauders wreak havoc on the people inside the amphitheater. As if she were afraid to look, Beth peeked at the VC from behind Bjorn. Only her head was visible as she rested her hand on his massive bicep.

"You don't have to look at this, Beth," said Mulati.

"And I don't think I will," she said while wiping away tears as she turned to leave the communication room.

They all thought of going with her, but no one could take their eyes off what was taking place in the amphitheater. Suddenly the image disappeared. Right in the middle of all the chaos, the signal was interrupted. For a moment no one spoke as they all stood there processing what they had just witnessed. Mulati walked out of the communication room and onto the bridge. As he sat in his captain's seat he started powering up the Whisper. Sampa joined him shortly thereafter. Like Mulati, she just got to work without saying a word. Next to enter the bridge was Francois. He sat behind them and strapped himself into one of the reserve seats without speaking. Bjorn and Corto were the last to leave the communication room. They walked out of the bridge headed for the main deck.

"Central City?" asked Sampa.

"Yes," replied Mulati.

Location: Central City, District County, Rights Province, Neutralia
The Grand Amphitheater of Central City

Having barely gotten out of the building alive, the three council members, Nastasia, and the two generals frantically strapped themselves into their seats in a JEDDO as it was quickly driven away by Friedrich.

"I hope you're proud of yourself, Steven!" said Judas angrily.

"Now is not the time, Judas," replied Chancellor Aldrich matching his tone.

"Then when is a good time? Vice Chancellor Lamont and I would like to know why you thought it was a good idea to keep this bastille away from us."

"Neither of you needed to know. It was of the utmost importance that it remained a secret," replied the Chancellor.

"I think you feared that we would argue against it," said Judas. "You knew that we wouldn't easily accept this. Your blind ambition kept you from seeing that the people would not either."

Chancellor Aldrich ignored Judas's last remark.

"Where are we being taken?" asked Theris Lamont. "I don't feel that it's safe to go to our personal dwellings right now."

"We're going to the Hidden Bastille in Southtown, we'll be safe there," answered Chancellor Aldrich. "That facility is impenetrable. I have personally toured it."

"I bet you have," said Judas. "And you? Have you been there, Nasty?"

Nastasia Rodmanovic glared at Judas but held her tongue.

"That's enough from you, Councilman Benedict!" said Chancellor Aldrich. "Any more out of you and you'll find yourself amongst those angry Sapiens!"

"At least I know what they stand for," said Judas. "I rather like those odds!"

They continued to bicker as the JEDDO left the rear of the facility and traveled through the streets immediately surrounding the Grand Amphitheater. Their JEDDO was pelted by large stones and anything else the people could find to throw at them.

Inside the Grand Amphitheater the Mayhem Marauders continued to push the panicked crowd through the front lobby of the building and onto the street.

The captain, being the high-ranking Mayhem Marauder left in the building, led the way as he made the decision to continue the onslaught. "Follow me, we'll teach them to attack us!" he yelled as he pushed open the massive wooden door that led to the outside with his left hand. Looking back, he waved the other Mayhem Marauders forward. But as he looked forward and attempted to exit, he saw a silver blur flash downward. It was accompanied by the sound of air being sliced. He felt a jolt of pain. He looked down through spraying blood and saw his own arm on the floor.

Rokuro Onishi stepped through the door from the outside with both hands on his sword. His next swing removed the captain's head from his body. As the headless body fell backward to the floor, the DOD entered the building in droves.

"Kill everything wearing a uniform!" said Rokuro Onishi.

The stunned Mayhem Marauders retreated into the amphitheater. As a few stood and fought, and lost their lives, the others stumbled over one another trying their best to get backstage so that they could escape through the back door. One hundred DOD members filed through the doors and into the amphitheater. Alexei stayed by Rokuro Onishi's side as they both killed any Mayhem Marauder who made the mistake of getting in their way. Alexei used his twice emitter with great precision. Before long, the floor of the amphitheater was littered with freshly killed bodies. The blood of Mayhem Marauders mixed with the blood of the Sapiens they had destroyed only minutes earlier.

Twenty Mayhem Marauders, the lieutenant and nineteen squaddies, made it to the back door. As the first squaddie opened the door to exit he was immediately emitted. The fluorescent glow of the green tracer illuminated the doorway. After the second projectile entered his chest cavity his blood and internal organs exploded backward from his body. He collapsed. The door slammed shut. The others knew then that they had nowhere to go. As they turned to go back toward the amphitheater they encountered Rokuro Onishi, Alexei, and ten more DOD warriors. Rokuro Onishi already had his sword unsheathed.

"One of you will live," said Rokuro Onishi, "and that is he who will show us this Hidden Bastille. You have ten seconds to speak."

"My men will not tell, you'll have to kill us all," said the lieutenant as he stepped forward immediately.

Rokuro took a huge step forward with his left foot leaving his right foot behind creating a wide combat stance. With both hands he drew his sword back to his right side at shoulder level in an exaggerated fashion. His blade was pointed toward the lieutenant's chest. With one quick and powerful thrust he drove it forward and through his heart. The lieutenant slid forward on Rokuro's sword with his mouth and eyes wide open. He tried but could not speak. Slowly Rokuro lowered his own center of gravity so that the lieutenant would continue to fall forward onto his blade. As Rokuro got down to his knee the lieutenant's chest finally reached the guard of his sword. Grabbing his shoulder and pulling him closer, Rokuro whispered into his ear, "Death embraces you." He then stood up, and as he did so, the lieutenant's body slid from his sword and crumpled to the ground. He breathed his last breath there. "Five, four, three, two, one," continued Rokuro as the puddle of blood under the lieutenant's body grew quickly and evenly.

"I can show you where it is!" said one of the squaddies.

"What is your name, Marauder?" asked Rokuro.

"My name is Brian," he replied with his head down.

"Kill the others," ordered Rokuro, "but save one."

The DOD proceeded to massacre seventeen of the squaddies with their swords, hatchets, and twice emitters as Rokuro Onishi watched. Only Brian and one other squaddie remained. Both men stood almost motionless. They were afraid.

"Do you believe in symbolic gestures, Brian?" asked Rokuro.

"N-No, I d-don't," he answered as he trembled with fear.

"Neither do I," said Rokuro as he handed him a twice emitter. "Kill that other Marauder."

Brian reluctantly accepted the twice emitter from Rokuro. He raised it, aimed it, and fired the first projectile. The other squaddie became paralyzed. Nothing on his body moved except the single tear that rolled down the side of his face. Brian lowered the weapon to his side and turned his back toward the other Mayhem Marauder. He dropped his head and he slowly squeezed the trigger a second time. The concussion of the blast made Brian jump. The sound of the body hitting the ground made him sorrowful, angry, and ashamed of what he had done.

Rokuro Onishi took the twice emitter from him and pointed toward the door. "Now show us the way!"

Chapter 18: The Reckoning

Location: Southtown, District County, Rights Province, Neutralia
The Hidden Bastille

For the first time since his arrival at the hidden bastille two years prior, Bahadur felt completely at ease. He stared at the ceiling as he laid supine on his bed. His hands were behind his head and his ankles were crossed. Just beyond the door of his dwelling, Klaus paced back and forth between his cell and that of Onin Gesh's. Despite the relatively cool temperature of the facility, Klaus perspired profusely. His knuckles were white from the force with which he gripped his troll. He had previously used it to control both men. What was once a device he used for torturing them, and for his own personal amusement, was now a tool that he felt was vital to his own personal safety and survival. With him were two squaddies, one assigned to each cell, who stood close by.

Bahadur had reminded Klaus repeatedly on the ride from the amphitheater to the bastille that his days were numbered. Until that point, those threats had never seemed real to Klaus. However, something in the certainty with which Bahadur spoke those words on this day unnerved him. Even more unsettling to Klaus was the utter lack of concern now displayed by Bahadur as he rested.

Onin Gesh stood in his usual spot as he watched Klaus's every move. That Klaus was behaving differently did not go unnoticed by Onin Gesh. He had seen that type of fear before. "No matter how many men you put between us, I will watch you breathe your last breath," he said. "That I can promise you."

The low register and gravelly texture of Onin Gesh's cold voice felt like long fingernails slowly scraping the hard surface of Klaus's soul. He dared not use the troll for punitive measures at this point. Only now was the malice of his previous actions toward both men viewed, by him, with the clarity it required. Fear had consumed him. Klaus looked into Onin Gesh's cell but could find neither the words nor the desire to respond. Klaus's silence spoke volumes.

Onin Gesh turned around, walked away, and disappeared into the blackness of his cell's depth. He sat on the edge of his bed. From the darkness, his wicked voice emerged. "I'm going to enjoy killing you, Klaus."

He said the words slightly above a whisper, but Klaus heard them clearly. As he backed away from the cells his face turned white. "My EPIC is open," he uttered nervously to the squaddies who stood guard outside the cells. "If anything changes, alert me. I'll be in the control room." As he turned to walk away, he plunged both of his hands deep into his pockets in an attempt to hide the fact that he was shaking from fear. He was unsuccessful. Even his elbows and shoulders shook violently as he left.

In the garage of the bastille, the JEDDO carrying the supreme council came to a sudden stop. As the large garage door closed behind them, all the occupants, except for the driver, Friedrich, exited the vehicle.

"This way. Everyone, please follow me," said General Tolliver as he walked toward one of the many doors which led into the facility from the garage. This particular door was guarded by two squaddies who were armed with twice emitters. Behind the door was a long, well-lit hallway with a single door at the other end. The white walls and cement floor leading to the dark door seemed to highlight it as they all approached. The hallway was long and there were no windows or other exits anywhere in it. When they reached the door, General Tolliver punched in a four-digit code on the keypad which was located just to the left of it and about half way up. The door slowly opened inward to a large room filled with plush couches, two VC tables, and many more items suitable for a long comfortable stay. "Make yourselves comfortable," said General Tolliver as he walked over to one of the VC tables. "Communication mode: contact Captain, Grand Amphitheater," he said. There was no response. *Hmm, that's interesting* he thought as he waited an extra second for the VC to answer. "Communication mode: contact lieutenant, Grand Amphitheater," he carefully enunciated. Again, there was no response. "Function check," he said sounding frustrated as he paid close attention to the VC.

"Visual Console is fully operational," said the automated voice that came out of the VC.

"What's going on?" asked Chancellor Aldrich.

"I don't know," replied a concerned General Tolliver. "I can't seem to reach my leaders. I need an update from the Grand Amphitheater."

"Then expand your call criteria, surely someone is available," barked Chancellor Aldrich.

For a moment General Tolliver thought and then modified his call. "Communication mode: all Mayhem Marauders, Grand Amphitheater."

The image of a squaddie appeared above the surface of the VC. Clearly shaken, the man began to speak. "I need help, sir! We've been decimated. The DOD are here!"

"Where are the captain and lieutenant?" asked General Tolliver.

"The captain is dead. I have not seen the lieutenant. I don't know if anyone else besides myself is even alive at this point," he said.

The room fell silent.

The frightened Mayhem Marauder pleaded, "Please, sir, it won't be long before they find..."

"End transmission! Block most recent correspondent," said General Tolliver as he abruptly discontinued the conversation. "We had two hundred men in that amphitheater; that was one percent of our forces wiped out in minutes. Fortunately, he is not one who knows where this facility is located. They will torture him in vain."

"How many troops do you have at this facility?" asked Chancellor Aldrich.

"There are two hundred here," replied General Tolliver. "That includes everyone from squaddies to food service personnel. We are well fortified."

Holding her EPIC up and at an odd angle, Nastasia Rodmanovic spoke. "Why is it that I cannot transmit from this place?" she asked.

"Both of these VC tables are hardwired to a satellite dish that sits outside of this facility," answered General Tolliver. "This room is secure by design. Any transmissions made from inside it have to be communicated in the open from one of these two VC tables."

Nastasia rolled her eyes as she put away her EPIC. She walked over to the nearest couch, flopped down on it, and immediately crossed her legs and folded her arms. Her pouty face showed the frustration she felt.

Chancellor Aldrich stepped up to the VC on which General Tolliver had been communicating. "Surveillance mode: Grand Amphitheater of Central City."

Immediately the image of the inside of the amphitheater appeared. They all watched as five DOD warriors, who stayed behind, systematically canvassed the floor of the amphitheater for survivors. They also watched as the lone surviving Mayhem Marauder, with whom General Tolliver had just communicated, was discovered hiding in a closet. "End transmission," said Chancellor Aldrich after they watched the DOD pull a sharp machete through his neck beheading him completely. "Savages," he said scornfully as the image faded and he turned to walk away.

Location: Above the Southern Continent of Neutralia
Aboard the Whisper

As the Whisper ascended through the atmosphere over the southern continent of Neutralia, Mulati and Sampa focused on plotting their course to Central City. Sampa suddenly removed her hands from the control panel and took off her headset. She leaned back in her chair. *That has to be it, Director Rand is in cahoots with the Mayhem Marauders. That means they could control everything.* "Mulati, I think there's a bigger problem," she said suddenly.

"Bigger than what we just saw?" he asked as he looked over at Sampa. Immediately he saw that she was both in deep thought and concerned. Something was seriously wrong. "What is it, Sam?"

"Mulati, remember how I said that it was odd that the island on Evropa wasn't on the map?"

"Yea, you said that someone had to have purposely omitted it."

"Who do you think, of all people, would have wanted that feed to the Grand Amphitheater to get interrupted?"

"My best guess would be either the council or the Marauders, Sam."

"Or both!" she replied sharply. "The only one who has the power to make that happen that quickly is the leader of CA, Director Rand. They had to have communicated directly with him to do that."

"I'm not seeing the connection, Sam."

"Mulati, if they have that direct link to him and they also work directly with that general you saw torturing Lihua, then it's not a stretch that they're all working together. Director Rand intentionally hid that island for them!"

Suddenly it dawned on Mulati what they were up against. *That makes them more powerful than I thought. They can monitor anyone at any time.* "What are you thinking about doing, Sam?"

"I need to go back, Mulati. I can go alone; I don't need anyone else."

"Are you sure? I can send Bjorn, Corto, or Francois with you."

"You'll need all of them in Central City. I'll be fine in the city of Sherrod."

"What are you going there to do, Sam?"

"There are some CATs I trust. We've always had a contingency plan in place to prevent certain individuals from using our technology for nefarious reasons. This is that time. They need to know what we know, and I have to tell them in person."

"Do you think they're monitoring us already?"

"At this point it's difficult to tell what they are doing. It's better for us to be cautious. I'm going to take Shadow One and head back. I'll keep my EPIC open, but keep it to emergency transmissions only, and keep it cryptic," she said as she got up from her seat. She quickly crossed both of her fists over her chest. After Mulati returned the Whisper salute, she turned to leave the bridge. On her way out, she briefly touched Francois' shoulder. In return he tapped the back of her hand as she walked by.

After briefly meeting with Bjorn, Corto, and Beth to tell them her plan, Sampa made her way to the portside gunner's pod and strapped herself in. She remained focused as she prepared the pod for shadow mode. She also programmed the exact coordinates of her destination into the mapping system. The overhead entrance was then sealed as the opening quickly closed creating a hard roof above her. "I'm prepared to detach," she said as she communicated directly to Mulati through her headset."

"Unlocking now," he replied as he initiated the sequence to release the shadow fighter.

The clamp securing the top of the shadow fighter to the Whisper slowly opened as the pod was simultaneously demagnetized. The pod began to free fall away from the Whisper and immediately the wings and horizontal stabilizers extended from both sides. A small vertical stabilizer also popped up at the rear.

"Shadow One away," said Sampa as her rear thruster engaged.

"I copy, Sam. Listen to your conscience."

"I will, Mulati, and let yours lead the way."

"You're up, Francois," said Mulati as he looked over his right shoulder to the seat behind him.

Francois moved to the co-pilot's seat normally occupied by Sampa.

"The coordinates are already set, we're going to one cel on my mark," said Mulati.

"I copy," said Francois as he positioned his hands on the control panel and waited for Mulati to give the word.

"Engage!" said Mulati.

"Engaging," said Francois as he pushed the levers into position propelling the Whisper to one third the speed of light and toward Central City.

As Sampa sped toward the city of Sherrod she tried to focus on her task and not worry about what the rest of the crew were about to encounter in Central City. *They can handle themselves, Sampa. They know what they're doing* she thought to herself. With the darkness of space behind her she realized that she was minutes away from her destination. She made it back to the airfield a short time later. As she got close to the ground, she initiated the landing sequence. Three wheels, one at the front and two in the rear, lowered from the shadow fighter. Ground thrusters engaged from the bottom as the craft slowly descended straight down. She landed her shadow fighter with relative ease. Sampa taxied the shadow fighter to a spot that would easily accommodate the six-thousand-pound vessel. Carrying only her EPIC and her conscience, she quickly left the shadow fighter and entered the rear of the air station. Moving as if every second counted, she ran toward the front door once she was inside. Once outside, she entered the first available JEDDO. "Driver, I need to get to the CA headquarters near Bell Square."

"Right away," the driver replied. He closed the door behind her and got into the driver's seat. For a while there was silence as they headed toward her requested destination and Sampa was content with that. She wasn't in the mood for small talk anyway. That, however, did not last long.

"Have you heard about what happened in Central City?" asked the driver.

"I have," said Sampa reluctantly, not wanting to engage in a conversation about the tragedy with the driver. She, however, did not want to be rude so she feigned interest.

"You know, I brought my family here to get away from that type of stuff," the driver continued. "No place in Sapien is safe now. I don't know what we're going to do. Now they're talking about monitoring twice emitters. I'll tell you what, I need to get me a few now!"

"That may be true for all of us," said Sampa as they entered Bell Square. Shortly thereafter they were in front of the CA headquarters.

"Here we are, that'll be ten DANs," said the driver.

Sampa transmitted the funds from her EPIC along with a small tip.

"Thank you. Thank you very much," said the driver as he scurried around to open the door for her. "I can wait here to take you back if you like."

"That won't be necessary," said Sampa. "Besides, I don't know how long I'll be."

As Sampa entered the familiar fourteen story building, she headed straight for the elevators. The lobby was alive with CATs who were moving about frenetically. Many of them had concerned looks on their faces. Some of them even looked panicked. The offices of the director and his two deputies were in the basement of the ornate building. The spacious lobby was filled with white columns that rose up from the white marble floors; floors that had light gray veins that looked like tiny rivers. The walls were light gray with fancy white crown molding that connected them to a white ceiling. The highly glossed black elevator doors seemed to blend in with the elegant modern motif of the building. Large plants sprang up from beautiful black vases which were spaced evenly throughout the floor. Sampa was there to see her longtime friend and CAT, Sahil Kapadia, who was from India. Sampa and Sahil became CATs at the same time. Although he was one year older than Sampa, they had worked closely together on numerous projects while she was a part of the CA. She patiently waited for an elevator to arrive with several other people. When one of the doors finally opened, she stepped into the empty elevator, quickly pressed the fourteenth floor, and stepped to the back wall as others filtered into the elevator.

After several stops, she had finally reached the fourteenth floor. She stepped out and immediately headed towards Sahil's workshop which was the second door on the left. All the CAT workshops in the building had dark red doors. As she got to his door she entered a personal code that he had previously given to her. She knew he wouldn't have changed it because the digits he used had sentimental value to him.

Sahil looked up from a project he was working on when Sampa walked in. "Sampa? Is that you?" he said as he removed his glasses. "It is you!" he said as he put his glasses back on and quickly walked over to her. He gave her a warm embrace.

"I've missed you too," she said as she smiled and hugged him back.

"This is a pleasant surprise. You look terrific!" He paused as he seemed to be confused about something. He gently pushed her out to arm's length and looked into her eyes. "Is your EPIC not working? Why didn't you call first?" he asked.

"That's what I'm here about," she replied. "I'll get straight to the point. I think Director Rand is selling out the CA to the politicians in Central City. Neutrality is the prime directive of the CA. Non-partisanship was at the core of its inception. That policy is clearly being violated."

"Tell me something we don't know," said Sahil. "We've been onto him for some time now. We have reasons to believe that certain ones of us have been hacked and spied on. What we can't figure out is if only one of his deputies has gone rogue, or both. The only way he can do anything at all is with their help; he has no technical ability whatsoever. It took us several days to show him how to work his EPIC. I'm still not sure he knows how to use it. Last week he accidentally messaged every CAT while he was trying to speak directly to one of his deputies. He's pathetic."

"So, is the back channel up and running?" she asked.

"Yes. In fact, we've activated several. A few of them are dummy accounts that can easily be uncovered with a little work. We have honeypots scattered throughout those. That way if anyone reports them, we'll at least know who's snooping around by their digital footprint," he said as he folded his arms and nodded confidently. "So yes, the Black CATs are hard at work."

"Good," said Sampa. "I'll give you the digital signatures of all of my relevant contacts. If you can put them all on an encrypted frequency that would be great."

"Transmit those to me and I'll make sure that happens. Obviously, you still want them patched into the main line as well, correct?"

"Absolutely. I'm not ready to unplug completely just yet," Sampa replied with a chuckle.

"Consider it done," said Sahil. "Any chance you'll be coming back to us? We could use a brilliant mind like yours, up top and down below."

"If I ever did it would be for the latter, but I can't right now. I'm happy where I am. As long as I have allies like you on the inside I'm good."

"Fair enough," said Sahil.

"Also, I think you should know that they are tampering with the mapping system as well. I'm talking total omissions! We found an island on Evropa that was completely missing from the databank."

"Really? An entire island?" said Sahil as he stretched his arms as wide apart as he could.

"Yes, in the Macabre Sea," she replied. "We stumbled upon it by accident."

Sahil dropped his arms to his side while shaking his head. "That makes sense, we only found out about the Southtown mines ourselves this morning."

"The Southtown mines?" asked Sampa. "What about them?"

"That's where they have that Hidden Bastille," said Sahil. "They told us because they were going to reveal it to the rest of Sapien anyway."

"Incredible. I'll tell you what, Sahil, include yourself on that encrypted frequency you're going to create for me. That way we'll have a direct line of communication outside of the main line."

"I'll do that, Sampa. Once it's up and running I'll contact you on the main line to let you know. I'll say *look to the East* somewhere in the conversation. Your next communication will come from the encrypted line. I assure you that all non-repudiation protocols will be in place. It'll be good to go for all of you at that point."

"Sounds like a plan. Thanks a lot, Sahil, I really appreciate this."

"You're welcome," he said. After another embrace, he walked her to the door. "Don't let this much time pass again without me seeing you, Sampa. True friends are hard to come by around here."

"I know what you mean. I'll do better," she said as she smiled and left the workshop headed for the elevator.

"Listen to your conscience, Sampa," he said as he watched her walk away.

"I will and let yours lead the way."

Location: Westborough, District County, Rights Province, Neutralia Aboard the Iron Raven, 1400 hours

Heeding the advice of Sunday Okonjo, Rokuro Onishi brought Brian to the Iron Raven instead of heading directly to the Hidden Bastille. The captain of the Iron Raven felt the probability was high that Brian would lead them into a trap. With some urging from Alexei, Rokuro Onishi agreed. Along with a few more prominent DOD warriors, they all assembled in the war room of the Iron Raven intent on gathering as much pertinent information as they could from Brian. They would devise a plan of attack based on what they learned. The well-lit war room featured a large U-shaped table, capable of seating twenty people, positioned in the center of it. Approximately five meters beyond the open end of the table and centered stood a large VC. Seated at one end of the table was Rokuro Onishi. Beside him was Alexei. At the other end of the table, across the room, sat Sunday Okonjo. Standing at the VC with Brian beside him was their chief battle strategist, Hania, the spirit warrior of the Hopi Nation, from America.

"Geography mode: Southtown mines," said Hania.

As the image of the mountainous terrain appeared before them, Brian stepped forward and started pointing to where he knew the Hidden Bastille was located. "It doesn't show up on these images because it has been omitted intentionally," he said. "The entrance to the bastille is on the face of this mountain base."

"Facing west?" asked Sunday Okonjo.

"Yes, facing west," Brian continued. "For the most part, the facility is completely underground. It has a large garage in the back on the east side."

"Are those the only two points of entry?" asked Sunday Okonjo.

"They are," answered Brian.

"How can we be sure that this facility is where you say it is?" asked Sunday Okonjo. "If I were in your situation I'd lead my adversary to a DOD stronghold."

"I understand," said Brian. "The only assurance I can give you is my word."

Hania extended his arm with his palm facing toward the men who were seated at the table. They held their questions. "I am sending these coordinates to the seven scouts. They will go to this place and they will either confirm or deny its existence. Once we have started our assault on the bastille, I will personally monitor it from here. Brian will be by my side. That way I can make adjustments for our men on the ground in real time."

"Surely there is a defense system in place?" asked Rokuro Onishi.

"Externally? No," said Brian. "The fact that no one knew it was there was the defense they relied upon. Until now that was an effective strategy. This was never meant to be a permanent facility."

"So, it's true then that their intent is to turn Hades into a penal colony," said Rokuro Onishi.

Brian looked at Rokuro inquisitively. *How could he have known that?* "Yes. Yes, that is correct. That is the plan. It's supposed to take some time, but that is their intent."

Rokuro Onishi leaned back in his chair and folded his arms. *Judas Benedict will be very beneficial to the DOD with all that he knows.* "What more can you tell us about this facility?"

"It goes two levels deep," said Brian. "The deepest level is where the prisoners are housed. The top level is where the control tower is located as well as the cafeteria and administrative offices. That's all I know about the building."

"What do you know about the manpower?" asked Sunday Okonjo.

"There are two hundred men there," replied Brian.

Rokuro Onishi stood up from the table. "I want you to understand one thing, Brian. If any piece of this information is not accurate, you will die immediately."

"I understand," said Brian.

Rokuro Onishi, Sunday Okonjo, and Alexei left the war room. Hania stayed behind with Brian and continued to collect whatever information he could from him.

Location: Central City, District County, Rights Province, Neutralia Central City

Mulati and Francois landed the Whisper in East City. Beth

remained aboard as the rest of the crew traveled from there to Central City in a JEDDO but Sampa had yet to return. As their JEDDO got closer to the Grand Amphitheater, they could hear the chaos that was occurring in the surrounding streets.

"That shit doesn't sound good!" said Corto.

"It's about what I expected given what we just witnessed," said Francois as he performed a function check on his twice emitter. "It's going to be a while before things are back to normal around here."

"Maybe this is the new normal," said Mulati. "I can't see things ever going back to the way they were after this."

The JEDDO suddenly stopped approximately two blocks away from the Amphitheater. The driver went to the side of it and slid the door open. "This is as far as I'm going, men. I don't want to get sucked into that mess around there. That'll be thirty DANs."

"Thirty DANs?" said an incredulous Bjorn. "That trip normally costs no more than fifteen!"

"And I normally don't transport men carrying twice emitters into a war zone," said the driver. "That's my price."

"That's fair," said Mulati as he pulled out his EPIC and transferred the thirty DANs to the driver. "Let's go, men."

With their twice emitters at the ready, they all exited the JEDDO. Mulati's EPIC signaled an incoming transmission from Sampa.

"Receive," said Mulati as they all stopped to focus on the message.

"I'm done here, Mulati. Where can we rendezvous?" she asked.

"The Whisper is in East City, right where we were before. Beth is onboard by herself. Go there and be with her. The rest of us are already in Central City headed to the Grand Amphitheater to get Theris Lamont. Hopefully he's still alive."

"I copy," said Sampa. "You guys be careful out there. I'll call Beth to let her know I'm on my way. End transmission."

As soon as Sampa's image faded away, Mulati secured his EPIC in a cargo pocket on the side of his trousers. They continued on their way and as they got closer, the shower of noise they had heard from a distance became individual droplets of taunts, complaints, threats, insults, and cries for help.

"Make sure we keep it tight," said Mulati as they continued to move.

Mulati, Bjorn, and Francois walked shoulder to shoulder. Mulati was in the center. Corto walked two paces behind them. Every five steps or so, Corto would turn to see if anything or anyone was creeping up from behind them. Visibility decreased significantly the closer they got. The streets were dense with people and the cover of smoke from fires that had been set. The crowd was thickest in the immediate area surrounding the Grand Amphitheater. As the four men made their way through the crowd and toward the front of the venue, the Sapiens on Main Street moved out of their way. They weren't wearing Mayhem Marauder uniforms, so the crowd didn't see them as a threat even though they all were carrying twice emitters. The closer they got, the clearer the source of confusion and chaos became. The crew raised their twice emitters to the ready position. Just beyond the front stairs of the Grand Amphitheater, the Sapiens had captured two of the squaddies who had attempted to flee from the DOD. Even though they were badly bruised, severely injured, and unconscious, the bloodthirsty crowd continued to beat them mercilessly.

"Stand down, they're Marauders," said Mulati to his crew as he saw the uniforms. "Let the Sapiens have their revenge."

The men lowered their weapons as they continued through the crowd and up the stairs toward the front door. As they slowly climbed the stairs with their twice emitters at the ready, Corto continued to follow behind them. This time he walked backwards as he kept his twice emitter pointed toward the rowdy crowd. He reached behind with his left hand and placed it flat on Mulati's backside, so he would not lose contact.

When they reached the top of the stairs, Francois lowered his weapon and pulled the massive front door open. Taking short choppy steps to his right, Mulati slowly cleared the lobby visually as Bjorn stayed attached to his right shoulder.

"Move!" said Mulati as he and Bjorn quickly stepped into the lobby being careful not to trip over the headless body of the Mayhem Marauder captain. Next to enter the building was Francois. He immediately reassumed his position at Mulati's left shoulder. Finally, Corto entered the building and got behind them again. They continued to move toward a large wooden door that led from the lobby to the amphitheater seats. Again, Francois grabbed the handle of the door and pulled it open. Mulati and Bjorn entered the room the same way they entered the lobby. On stage was an Evropan man holding a twice emitter. He immediately looked toward the door and raised his weapon.

"Who are you?" the man asked seeing that they were carrying twice emitters but not in uniform.

Just then, Francois entered the amphitheater. "Shit! That's DOD!" he said.

"It's Francois!" the DOD warrior yelled as he fired his weapon and missed striking the wall behind them. His second projectile blew a hole through the wall spraying debris into the lobby. From behind the stage four more DOD warriors entered the amphitheater.

Bjorn, Mulati, and Francois immediately split up concealing themselves within the rows of seats as they tried to get a good shot on the advancing men. Mulati remained in the middle section while Francois scurried to the far left and Bjorn moved quickly to the far right. Corto had yet to make his way into the amphitheater from the lobby but had heard the commotion coming from inside. As the crew of the Whisper fired upon the DOD warriors, it slowed their advance considerably. Corto wanted desperately to get into the fight. However, he knew to not open the door as it would likely draw the fire of the DOD warriors. Suddenly, he saw a utility closet approximately twenty steps away from where he was in the lobby. He quickly went over to it and attempted to open it. It was locked. He pulled a small dagger away from his vest and started manipulating the strike plate. In Mulati's section about five rows from the stage, he could see the top of one of the DOD warriors' head. He sighted in and fired his round. It was a direct hit. He immediately released the second projectile and upon impact a bloody red mist filled the air where the top of the DOD warriors' head once was. At that moment the volume of return fire increased. The four remaining DOD warriors rained suppressive fire in Mulati's direction. Although he was not being hit, he did not move for fear that he would be.

Corto got the door open.

After he entered the utility closet, Corto quickly found the main breaker and he pulled it down. Immediately the lights went out. All the power in the amphitheater was off.

"What the fuck just happened? I can't see shit!" yelled Francois as he searched for the wall with his left hand.

And neither can they Bjorn thought to himself as his infrared vision kicked in. Everything in the amphitheater became illuminated with a greenish hue inside his goggles. Quietly, but confidently, he stood. Like an apex predator stalking his prey, he slowly walked down the right side of the amphitheater where he saw the four remaining DOD warriors squatting behind chairs in different rows. Bjorn tapped the button on the side of his goggles and the distance readout appeared. The closest man was twenty meters away from him. He quietly got stockweld on his twice emitter, lined the crosshairs up on his torso, and he squeezed the trigger. The tracer round sliced through the darkness. As the first projectile made contact, Bjorn immediately changed his location. The paralyzed DOD warrior was now a defenseless target. Once he was far enough away, Bjorn squeezed the trigger again. While the three other DOD warriors fired on his previous position, the fourth died. The fluorescent tracer rounds of the DOD warriors' twice emitters told Mulati and Francois where they were. They both fired to positions where the rounds originated, and they killed two of the three remaining men. The last one was smart enough to refrain from firing his weapon again while moving from his previous position. For the moment, Bjorn could not see him. Mulati fired another round giving away his own position. The last DOD warrior started low crawling up the center aisle, through the dead Sapiens and Mayhem Marauders, toward his position. Bjorn continued down the right side of the amphitheater all the way to the stage. He started scanning the entire seat section as he quietly moved left. When he spotted the DOD warrior he was five feet away from where Mulati was hiding. Slowly the DOD warrior stood as Mulati's heavy breathing gave away his position. He aimed his weapon at where he estimated Mulati would be. Mulati had no idea he was there, however, by standing, the DOD warrior gave Bjorn a clear shot at his back. Bjorn quickly sighted in, as the readout measured a range of fifty meters, and he squeezed the trigger. The tracer round illuminated the dead bodies underneath its path as it traveled through the pitch blackness and struck the DOD warrior in the back of his head.

"I got him! That's all of them!" said Bjorn as he went running up the center aisle toward the living statue. Mulati and Francois both stood up. Bjorn squeezed the trigger again firing the second projectile. Mulati could not see the man standing in front of him, but he heard the impact of the second projectile as it hit the back of his head and he felt the blood from the DOD warrior as it splattered all over his face. The body collapsed to the floor as Mulati forcefully spat the man's blood, bone fragments, and brain particles out of his mouth and wiped the messy debris away from his face and eyes.

"That's disgusting! I didn't realize he was that close to me. Thanks, Bjorn," said Mulati.

"No problem," said Bjorn as he walked past Mulati and into the lobby. After looking in both directions, he saw Corto standing by the utility room to his left. "Turn 'em back on, Corto!"

"Doing it now," said Corto as he pushed the main breaker back to the on position.

As the power returned to the building, the lights illuminated the Grand Amphitheater. Bjorn waited by the door for Corto as he walked to his position. "That was some quick thinking, Corto. You saved the day, buddy."

"It came to me at the last second, big guy. I wanted to be in there with you guys, but I couldn't chance opening that fucking door. I knew you'd know what to do once the lights went down."

"Yea, it was pretty obvious," said Bjorn. "Come on, let's get in there with Mulati and Frenchie."

As Bjorn and Corto walked into the seating area of the amphitheater, the first thing they noticed was Mulati's bloodied face and upper body.

"Shit! What'd you do eat the guy, Boss?" said Corto as he looked from Mulati's face to the partially decapitated DOD warrior laying on the floor in front of him.

"One would think," said Mulati as he continued to wipe the blood from his face.

Francois walked over to join them. For a moment they all stood and looked down the aisles of the amphitheater at the carnage before them. Dead bodies were all over. Some were seated in chairs, some were on the floor in front of the chairs, and many were in the aisles.

"This was a fucking massacre," said Bjorn as he shook his head.

"I'm guessing the DOD came through and handled the Marauders after those idiots paraded Bahadur out there," said Francois. "Bad move. I knew it when I saw it."

"Spread out," said Mulati. "We need to make sure no one else is here. We don't need any more surprises. Bjorn and Corto, you two take the right side. Francois, you come with me down the left side. We'll meet behind the stage. Be focused and watch your backs. Move!"

"Moving, Boss!" said Corto as he and Bjorn headed to the right side of the amphitheater.

All four men systematically searched every inch of the room. Backstage Bjorn and Corto waited by the back door for Mulati and Francois to join them. Moments later they appeared.

"You see this shit?" asked Corto referring to the dead Mayhem Marauders near the back door. "They got their asses handed to them back here!"

Francois shook his head as he took in the ominous scene. "Rokuro Onishi got this one," he said referring to the dead lieutenant. "He's singled out and there's a hole right through his heart. That's typical Onishi shit right there; he's dramatic that way."

"So where do you think he is now?" asked Mulati.

"He's most likely gone to get Bahadur," answered Francois.

"You don't think he'd go devise a plan first?" asked Corto.

Francois thought for a moment before answering. "That depends on a number of factors. If Sunday Okonjo or Hania are involved, then yes. If Rokuro Onishi is leading the way, then they are fighting right now. He believes he can defeat everyone in the solar system. He likes to attack while his rage is boiling."

"That's why he can be beaten, he fights with his emotions and not his brain. Search each Marauder," said Mulati. "If there's an open EPIC, I want it in my possession. We need to find out where Theris Lamont is right now. He's not safe with the DOD looking for him."

The men started searching all the dead Mayhem Marauders for their EPICs starting with the lieutenant. Mulati decided that he would start at the entrance to the amphitheater and work his way back to the others. Walking through the auditorium proved to be a macabre experience. The sea of bodies lying there, devoid of life, angered Mulati. Unarmed Sapiens were dead. *Same ol' Marauders* he thought as he navigated his way to the front door through the lifeless mass of humanity. Once he made it to the front door he squatted beside the headless body of the captain. With the weight of his body teetering on the balls of his feet, he rummaged through the outer garments of the headless corpse. As he moved the body to one side, an EPIC was uncovered. Mulati picked it up and he immediately observed that it was left open. *He must've been continuously communicating with someone which means he had to be important* he thought as he searched the data. Then he found the information that he was looking for. While in route to the Hidden Bastille, Nastasia had sent a message to the captain letting him know that the politicians were being taken there. Mulati stood up and tucked the EPIC into his cargo pocket before walking back into the auditorium of the amphitheater. "I have what we need," he said to the others from the back row. "Let's get out of this place before the DOD decide to come back."

"You'll get no argument from me," said Francois as he stopped what he was doing and started walking toward Mulati.

Bjorn and Corto also headed his way.

"They're at the Hidden Bastille," said Mulati once the others were in front of him. "We've got to get in contact with Ean and we need to go there." He pulled his EPIC from his pocket. "Contact Sampa," he said.

"Go ahead, Mulati," she said as her image appeared.

"I've found out where Theris Lamont is located, Sam. He's at the Hidden Bastille. I need you to work on finding out where that is."

"That won't be necessary, Mulati. I already know. The Southtown mines is the Hidden Bastille. That's where it has been the whole time. And what happened to your freakin' face?"

"I'll tell you later," he replied. "We're on our way back. End transmission."

As Sampa's image faded away, Mulati turned to Bjorn and Corto. "Let's move."

"You really do need to get that shit off your face first, Boss," said Corto.

"Yea, if you walk out into that crowd like that there's no telling what might happen," said Bjorn. "They're spooked enough already."

"It's that bad, huh?" said Mulati.

Francois simply nodded without saying a word.

"Say no more," said Mulati. "I'm going back down there to find a head. I'll be back in a few."

Mulati found the backstage bathroom. As soon as he walked in, he checked the stalls to make sure no one was hiding inside and proceeded to walk up to one of the six sinks along the counter while looking into the mirror that extended the same length as the counter. He laid his twice emitter on the counter to the right of him so that he could turn on the faucet to fill his hands with soap from the dispenser on the wall and lather his face and hair. He leaned over into the sink putting his face as close to the water as possible to allow the running water to rinse the soap from his face until the water flowing down the drain changed from dark red to pink to clear. As he turned his head to the right to make sure that his entire head was clean he noticed his twice emitter was gone. He reached to his waist, grabbed his dlhá násada, and opened it as he spun around into attack position. The water from his face and hair sprayed the wall and mirror. Struggling to blink the water from his eyes, Mulati noticed Ean was standing behind him holding his twice emitter.

"Be careful where you lay this, Mulati," he said as he stood with the twice emitter in his hand and extended toward him.

"Shit! Where'd you come from?"

"We just got here and came through the back door. I heard the water running so I came in. I assume you're here for the same reason we are, to find Theris?"

"That's correct," Mulati replied as he closed his dlhá násada. He dried his face with the disposable paper he pulled from the receptacle on the wall. "Actually, I'm glad to see you. I was going to contact you. Theris is at the Southtown mines, that's where that bastille is."

"Where are the others?" Ean asked.

"The rest of my crew, minus two, are waiting for me at the entrance. Where are Louis and Eric?"

"They're waiting for me outside of the head. I didn't know who I'd find in here and I didn't want them to get hurt so I made them stay out there."

"Yea, I'm sure *made* is a pretty generous description of what actually happened. Let's go get the others and get out of here. You almost scared me to death," said Mulati as they exited.

Mulati and Ean walked out of the bathroom to the relieved faces of Louis and Eric. Mulati nodded to both men before leading the way to the front of the amphitheater.

"It's worse than I thought," said Ean as he took in the gruesome scene on their way to the front entrance.

"It's about to get even worse, I fear," said Mulati as he pressed on.

Once they got to where Bjorn, Corto, and Francois were standing, Bjorn and Ean locked eyes.

"Does he know what team he's on?" asked Bjorn referring to Ean.

"If I were on the other side, you'd be down a man already," said Ean.

"Don't be so sure of that," said Mulati. "As it stands, Bjorn and Ean, we are all together. Right now, our job is to get Theris Lamont to safety."

Mulati led the way as the seven men exited the Grand Amphitheater and entered the crowded streets of Central City headed back to the Whisper.

Chapter 19: Blood in The Bastille

*Location: East City, District County, Rights Province, Neutralia
Aboard the Whisper, 1500 hours*

The crew of the Whisper, along with Ean, Louis, and Eric, assembled in the ship's lounge. Mulati stood as everyone else sat and listened intently to what he had to say.

"Because it's hard to predict what Rokuro Onishi is going to do, time is not on our side," he said. "What we do know is that they are definitely going to the bastille to free Bahadur. We also know, from what we got from Francois, that their intent is to assassinate both Theris Lamont and Chancellor Aldrich. My guess is that the Marauders have to suspect that they are coming. Therefore, I think there will be a lot of manpower present on their behalf. What they do not expect is for us to show up. That's to our advantage."

"We don't know the facility," said Bjorn. "We have no idea what we're walking into."

"You're right, Bjorn. However, ours is the path of least resistance. We're going to rescue someone who wants to be saved. The DOD are guaranteed to meet resistance. In fact, they're blood thirsty and will be looking for it. If we're careful enough we may be able to avoid it."

"If they waited, they'll want to attack at night," said Francois. "Hania likes to have everything accounted for. Okonjo is a thinker, he wants to beat you mentally as much as physically. If we get there before they do, we can probably have Theris Lamont freed before the shit starts. I don't believe they'll want to do anything more urgently than they'll want to free Bahadur. They'll do that first."

"That makes sense, Francois," said Sampa. "You're sure they can't do both at the same time?"

"That depends on the number of Marauders that are there," said Francois. "The Iron Raven holds two hundred warriors; I suspect they'll have at least half that many on their raid."

"We can't fight all of those!" said Corto.

"If things go as planned we won't have to, Corto, but we will be prepared just in case," said Mulati. "We leave in an hour. Beth, you're staying here. Ean, are those two fighters?"

"No, they are not," Ean replied. "Louis and Eric are assistants. That is all."

"Then you two will stay here with Beth," said Mulati. "We will travel on the Arachnids. I think our best bet is to stay away from the main roads."

Location: Westborough, District County, Rights Province, Neutralia Aboard the Iron Raven, 1700 hours

The seven scouts, comprised of two Lipan Apaches, three Mescalero Apaches, and two Warm Springs Apaches, all from America, returned to the Iron Raven with valuable information about the Hidden Bastille. They were adept at reconnaissance, tracking, and surveillance. After receiving their information, Hania summoned Rokuro Onishi, Sunday Okonjo, and Alexei to the war room to go over his proposed plan of attack. Brian was being held in the living quarters of the Iron Raven under the watchful eyes of two DOD warriors.

"The seven scouts have confirmed to me that the bastille is exactly where Brian indicated it would be," said Hania. "The road that leads to it is surrounded by terrain that is difficult to navigate. It is also straight and narrow. There are three kilometers of road that lead directly to the front. It appears that it is designed that way so that they can see the enemy coming long before they get there. The road ends at a clearing in front of the bastille. Two smaller roads split from the main road and go around the north and south sides of the facility. They go through the mountain and lead to the garage on the east side of the building. That is the rear. There are guards posted at the front entrance. The outside of the rear is guarded as well."

"How will we get there without them seeing us coming down the roadway?" asked Alexei.

"We won't come down the roadway," said Hania. "We should take the horses over the mountains and approach the bastille from the rear."

Sunday Okonjo cleared his throat.

Hania looked his way. "Is there something you would like to say, Okonjo?"

"Yes, there is," he replied. "It would stand to reason, Hania, that if they wish to funnel their enemies down a particular path, then they would also prepare for them taking an alternate route should they be wise enough to avoid that trap."

"So, you think they'll be waiting along the alternate routes then?" asked Hania.

"I do," replied Sunday Okonjo. "However, if we can convince them that we somehow overlooked that minor detail, it may effectively disarm them."

"Then what do you propose?" asked Hania.

"I suggest we send a team down the main road," said Sunday Okonjo. "Make it obvious that we're coming. They should be well armed and some of our fiercest warriors. Alexei, for instance, would be a good candidate to lead them. They'll, in all likelihood, be engaged by the Marauders on that very roadway. We can then send everyone else through the back door while their attention is focused on the most imminent threat. That's what I think we should do."

"It would work," said Rokuro Onishi. "No one wants the bad man to kick in their front door."

"I agree," said Alexei. "I will lead them."

"Then that is settled," said Hania. "They have also made what is, in my opinion, a catastrophic mistake. Their auxiliary power supply is generated from the outside. There are four generators on top of the facility, one on each side. According to the scouts, none of them were on. That means that they are used as reserve power."

"Leave that up to me," said Rokuro Onishi.

"Good enough. I suggest we attack at 2200 hours," said Hania.

Location: Southtown, District County, Rights Province, Neutralia One kilometer north of the Hidden Bastille, 1930 hours.

"This is far enough for now," said Mulati as they brought their Rapid Arachnids to a halt in a grassy area just beyond the mountainous landscape surrounding the Hidden Bastille.

Following closely behind him were Bjorn, Francois, Ean, Sampa, and Corto. They all carried twice emitter rifles, except for Sampa. She preferred the smaller twice emitter pistol because it was easily concealed in her thigh holster. She thought the amount of distance she would lose by carrying that would be made up for by its ease of carry. She also carried her hand forged warrior Naginata which is her close combat weapon of choice. The long weapon was one fourth razor sharp sword and three fourths wooden staff, almost as tall as her when she stood it upright.

"Hide 'em," said Mulati referring to the Rapid Arachnids as he stood to survey the landscape with his high-powered binoculars. The rest of them placed vegetation into the chameleon ports so that the machines quickly blended into the landscape.

'It's a good thing we didn't come down that main road," said Mulati. "I see Marauders all over the mountain. They appear to be waiting."

"That means either Hania or Okonjo convinced Rokuro Onishi to wait until later then," said Francois. "I think we should do the same."

"I think you're right," said Mulati. "We'll stay together right here."

Sampa walked up to where Mulati was standing carrying her Naginata.

"You look ready for battle," he said as he lowered his binoculars.

"Whether I am or not, it's going to happen," she replied. "Do you think we can make it out intact?"

Mulati pondered the question for a moment. "Can we? Sure. Will we? I don't know. We've been a lot of places and have done a lot of things. We haven't lost yet. I don't see us losing now. That's the best answer I can give you, Sam."

Sampa nodded and gently touched him on the shoulder before walking back to join the others. As she walked away, she received an incoming transmission on her EPIC. It was Sahil. "Receive transmission," she said.

The image of Sahil appeared and began to speak, "If you look to the East in the morning the sun will surely blind you, Sampa. End transmission."

As his image disappeared, Sampa received a message on an encrypted channel which read *listen to your conscience*. Her reply was *let yours lead the way*. She raised her voice and spoke to the group. "Stand by for our new channel frequency." She waited for a moment as they all prepared their EPICs for the change. "Channel PHA3B5C7T. Lock it in." She then put her EPIC away as everyone else did the same.

Mulati raised the binoculars back up to his eyes and continued to scan the area surrounding the Bastille for activity and intel.

Location: Southtown, District County, Rights Province, Neutralia
The Hidden Bastille, 2200 hours.

Two kilometers down the road from the front of the bastille stood fifty DOD warriors. They were led by Alexei and all the men carried circular shields engraved with the DOD emblem and had twice emitters strapped to their backs. Some carried short swords or daggers, and the others carried hatchets. Alexei also carried his spear. They stood in the middle of the road and in unison they began repeatedly banging their hatchets, daggers, and short swords against their shields. The rhythmic sound echoed through the valley like thunder. Down the narrow road and all the way up to the front door of the bastille the ominous metronome could be heard. The startled squaddies, who were posted at the front entrance, sounded the alarm which sent the Mayhem Marauders into a frenzy.

Instead of advancing, the DOD warriors held their ground because they wanted to draw the Mayhem Marauders out to meet them. Through the darkness, Alexei observed the light emanating from the interior of the bastille as one hundred Mayhem Marauders exited the structure to confront them.

The Mayhem Marauders marched in four lines of twenty-five fighters down the road and toward the DOD warriors. As they closed to within twenty yards of the DOD warriors, they stopped. Lieutenant Tamm, a tall and strong Estonian, stepped forward and turned around to face his Mayhem Marauder contingent. As the DOD warriors behind him continued to pound their shields, he gathered his wide-eyed men for a speech.

Alexei retrieved an illuminator from his pocket. The illuminator, a six-inch metal tube consisting of two identical parts that twist together in the center, emits a brilliant glow that lights up a ten-meter radius when the two halves are separated.

As Lieutenant Tamm began to speak, Alexei raised a fist in the air. The DOD warriors stopped pounding their shields and they listened.

"Do you hear that silence? Even they recognize what danger they face!" said Lieutenant Tamm to the Mayhem Marauders in front of him. "Tonight, we become legends. This is close quarter combat; let them feel the steel of our blades. What we do here tonight will echo throughout time, long after we are all dead and gone. Every man fears death, and we should as well, but what I fear most is to be forgotten. If I die tonight, I will do so having staked my claim amongst the greatest men to have ever fought. However, ... I am an honorable man. So tonight, we'll let them be martyrs, and we will let their women suck our dicks to honor their memory!"

The Mayhem Marauders erupted with cheers and raised their weapons high above their heads with jubilation as Lieutenant Tamm nodded with approval knowing that they were ready for battle. As they readied their shields and raised their weapons, Lieutenant Tamm turned to face the DOD.

Alexei twisted open his illuminator and tossed it in the center of the roadway. It landed halfway between himself and the lieutenant. Through the light glowing from the illuminator each group observed what they were up against. Alexei and Lieutenant Tamm stared at one another. Alexei repositioned his spear in his right hand from a carrying posture to a throwing posture. With a loud grunt, he let it fly. His spear traveled directly over the illuminator and through the throat of Lieutenant Tamm. He fell backward with his eyes open, hitting the ground while the vertical spear continued to wobble as it protruded from his neck. He died instantly. Alexei unsheathed his short sword and took a step back. The DOD warriors stepped forward and created a wall with their shields. Projectiles from the twice emitters of the Mayhem Marauders pelted their shields like hail and fell harmlessly to the ground. No one was hit. The DOD and the Mayhem Marauders clashed in the middle of the road. The Battle of The Hidden Bastille had begun.

Although they had a two to one advantage in manpower, the Mayhem Marauders were being beaten easily. Within minutes twenty of their men were dead while the battle-hardened DOD warriors had yet to lose one. Alexei had already killed two more men by himself. Thirty Mayhem Marauders had retreated to the front of the bastille, fearful that they would die. Fifty Mayhem Marauders remained in the fight. Alexei, the Apache scouts, and the rest of the DOD warriors continued to battle through the beleaguered combatants. Time after time, Alexei would raise his shield to thwart incoming blows while delivering devastating strikes of his own. Mayhem Marauders who weren't killed were severely maimed and unable to continue fighting. With the rage of mad men flowing through their veins, the DOD devastated the physically and tactically inferior Mayhem Marauders. Before long they stood tall amongst the vanquished. Seventy Mayhem Marauders laid defeated before them. In all the vicious fighting the only casualties sustained by the DOD were ten severely wounded men, however, they were all still alive.

The sound of emergency sirens blaring through the bastille awakened Bahadur from his sleep. Instantly he sat upright. On many previous occasions in the past, the Mayhem Marauders had conducted emergency drills. The intent of those drills was to allocate manpower to a specific area of the bastille as efficiently as possible. As he watched the Mayhem Marauders scurry about in the corridor beyond his cell, Bahadur's heart began to race. Slowly he stood and without even realizing it, his fists were clenched. The hair stood up on his neck. At long last it was happening. He knew the DOD had found the bastille. There were no longer two squaddies outside of the cells of Bahadur and Onin Gesh. In an instant, most of the manpower had disappeared. Bahadur walked to the cell door and he looked out. The sirens continued to blare with each screech coinciding with flashing emergency lights that were positioned several feet apart where the ceiling and wall met.

Onin Gesh removed his blanket from his bed, draped it over his head and upper body, and turned to face the back wall. The flashing lights were an annoyance to him.

Under the cover of darkness and aided by the distraction being created by the contingent of DOD warriors led by Alexei, Rokuro Onishi led fifty warriors around the south side of the mountain. Their destination was the rear entrance on the east side of the bastille. Also accompanying him were two electrical engineers from the Iron Raven. The plan was for them to find the utility room and disable the internal power source once they were inside the facility. The warriors traveled in two lines around the dark mountainside. Before long the flat surface of the roof of the bastille was in front of them and the four massive outside generators were visible. Acting in accordance with Hania's plan, Rokuro Onishi sent two men toward each generator. He and the other forty-one men continued toward the back entrance. What was once two squaddies guarding the east entrance had now grown to fifty. Near the well-lit entrance to the garage, the Mayhem Marauders fanned out in a convex semicircle creating a defensive perimeter. After Rokuro Onishi gave the go ahead, green tracers filled the air. Several of the squaddies were hit while the remainder of them scrambled for cover. As they did, the DOD warriors delivered their second projectiles killing the already emitted Mayhem Marauders instantly. The DOD stormed the rear entrance as the Mayhem Marauders returned fire. While descending the mountain toward the garage door, the DOD took heavy casualties. Five warriors were killed but Rokuro Onishi and the others pressed on being careful to stay behind their shields. Once they were on the ground near the rear entrance, they savagely assaulted and killed all the squaddies they encountered.

In the distance, Mulati and Bjorn watched from their position on the northern outskirts of the mountain. The crashing of the swords and shields had gotten their attention. They watched as the DOD took out the Mayhem Marauders on the road leading up to the front entrance. They also watched as Rokuro Onishi and the others stormed the rear entrance.

"Rokuro Onishi is at the rear," said Mulati. "They're attacking the Marauders."

Francois stepped forward. "You mind if I take a look, Mulati?"

Mulati handed his binoculars to Francois who commenced to scan from left to right until he found the rear of the Bastille.

"It's done! They're making their way inside now," said Francois.

"Get ready to go," said Mulati. "Now is the time. While he's looking for Bahadur, we'll look for Theris Lamont. They're doing the hard work for us."

Mulati crossed both arms across his chest in an exaggerated fashion. The rest of the crew did the same and in unison they executed a six step Whisper Yell.

They walked over to the Rapid Arachnids and turned them on. Once they were all powered up, the crew of the Whisper mounted the machines and started their trek to the east entrance. Mulati led the way, followed by Sampa, Francois, Ean, Corto, and Bjorn.

Inside the bastille, Bahadur and Onin Gesh were now fully aware that the building was under siege. The sirens and flashing lights had stopped and the Mayhem Marauders had already mobilized. This time, Bahadur stood as close to the cell door as he possibly could even as Klaus returned to their cells with his troll in hand. For a moment the lights flashed and instinctively everyone looked to the ceiling. However, it is was only a flash. Then they went out completely and all the cell doors slid open but this time when they did, Bahadur slid out. Onin Gesh was too far away from his door to make an escape. As the power came back on, the cell doors closed, and Klaus immediately pressed the button on his troll causing Bahadur to fall to his knees in agony. Onin Gesh also collapsed inside his cell. With two hands Klaus gripped the button, shaking it as if that would generate more power from the device.

"Emit him!" Klaus screamed to the squaddie.

Without hesitation, the squaddie delivered the first projectile to Bahadur's torso. Bahadur became paralyzed as the effects of the twice emitter and the pain from Klaus's troll overlapped. He grabbed his restraints and used them to secure Bahadur's hands behind his back. After the twenty seconds passed, Bahadur laid on his side almost in a fetal position hyperventilating. Suddenly the power failed again and the doors to the cells opened and shut once more. Onin Gesh got up, stepped out of the darkness, and got closer to the cell door.

Klaus pulled out his EPIC to communicate with the tower. "What's going up there?"

"The main power has been disabled from the inside," said the voice on the other end. "That was the first generator going down as well."

"We need more squaddies down here!" screamed Klaus. "I have twenty prisoners trying to get out!"

Again, the power went down. The cell doors flew open. Klaus immediately pressed the button on his troll sending Onin Gesh to the floor. As he held the button down, the third generator kicked in restoring the power. Again, Bahadur screamed in agony. The cell doors closed instantly. Only this time fifteen of the other prisoners managed to get out but seven of them were instantly emitted and killed by squaddies. However, eight of them got away and were now running freely through the facility trying to escape. Klaus panicked. It was clear to him that the system was being sabotaged and that it was only a matter of time before the last two generators were disabled.

"Stay here, I'm going to get you help," said Klaus to the squaddie who was guarding Bahadur and Onin Gesh. The disappointed and pitiful look on the squaddie's face let Klaus know that he knew he wasn't coming back. Within seconds Klaus was gone.

Bahadur looked to the squaddie after Klaus left. "It's not you we want to kill. Klaus has left you to die because he knows my men are in the building. Take these restraints off my hands and you will live. I promise you that."

"If they find out I let you go then they'll kill me," the squaddie replied.

"Do you not see what is happening? In a few minutes Rokuro Onishi is going to come through that door," said Bahadur. "The only one who can stop him from impaling your decapitated skull on a spear is me. If you want to live, you'll do as I say. That's my last time asking."

Fearing that what Bahadur said was true, the squaddie reluctantly reached down and loosened his restraints. As Bahadur stood he briefly massaged both of his wrists in an attempt to alleviate the discomfort caused by the restraints. The squaddie backed away as the expression on Bahadur's face suddenly changed. His flaring nostrils, tightened lips, and pushed together brows let the squaddie know that he had made a terrible mistake.

"No! Please don't," said the squaddie as he attempted to raise his twice emitter.

Bahadur rushed toward him and palmed his face with his right hand. With his left hand he pressed down on the front sight post of the twice emitter. The squaddie managed to squeeze off the first projectile which ricocheted off the floor. The momentum Bahadur gained from running carried him with great force. He slammed the back of the squaddie's head into the glass. The force of the impact crushed the back of his head and cracked the thick glass. He slid down the door leaving a thick streak of blood where his head once was. Bahadur casually removed the squaddie's twice emitter from his hands as his unconscious body toppled over to the side. He was still alive. Bahadur racked the weapon extracting the useless second projectile. He pointed the twice emitter at the squaddie's head and squeezed the trigger. He fired both projectiles in rapid succession. He was already walking away as the squaddie's head exploded all over the wall. Again, the lights went down.

Bahadur walked over to the next cell. "Come out, Gesh. We're free!"

Onin Gesh slowly turned around, but the doors closed, and the lights came back on before he could move. "Check the squaddie for a dagger," he said. "I'll wait until the last generator is down before I come out. I work better in the dark."

Bahadur went over to the dead squaddie and searched him for a dagger. He found it and he showed it to Onin Gesh. "I'm going to leave it here on the deck for you, Gesh." He placed the dagger on the floor directly in front of his cell and turned to walk away but stopped and turned back around. "I never asked you this before, Gesh, but I'm curious. How did they catch you?"

Onin Gesh walked close to the cell door and looked Bahadur in his eyes. "One and The Other," he said. "I will have my revenge on them." He slowly stepped back into the darkness of his cell.

Bahadur emitted several squaddies as he made his way through the corridor. In all areas of the bastille, the Mayhem Marauders were being wiped out. Finally, the lights went down again but this time they stayed off. Onin Gesh slowly walked to the opening of his cell, squatted to grab the dagger, and he pulled it in.

As Bahadur made his way to the end of the corridor, he found the door to one of the many stairwells leading to the top level. When he stepped onto the bottom landing, an illuminator came bouncing down the stairs and stopped close to his feet. He looked to the top of the stairs to see Rokuro Onishi.

"If I had known you were still alive, I would not have stopped looking until I found you," said Rokuro Onishi. "Please forgive me."

Bahadur slowly walked up the fourteen steps to the landing where Rokuro Onishi stood. Once they were face to face, they embraced. "It's good to see you, Rokuro. I knew you were coming for me," he said.

Rokuro Onishi summoned another DOD warrior to the landing who was carrying a short sword and a hatchet, his two favorite weapons. "I brought these for you. Let's kill some Marauders."

Bahadur strapped the twice emitter to his back and walked back down the stairs with his short sword in one hand and his hatchet in the other. When they opened the door, they tossed the illuminator into the corridor. As the Mayhem Marauders struggled to focus their eyes, the DOD stepped in. Bahadur led the way and encountered the first squaddie. Before the Mayhem Marauder could raise his weapon, Bahadur thrusted his short sword into and through his abdomen. He brought his hatchet down on his neck in a chopping motion with his right hand. A large quantity of blood from his carotid artery sprayed the immediate area. Next, he reverse pivoted to his right leaving his left foot in place as he executed a backhanded horizontal slash with his hatchet to the midsection of the next squaddie who approached from the rear. Pulling his short sword away from the first squaddie, he brought it downward into trapezius muscle of the second one who had already collapsed to his knees. With great force he kicked him in his chest leaving him prostrate on the floor. Both men were dead. He, Rokuro Onishi, and the other DOD warriors continued to effortlessly cut their way through Mayhem Marauders as they headed toward Onin Gesh's cell.

Outside of Onin Gesh's cell were three more dead squaddies with fatal dagger wounds. The floor in front of the cell was covered with blood from the two men's slit throats and the third's punctured jugular vein.

"Gesh, are you still in there?" asked Bahadur.

There was no reply. He grabbed the illuminator and tossed it into Onin Gesh's cell. The light revealed two more dead Mayhem Marauders but no Onin Gesh. He was gone.

"He had to have taken one of the other stairwells," said Bahadur. "He's going for Klaus."

"Who is Klaus?" asked Rokuro Onishi.

"Klaus Moken. He's the one man who has done more to earn his own death than any man I have ever known," said Bahadur.

"Then why would you leave the satisfaction of taking his life to another?" asked Rokuro Onishi.

"Because Onin Gesh is the one man I'm sure is capable of the torment and pain that I myself would inflict," he replied.

Bahadur turned and walked back down the corridor to the stairwell where he had originally encountered Rokuro Onishi. With his sword in his left hand and his hatchet in his right, he moved with a purpose. The Mayhem Marauders had already killed the five remaining prisoners. The other eight were still outstanding.

Sounds from the chaos occurring inside the bastille could be heard clearly inside the safe room where the politicians and generals were. Because it operated from an isolated power source, the lights in the safe room never turned off and only a select few Mayhem Marauders even knew the room existed. While Chancellor Aldrich, General Tolliver, and General Branimir huddled together discussing how to get out of the bastille alive, Nastasia sat alone in a corner of the room with her arms folded and her legs crossed, her rapidly swinging foot signified that she was either worried, annoyed, or both. She had not spoken a word since her earlier failed attempt to use her EPIC.

Judas Benedict walked across the room and sat next to Theris Lamont. "Look at them," he said referring to the Chancellor and his generals. "The solar system is at the dawn of oblivion and they're acting as if they can raft amongst leviathans."

Looking forward, Theris Lamont replied stoically, "Sailors look for the lighthouse when in choppy waters. Perhaps it is better that they are calm."

Judas was taken aback by what he perceived to be a somewhat veiled defense of the men by Theris Lamont. "Can you not see that we are in extreme danger?" asked Judas.

"That is a danger I can see," said Theris as he nodded toward the men. He looked Judas directly in his eyes and said, "It is that which I cannot see that I fear."

Judas sat back on the couch as it was clear to him that Theris's allegiance had shifted. His previous neutrality was an annoyance to Judas. However, his perceived partiality to the other side was a problem. *They have him brainwashed. I can't believe he has fallen for their rhetoric.*

General Branimir walked away from the other two and toward the VC. After texting a message from it he walked away. "I have work to do," he said, "and I don't feel I can get it done from in here." He walked toward the exit of the safe room.

"Wait!" said General Tolliver as he walked toward one of the VC tables. "Surveillance mode: garage interior," he carefully enunciated.

Inside the garage he could see ten parked JEDDOs. He also saw the dead bodies of the two squaddies who guarded the door that they walked through to gain entrance into the safe room. Other than that, there was no visible activity in the garage.

"Surveillance mode: garage exterior," said General Tolliver carefully to the VC as he expanded his probe. Outside of the garage he saw at least eight DOD warriors standing by the door. The warriors who disabled the generators had transitioned to the rear for security. The bodies of dead Mayhem Marauders were strewn about. "Surveillance mode: front entrance," he continued. Outside of the front door he saw the thirty Mayhem Marauders who had retreated to that location. "That's our only way out," he said. "The entrance to the bastille appears to be clear. General Branimir and I will go there. Once we are assured that the way is clear, we will come back for you. Keep this door secured!" General Tolliver walked back to the VC and left it on surveillance mode of the garage interior. "This is how you will know that it is us when we return. If we're not back in twenty minutes, you're on your own. Get out the best way you can."

Both men grabbed the only two twice emitters from the weapon locker and exited the safe room to head for the garage. Because the bastille was still completely dark, they were able to quietly slip into the garage, sneak past the JEDDOs and make their way into the interior of the building without being seen by the DOD warriors who were posted as guards on the outside.

Meanwhile, in the control tower Klaus stood alone behind the locked door, hiding. Positioned at the north end of the building, the tower was elevated high above the floor with twenty metal stairs leading from the highly glossed cement floor to the entrance of the control tower. On three sides of the room the walls were solid from the floor to about four feet high and from that point to the ceiling they were made of glass for maximum visibility. Only the northside wall was completely opaque. In the center of the room was a large island with a VC and other electronic devices. Klaus's EPIC and his troll were also sitting there. He remained as quiet as possible until he heard what sounded like a very heavy footstep on the bottom stair. Then there was another, and another. Someone was coming toward the door. Klaus kneeled behind the back side of the island barely looking over the top. By the heaviness of the footsteps he could tell that the person on the outside was getting closer and whoever it was, he was not in a hurry. The door handle shook and for a moment Klaus felt a sense of relief thinking that it had to be one of the squaddies. He grabbed an illuminator and crawled toward the door. It was still too dark for him to see who it was with his naked eyes, so he got closer to the door, but he could hear the lock being manipulated. Still crouching down, and mere feet away from the door himself, he held the illuminator slightly above his head and gave it a quick twist. The flash of light revealed Onin Gesh standing at the door and staring right into Klaus's eyes. Klaus quickly closed his illuminator, dropped it, and scrambled back behind the island as Onin Gesh calmly continued to tamper with the lock. Klaus whimpered like a frightened child as he reached to the top of the island frantically searching for his troll. He found it. Thinking quickly, he decided that he would wait until Onin Gesh got the door open before he delivered the debilitating electric shock to his body. He would then flee from the tower while Onin Gesh was on the ground suffering. Slowly he stood with both hands on his troll and walked around to the front side of the island. He shook like a leaf in the wind as he anticipated the inevitable meeting. At this point, the only thing separating him and Onin Gesh was the door which was mostly metal. Finally, Onin Gesh popped the lock. Slowly he pushed the door open and walked into the control room with the dagger in his left hand. He left the door open behind him and he took another step forward. Klaus quickly pressed the button on his troll. It had no effect.

"No!" said Klaus as he backed away and bumped into the island.

Again, he pressed the button, this time more emphatically, but with the same result. No effect. As Onin Gesh took another step, Klaus's worst fears were confirmed. As his eyes adjusted to Onin Gesh's pale white body he could see chunks of flesh missing from both of his upper pectoral muscles. With his dagger, Onin Gesh had removed the subcutaneous electrodes from his body.

Onin Gesh laughed. "Fight for your life, bitch!" he said through clenched teeth.

Klaus attempted to run past him and out the door. Onin Gesh grabbed him by his throat with his right hand stopping him in his tracks. Klaus immediately reached up with both hands and tried to loosen Onin Gesh's grip. He was unsuccessful. The sound of Klaus's urine running down his legs and dripping onto the floor was the only thing louder than his heartbeat. Looking Klaus directly in his eyes, Onin Gesh plunged the dagger into the right side of his abdomen. He slowly dragged the sharp blade from one side of Klaus's stomach to the other. Klaus's grip released from Onin Gesh's right hand and his hands dropped to each side, dangling, as he drifted into unconsciousness. Klaus's blood and intestines spilled out of his body and onto the control tower floor.

Onin Gesh pressed his lips against his left ear and said, "I told you I was going to kill you, Klaus."

The generals methodically made their way through the massive facility to reach the front entrance. Stepping over the bodies of murdered Mayhem Marauders, they were careful to make sure that they stayed close to one another and kept an eye out for the DOD. The sounds of intense battle and death filled the air as they made their way through the turbulent facility. A few minutes later they were in the main hall where the control tower was located and through darkness, they eventually found the stairwell leading to the control tower itself. They were halfway to the front of the bastille.

"Let's go up and see if anyone is in there," whispered General

Tolliver.

"For what?" asked General Branimir.

"Just in case we don't make it to the front. We can secure ourselves in there," he replied.

"Alright," said General Branimir. "I'll take the left side and you take the right side. Ready? Go!"

Making sure to stay abreast of one another, the men quietly ascended the metal stairway with their twice emitters at the ready. As they got to the top, they saw that the door was wide open.

"Anybody in there?" said General Tolliver softly. Hearing no response, he asked again, this time a little louder. "Is there anyone inside the control tower?" Again, there was no reply.

Both men lowered their twice emitters and walked inside.

Before he was even two steps in, General Branimir kicked the illuminator that was on the ground. "Just what we need," he said as he picked it up from the ground and twisted it open.

Immediately he dropped it on the floor. "Oh shit, it's Klaus!" he said.

Both men jumped back, raised their twice emitters to the ready, and got back to back. They quickly scanned the room to see if anyone else was in there with them. What startled them was the sight of Klaus's disemboweled body propped up against the island with his eyes wide open. His legs were straight out, and his intestines were on his lap. A dagger was buried four inches into his forehead with a stream of blood flowing from the wound. His severed penis and scrotum were stuffed into his mouth. His entire body was soaked with blood.

"Back out! Back out! Back the fuck out!" yelled General Tolliver. Both men hurriedly descended the stairs and headed to meet the other Mayhem Marauders at the front door. Onin Gesh walked out from under the stairs in the other direction.

Unbeknownst to the eight DOD warriors outside of the rear of the bastille, Mulati and Corto had quietly made their way to the roof of the facility. The others remained a few feet away on the hill waiting beyond the edge of the clearing. Although the DOD warriors on the ground appeared to be on high alert, they neglected to scan the roof. Mulati guessed correctly that the roof would be a good place to be since the eight men had recently been there and would probably assume that it would remain clear of hostiles.

Mulati crept to the edge of the building and took a knee while holding his fully extended dhla nasada. He looked back over his shoulder at Corto. "Whenever you're ready, you can do your thing," he said.

Corto simply nodded as he walked up to the ledge while removing two daggers from his vest. After taking a moment to focus, he quickly tossed the two daggers from the rooftop and two of the DOD warriors fell from daggers to their neck with blood spewing profusely. Mulati and Corto retreated toward the center of the roof. The six remaining DOD warriors backed away from the building as they tried to look for them. From the hill, Bjorn's green tracer round entered the back of one of the men. As his chest exploded outward from the second projectile, the others realized that they were surrounded, and they scrambled to find cover. Sampa, Francois, and Ean had made their way to ground level together. The five remaining DOD warriors huddled together at the base of the hill closest to where Bjorn's shot came from.

That maneuver created a blind spot for Bjorn. "I can't see them anymore," he yelled from atop the hill. "They're at the base of this hill under me."

"Split up," said Francois. "Ean, you go toward the garage and Sam you go toward the south side. A few seconds from now I'll fire to the base of that hill where Bjorn said they are. When they fire back, light them up. Go!"

Francois waited for the others to get into place. He fired a shot at the DOD warriors and ducked behind a large rock. Immediately they returned fire allowing Corto and Mulati to aim and fire from the rooftop. Ean also fired his twice emitter but Sampa held her fire because her pistol did not possess the effective range to reach them. Three of the DOD warriors died while a fourth ran from the base of the hill. Sampa could hear him getting closer to her and when he got within a few meters, the DOD warrior opened an illuminator and rolled it in front of him. As the light flashed, Sampa could see that he was nearly on top of her and raising his twice emitter to fire. She went to one knee while executing a diagonal slash across his body with the blade of her naginata. As his flesh ripped open from his right shoulder to his left hip, he struggled to raise his weapon again. He squeezed his first projectile into the ground as he fell backward dropping his twice emitter in the process.

"Stay down!" said Sampa as the DOD warrior rolled over to his stomach searching for his twice emitter. She sliced downward to the ground and through his hand chopping off four of his fingers. The defeated DOD warrior rolled over to his back and drifted into unconsciousness as Sampa backed away from the glowing illuminator.

"I give up!" said the one remaining DOD warrior. "Don't shoot, I'm walking toward the illuminator. My twice emitter is strapped across my back."

"Fuck! I know that voice," said Francois.

As the man appeared in the light of the illuminator, Francois saw that it was Roderick, his only friend in the DOD.

"Easy, Roderick, we won't hurt you," said Francois as he also walked toward the light. He had his twice emitter lowered.

"What are you doing, Francois?" asked Sampa. "Keep your guard up!"

"This one won't try to harm me," said Francois. "We're friends."

The others held their positions as Francois talked his friend through surrendering.

"Everything is gonna be alright," said Francois. "Just unstrap it and lay it down by the illuminator. These are good people."

Roderick went down to one knee with his hands still in the air. He reached to his back and grabbed the twice emitter with both hands. In one motion he oriented himself toward Francois and fired a shot in his direction, narrowly missing Francois as the green projectile whizzed past his ear causing Francois to fall backward. Before Roderick could shoot again, Corto had already delivered a projectile to his head. A fraction of a second later Bjorn's first projectile struck his torso. Both men delivered their second shots decimating Roderick's head and body. Ironically, Francois felt betrayed. He rose to his knees with his twice emitter across his lap and started to weep. As he brought his hands to his face and cried the others watched, not sure what to make of what Francois was going through.

Chapter 20: The End?

*Location: Southtown, District County, Rights Province, Neutralia
Hidden Bastille*

"Are you done?" asked Mulati as he looked down at Francois. He and Corto had come down from the rooftop while he was on the ground crying.

At first Francois thought it was a cold and insensitive question for Mulati to ask but thinking for a moment about the situation, he dried his hands on the front of his trousers and extended his right hand toward Mulati.

Mulati reached down with his right hand and helped him to his feet.

"You never know how something like that will affect you," said Francois as he quickly pulled himself together. He sounded as if he was almost apologizing for his lapse in judgement. "I guess Roderick was more committed to the cause than he let on."

"Will you miss him?" asked Mulati.

"No. Fuck him," said Francois. His facial expression went from one of sorrow to a scowl. "He tried to kill me. He can get sucked into a blackhole for all I care. I'm over it." He hurriedly strapped his twice emitter to his back. "Thanks for checking me, Mulati. You don't have to worry, I'm all in."

"We've gotta move," said Mulati with an elevated voice. "I suspect we don't have much time. Mask up, everybody. I don't want this Judas Benedict or that fat general to see our faces. Ean, you keep your face exposed. That way it won't look suspicious when Theris comes with us voluntarily."

The crew pulled out white silk face masks. The eye sockets and mouth slit were black mesh. The material allowed them to see and to breathe but shielded their identity completely. The top of the masks had a hole that exposed the crowns of their heads to allow their body heat to escape. Their hair sprouted from the hole like plants from a flowerpot.

"I understand," said Ean. "I will lead the way."

"Corto, I want you and Sampa to stay out here," said Mulati. "Make sure no one comes in after us."

"Got it, Boss," said Corto.

"Sure thing," said Sampa. "We'll be waiting."

Mulati, Bjorn, Ean, and Francois moved their twice emitters to the ready position and walked into the garage. As they walked past the parked JEDDOs they saw several doors that led into the facility. Beside the door to the far right were two dead squaddies.

"Which door do we take?" asked Francois. 'Who knows where they lead?" he asked rhetorically.

"We'll take this one," said Mulati as he nodded toward the door in the center.

They all started to walk forward. As they moved, the door to the far right opened and immediately they all turned their twice emitters toward the movement.

"Don't move!" said Mulati to the person standing in the doorway.

"Ean, it's me, Theris Lamont!" he said. He had seen Ean enter the garage on the VC inside the safe room. "There are others here with me. We are trapped."

"Stay where you are," said Ean. "We'll come to you."

"Bjorn, Francois, stay out here," said Mulati. "I'm going in there with Ean."

Bjorn and Francois turned to face the interior doors as Mulati and Ean walked toward Theris Lamont.

"They're in that room," said Theris Lamont as he pointed down the long hallway toward the safe room.

Quickly the three men moved down the hall and toward the door. Once they were there, Theris knocked hard three times. Chancellor Aldrich opened the door. Before he could say anything, Ean, who he recognized as Theris's personal bodyguard, stepped into the room.

"Move quickly!" Ean said. "We're going to get you out of here!"

As Judas Benedict slowly pulled himself up from the couch, Chancellor Aldrich and Nastasia Rodmanovic hurried toward the door. Mulati stayed behind Theris Lamont in the hallway. Frustrated with his lack of haste, Ean went over to Judas Benedict and grabbed him by his left arm around his bicep and tricep. His fingers were under Judas's armpit and they pressed against his EPIC. Inadvertently, he pushed his snitch. Judas's feet barely touched the floor as Ean dragged him toward the doorway. Once he got to the exit of the safe room, he pushed Judas in his back toward the others. Ean closed the door behind him and Mulati led the way to the garage as they moved quickly through the long hallway. As they exited the door into the garage, Judas's EPIC received a signal.

"Moving, Sam!" said Mulati as they all sped up to a jog.

Francois and Bjorn joined them as they all exited the building.

"This way," said Sampa as she moved across the north side road toward the path that they had used earlier which was on the hill.

All the others followed as she led the way.

On the bottom floor of the Bastille, Rokuro Onishi, Bahadur, and the other DOD warriors continued to slay Mayhem Marauders. Startled Rokuro Onishi felt the vibration of his EPIC and moved behind Bahadur long enough to take it out and take a glance at it.

"They are here!" said Rokuro Onishi. "I have the coordinates of the politicians. Fortune has favored us. Follow me!"

He led the way as they fought their way back to the stairwell from which they had entered. Rokuro Onishi had one thing on his mind as they made it to the top level, find the politicians.

Outside of the Bastille, Alexei and his men pressed down the road to finish off the Mayhem Marauders who had fled from them. As they attacked, the Mayhem Marauders retreated further back into the building. General Tolliver and General Branimir had joined them only to realize that the situation was dire. Having not yet made it to the front door, they decided that they would head back to the safe room. As the two generals ran by, Onin Gesh stepped out of the shadows. He had been concealing himself under the tower stairs. For a moment he contemplated pursuing them and killing them both, However, the commotion coming from the front of the Bastille was more interesting to him at the time. He pulled another dagger from one of the dead squaddies on the floor and slowly walked toward the door.

"Behind you, Gesh!" said Bahadur as he, Rokuro Onishi, and the other DOD warriors moved up to join him.

Onin Gesh turned and looked at the men. "No illuminators," he said gruffly as he turned back toward the door.

Seconds later, the fleeing Mayhem Marauders came around the corner into the waiting arms of death. They were trapped. Onin Gesh ran full speed into the Mayhem Marauders throwing caution to the wind. With reckless abandon he sliced the visually challenged men. Like a whirling dervish of pain, he sliced or stabbed everything he touched. Just as quickly, he fell back into the fold as the DOD moved forward to finish them off. As Onin Gesh faded into the darkness, Bahadur opened the illuminator and tossed it toward the Mayhem Marauders. Green tracers suddenly filled the room along with the resounding sound of swords clashing.

The Mayhem Marauders who were fortunate enough to survive the onslaught made their way to the garage along with some of the men from the lower level who had also survived. They were headed for the JEDDOs. Of the two hundred Mayhem Marauders who were at the Bastille, only forty survived. They packed themselves into four of the JEDDOs and exited the rear of the Bastille. Not long after, the DOD flooded into the garage just in time to see the JEDDOs driving away. Six JEDDOs remained.

"Let's go after them!" said Bahadur.

"No!" said Rokuro Onishi. "We have a plan for that. Plus, the politicians are a higher priority."

Inside one of the remaining JEDDOs, Friedrich slumped down in his seat. He had seen the DOD enter and kill the squaddies. He witnessed the generals go and return. He witnessed the eight Bastillians as they made their escape. He also saw Mulati, Ean, Francois, and Bjorn when they entered and left with the politicians. As Bahadur opened his illuminator and threw it to the middle of floor Friedrich slumped deeper into his seat. Over the dashboard he could see the shadows of the DOD as they walked around the garage checking doors.

Inside the safe room the generals heard them as they got closer.

"Help me," said General Tolliver as he grabbed one end of a large sofa.

General Branimir grabbed the other end and together they pushed it forward. Underneath the sofa was a trap door. General Tolliver slid the top open to reveal ladder rungs extending from the rock wall beneath. General Branimir got in first descending the ladder rungs with General Tolliver following. He grabbed a handle underneath the sofa and pulled it as close to the trap door as he could. He then slid the door closed behind him. Once they got to the ground, they felt a strong breeze in the tunnel beneath the Bastille. Slowly they walked against it with General Tolliver leading the way.

Rokuro Onishi followed Judas's signal to the rear of the garage. Orienting himself he realized that the signal went north, up the hill toward the mountain so he crossed the northside road toward the hill and stopped to listen. The mechanized noise sounded like more than the four JEDDOs that had exited the garage previously.

"Something is not right," he said to Alexei. "Follow me."

He walked around the road and through the northside tunnel. In the distance he could see what he expected. Four JEDDOs had turned into fifteen. The Mayhem Marauders had reinforcements.

"Okonjo was right," said Rokuro Onishi.

Moments later, his EPIC signaled an incoming message.

As Hania's image appeared, he said to Rokuro Onishi, "We see them, and we will proceed as planned."

"Send them. End transmission," said Rokuro Onishi.

The transmission from the Iron Raven disrupted Rokuro Onishi's signal to Judas Benedict. He no longer had his location. From the tunnel the DOD warriors watched as the JEDDOs carrying the Mayhem Marauders slowly made their way back to the Bastille. They were close enough for them to smell the engine oil when five Sparrows emerged over the western horizon. With pinpoint precision, they launched their SPIMs into the unsuspecting JEDDOs. One by one they burst into flames as the missiles pierced their armor and burned them from the inside out. One hundred fifty more Mayhem Marauders were dead.

"Let's go to the horses," said Rokuro Onishi after he witnessed the destruction. "We are done here."

As the DOD walked westbound through the tunnel, Onin Gesh turned and walked in the opposite direction. He went east toward the rear of the bastille.

Bahadur stopped. "Gesh, why don't you come with us?"

"I've been imprisoned long enough," he said as he stopped walking. He did not turn to face Bahadur as he spoke those words.

Bahadur knew exactly what he meant by that and did not press the issue. Onin Gesh was his own man. He walked his own path. It wasn't in his nature to submit to anyone else's authority. "Listen to your conscience, Gesh," he continued.

"If my conscience had a physical form I would have slit its throat by now," he replied. He walked out of the tunnel and re-entered the Hidden Bastille.

That was the goodbye that Bahadur had expected, and he was satisfied with it.

Rokuro Onishi raised his EPIC. "Contact Iron Raven," he said. As Hania's image appeared he continued saying, "Do not destroy the Hidden Bastille. Call off the Sparrows. End transmission." Hania's image then disappeared.

As the tired DOD warriors walked westbound on the road toward the smoldering JEDDOs, the Sparrows abruptly turned around and headed back west toward the Iron Raven.

As Onin Gesh entered the garage, he walked past the six remaining JEDDOs and toward the interior door. Before reaching the door, he stopped. He turned and looked toward the JEDDO in which Friedrich was hiding. "Come out," he said.

Slowly the driver side door opened. Friedrich stepped out with his hands held high. "I'm just a passenger driver for the politicians. I am in no way affiliated with the Marauders."

As Onin Gesh studied him he saw that he was not wearing a uniform. "I want you out of here right n..."

Before he could finish, Friedrich was already running out of the open garage door. For a moment he paused at the rear as he decided which way he wanted to go. He eschewed both tunnels and opted for the path which led to the north side of the mountain.

Onin Gesh closed the garage door. He continued through the main floor to one of the stairwells which led to the lower level. Through the dead bodies he walked back to the only home he had known for the last two years, his cell. The Hidden Bastille was well stocked, and he thought that there would be no better abode for him to reside in for the near future. He laid down in his bed looking up at the ceiling. Before long, he was asleep.

Location: East City, District County, Rights Province, Neutralia
Aboard the Whisper

Mulati had delivered the politicians safely to the outskirts of the mountain. After securing them on a JEDDO and sending them on their way, they returned to the Whisper. Beth, Louis, and Eric were still awake and in the cargo bay when they got there. Beth rushed to greet them. Just as quickly as she touched each one of them she let go and went to the next. She was making sure that they all made it back alive and unharmed. The near panicked look on her face transitioned to relief as each member of the crew was accounted for.

"Ean will meet you two in the morning," said Mulati to Louis and Eric. Right now, he's taking Theris Lamont to safety.

"Anybody injured?" Beth asked.

"No, we're fine," said Mulati. "We're all just tired."

"Tomorrow should be interesting," said Sampa as they busied themselves with putting away their weapons and Rapid Arachnids.

"If it's okay with everybody, I'm gonna rack out," said Bjorn.

"I'm right behind you, Bjorn," said Corto as he walked to the cargo bay exit.

"Me too," said Francois.

The three of them waited quietly for the elevator. When it arrived, they rode it to the main deck and entered their respective sleeping quarters.

In the cargo bay Beth studied the faces of Mulati and Sampa. She imagined, for a moment, what they had just gone through. She wondered how they could go through something so terrible and then act as if they had just come home from a long day of work. As she stood there with her arms folded, she shook her head watching them go about their business. Sampa placed her back against the wall closest to the weapon locker and allowed herself to slowly slide down to a seated position on the floor. With her knees pulled up to her chest, she rested her elbows on them and her face in her hands. She closed her eyes and let out a long sigh. When she opened her eyes, she tossed her head back with her eyes fixed on the ceiling with her arms resting on her legs and her hands dangling between her knees.

Mulati walked over to Sampa and squatted in front of her looking straight into her face. She lowered her eyes to meet his.

"You good?" he asked.

She simply nodded and returned her gaze to the ceiling. That was good enough for Mulati.

He looked to Louis and Eric and said, "You two come with me. I'll take you to your quarters."

All three men left the cargo bay and headed toward the main deck. Beth walked over to Sampa and sat beside her against the wall. She reached over her head and wrapped her arm around her shoulders. Sampa leaned into Beth, wrapped her arms around her waist, and rested her head on her bosom. Softly Beth sang a Gaelic tune that she had learned in her youth. Sampa drifted off to sleep.

Location: Central City, District County, Rights Province, Neutralia Main Street, in front of the Grand Amphitheater, 0600 hours

Chancellor Aldrich and Nastasia Rodmanovic exited the JEDDO onto Main Street. Although neither of them had had the opportunity to sleep they were both clean and eager to see their city. Dawn in Central City had never looked so tattered. As the darkness and sunlight waged war against one another, the calm streets offered a surreal commentary on what had occurred the day before. Trash was everywhere. Black smoke rose from abandoned JEDDOs that had been set on fire. The once flowing modern architecture was interrupted by broken glass and burning buildings. Doors to buildings were left open, evidence that some looting had occurred. The smell of smoke was heavy. Slowly they walked through the streets taking it all in. Dead bodies were scattered here and there. Chancellor Aldrich walked to the base of the stairs leading up to the Grand Amphitheater. The rising sun cast his shadow sideways as it peaked through the large buildings. He did not go up the stairs. He had seen enough. He didn't say a word as he turned and walked back toward the JEDDO. Nastasia followed him.

"I want a meeting in the Council Chambers at 1600 hours today," he said to Nastasia as he got comfortable in his seat. "Make sure that everyone is there. Have the generals meet me in my office an hour earlier."

Nastasia pulled out her EPIC and added the event to her schedule. "Is there anything else, Chancellor?"

"Yes. Tell Director Rand that we will need to broadcast to the entire solar system at 1630 hours."

"As you wish," she said as the JEDDO started to drive away.

Location: East City, District County, Rights Province, Neutralia Aboard the Whisper, 0900 hours

"Receive transmission," said Sampa as she raised her head from her pillow. She pulled her EPIC close to her face as she focused her eyes. Upon seeing that it was Sahil transmitting on the encrypted channel, she sat up.

"Good morning, Sampa," he said. "The Black CATs have brought something to my attention that I think you should know about."

"What is it?" she asked.

"I told them what you said about that island on Evropa. That combined with what they did with the Southtown mines made us wonder, naturally, if they had done more of this."

"Go on."

"Well...it appears they have been very busy. There are more hidden locations. They used a different program to hide each place. They were careful to omit any common characteristics. Therefore, we had to contrast the new system with our last major update, which was five years ago. Since we have no program that can account for subtracted land masses, we overlapped the maps with the older one on top and asked the new system to highlight anomalies."

"How many were there?" she asked.

"There are ten, and we have the location of each one. Except for Alkebulan and Neutralia, they're on every planet," Sahil said with certainty.

"Send me the coordinates of each location," said Sampa. "Thank you for this valuable information. End transmission."

Sahil's image faded away and Sampa got out of her comfortable bed, stretching, and thinking about the previous night. She wondered how Francois was doing. The night had been particularly hard for him. She was sympathetic about his ordeal with Roderick. She imagined how she would feel if, for some reason, she had to take up arms against the crew of the Whisper. She quickly shook her head in an attempt to toss away the unpleasant thought. She raised her EPIC to speaking distance. "Contact Mulati," she said.

"What's going on, Sam?" he responded as his image appeared.

Quickly observing his background, she said, "Good, I see you're on the bridge. I'm on my way. End transmission."

Moments later she walked onto the bridge to see Mulati and Francois sitting in their usual seats. She walked over to her seat, sat down, and swiveled inward toward both of them. "Francois," she said as she nodded to him.

"Morning, Sam," he said.

Both men sat quietly as they waited to hear what Sampa had to say.

"I got a transmission from Sahil on the encrypted line just now," she said. "They did some CAT magic and discovered that there are ten more locations in the solar system like that island in the Macabre Sea."

"Do they have the exact locations of each one?" asked Mulati.

"They do, and now we do," said Sampa.

"This is the break we needed," said Mulati. "Contact Ean and tell him to put Theris in contact with us. It's time to make our move."

"I will do that," said Sampa as she got up to leave the bridge. While walking toward the door her EPIC buzzed with a text message: *Broadcast for the entire solar system has been scheduled for 1630 hours. Something big is about to happen.* The message stopped Sampa in her tracks.

"Sam?" said Mulati.

She turned around shaking her head. "Sahil says that they're broadcasting to the entire solar system at 1630 hours. That can't be good. Stand by." She left the bridge.

An hour later Ean and Theris Lamont arrived in a JEDDO. Francois met them in the cargo bay and escorted them to the lounge on the main deck. The rest of the crew were already there awaiting their arrival.

Mulati stood as Theris and Ean sat and made themselves comfortable. "There's a good chance that we will find your people, Vice Chancellor Lamont. We have it narrowed to ten specific places to search. We've decided to begin our search tomorrow. We will communicate with you on the encrypted channel only. From this point on my plan is to never be seen with you again. We will communicate with Ean if we have to see someone in person. Preferably that won't be on Neutralia. Have you any questions?"

"No, I don't have any questions," he said as he slowly rose to his feet. "This news pleases me."

"Good," said Mulati. "Francois will see you out."

Everyone in the room stood as Francois led Theris Lamont, Louis, Eric, and Ean out of the lounge. Minutes later they were being driven back to Central City in their JEDDO.

Location: Central City, District County, Rights Province, Neutralia Council Chambers, 1600 hours

Chancellor Aldrich stood in front of the large window looking out at the city streets from inside the Council Chamber. He had his back to the rest of the room. Theris Lamont sat in his usual seat on the sunny side of the table. Beside him was Nastasia Rodmanovic. Standing behind them were General Tolliver and General Branimir. The other side of the table was empty. Chancellor Aldrich had personally arranged for Friedrich to drive Judas Benedict to the meeting. At 1600 hours Judas Benedict walked into the room. The heavy door slammed behind him as he made his way to the dark side of the table. The room remained silent as he entered.

"No need to stand for my sake," Judas said sarcastically. "There was once a time when we at least pretended as if we liked one another."

Chancellor Aldrich turned around to face the room. He nodded toward the two generals who walked toward Judas. "No need to sit, Judas Benedict," said Chancellor Aldrich as the generals positioned themselves behind him.

"What is the meaning of this?" asked an incredulous Judas.

Chancellor Aldrich walked toward Judas as the generals grabbed an arm each. Judas had a panicked look on his face as he looked side to side at both generals. They tightened their grips as he tried to yank away.

"You have been proven to be a traitor, Judas Benedict! Two months from today you will be hanged for your treason," said Chancellor Aldrich.

Judas looked directly into Theris Lamont's eyes. Theris lowered his head and looked away. Judas's body went limp as he was suddenly overcome with grief.

"Take him away," said Chancellor Aldrich.

Theris Lamont and Nastasia Rodmanovic both watched silently as Judas was dragged out of the room.

"Congratulations, Councilwoman Rodmanovic, you've been promoted," said Chancellor Aldrich.

"Thank you, Chancellor," she replied. "I'll try not to disappoint the council."

Chancellor Aldrich turned back to the window to gaze out into the streets of Central City.

Both Theris Lamont and Nastasia Rodmanovic remained stoic. For minutes the Council Chamber remained quiet. Nastasia was surprised that she did not feel better about her ascension to her new position. Judas Benedict had been a thorn in her side, but she respected his toughness. She also coveted a seat at the council table but imagined that it would eventually come as a result of her hard work and not the failure of another. Moments later both generals walked back into room.

"We make the announcement to Sapien in ten minutes," said Chancellor Aldrich. "We have to present a united front. Remember, our goal is to get the citizens on our side at all costs. That is of the utmost importance."

Theris Lamont thought that it was strange that Chancellor Aldrich felt the need to say that, but he agreed.

At 1630 hours, every VC and every EPIC in the solar system received the signal from the Supreme Council. As the image showed, Chancellor Aldrich stood front and center. On his immediate right stood Theris Lamont. On his immediate left stood Nastasia Rodmanovic. General Branimir stood next to Theris Lamont, and General Tolliver stood next to Nastasia Rodmanovic.

"Sapiens, I come to you with a heavy heart," said Chancellor Aldrich. "Yesterday's events can be seen as nothing less than a disaster. For that I apologize. The Supreme Council takes full responsibility. However, what transpired was the result of an attempted coup. At the direction of former councilman, Judas Benedict, a faction of rogue Mayhem Marauders sabotaged the convention in an attempt to make us look like tyrants. He tried to have myself and Vice Chancellor Lamont killed as well. Because of his actions, Judas Benedict has been tried and convicted of treason. He is scheduled to hang in two months' time. All his fellow saboteurs have either been captured or killed. At the conclusion of this broadcast we will march him from the front doors of the Council Chambers to his destiny."

Theris was not prepared for what he was hearing. It was true that Judas had conspired to murder him and Chancellor Aldrich. However, the mishap at the Grand Amphitheater was clearly the failure of Chancellor Aldrich and his generals. *Now I know what he meant by presenting a united front* he thought to himself.

"From this day forward, all members of the DOD are considered fugitives," Chancellor Aldrich continued. "Anyone who brings one of their members to justice will be awarded ten thousand DANs. Dead or alive! A monument will be constructed in front of the Grand Amphitheater to honor the brave Sapiens who sacrificed their lives standing up to Judas's evil regime. Neutralia is once again safe. We will not allow one bad day to discourage us from living freely. Listen to your conscience, and we will let ours lead the way. End transmission."

As the VC went dark Theris Lamont and Nastasia Rodmanovic both stared angrily at Chancellor Aldrich.

"There was no coup," said Theris Lamont. "You lied to the people."

"Would you rather they despise us all, or just him?" asked Chancellor Aldrich. "Because of his own actions he was a doomed man anyway. His punishment could be no harsher. He may as well bare our share of the blame."

"Our?" said Nastasia Rodmanovic. "It's good to see that you've learned to share, Chancellor."

The Chancellor squinted his eyes at Nastasia Rodmanovic. He reached up and stroked his salt and pepper beard once. He turned away and walked to the large window that looked out onto the streets of Central City. "Meeting adjourned," he said as he looked down upon citizens gathering in the street in front of the building.

Councilwoman Natastia Rodmanovic and Vice Chancellor Theris Lamont got up to leave the room.

As Judas Benedict was escorted from the doors of the Council Chambers to a waiting JEDDO by the Mayhem Marauders, a gauntlet of angry Sapiens formed along the stairwell. As he passed by, they punched, kicked, and spat on the Albino. They called him, traitor, murderer, and any other terrible names they could think of. The Mayhem Marauders were in no hurry to get him to the JEDDO. After sustaining a significant amount of abuse, he was inside. When they seat belted him into the vehicle, he hung his head in shame. His fall was complete. With two squaddies armed with twice emitters riding in the back with Judas, Friedrich drove the JEDDO and the humiliated Albino to a secret location. The entire Sapien Solar System had watched Chancellor Aldrich's speech. They were also shown the surveillance feed as Judas Benedict was escorted to the JEDDO. Night soon fell, and the city was quiet, but it no longer felt safe.

About the Author

T. O. Burnett is in many ways a typical inner city man. Having moved to the southeast section of Washington, D. C. by the age of one with his single mother, he spent his adolescent years in the school of hard knocks as he grew up there in the Barry Farms community. Like every other child his age, he loved sports, girls, and Kung fu flicks.

Despite not having much, he managed to excel academically very early on. Always inquisitive, T. O. quenched his thirst for knowledge through school and public television. He also prided himself with acquiring trivial knowledge of a multitude of subjects which came from a vast array of sources.

After moving further south to rural Alabama to start high school, T. O. began to explore and develop his writing which came naturally to him. His literary skills and overall writing talent were cultivated by his father who was a respected educator and dedicated public servant.

A tour in the United States Marine Corps as a machine gunner, some college, a few odd jobs, and a career in law enforcement helped to develop what T. O. himself considers to be a well rounded personality.

T. O. has never been married and does not have children. He endeavors to unplug from the rat race by becoming a full time writer.